NEIL GRIFFITHS
BETRAYAL IN NAPLES

VIKING
an imprint of
PENGUIN BOOKS

VIKING

Published by the Penguin Group
Penguin Books Ltd, 80 Strand, London WC2R ORL, England
Penguin Group (USA) Inc., 375 Hudson Street, New York, New York 10014, USA
Penguin Books Australia Ltd, 250 Camberwell Road, Camberwell, Victoria 3124, Australia
Penguin Books Canada Ltd, 10 Alcorn Avenue, Toronto, Ontario, Canada M4V 3B2
Penguin Books India (P) Ltd, 11 Community Centre, Panchsheel Park, New Delhi – 110 017, India
Penguin Books (NZ) Ltd, Cnr Rosedale and Airborne Roads, Albany, Auckland, New Zealand
Penguin Books (South Africa) (Pty) Ltd, 24 Sturdee Avenue, Rosebank 2196, South Africa

Penguin Books Ltd, Registered Offices: 80 Strand, London WC2R ORL, England

www.penguin.com

First published 2004
1

Set in Monotype Dante
Typeset by Rowland Phototypesetting Ltd, Bury St Edmunds, Suffolk
Printed in Great Britain by Clays Ltd, St Ives plc

A CIP catalogue record for this book is available from the British Library

BETRAYAL
IN NAPLES

Neil Griffiths was born in 1965. He has lived for extended
periods in New York and Paris. He has previously written for
radio and film. He currently lives in London. *Betrayal in Naples*
is his first novel.

For Michael Stewart & Lena Aspri

Terra di baci d'onore e non d'amore
Land of kisses of honour, not love

Gabriella De Fina

sickness
crime
sex
death

Fact: you cannot predict the outcome of acts of the heart. I learned that in Naples, when on Piazza Garibaldi, at 7 p.m., during the late Italian rush hour, I was shot in the stomach. All I felt was the snub barrel of a gun pressed into me, to the right of my belly button. Take two fingers and press there. That's all I felt: a little give before meeting the resistance of muscle. Then I began to fall.

The pain was sharp, like a long silver sword run through me. A precise pain. I heard myself saying, 'I've been shot.' It was so clear to me, even the image of myself in that moment, dropping to my knees, listing over, clutching my belly. It was as if I could see myself in long shot, from way up high, a man stumbling, out of step with the crowd – shot, or perhaps knifed, but attacked from close range, singled out as the target and neatly killed. That's how it happened . . .

I wasn't dead, but I was dying. My breathing was quick and shallow; the screams around me muffled, compressed. With my face pressed into the mirror-grey paving all I could see was shadows, and blood in rivulets running between the stones.

I made out a single voice. Medico! Presto! Presto! *It was a male voice – deep but melodious – a baritone: Italianate, passionate, commanding, without hysteria or panic. Bel canto in a crisis. He'd taken charge. I wanted to call out but all I could do was stare at the blood emptying out of me, pooling over the worn stone, making the street look like the surface of a strange planet – grey rock and red seas.*

Then I was turned over; a body washed up on a beach. A woman was kneeling over me, issuing instructions, asking me questions in Italian. She ripped open my shirt, away from the wound; it was heavy, soaked, adhering to my skin. She then plugged the wound with her fingers. Take two fingers and press them into your belly – that's how she did it. It felt just like the gun, but this time there was no resistance, no pain. I felt cold. It was a hot, humid evening and I was cold, shivering – just like the day I arrived in the city. But this time I was going to die.

You don't expect it, do you? It's not something you foresee as your lips touch another's and briefly your world feels perfectible. You don't think that within a few days you'll be dying on a street, shot at close range, a contract fulfilled. But then you cannot predict the outcome of acts of the heart. Fact.

It was supposed to be a long weekend. A time to relax before I started a new job. I was going to be a senior counsellor at an addiction treatment centre specializing in the homeless. Don't think well of me – it's a job like any other. It's not worthy work: that's soup-kitchen stuff. Counselling addiction in the homeless requires emotional toughness. It is dangerous also. The embittered take offence easily: the street is violent, counselling intrusive; there is little trust. I've been ridiculed, insulted, threatened, attacked even.

Ten years in the same job, talking to the lonely, isolated, frightened, desperate, I had to quit. It's thought of as a soft job. Rewarding. But you lose more than you gain. Striving for empathy takes it out of you. To connect with the dispossessed means a part of you has to connect with their fear, loneliness, pain. You can only do that for so long. It's like being a city trader: burnout arrives quickly.

I needed time to work out what I wanted to do with the rest of my life. I quickly discovered it's all I'm good for – thirty-five years old, years of experience, a reputation. After six weeks of indecision – courses paid for and not attended, applications made but the interviews ignored – I was offered this job. Three days' actual counselling, the rest of the week liaising with the government's policy unit for the homeless. I accepted reluctantly. My cowardice infuriated me. A friend suggested I get away, 'Take yourself off for a few days.' It was that simple – I was following advice. I should have known then it would all go wrong. Who, these days, follows advice?

Why Naples? Why did I go to a place where I knew nobody, a place I had never thought of going? I have a good friend in Amsterdam – why didn't I go and see him? If I needed to be on my own, why didn't I choose Florence, Rome – any of the other cities within a few hours' flight? There was this question, on a radio quiz show. From where does the phrase 'See Naples and die' originate? It's something you hear, but I had no idea where it came from. If pushed, I would have said from a poem by Shelley – he had a terrible time during his stay there. One contestant said that it was the title of a film starring Humphrey Bogart; another that it was due to the city's typhus and cholera epidemics; and the two other contestants passed. In the end we were all wrong. The phrase was a piece of nineteenth-century advertising copy from a Thomson Holidays campaign for the Grand Tour.

Naples? I lifted myself off the sofa, logged on to the web and looked for a cheap flight. There wasn't a lot of choice. Only a few flights a day. A couple extra at the weekend. I entered my requirements, and after a frustrating few minutes' wait a selection of airlines and departure times appeared. The only price available was the highest. I clicked. *Please enter your payment details.* I did so without really thinking; I could always just close the page if I wanted. *Confirm your reservation?* I was one click away from purchasing a four-day return flight. Thursday to Sunday – arriving home the evening before the start of my new job. I circled the cursor around the icon. I asked myself out loud, 'Is this what I want to do?'

I leaned back in my chair and imagined what might happen. My hope was to meet a beautiful Italian girl, dark, voluptuous, full of Catholic abandon. I remember an ironic snort; my recent past promised three days of loneliness. It didn't matter – I would be away from London and I could pretend my life was full of adventure and possibility.

I clicked. I clicked impulsively, decisively. I felt a rush of adrenalin, fluid, pulsing. Suddenly a place I'd never thought about was the only place I wanted to go. And I was going.

What I think made my reaction so intense was how different this decision was from my normal behaviour. I'm not intrepid, I'm not impulsive; I'm usually very responsible. Choosing to go to Naples only days before I started a new job contradicted something fundamental in me. It represented a point of change in me.

sickness

I

As I board the plane I realize I have a sore throat. By the time I arrive in Naples I am feverish. Stumbling from the plane to the airport building I know I should turn back, reboard and fly home, but I am delirious and all I can think of is hotel, bed, sleep.

At passport control the officer waves me through without caring that the man in the photograph in my passport looks like a terrorist and the man before him is sweating profusely and hardly able to stand. I stumble through the arrivals lounge, following the directions to the taxi rank as though they are hypnotic signs guiding me, tempting me somewhere mysterious, exotic. My guidebook, which I bought at the airport and have hardly looked at, warns about Neapolitan taxi-drivers in the introduction. Firstly, make sure they turn on the meter; secondly, make sure they don't kidnap you. Right now I am too sick to care and head for the first cab I see. The driver, a man in his mid forties, unshaven, unsmiling, is standing by the open rear door like a chauffeur. I make some vague gesture asking him whether he is free. He nods and places a lighted cigarette in his mouth.

I collapse into the back seat. He walks around the front of the car. I need to lie down but remain upright by propping myself up on my bag. After inspecting me in his rear-view mirror, my driver wraps his arm around the back of the passenger seat and turns to look at me directly. Is he assessing what kind of kidnap victim I might be? I feel cold sweat on my forehead, on the back of my neck, running down my back. My shirt is drenched and clings to me. My jeans, damp like sodden cardboard, are heavy and resistant to movement. Even my hands are covered in a film of moisture. Is this all a symptom of fever or is some of it fear, I wonder. I take a deep breath and say in English, 'Sorry, give me a moment . . .'

The driver doesn't respond, just continues to stare at me. When he does eventually open his mouth it is to expel a thick cloud of smoke. This is followed by a deep glottal rasping. At first I think he is just clearing his throat but then realize words are embedded in the low growl. He is speaking to me. His accent sounds like a kind of a warrior Italian, an Arabic Italian, harsh, irritable, masculine, quite different from the gentle lilting cadences I have heard from all the young Italian tourists in London.

Raising my hand, I say, 'Wait . . . please,' and drag my bag onto my lap. I open it fumblingly and pull out my guidebook. I haven't booked into a hotel. My plan, based on my newly acquired boldness, had been to arrive early enough to head into the city and find one – a real Neapolitan place, small, family-run. But after three hours of flight delays it is now evening. And hot. Very hot. A digital display fixed over a large advertisement for Banco di Napoli is flashing the time and the temperature. It is 19.45/34°. For a moment I wonder whether I am ill at all. It hasn't occurred to me that the heat is on the outside, that I am burning up because of the unexpected humidity closing in around me. I feel a wave of relief. It is simply the metabolic shock. The climatic change from cold, damp London to hot, humid Naples. I am wrong – again: my hands are barely able to hold the guidebook and my thumbs, thick and dull, refuse to divide the pages. Even when I manage to find the accommodation section my eyes are unable to focus on the tiny print. The words swim and stretch and slide down the page. I feel like crying. I throw the guidebook down and slump back in the seat.

Through all this my taxi-driver hasn't taken his eyes off me, cigarette hanging from his lips, arm still slung over the back of the passenger seat. Then, for no apparent reason – and certainly not on any instruction from me – he swivels around in his seat, flicks his cigarette out of the window and starts the engine. I think, but only vaguely, why's he doing this, he doesn't know where I want to go. But it has ceased to matter. For some inexplicable reason, from the moment I tossed the guidebook aside, I have decided to trust him

– to trust myself to him. I think, and this time not vaguely – the illness somehow providing me with a perverse clarity for a moment – what can happen, really? There are only four possible outcomes, surely. He can take me to a hotel – some place he might make a little extra if he brings in business; he can take me to his home – you hear these kinds of stories from people who have travelled, the generosity of strangers when things get tough; he can take me to a hospital – I obviously have nowhere to go and am too sick to look after myself; or he can drive around until I pass out, rob me and dump me somewhere to live or die according to my own instinct for self-preservation. That's it. I don't see kidnapping as a possibility – it is clear I am worth little.

As we leave the airport I stare out of the window and attempt, with my sweat-blurred vision, to read the road signs. If we follow the directions to Napoli, I can relax a little. Sometimes we do, sometimes we don't. Either way, we seem to be heading into the city. There is a large black mass on the horizon I take to be Vesuvius. I have never seen a volcano before. Sick as I am the sight gives me a real thrill. 'Wow, Vesuvius,' I say weakly, hoping to elicit a response from my driver, to make a connection with him. He is silent.

We come to an abrupt stop next to Naples' central railway station. It has a long low grey roof, jutting out into a point, with only a McDonald's to give it any colour. The external concourse is busy, Neapolitans hanging about talking and smoking. No one seems in a rush to catch a train. This is the first group of Neapolitans I've seen. Nearest to me is a group of young men. Men in their mid thirties – my age. They are all dressed in dark suits, white shirts, top buttons open, ties perfectly skewed. Their faces are dark, also. Some are handsome; most tough-looking. None is pretty or smooth. In my sick state I feel a little threatened.

I turn away and look out over the large piazza; buses and coaches nestled up to the grass verges which demarcate the car parks and the roads. There is little atmosphere in this area of Naples.

The car lurches into space and we filter into a slow-moving

lane crossing the piazza. We stop again. This time I can't see a way through, the roads are jammed. Cars, taxis, buses, trams and scooters all vying for two lanes. I imagine that from above, from the heavens, the traffic looks like an underwater mosaic, intricate, amorphous, shifting.

The image makes me dizzy. My driver is talking to himself, declaiming to other drivers, punctuating the low rasp of his voice with raps on the horn. Every so often he looks around at me. The expression on his face is unreadable. Concern, irritation, suspicion? All I manage is a feeble smile – a helpless baby to a parent, an encouragement to love, responsibility, security. He lights another cigarette, drops his arm out of the window and taps his finger on the door. As we move slowly forward a large hotel – the Cavour – comes into view, an eighteenth-century building, ornate and grand, its façade blackened by the exhaust emissions of perpetually grid-locked traffic.

The next hotel on has a large neon sign across its roof. *Luxotica*. That's what I need, I think, some exotic luxury. I peer in as we pass, imagining the interior will display in some way what its name promises, but it's like every other large European hotel: revolving doors, staff in ill-fitting uniforms, tall flowers in tall vases – everything in gold leaf. Corporate opulence. A level of comfort and service guaranteed. I say to myself, check in there, they'll look after you, they'll speak English, they'll have access to a doctor – do it, do it. But I can't. Or rather I don't. Something stops me. However sick I am, however stifling the heat in this cab, I have decided to submit to the momentum that has got me this far, which means I am going to persevere with my cab-driver and his plans for me.

The traffic shunts forward and the hotel disappears behind me. We enter a long, wide street lined with small shops, windows brightly lit and crammed full of clothes, shoes, underwear, electronics. The shops are open yet there are few people about. If you look to the pavement, Naples seems empty, abandoned, as though

Vesuvius is about to erupt and everyone has fled; yet, if you look to the road, it is a city full to overflowing, abundant with life. Vespas shoot past us in both directions, with two to a bike, shirts and blouses rustling rapidly in the breeze, not a helmet in sight. Before us, beside us, behind us, trams, buses, cars weave their way down the street as though it is illegal to stay in the same lane for longer than a minute. We seem to be parked at an angle across the traffic with no space to move in any direction. My driver turns on the radio. Italian pop. The song seems to consist of a single melody, high and sweet, endlessly repeated as if repetition is the only way it has any chance of being remembered. My head begins to throb. I grab the top of the passenger seat and heave myself forward. I want to protest, gesture to him to turn it off, or at least reduce the volume. But having leaned forward I immediately notice two things – one, my driver's name is Massimo; two, the meter isn't running. I slump back. If he isn't charging me he can do what he likes; if he isn't charging me he *plans* to do what he likes. My heart begins to beat rapidly – tight, hard punches in my chest. My body temperature plummets and I'm covered in a cold sweat, each droplet of perspiration freezing in my pores. I feel as if I am embedded with crystals. Each tiny movement crackles in my inner ear, each tiny movement cuts me. I shiver. This is followed by an instant rocketing in body temperature and the crystals drop out of my pores like hot wax dripping down my skin – I am burning up again, melting, liquefying . . .

Massimo swings the car sharply right and we are on a side street. The alley is so narrow he is forced, with cigarette nestled in his knuckles, to hold back his wing mirror so it doesn't scrape along the wall. The people we encounter are forced to back up against the walls, thinning and elongating themselves to let us past. The buildings on both sides are tall and made of black stone. The only source of light is the shallow fluorescence of strip lighting coming from the windows high above us. Every now and then the street opens up into a small, dark piazza, and the Vespas gathering impatiently behind us stream past like water breaking around a rock. It is obvious to me I am in the back streets of Naples, precisely where I've been warned not to go by the guidebook, friends, the mythology. The darkness is deep, and the air pressed in through the taxi windows due to the proximity of the buildings is stale and meaty. This place feels forbidding and oppressive. It feels dangerous. I can tell that it will differ little during the day; the height of the buildings in relation to the width of the street means sunlight will not reach down here. I am being driven into permanent night. I don't have the strength to panic so I pass out instead.

I am hardly aware that we have stopped. It is a dead end. Headlights spread over the wall. I am being pulled from the car. I try to grab my bag, but a hand is pressing down on my head the way the police always seem to guide people down into the back of a car. I am steered through a small door; I have to bend over, again there is a hand on my head.

I am in a courtyard. Small. Square. Tiled. Lemon-and-lime tiles. Washed clean. There are plants. Tall ferns in terracotta pots. Small palm trees. I could be in Morocco, Tunisia. I attempt to stand up straight, but I am too weak, shaky, cold. I hug myself, both for warmth and any sensation of security I might muster.

There is conversation around me, whispered, insistent. A man, a woman. I can't see them. I look up at the building surrounding the courtyard. Five storeys; I count them carefully for some reason. Each floor has a hallway overlooking the courtyard. Plants cascade through the ornate railings. Directly above me, framed by the four sides of the building, is the night sky, a high, squared-off dome of blackness. Squinting, trying to focus, I can just make out the stars: tiny, irregular pinpricks of white light. Needle stabs in black card. I have a moment of recognition – these are the same stars, the same random pattern of lights I can see from the roof of my building in London, clearer perhaps, but the same, and for a moment I feel free from fear, sickness, helplessness – I feel safe. Then I begin to fall, like a man shot in his tracks. Spiralling down. A human twister unable to stay upright. I hit the floor hard and black out. When I come to, all I can see before me are the lemon-and-lime tiles, stretching for ever like citrus groves flattened by a god's footsteps.

2

I awake in a small single bed, wrapped in soaked sheets, fixed in the scoop of a collapsed mattress. I awake with a start, as if shaken. My eyelids are heavy and resistant to opening. The room I am in is large, empty – almost. There is a chest of drawers in the corner with an enamel jug and bowl on top. Next to the bed is a chair on which my clothes are hung, my bag pushed neatly underneath. I don't think it's a hospital. Opposite, through a tall shuttered window, a little light comes in, shredded, slanting downwards, reaching halfway into the room.

The room feels like a cell, as if it has been designed this way by someone who has made the decision to live minimally, untroubled that a little plaster has fallen from the walls, that the paint is peeling and discoloured, or that the floorboards, unvarnished and dusty, look like the carpet has just been removed. I don't think I'm in a hotel. Behind the shutters, a window is open. I can hear Italian being spoken. A family arguing. Around a table. Setting a table. The clinking of cutlery and crockery is clear, close. Is it breakfast, lunch, supper? Breakfast. From the small amount of light, I judge it to be morning. There is a radio on somewhere. Music. More Italian pop. It is almost as close as the family.

I heave onto my side and look over the edge of the bed. A small, brightly glazed terracotta jug of water and a small glass. I carefully pour myself a drink. The cool water is a shock to my dry mouth and throat. After a few sips, I try to stand, but the manoeuvre proves too much, my joints are stiff, my muscles ache – I am instantly tired. I lie back down with a low groan. I hear a sound outside the room, the swish of a brush, a scratching at my door. I call out, 'Hello . . .' My voice echoes feebly in the bare room. I draw in a deep breath to shout more loudly. But then just as I am about to form the first syllable of 'buon giorno' the door opens and an old woman walks in. She is wearing a light-blue housecoat over a black dress, her hair is thick and grey and amassed into a small wiry bouffant that has collapsed slightly to one side. Her face is small, dark, lined. She has small, dark eyes underscored with lapping wrinkles.

She addresses me in a quick burst of Italian. The only word I recognize is 'mal'. She is either telling me how sick I *was* or asking me how sick I *am*.

I shrug and look at her gravely.

She studies me – her small eyes hard, direct – before speaking again. This time I don't understand a single word. I stare back at her, shrug. She tries another tack.

Pressing the fingers of one hand together and bringing them up to her mouth, she says, 'Affamato? Mangiare?' and points to me.

Hungry? Eat? Am I hungry? I don't know. Am I?

I nod. 'Yes . . . sì . . . grazie.' I notice my breathing is shallow.

'Prego,' she says lightly, and nimbly slips out through the door.

Wherever I may be at this moment I know this: there is a bed, water, a woman who as far as I can tell doesn't mind me being here and is going to feed me. So I should relax. I close my eyes and try to attune my ears to what is going on outside. The family across the street are now talking more amiably, laughing. It's a mother, father, young daughter. Below the window I hear cars and Vespas passing, the constant squeal of their horns. I try to lift myself out of bed for a second time. I place my feet on the floor and haul myself into a sitting position. Easy stages. Like a weightlifter, readying himself for the thrust upwards. It's no good. As soon as I am fully upright, the dizziness returns. In addition, I am naked. Someone has undressed me. I lower myself back down on the bed just as the door opens and the old woman walks back in. In one hand she is carrying a bowl, in the other a stiff, clean sheet, neatly folded. I grab a pillow and cover myself. The old woman approaches, places the bowl on the chair and holds the new sheet out to me. 'Grazie,' I say and take it. She then turns to allow me to lie back down and arrange myself. I only have the energy to pull the old top sheet off and replace it loosely with the new one. When I am settled she turns around. Her eyes flash to the bowl she has placed beside me. I lean over and pick it up. A small spoon sits in the soup, the handle resting on the side of the bowl.

'*Zuppa*,' she says encouragingly. '*Fagioli. Bene.*'

'Thank you. *Grazie, signora*,' I say, trying to express extra gratitude with a thankful expression.

'*Prego*,' she says once again, but this time remains where she is, her hands in the front pockets of her housecoat.

The soup is a white-bean broth, thick, heavy, alive with ground black pepper. My palate is so rough and dry from dehydration I am forced to wash each mouthful down with sips of water. I manage about half of the soup before I lose my appetite. Eating has exhausted me. I push the bowl back onto the chair and repeat, '*Grazie, grazie*,' over and over to make sure my appreciation is clear. The old woman gathers the old sheet up from the floor. As she is about to leave I call out, '*Scusi, signora?*'

She stops and turns. '*Sì, signor?*'

'Hotel. Is this a hotel?' I ask and point to the floor.

She pauses, thinking about it, then says unsurely, '*Sì, signor . . .*'

Is it a hotel? I wonder. The answer is far from certain.

'*Pensione?*' I ask.

All she does is repeat the word back to me, neither affirming nor denying. I am beginning to suspect the Neapolitans are an opaque people. This woman is as inscrutable as my cab-driver.

'Massimo?' I ask, having reminded myself of his name, and mime holding a steering wheel. Maybe I can at least make a connection between the man who brought me here and this woman – is she his mother, his wife? Is this their home?

She shrugs, her expression blank.

'*Grazie*,' I say and leave it at that.

She then says something ending in *riposo*, which I take to mean 'rest', and leaves.

After she has closed the door behind her I notice a newspaper at the end of the bed. Flat and unread. I am sure it wasn't there when I changed the sheets. I don't remember the old woman bringing it in either; her hands were empty the first time, the second time she was carrying the soup and sheet. I lean forward with an outstretched arm and pull it over the bed. It is a tabloid. *Ultimissime*. The headline is large: *Il Pentito*. Directly below there is a picture of a young man: handsome, elegant, dapper even. He was obviously posing for the photo. The caption underneath reads: *Giacomo Sonino. Pentito di Camorra.* Camorra? I vaguely remember it's the name of the Mafia in Naples. Or something like that. Who is he? I wonder. What has he done? Surely 'penitence' is not front-page news. Not even in Italy. I turn to the text to try to discover what the story is about. I give up after the first short line. My mind is heavy, lumbering, and I cannot concentrate. I go back to the photo and study it. Certainly not penitent when this was taken. Leaning against a lamp post he looks as if he is pointing to the photographer, jokily warning him not to take his picture. But then on closer inspection I realize he isn't pointing at all. As well as his outstretched forefinger, his thumb is raised. Now, not so jokily, he is warning the photographer: take my picture and I'll shoot you. On first glance the picture seemed posed, but now it is clear it was taken on the spur of the moment: Giacomo on a street corner, too cool to walk away, to hide, cover his face, yet quick enough to raise his hand and issue his warning. With a smile. I smile. This man is a gangster.

I drop the paper to the floor and close my eyes. I am just about to doze off when I realize I have no idea how long I have been here, wherever that is. I am taking it for granted that I arrived in Naples last night, passed out and it's now the following morning – yet I have a strong sense more time has elapsed. I grab the paper from the floor: *sabato 24 maggio. Sabato?* Is that Saturday or Sunday? *Sabato* – Sabbath – Saturday. I arrived Thursday. One whole day missing. I have been unconscious for a whole day and night. I try to think back. The last thing I remember is standing in a small courtyard staring up at the night sky. Maybe some sense of time passing, of sleeping, but this room, the old woman – nothing. A blank.

Panicked by this, I try to stand. I need some control. To be able to walk, to get out of here if that's what I decide. I push myself to my feet, ignoring the dizziness, the weakness in my legs, and take a few faltering steps. A single hot bead of sweat runs down my back, snaking over my backbone. I head for the window and open the shutters. There is a rush of hot air. There is a small, shallow balcony, two feet deep at most. I step out tentatively and grip the railing; flaky white paint crumbles in my hand. I look up. The heat of the sun cracks me on the skull and I reel back. I look down, over the railing to the street. I'm high up – the top of the building. Vertigo mixes with the heat and this time I all but faint. I grip the railing tightly to stop myself collapsing; more paint crumbles away. Across the street, only ten feet away, sitting around their kitchen table, is the family I heard earlier – they are all staring at me. When I've fully recovered, I force a smile. There is no response – three more expressionless Neapolitans. Expressionless, staring at . . . my genitals. I quickly cover myself, back unsteadily into the room and close the shutters. I rest against the chest of drawers until another bout of dizziness passes.

I pour some water into the bowl and immerse my face. The water is cold. I blink rapidly, and with two fingers of each hand clean away two days of sleep embedded in my eyes. When I emerge I feel better. Clear eyes, clearer mind. I squat down by the door and peer through the keyhole. A long hallway, dark and empty. No sign of the old woman. I contemplate dressing and trying to leave, but dismiss it as impractical. Where would I go? What if I collapse out in the street? I doubt I could lift my bag, never mind carry it. I climb back into bed. I will finish the *zuppa* and then sleep for a while after which hopefully I'll feel strong enough to go out. A day in Naples. That will be my holiday!

3

The back streets of Naples *are* the streets. There are no other streets. There may be two or three main arteries leading down to the port but the heart of Naples is its back streets: narrow, ancient, dangerous. The Historical Centre, the Spanish Quarter, Forcella – there is nowhere else to go. That's why there are so few tourists. They are afraid. They pass through the city on private coaches from their hotels on the outskirts of the town, heading for the port to catch boats to Capri, Ischia or Sorrento. They don't stop. They might get robbed, stabbed – a stiletto between the ribs. And let's not forget the kidnapping. How easy it would be when walking along one of those narrow streets, perpetually crepuscular, to be pulled in through a doorway. One minute you're marvelling at the quaintness of the *bassi* – the tiny street-level single-room homes – and the next you're bound to a chair in a dark room that reeks of fear and torture stretching back centuries.

When I leave my room for the first time I find the old woman sitting at a round table in a small room that opens up at the end of the long, gloomy hallway; she is smoking and watching a small television, an American soap dubbed into Italian. As I approach she indicates I should sit. I remain standing.

'*Caffè, signor?*' she asks.

'*Non, signora . . . Grazie.*'

She again indicates she wants me to sit. This time I do as I am told. Satisfied, she stands up and walks into a little kitchenette opposite. She returns with a small notepad. She produces a biro from a pocket of her housecoat. In soft, looping letters she writes *Signora Marina Maldini*, and points to herself. I point to her and say out loud, 'Signora Maldini.'

'*Sì,*' she confirms and then hands me the pen.

I write *Jim Wolf* and point to myself.

'Signor Wolf,' she says, pronouncing it Vulf.

'Jim,' I say.

'Sì,' she says and repeats, 'Jim,' pronouncing it Yim.

I smile. '*Sì.*'

She then takes the pen from me and writes on the next sheet of paper: 1 *Via Radici*, and then the telephone number. If I am going out she doesn't want me to get lost.

'Thank you . . .' I say; somehow '*grazie*' doesn't seem enough.

Signora Maldini then reaches again into the front of her housecoat and produces a long key. She holds it up to me. I nod appreciatively. She directs me to the front door, where she demonstrates the key needs four turns in the keyhole to lock or unlock the door.

'I *comprende*,' is all I can come up with.

'*Bene.*'

We are beginning to understand one another.

I say, '*Uno minuto*,' and open my phrase book to look for 'how much?' I think it is best to sort out what I am paying for the room now, pay for it, and prevent any confusion tomorrow when I leave.

'*Qual'è il prezzo?*' I say with a terrible accent and resort to pointing again: over the shoulder for nights passed and in the air for one more night.

Once again Signora Maldini looks at me blankly. I pull out my wallet and open it, displaying a fan of notes. '*Qual'è il prezzo?*' I repeat, adding 'for *tre notte* . . .'

She shakes her head, but before I can close my wallet she plucks out all the money. It is a swift, sharp motion, like clicking your fingers. One moment her hands are empty, the next she is holding all my money before me, spanned out, like a deck of cards at the top of a trick. She registers the shock on my face, but remains expressionless. With her free hand she then plucks my empty wallet from me and tosses it onto the table. All the while she has been trying to explain something to me; it seems more complex than the price of the room for three nights. She then shuffles the money into a neat pile and hands it back to me. It is my turn to look at her

22

blankly. A little exasperated she snaps the money back a second time, and with as swift, as deft a motion as she whipped it from me the first time, she slips it into the front pocket of my jeans. I would have missed the whole manoeuvre had it not been performed quite so boldly before me.

'*Ecco fatto* . . .' she says and gestures dramatically with her hands – finally now we are done.

Then I realize: it's the same in New York. Wallets in the back pocket are an easy target. Notes in the front the hardest to steal. I try to show my comprehension. 'Ah, *sì* . . . *sì* . . . pickpockets. *Comprende*. Thank you . . . *Grazie* . . .' She nods and hands me the long key. I am now ready to leave.

The exterior landing is bathed in the bright sunlight flooding in through the open roof. I look over the railing. The lemon-and-lime courtyard. It is reassuring to know that I am still in the place I was brought to the first night and I wasn't moved without realizing. I head down the stairs. Each floor is made up of two adjacent landings and two interior balconies. Hanging plants cascade and pot plants flourish in the direct sunlight. I can't quite believe I have found myself in quite such an extraordinary place. Two nights ago it felt like North Africa, the heat humid, tropical, malarial; now it is brightly Mediterranean, the heat similarly humid, yet emanating from a benevolent sun. On each floor I seem to pass someone coming up the stairs and, although not smiling, they greet me with a hearty '*buon giorno*'. At first I respond timidly, but by the time I reach the courtyard I am giving it the most vigorous Italian inflection I can manage. It helps that a certain amount of impacted phlegm is loosening up, giving my delivery a kind of throaty regional accuracy.

To my left is the small door I was bundled through two nights before. It is even smaller than I remember, quarter-size; it is built into a much larger wooden, arched, castle-like door. I open the smaller door, crouch down and step through. The alley is jammed with two parked cars. I slide sideways past them and onto the marginally wider street. I open my guidebook and locate where I am on the map, noting landmarks around me. Opposite there is a small, rectangular piazza, no more than ten yards across with a small church covered in scaffolding to the left. The street is Via Santa Maria la Nova. I turn right. Despite my prediction of eternal night, the street is punctuated with bright pools of light, as if once the sun has located a rare break between the buildings it has deliberately sent down beams of imperious intensity. However, for long stretches it is as dark as my first night. This seems to do less with the absence of light than with the years of perpetual shadow somehow amassed along the walls like centuries of dust. A chiaroscuro world created by sun and shadow. It is very unsettling and I stay in the centre of the street, vigilant to my surroundings. I pass tiny shops, cave-like, entirely lit from within. On the street corners, in the tiny piazzas, I am watched by young and old. They don't stop their conversations but my presence is noted. I notice there are no other tourists about. I try not to look perturbed. Every now and then I slip on the worn paving stones trying to dodge the Vespas tearing around me. There are times when the street is so narrow that I can touch both sides with the open span of my arms.

I am a little relieved when I finally hit a main road. Cars hurtle up and down with no respect for lane demarcation or sensible speed limits. To my left a café is just opening up. A single waiter has ten or so tables to erect, along with shades and chairs. On the other side of the road is a marvellous-looking modern building, made entirely of huge black and white cubes of marble. I look it up in my guidebook. The Post Office. Built by the fascists in the thirties. Beside it, directly in front of me, there are some wide steps. Despite the noise of the traffic and the smog people are sitting there reading, talking, taking a breather. I decide I can't wait for the café. I'll take a break myself and consult my guidebook, work out what there is to see.

I notice the Neapolitans around me cross the street with a tacit understanding that the cars won't hit them however fast or urgently they are travelling. They step out quickly and stride over confidently. I try this myself, but soon realize that it requires the pedestrian to make life-or-death decisions as swiftly as the traffic speed itself. If you're going to go, go, and keep going, and only deviate from a straight line when absolutely necessary, and only stop when death is certain – because the cars are not anticipating anything but forward motion, theirs and yours, and to stop is to go against nature. I just make it; but not without some hesitancy, back-pedalling and a momentary freezing-on-the-spot. I am honked at, shouted at, gestured to, from every direction; I force cars to brake hard, to swerve, to stop. With one indecisive twenty-yard dash I temporarily undermine the whole system and unleash chaos.

By the time I climb to the top step and sit down I am sweating again, my breathing is shallow and I need to lie down. I doubt I have more than an hour's walking left in me. According to the map in my guidebook, much of what there is to see is either towards the port or in the direction I've just come from. I decide to head towards the port. Most of the big buildings are located around there. I've had enough of the back streets; I'm in search of a more Florentine or Roman Naples – sunlit and grand.

The route I choose is fairly straightforward – an oblique circle. Start at the Castel Nuovo, then right towards the Teatro San Carlo, left into the Piazza del Plebiscito, where the Palazzo Reale and the mock Pantheon are located, then up Via Roma, dip into the Galleria Umberto, back to the Post Office and home – that's at least six major buildings in one hour. Speed tourism.

I buy a bottle of water at the first kiosk I come across and replenish the fluid I seem to be losing by the litre. Unlike on the evening of my arrival, I am now very aware of the heat outside my body. If two days ago the sickness had been pressing the sweat out of my body, the sun is now sucking it out.

Heading for the thirteenth-century Castel Nuovo, I am overcome with an ennobling keenness to learn about the centuries of architecture I will encounter. I wish to imbibe as much information as I can, to be educated, edified, inspired. This is a great city with an impressive history, much of which is embodied in its great buildings. But within twenty minutes I am back at the Post Office, and that includes stopping off and buying a fresh T-shirt. I can take nothing in. There were moments when the grandeur had some effect – the Piazza del Plebiscito, the Galleria Umberto – but they were fleeting, and I found myself quickly moving on in search of something else to arrest me. It seems that this cluster of great buildings can't compare in richness, in mystery, to the dark and narrow streets I scurried along in my search for a finer, sweeter Naples. I had expected its big set pieces to deliver an experience of the place, but it is clear that they are irrelevant when searching for the spirit of the city, a spirit that is unavoidably, if a little threateningly, present in the back streets.

I sit down on the Post Office steps and look again at my guidebook map. There are two areas close by where the streets are densely packed, like tiny grid systems, like mazes. I'll walk there, and whenever I hit a main road I'll turn back. I slam my guidebook shut. My plan has given me new resolve, extra energy. I skip down the steps and with native nimbleness cross the road to the café I passed earlier, now fully open for business, but with only half its tables occupied. I sit down at one and order two espressos (the word for 'double' eluding me) from the waiter. I need a fix – there is much to do, and little time. I have the inexplicable feeling I have at last made some kind of deal with this city. If I am willing to push myself a little Naples will reveal itself to me. In some strange way it has been tempting me to do this from the day that I arrived; from the moment I fell into Massimo's taxi my role as a regular tourist was suspended and I was offered the chance of a different experience altogether. I am beginning to regret that I will be flying home so soon.

And it is precisely while I am thinking this that she walks past. A girl I think I know. I am sure I've made a mistake: a distant memory of a girl I once thought I loved has dislodged itself, escaped from inside my mind and somehow become entangled with an unknown girl walking down the street towards me. I say inwardly, it can't be her. But before I can stop myself I call her name.

She turns. Looks at me. Her expression, first quizzical then

26

incredulous, must mirror mine. Louisa Wright, a girl, now a woman, I haven't seen in ten years. She walks up to the table, eyes wide in disbelief. I stand and raise my hands in amazement.

'Jim? No! Wow . . .' she says, her voice pitched high and breathless; she was walking at a clip.

'Wow, indeed,' I echo.

I'm not sure that my exclamation is due so much to my surprise at running into Louisa in Naples after ten years as to my astonishment that during that time her beauty hasn't diminished in any way and that she is still as unerringly beautiful as the day we first met – her seventeenth birthday.

'What are you doing here?' she asks, her voice still breathless but now lowering to its normal register.

'Holiday,' I say. 'What about you?'

The question seems to surprise her. 'Me? I live here,' she says and absently drops the big brown leather satchel she is carrying over her shoulder to the ground.

'You live here . . .'

We sit down at the table, and with perfect timing the waiter brings out the two espressos I ordered and places one before each of us. Without troubling herself with the coffee's miraculous appearance, Louisa dumps a sugar cube into her cup and gives it a quick stir.

'This is amazing,' she says, 'I was just thinking about you the other day. How long are you here for?'

I explain the vicissitudes of my trip so far.

'Oh, you poor thing. Where are you staying?'

'I'm not really sure. I fell into the first available taxi at the airport, passed out and was taken to a place just up the street. I was almost unconscious when I arrived. It's not a hotel. I think it's just an apartment.'

'Where?'

'Just off this street.' I point behind me.

'I love it around here,' Louisa says, holding her cup midway between the table and her lips. 'I've just come from the university.

It's a shortcut through here. I'm taking a course in Italian history. I loathe it. There're too many names to remember. How many Medicis *were* there? I find I only remember the mean ones, and Lorenzo il Magnifico, of course. Very sexy.' She shifts subject slightly. 'Did you know there are only oral exams here? You don't have to write anything down. Not a single essay. That's amazing, don't you think? There's hope for me yet. Remember what I used to be like?' She smiles – a beaming, unaffected smile.

I laugh. I remember very clearly that although she was only really interested in parties, clothes, friends, gossip, she was so attuned to her own sexual allure triviality was somehow eliminated in her.

An awkward silence follows. I think her sudden reference to the past has reminded her for the first time of our brief and irksome affair. She reaches blindly into her bag, pulls out a packet of cigarettes, opens the box and counts the cigarettes inside with the tip of her finger. She then appears to do some calculation to determine whether she can smoke one or not. Evidently she can. She lights up with a professional smoker's swiftness.

'Well, what do you think of Napoli?' she asks with new enthusiasm, her sky-blue eyes flashing brightly, all memories of our relationship forgotten.

'What can I say? I've seen so little.'

'Jim Wolf, lost for words. It must have had quite an effect.'

It is true; ten years ago I was more talkative. When she knew me I was animated by idealism, by my need to make a difference. But then I was twenty-five. I have failed too many times since then. I am a shadow of my former self – my life force drained by patients with the same efficiency as their addiction wastes them.

'Come on,' Louisa urges, 'admit you love it.'

'I'm going to spend the rest of the afternoon exploring this bit.' I gesture behind me with my thumb.

'Good idea. It's the largest living museum in the world. Though I think to call it a museum at all is a bit of an insult.'

With her elbows on the table, her hands together, a cigarette burning, Louisa looks wonderfully European – cool, indifferent, sexy. And yet with her slender body, pale skin and delicate features she is strikingly different from all the young Neapolitan women I have seen today, every one small, dark-skinned and voluptuous.

'Is there anything you recommend I see?' I ask her.

Louisa thinks, absently, charmingly, knitting her brow and stroking her chin.

'You should walk the length of Spaccanapoli . . . "Split Naples",' she translates. 'It cuts right across the city. It's parallel to us now. Up there.' She points.

'Is it safe?' I ask.

'Don't believe all you hear about Naples.' She laughs. 'Just some of it.'

We are silent for a minute or two, politely if a little awkwardly, smiling at one another. Louisa then asks when I am leaving.

'Tomorrow at four-thirty. I start a new job on Monday . . .'

'Oh, that's a shame . . . I was going to suggest meeting Monday . . .' Her eyes begin to dart from side to side. She is thinking of when else she might be able to meet me before I leave. 'I can't tomorrow . . .' she says almost to herself.

'Look . . . don't worry . . .' I say, a little disappointed. During our minute of silence I found myself fantasizing that a brief reconciliation might be possible. A one-night holiday romance. Our affair was conducted in the heart of winter but I am overcome by desire for Louisa in this afternoon heat. I picture her in my empty room undressing – windows open, shutters closed – while I shift the sunken mattress off the bed and into the centre of the room. I can feel the presence of her naked body in the palms of my hands as she stands at the end of the mattress, hot and sticky, ready to kneel, ready to curl under me, to raise her arms above her head and stretch out – a languorous flexing S-shape. I remember her ten years ago in my cold flat undressing under the duvet.

Louisa sits up, an idea striking her. 'Come to dinner tonight. I don't know why I didn't think of it. Alessandro will love you. He's mad about the English . . .'

'Alessandro?' I ask.

'My husband,' she says as if I should know.

It is my turn to sit up. The image of her in my room fades like a cheap special effect.

'You're married?' I smile and sip the dregs of my espresso to hide my disappointment.

'Yep,' she says, obviously pleased with herself. 'Two years.'

'Two years,' I repeat. So much longer than my two months with her. I disguise my envy of her husband, my covetousness of his time with her. I ask whether she is sure she doesn't want to check with her husband first before we make an arrangement. 'I have a phone number.' I try to retrieve the piece of paper from my pocket.

'God, no. It'll be fine. Come at eight-thirty.' She is certain, insistent. She rests her hand over mine. Her palm is hot. I feel a faint charge, a tremor. Louisa feels it, withdraws her hand. She smiles, tight, cool, brief; her eyes narrow.

'Where do you live?' I ask.

She recovers herself. 'On the hill. Chiaia.' She picks up my guidebook from the table, flicks through to the map, bends back the covers vigorously and flattens it out on the table between us. I am given my instructions, her long slender finger tracing the route I am to follow.

'We're here, right?' she says and I nod. 'And I live here, right?' I nod again. 'So, what you need to do is walk along here.' Each time she repeats 'here' she glances up at me to see if I am following her. Each time, I stare further into her blue eyes, taking less and less in. 'Then cross here. Go up here. Then down here. That's Via Roma. You need the funicular here. Get out at the first stop. Walk down. Five minutes and you're there. My house. 404.' She sits back.

'Louisa, I'll never find it . . .'

She looks astonished that her simple, highly detailed explanation has failed me. 'Catch a taxi then . . .' she says a little impatiently, but then, sensing my apprehension, softens. 'OK . . . I'll send the car if that's what it takes.'

'The car?'

'Alessandro works for the city. It's a perk. We're not really allowed to use it for private – you know? But I'll say you're ill. He won't mind. I'll arrange for it to pick you up here. Opposite the Post Office.'

'What time again?'

'Eight-thirty. And don't worry if the driver's in police uniform, sometimes they are, sometimes they're not.'

'What does your husband do?' I ask, intrigued.

'He's a judge. Presidente della corte d'Assise. That's the court of murder. They kind of specialize over here. That's why we have the police driver. The Camorra . . .'

'The Mafia?'

'The Mafia is Sicily. It's the Camorra here. But it's the same sort of thing. Murder, extortion, drug trafficking. But Alessandro only deals with murder.'

'Hope they don't shoot me by mistake,' I say with some alarm.

'Shoot you?' Louisa says laughing. 'They won't shoot you. They might try and blow up the car. But don't worry, the car's supposed to be some kind of fortress.' She stands up, pressing her cigarette firmly into the ashtray. 'Anyway, they're not after you. But now you'll have to excuse me. I'm very late.' She heaves her satchel onto her shoulder.

'Well, stand up, kiss me,' she orders when I remain seated.

I stand and lean over the table and we exchange kisses on both cheeks, quick, soft, with a little clunk of cheekbones. Just as we part Louisa whispers 'bye' into my ear, her voice once more high and breathless.

Within a few paces she is at exactly the place where, fifteen minutes before, I called out her name. It is as though I haven't yet done so and in a second it will be too late: she will be at the main road, my voice drowned out by the noise of the traffic, the incessant horns. This is what would have happened had I not called her name. It is the strangest sensation. Even though I know I stopped her, talked to her, arranged to see her later, it feels as if it all took place in a unique pocket of time, and if I choose not to include it in my life . . . there in front of me is the same girl bowling along, satchel slung over her shoulder, taking the shortcut from the university to meet her husband, uninterrupted.

There is something vertiginous about this temporal dilemma and I grip the table to steady myself. I want to blame the sensation on a resurgence of delirium brought on by a strong shot of caffeine but I feel once again a profound sense that the city is offering me something, an opportunity to choose my destiny, to twist fate my own way. It is asking me: did you just meet an ex-lover after ten years or did you just see a woman pass who reminded you of a girl you once knew? It is as though my peculiar sickness has given the possibilities in my life a peculiar transparency, and if I look closely enough I am being allowed to see the fork in the road.

4

As instructed by Louisa, I spend the rest of the afternoon walking the length of Spaccanapoli, the *decumanus inferior* as my guidebook calls it, narrow and high, splitting Naples from east to west. Occasionally it breaks out into piazzas and I look around churches that appeal, but mostly I wander, cutting up side streets that look interesting. I stumble across a street of shops that seem to sell only small terracotta figures, almost exclusively sacred but with some modern characters as well. Every shop has tens of thousands of them. More. The stock in each shop, the workmanship, the arrangements are identical. Row upon row of angels, shepherds, Virgin Marys, cribs, animals – all spilling out onto the street, massed around the doorways like crowds waiting for a sale. But tiny. It is freaky, unnerving. The street is the darkest I've yet walked up and I quicken my pace to the end.

I am on Spaccanapoli as the sun begins to set. The street is very long, very straight and slices through the heart of Naples before climbing the Vomero hill, tapering to a precise point at the very top; it is like an arrow aimed at the falling sun. I stand and watch for the exact moment when the sun and the arrow-point of the street meet. The last second before the rim of the sun rests on the rim of the earth seems to last for ever, an endless forestalling of the moment. But when it finally happens it is as if the sun is suddenly pricked open and light pours out, hot, white, dense. It is visible, racing down the length of Spaccanapoli. It takes a whole minute to reach where I am standing. People around me aware of its approach search for sunglasses or span their hands across their eyebrows and drop their heads. Incredibly, even the Vespas slow down while they search for a place to turn off, to plunge back into the darkness. The moment it hits the world disappears. It takes less than a second. And everything is obliterated. Enveloped by the light. I step into a doorway and watch people pass, vague as spirits in the brightness.

It is a minute or so before the light begins to fade, drawn up the street like smoke. Its retreat is visible over the paving stones. I follow it, withdrawing quickly before me. I feel like a small boy chasing after a toy invisibly attached to a long piece of string, being tugged away, always just out of my reach. I'm sure the locals are looking at me. I'm not sure whether the moving line demarcating the shadow and light is all that distinct, but it seems so to me. By the time I reach the piazza close to where I am staying the light has become so diffuse there is nothing left to follow and I am surrounded once again by shadow. I experience a profound sensation of loss, of abandonment, of sadness even. I put this down to increased feelings of vulnerability caused by my general physical weakness – this is after all a strange and mysterious place and not somewhere you want to feel exposed in any way. What I don't think is . . . this is a *signal* of any sort. I might find metaphysical explanations seductive when they suit me, but I'm certainly not superstitious and I refuse to believe that following a path of light that leads to darkness has any meaning.

Signora Maldini is standing in the middle of the front room when I walk in. Give or take a few inches and a possible slight shift in the angle of her hair, she hasn't moved from this morning. We greet one another awkwardly. I smile, she nods. This is followed by more awkwardness as I dither, wondering whether I should ask before going into my room – I do not want to behave as a guest if I am not one – and then a very awkward exchange as I explain I need a shower. I am led into the bathroom and shown how everything works. I am given a clean towel.

In my room the bed has been made. The sheets are so tightly tucked the edges of the mattress curl up. I place my bag on the bed. What should I wear to dinner with a judge and his wife? I have little to choose from. Jeans, old Dockers, T-shirts, a shirt, a pullover.

I arrange the neatest combination on the bed. At best, I will look stylishly dishevelled; at worst, disrespectfully scruffy. I undress and wrap the towel around me. The newspaper that appeared so mysteriously this morning is on the chair. Louisa said her husband was a target for the Camorra; Giacomo here is a penitent Camorra member. Is there some connection? A trial? Is this the reason the story has made the front page: dramatic scenes in courtroom as Camorra soldier breaks down. Confesses. Penitent. I scan the copy for clues, for words common to both languages that might help me decipher the story. *'Criminale'* is easy enough, as is *'avvocato'*. *'Auto-bomba'*. *Auto-bomba!* Louisa wasn't joking when she said this was their preferred mode of assassination. There are nine names listed. Victims? Accused? Gang members? I can't tell. Then further down there is that title: *Presidente della corte d'Assise*. Followed by the name: *Alessandro Mascagni*. Little doubt this is Louisa's husband. Little doubt I will be riding in his official car during some kind of trial involving Neapolitan organized crime and car bombs. Big doubt there is any helpful advice in either of my two guidebooks to cover this type of situation. Lost passport. Disabilities. Gay Italy. All covered. Meeting ex-girlfriend now married to senior judge in the middle of a car-bombing trial. Notable for its absence. I lie back on the bed. Judges are always being killed in Italy. And not just in Sicily. Am I in any danger? Maybe this is normal for Naples. Not in the particular – but generally. Visiting Florence you are certain to experience the beauty of the city. In Naples the experience is danger. That's what the city offers. Every tourist here feels it. I'm not special. It's like going to New Orleans and hearing jazz – it would be odd if you didn't.

When I arrive at the Post Office the car is waiting for me, a big, dark-green Alfa Romeo. A man in plain clothes climbs out of the driver's side door and walks around the front of the car. He opens the rear door for me.

He says, 'Signor Wolf . . .' and gestures for me to climb in.

I say, *'Grazie,'* and oblige.

The driver takes his seat and hits the central locking. I expect a click but instead it sounds more like the heavy clunking of two train carriages buckled together. Even the door locks themselves are heavy handles moulded into the interior. I instinctively curl my finger under them to see if they have any give – nothing, they might as well be cosmetic. Louisa was right, this is a fortress. No one's going to get snatched from this car. Let's hope its bullet-proof glass and bomb-resistant undercarriage are as effective.

We stay on the wide roads until the first junction and then turn left up a steep street. Every fifty yards or so there is a sharp, blind bend. There isn't a single place for two cars to pass, but each time we meet oncoming traffic we somehow manage. It involves astonishingly subtle manoeuvres on the part of both drivers, and a complete lack of concern for bodywork; sparks leap up as we scrape the car along a wall. This might have been avoided had one of us stopped but Neapolitan drivers don't like to stop if motion is possible. I haven't yet seen a car in Naples that doesn't have a dent, a scrape, a missing wing mirror. Towards the top of the hill the streets begin to widen. The buildings, mostly apartment blocks, begin to resemble those of most other big European cities: examples of every twentieth-century architectural movement all homogenized over time. Below me is the Historical Centre, with Spaccanapoli a black vein across its heart. Even from this elevated position Naples is a dark city.

After about ten minutes' winding down the other side of the hill along a high coast road, with apartment blocks above and below, we pull up outside the gates of a big white house. I presume this is where Louisa lives, where I am to get out; my driver is motionless, upright, in his seat.

'Louisa's?' I ask, unsure what else to say.

He releases the central locking. I thank him and climb out. As soon as I shut the door he pulls away, the back wheels spinning so fast that gravel sprays over my legs like shotgun pellets.

The house is set off the road between two tall apartment blocks. I push open the heavy gates. There is a two-tiered front garden. To my left the high branches of a marine pine spread over me like a single storm cloud in the clear night. To my right three palms sway gently in the warm breeze. Wide terracotta tile steps lead up to the entrance, splitting around a small dry fountain halfway up. A palm frond lies across the empty bowl like a discarded fan after a party. On either side of the massive double front doors there are small fruit trees in large pots, illuminated by tiny spotlights. I feel conspicuous; the beams appear to be aimed upwards at me. I look around for CCTV cameras. I feel a little nervous. I wish Louisa had checked. What if I'm unwelcome? What has she told her husband? She bumped into an old friend, someone she hasn't seen in years, or that I am an ex-lover? What will he be like? A legal star, obviously. Successful. Eminent. Not like me, that's for sure: unfulfilled and cul-de-sac'd in a profession I now hate. I am tempted to turn and run, not risk the ignominy of comparison, but I force myself to knock loudly, confidently. I step away from the door. I wait a full minute. Then I hear Louisa's voice cheerfully call, 'It'll be him. Don't worry. I'll get it.'

One of the big doors opens and Louisa appears. She is wearing a knee-length black dress, her hair is tied up and she has a shoe in her hand. As she greets me, she leans on the doorframe, kicks back one leg and presses her foot comfortably into the shoe.

I hesitate on the doorstep. 'Are you going out? I told you . . . you should have checked . . .'

'Don't be silly – we're all going out. Come in.'

I step into a square hallway. It is smaller inside than I imagined. More homely. The lights are low. The wallpaper is rose-coloured. There is a coat stand heavy with coats. I can smell coffee, wine. The air is sweet, rich. The place feels a little Christmassy.

Louisa kisses me softly on each cheek and slips her arm through mine. 'Come and meet Alessandro.'

We walk through a door, along a hallway and into a large library. The bookcases are crammed, the lower shelves obscured by towers of unshelved books extending into the room like a miniature Manhattan. To the right there is a baby grand, also laden with books. By the window is a large desk, and behind that, rising from his seat, is Louisa's husband.

Alessandro Mascagni is in his early fifties, handsome, powerfully built, with greying hair and beard cropped short, a wide smile and clear grey eyes. There is something fearsomely intelligent about his face.

As we enter the room he stands and, with arms open to greet us, exclaims loudly, exuberantly, 'Jim. Welcome. I am so happy to meet you. Come in . . .'

Louisa ushers me further into the room.

Stepping out from behind the desk, he declares, 'I am Alessandro Mascagni. Louisa's husband. Welcome to our home.'

He reaches for my outstretched hand with both his big, thick hands and draws me closer to him. I am instantly seduced by his warmth.

'Jim Wolf,' I say easily. 'Pleased to meet you.'

'How do you like Napoli?' he asks staring directly into my eyes, my hand still buried in his.

'I love it. Love it. I don't know whether Louisa told you but I've been ill for most of my holiday, but since this morning . . .'

'Wonderful, wonderful,' he says interrupting, my illness clearly of no interest to him. 'Naples is a very mysterious city, very mysterious. It is not sweet. It is not pretty. We have a word in Neapolitan dialect, *nzevosa*. The city . . . like on the skin.' He rubs his thick forearms, wild with grey hair. 'You understand? The city . . . on your skin. The buildings, the people, the dirt . . . I can't think of the expression?'

I shake my head and Alessandro looks to his wife. But I then realize what it is he means. 'It gets under your skin,' I say, and massage my fingers in my palms to demonstrate the palpableness of the sensation he is trying to describe.

'Yes, yes,' he says delighted. 'That is right. *Nzevosa* . . . Naples gets under your skin.'

I look around at Louisa standing by the door. She looks delighted also, aware of the impact her husband has on people and pleased, it seems, about the impact I have had on her husband.

'I knew he'd like you,' she calls to me, as though her husband wasn't there.

As if noticing her for the first time Alessandro calls sharply, 'Louisa. An aperitif. For our guest. Please.'

'What would you like, Jim?' Louisa asks me, knitting her brow irritably at her husband's abruptness.

'Anything,' I say.

'White wine? Campari?' She wants a decision.

'Really, anything . . .'

'Aless?' Louisa asks her husband, pronouncing it 'Alice'.

'Campari, Louisa,' he says. 'Now, Jim,' he says, his sharp eyes settling on me once again. 'How can we persuade you to stay longer in Naples? Three days is not long enough. For other cities maybe.'

I hear Louisa chuckle to herself as she makes the drinks in the corner of the room.

Alessandro echoes her laughter. 'Louisa is laughing because I like to be in my house near Sorrento. You know Sorrento?'

I shake my head. 'I've only heard of it. It's one of those places.'

'It is like your Tunbridge Wells. I am fifty-three. I like to read in peace. But for you Naples is wonderful, wonderful. Louisa loves it.'

'Love it,' she calls out mock-wearily.

All the time Alessandro is speaking English I sense the great struggle he has with his pronunciation. His Italian accent is like rough marble, without surface polish, and English seems to him to be made up of sounds that need precise articulation, a language made up of words that don't require the husky expressivity he is used to giving his Italian; and so for the most part his English remains trapped at the back of his throat, causing him to force out each resistant sound – every 'c' or 'k' hawked up, every 'r' rolled out, every diphthong crushed; a process that finally gives his

English a kind of impressive, exotic, if somewhat incomprehensible, gravity.

Louisa hands out the drinks. 'Campari,' she informs me, and then turning to her husband she says, 'We should be ready to go in five minutes. I'm just going to finish getting ready.' I watch her as she leaves, her pale shoulders glowing in the warm light of the room.

Alessandro and I stand opposite one another sipping our Camparis. I notice on his desk, open and face down, the book he was reading before being disturbed. I try to make the title out upside down. *Scienza Nuova*. Vico.

'You're reading Vico,' I say, sounding more than a little pretentious.

Alessandro smiles broadly. 'You know Vico? When I have a perplexing trial I read Vico.'

I decide it is not appropriate to ask him whether he is referring to the trial in the papers.

'I read it a few years ago,' I say, trying to remember exactly what it's about.

'So in England you are an intellectual?' Alessandro asks me, his eyes burning with expectation.

I laugh. 'England doesn't have intellectuals. I'm a counsellor.'

'A politician?' He appears even more delighted by this.

'No, no,' I say. 'I counsel drug addicts, alcoholics. A kind of psychotherapist.'

I can see Alessandro is a little disappointed. I continue, 'I read Vico because I was looking at new approaches to understanding my patients.'

Alessandro nods, indicating his reasons for reading him during a perplexing trial are similar. 'Yes, yes. I must remember what they say and what they mean will not always be clear to me . . .'

I presume he is referring to the accused, the witnesses.

Louisa comes back in and says, 'Are we ready? The car is here.'

Alessandro sets his glass down on his desk. Louisa, noticing I am unsure where to place mine, takes it from my hand and returns it

40

to the drinks table. We leave the room, the house, in silence, Alessandro and I following Louisa.

As we walk down the path to the road, I say, 'Thank you very much, both of you, for inviting me tonight.'

Louisa says, 'It's our pleasure, isn't it, Aless?'

Alessandro stops by the fountain and stares into it. 'What? What?' he says distractedly.

'It's our pleasure Jim is coming out with us to dinner?'

I expect a sudden rush of agreement, an exuberant smile or gesture to confirm this to me, but there is nothing. Alessandro just looks at me as though he is seeing me for the first time and isn't sure who I am, why I am there. He then remembers and squeezes my shoulder. 'I am very happy.'

The car is not waiting. We wait on the side of the road. Louisa leans against Alessandro. I stand awkwardly next to Louisa. It is still very hot and I am beginning to tire. Conversation over dinner will exhaust me further. Deciphering Alessandro is tough enough, but tougher still is having to be interesting myself when not at my sharpest. And I sense this is what Louisa wants from me. To impress her husband.

The car pulls up. The same driver climbs out and addresses Alessandro as Presidente and Louisa as Signora Mascagni. Hearing her called this I am forced to look at her afresh. She was just plain Louisa Wright when I last saw her in England. Somehow this now seems utterly wrong, ordinary, prosaic, suburban. Whereas, young as she still is, Signora Mascagni fits her perfectly, finally revealing why years ago, when other girls were shy and sexually inhibited, or loud and sexually brash, there was about her such elemental elegance, such sexual coolness. They were going to be the qualities that attracted the charismatic Italian judge she would marry, the man she would love (it is clear to me she loves him and loves him easily), and the man who would love her seriously, passionately, unashamedly. Even their age difference is somehow cancelled out by the inevitability of their match and the equality of their impressiveness.

I suddenly want to be better dressed. And not just for this evening, but from now on. I want a better job – influence, power, prestige. I want a house, a wife. A beautiful wife. I am not un-handsome, or without intelligence. Yet at thirty-five I am scruffy, single, living in a rented flat and about to start a new job I've been doing for years. My life curve hasn't curved much since I was with Louisa ten years ago.

We all climb into the back of the car. We squash up together with Louisa in the middle, her hand on Alessandro's knee. The locks come down.

'All safe and sound,' Louisa says and pats me on the knee.

As we circle our way back into the centre of Naples, Alessandro points out the various sights below us just distinguishable in the moonlight, grading them Very Important, Important, Not Impor-tant. I look in the general direction and make phatic sounds of comprehension. Louisa points out into the darkness of the bay.

'See those lights out there?' she asks me, knocking my knee with hers.

I squint. All I can make out is a small dark shape with a cluster of tiny lights in the middle. It looks like a section of the starry night sky has fallen into the sea.

'It's Capri. Very important,' Louisa says, and turning to Alessandro adds, 'isn't it?'

'Armani, Gucci, Versace,' Alessandro lists. 'Very, very important.'

We are now back in the old part of the city, the car snaking through the streets.

'Where are we going?' I half-whisper to Louisa.

'Aless's favourite restaurant. Very Neapolitan. Very important.' The last two sentences she says gruffly, mimicking her husband's accent. She then adds, whispering conspiratorially, 'I'm afraid he will order for you. I hope you're hungry . . .'

Before I can respond, Alessandro leans around his wife and says, 'Jim. This restaurant is very Neapolitan. Very important. When I'm in London I like to go to Brick Lane for curry. Very British.' He is pleased with this and laughs.

'I don't live far from Brick Lane,' I say.

Alessandro is visibly roused by this and sits forward, his impressive head half in shadow, the streetlights flitting across his face. 'It is an immigrant area, yes? We don't have many immigrants in Naples. In the north it is a problem. The north is rich. They want to keep their money.'

Louisa, having leaned back to allow us to talk, interjects, 'Alessandro is a *sessantottino*. He doesn't believe in national boundaries.' Then, turning to her husband, she says, 'Do you, darling?'

It is my turn to lean forward, around Louisa. 'What's a *sessantino*?'

'*Sessantottino*,' Alessandro corrects me, smiling. 'I was twenty-one in 1968.' He regards this as clearly explanation enough. Louisa elaborates. 'It is the name for the generation of 1968 – you know, after the riots and protests, the generation who wanted to change the world.' She then adds, 'Alessandro was a communist for twenty years.'

'You were a communist?' I say, turning to Alessandro.

Unexpectedly Alessandro presses his hands together as though about to pray and waves them at me imploringly. I am unsure what to make of this.

'You still *are* a communist,' I offer.

He repeats the gesture; I look to Louisa. 'I don't understand.'

'It means: "Do you have to ask?" It's very Neapolitan. They take for granted a certain amount of clairvoyance. Especially the men. They can have whole conversations this way. Football, politics, women.' She then closes the fingers of one hand together, very much like Signora Maldini did when asking me whether I wanted something to eat, and shakes it in front of her chest firmly. 'This means you're talking bullshit or you're being ridiculous. You'll see a lot of that.'

Alessandro thinks this is very funny. 'One day she will be a true Neapolitan woman.' He resumes praying, this time I presume to underline how amusing the image is, an image he takes for granted we all find as amusing. I decide to adopt these gestures with my patients. That way I won't have to say anything.

The car pulls up outside a small restaurant with an empty fish tank in the window. Inside there are square tables covered with plastic gingham tablecloths. High in the corner is a small TV showing a football game that the two waiters, both young men, refuse to divert their eyes from even while listing the specials, taking down orders and serving the food. The place is almost full. Ordinary Neapolitans eating, drinking, watching the football.

'Napoli, Lazio,' Alessandro informs me as we are shown to our table. He takes a seat with his back to the television.

'You don't like football?' I ask.

'He prefers his food,' Louisa answers for him as she sits next to her husband. Alessandro invites me to sit opposite him.

'Do you like football?' he asks. I can sense the answer he wants. I shake my head. 'Not really.'

'Too intellectual?' he asks. I take it he means me rather than football.

I laugh. 'Far too intellectual.'

A waiter stands over us and greets Louisa and Alessandro informally. I am introduced. His name is Angelo. We shake hands. He asks whether I speak any Italian; I say, 'No, sorry.' He then starts to talk to Alessandro about something I can't follow. Every now and then he sneaks a look at Louisa. Whenever she returns his gaze he coyly dips his eyes. I imagine him wondering how it feels to kiss her faintly tanned shoulders. I imagine it myself; I remember it. I turn to Alessandro and note for the first time the vast physical contrast between him and his wife. Beneath his expensive white shirt, he has a hardy, bullish, peasant body – a body of labour, exertion, force. I feel a surge of sexual jealousy for the first time. I want Louisa. I want her because I am taller, slimmer, younger than her husband.

My thoughts are disturbed by Angelo listing the specials and by Louisa explaining to me that this, the first course, will be soup or pasta. I listen to the names of the dishes in Italian followed by Louisa's description of them in English. Angelo and Louisa speak alternately, in a measured metre, as though participating in a bilingual litany. When they are finished Alessandro insists I have the *pasta e patate*.

'What is it?' I ask Louisa.

'Pasta and potato,' she says, adding, 'Don't be put off, it's delicious.'

I feel stupid for not understanding the first time. I compliantly agree although I am concerned my reduced appetite is going to offend someone this evening.

Waiting for the first course to arrive I am required to live up to my new role as England's pre-eminent intellectual. Alessandro wants to discuss British politics, Britain as a post-colonial power, London as the cultural capital of the world and Britain as a place he loves. He is overwhelming – a bulldozer of a conversationalist, garrulous, energetic, passionate. Even once the food has arrived and we eat he continues to talk, ask questions, probe my answers, all the time sucking up spaghetti, supping red wine and breaking open the bread with his powerful hands; the whole range of noises acting like punctuation to his discourse. Louisa constantly tells him to slow down, eat *then* speak, to speak more slowly, *he* might understand what he's saying but no one else does. At all this he laughs heartily. I understand what he is saying, he says. I am invited to confirm this. I nod. Louisa shrugs resignedly.

'I told you he loves the English,' she says.

I ask Alessandro what's so great about the English. I expect the praying gesture. But no, he washes down the last of his spaghetti with the dregs of our second jug of wine and mops up the sauce with a lump of bread. 'You are a strange people. *Pratico*. Without emotion. But eccentric. You are not religious, political . . .' I raise my eyebrows at this. He continues, 'I love London. In London I feel safe. Not because it is more dangerous here for me, I do not mean like that. But because without religion, politics, there is no danger of intolerance: *fascismo* – you understand?' He clenches his fists and presses them to his chest and then slowly opens out his hands. It looks like he is emptying his heart to me. But all he wants

45

is complete comprehension with his limited English. I implore him to continue by nodding and sitting forward.

He says with a smile, 'You are a philosophical people.'

I cut in. I can't resist, I'm so surprised by such an evaluation. 'I can't accept that. I think we're the least philosophical country in Europe. Politics, religion are the principal begetters of philosophical thought. We have so little, at least in any original sense.' I am pleased with this.

So it seems is Alessandro – it is the first time I have contradicted him. But then with an extravagant wave of his hand he says, 'I do not mean you are a country of philosophers. But without religion, politics there is . . . there is . . . there is . . .' He looks to Louisa for help.

Louisa rolls out his options as if she's done it a thousand times, 'there is hope, there is time, there is room, there is the chance . . .'

'Yes . . . there is room . . .' he says, but then comes up with a better word for himself. 'There is the freedom for *pluralismo*, you understand . . .'

'I find we are a dull country, a dull people,' I say.

Alessandro shrugs. 'Perhaps.'

Louisa says, 'Alessandro thinks the English and the Italians are the two extremes of Western Europe. We are like other countries, but not like each other.'

Instead of caring whether his wife is interpreting him correctly, Alessandro pushes his chair away from the table, stands up, brushes the large crumbs of bread from his lap and wanders into the kitchen at the rear of the restaurant.

'He's selecting our food,' Louisa explains when I look perturbed by his sudden disappearance. She then smiles warmly and asks me whether I'm enjoying myself.

'Alessandro is quite something,' I say. 'I wish I was on better form.'

For the second time today Louisa reaches over the table and rests her hand over mine. 'It really is lovely seeing you again. I was thinking a while back if there was one person I knew Aless might like it was you. He thinks all my friends are silly, and his friends are all so much older than me, and are really, really serious. Politics, politics, politics.' She says this in a deep, boring voice to make her point. 'There are some young lawyers, but Italian men are nothing but trouble.' Then, just like earlier today, she ever so slightly shifts subject. 'But as you can see I'm a little more grown up now . . .'

She is, but compared to Alessandro we both seem like children. And because of this I feel a connection forming between us. It is harmless, I am sure, based on little more than a culturally shared amusement at his Italianate extravagance, but I suspect it also includes an element of private, remembered flirtation. When he is present Louisa looks like his wife; when we are alone she looks like my girlfriend. I sense she feels this. I want to make a joke about it, but decide not to. Instead I say, 'What's this stuff in the paper about Il Pentito? I saw Alessandro's name . . .'

'It's a trial. Giacomo Sonino is Il Pentito.' She says this as though she's announcing a star actor as a lead character in a film.

'What does it mean?'

'It's like a supergrass, you know, someone who names names. The official term is *collaboratore*, but the papers say *pentito*.'

'I see . . .' It seems strange to me the newspapers would use a word that has a moral overtone, whereas the official term has more negative connotations.

'It's important because he's named nine members of his own gang.'

'Was it a car bomb?'

'Four members of a rival gang were killed. And three bystanders. But it wasn't just one bomb; there were loads. One morning. The whole city heard them.'

'Why?'

'It's very complicated. It goes back years. Alessandro can tell you all about it. But basically there are now two major gangs in Naples. Sonino was the head of one, the newest. And then there is the old lot. Every now and then they start killing each other. You get used to it.' I look sceptical. 'You do! The Camorra are part of life here.

47

Two years ago, when we were first married, where Alessandro works, the criminal courts . . . they were being moved into a massive new tribunal, built especially. First day – the Camorra blew it up. Bang.'

I laugh.

'It's serious stuff,' she says seriously; then adds, 'It's hard to get a conviction with a *pentito*. Especially one as complicated as Sonino. If you were staying longer you could go and watch. It's fascinating.'

Alessandro returns to the table and sits down. Louisa turns to him, laying her hand over his. 'I was just saying to Jim, if he was staying longer he could come and watch you at work. See the gangsters in their cages.'

I notice Alessandro stiffen for a moment, but he then relaxes. 'Of course, of course. I have a very interesting trial, Jim, very interesting.'

He then proceeds to tell me in a little more detail the same story Louisa has just related to me. The trial has lasted ten months, it is very perplexing, many accused, a *pentito*, political pressure from the Justice Department, responsibility to the families of victims, publicity. And on top of all that it must end soon. It is a headache, he says and raps his temple with his knuckles.

When he finishes I ask him, 'Why did you choose the court of murder?'

Alessandro looks at Louisa and I wonder whether I've said something wrong. But before I can apologize our second course arrives. On each plate there is a large grilled squid, porcelain-white, split open and empty like a cadaver after an autopsy. That's it. Then more plates, smaller ones, are brought out and placed before us. Mushrooms and a green vegetable that looks like overcooked broccoli.

Louisa explains. 'I think these are the best mushrooms in Italy. And this,' she points to the green stuff, 'is *friarielli*. A local delicacy. It may not look very appetizing, but it's delicious.' Her eyes are ravenous.

I help myself. I am aware I have asked a question that has not been answered. I am not sure whether it was ignored for some reason or just drowned out by the increasingly loud ambient noise. I repeat it.

Alessandro rests his knife and fork on his plate and places his elbows on the table, clasping his hands together to form an arch over his food. 'It is simple, Jim. It is very serious to kill someone. It's not like other crime, like robbery. It can never be a question of need. You do not *need* the life of a man. It is not possible. The many excuses I can make for the man who steals, I cannot make for the man who murders. When I was just an ordinary judge, if you committed a crime, come to Alessandro Mascagni's court – he will understand. He will let you go free. Not true, but that is what they thought. There are many poor people in the south of Italy. It is not a simple situation. Organized crime supports many people, many ordinary people. Many times I blame society first, the criminal second. But not so easily for murder. Here in Naples we have many murders. It is not like London. I must know the man who commits this crime. The society I know. Without understanding the psychology, every murder in Naples is the same. Camorra. So it is very important.'

He says this casually, anecdotally almost, but I am aware of the enormous seriousness behind it. His affability has been so disarming, his exuberance so charming, I haven't really understood what it is he does, what he is. I've never met a judge before and it's doubtful in England I ever would; but if I did, I am certain they would not be like Alessandro. He might be forced, in speaking a foreign language, to articulate his thoughts simplistically, but in his last three statements I sense a kind of Dostoyevskian fascination with the man who murders; a profound moral necessity to understand why such a grave act, each grave act, of murder is committed. The decision to do this work was not taken for its gangster glamour, the obvious allure of such crimes compared to lesser offences, but because in a city like Naples it is a social imperative that a man with his sensibilities undertakes this kind of work. For Alessandro presiding over the court of murder is clearly a civic duty underpinned by a kind of political morality; the legality of the offence is secondary, I sense. I want to ask him about this, but Louisa says, 'Alessandro's trials are legendary. They go on twice as long as anyone else's.'

Her husband laughs. He is plainly aware his obduracy allows for a certain warm-hearted mockery.

'In Italy it is not like in British justice,' he explains. 'The judge is after the reality of the reality, not the reality of the courtroom.' Here Alessandro draws out a frame in the air. 'The picture in the courtroom is not trustworthy. In Italy if something is not clear to me I can stop the trial and order investigation, more investigation. I have to be satisfied.' He laughs. 'I am happy if I am satisfied.' And picking up his knife and fork he starts to eat.

It is now my turn to speak about my work. Louisa prompts me. Asking me about my new job. I am aware she wants me to impress her husband. My enthusiasm is low but I do my best hoping Alessandro will be interested because my work similarly deals with the individual fallout of socio-economic problems, and because addiction and homelessness are political issues if you believe capitalist society tacitly preserves an underclass, which he must do given his left-wing politics. But this does not interest Alessandro. I can tell as I'm speaking he is forming a question, a question I fear will be as straightforward as mine to him earlier. And I fear it because my answer will not be as persuasive. If I'm honest with myself I know I cannot be as impressive and this galls me. I don't want to appear inconsequential in comparison. But I am wrong. He asks me something quite unexpected and the manner in which he asks it takes me by surprise.

Leaning back in his chair he says lightly, seemingly without reason or any particular intent, 'Tell me, Jim, why are you interested in addiction?'

I am surprised because it's a lawyer's question. It might have seemed casually delivered but it was deliberately phrased. He is not interested in addiction, he's interested in me. Answering this question I have to reveal something of myself. It feels a little manipulative.

I answer as honestly as possible. 'I have an addictive personality, it is true. But that's not what interests me. Interested me. Nothing about my job interests me now. Once it was everything, when I first met Louisa. But these days I feel like I'm being sucked dry by anyone who needs help. I have nothing new to say. I don't believe in anything I say.'

Alessandro asks bluntly, 'So why do you carry on? Why work at something that makes you unhappy?' He has adroitly shifted from lawyer to psychologist.

'I'm probably as bored with me as I am with my job so I don't care what I do.' I snort wryly and take a large gulp of wine.

'You are very honest, Jim, and I think it is true what you say.' An older, wiser man counselling the young and foolish.

I feel this man has with one well-chosen question revealed something important about my current state of self that I have been unable to face, and he has done so because he finds me wanting, yet at the same time finds me interesting enough to be bothered. I look over to Louisa.

'Annoying, isn't he?' she says brightly.

'Very,' I say, smiling.

Alessandro also is smiling. He is pleased we have come out to dinner and got along so well. He reaches behind to his jacket hung on the back of his chair and draws out his wallet and a pen from the inside pocket. He opens the wallet with his big, undexterous fingers and pulls out a business card. He turns it over and writes on the reverse. Hands it to me. 'Our address.'

'Thank you,' I say.

He says, 'Yours?' and offers me his expensive fountain pen.

I look about me for something to write on. Alessandro draws out another business card and hands it to me, reverse side up. I write my address.

'We are in London in November. We will come and see you?'

'Please do,' I say, a little surprised at his eagerness. 'You're welcome any time.'

'And if you come back to Naples,' he says in reply, 'you will stay with us.'

51

Come back? Of course, I'm leaving tomorrow. This feels like the first night of my holiday.

'Maybe in the summer,' he says.

Louisa, who has remained quiet during our invitation negotiations, suddenly speaks up. 'After the trial we are going to China.'

'Wow,' I say.

'I know. It's very exciting, but do come back. Soon. Aless works so hard. I need a playmate.'

I am feeling a little drunk, too drunk to regard this request as anything but sweetly charming. Besides I can't covet the wife of a man who has just seduced me in this way. I want to see them both again as a couple and I want them both, as a couple, to want to see me again, and to share my feeling of connection, warmth – I am drunker than I thought.

Over *limoncello*, the local liqueur, the conversation is more general, and Alessandro participates less, occasionally looking over his shoulder at the football. Louisa and I reminisce about the few people we know in common or used to. Alessandro sometimes laughs along with us. I'm not convinced he fully understands why something we've said is funny. Though this should only emphasize the difficulties of following another language when spoken by two native speakers, it also makes him seem older, out of touch. I sense Louisa also feels this and is a little embarrassed.

When we are finished Alessandro insists on paying and leaves a pile of notes on the table, without it seems receiving a bill or even a verbal price for the food. He admits he is tired and yawns broadly. He tells me they have to go and see his mother tomorrow. Louisa rolls her eyes at this. Alessandro says, 'In Italy mother is best!' and from his laughter I judge it is the joke of the day for him.

By the car, I am informed we are just three blocks away from where I'm staying; even so they offer to drive me there. Feeling bold, I opt to walk. As we part I offer Alessandro my hand but he says we are in Italy and embraces me. I feel his cropped beard rub against my cheek and it reminds me of hugging my father when I was a child. Louisa's cheek, however, pressed against my lips only reminds me of Louisa, and for a split second the ten years between our brief affair and this moment are crushed to nothing, creating inside me a continuous, unbroken thread of desire. I hold on to her and take a deep breath, drawing in the faintest odour of her body beneath her fading perfume. When I am full – as intoxicated by her as by all the wine I have drunk – I let go. Alessandro, yawning again, doesn't seem to have noticed my indulgence, and Louisa just asks whether I'm sure I'm OK to find my way back. I assure her and we part finally with more promises to see one another soon.

As I leave them, I hear Alessandro address Louisa in Italian. Her response is fluent with a softly undulating accent. Not once during our two meetings today have I asked her whether she speaks Italian, presuming she could not. I decide I will take an Italian course myself when I get back to London.

5

I sleep late. I have to. Exhausted by dreams – a confluence of my explorations yesterday and memories of Louisa ten years ago. I awake with my heart beating hard. I think it's a hand pounding on the door. I sit up prepared for attack. Camorra henchmen coming to kidnap me. Having been seen last night with Alessandro Mascagni I am mistaken for an important member of his family; I am collateral for the freedom of the nine Camorra family members on trial. The sheets, once again, are damp and twisted around me. I wrestle free and sit up. It is only then I realize the hammering is not at the door but inside my chest. I slump back down on the bed. For the first time I feel quite glad to be leaving this afternoon. Naples is an extraordinary city but these days I'm not sure I possess the robustness of spirit that such a place requires. I am disappointed in myself.

I climb out of bed, dress and step out onto the balcony. I salute the family opposite; they wave back. It seems I am forgiven for yesterday's exhibitionism. Signora Maldini is standing on the balcony to my right. She is unchanged, in a black dress, blue housecoat, her hair leaning precariously. She smokes. 'Buon giorno, signora,' I say.

'Buon giorno, signor. Caffè?' she says.

'Sì, grazie,' I say and indicate I will be ready in a moment. She disappears inside. I look down to the street. From this height the paving stones are shiny and smooth, diamond-shaped, and look like the sections of a long black velvet cloth. Three young kids appear with a football. They kick it to each other, ricocheting it off the walls. The sound is dull, soft, deep. Their cries of 'Napoli, Napoli' are sweetly edged with the huskiness of the native dialect. My earlier anxiety leaves me. I like it here and I will return soon.

I have coffee with Signora Maldini. The television remains on

54

throughout. She offers me a vacuum-packed brioche. I don't want it but don't like to refuse. She heats it up in a microwave and hands it to me. It is foul, its apricot filling acidic. I am forced to drink more coffee to wash the taste away and this makes my stomach churn. I rush for the toilet.

When I return Signora Maldini, unperturbed by my dash from the table, is quietly looking through my guidebook. She turns the pages slowly, stopping at the photographs – photographs she regards intently as if she is looking for mistakes in a drawing of a place she knows well.

As I approach she says, '*Bella*, Napoli. *Si?*'

'*Si, bella.*' I agree.

Signora Maldini then nods sagely to herself and hands me the book. I try to explain that I am leaving this afternoon and she claims to understand but I'm not sure she does. I tell her I'll be back at two-thirty for my bag. She again intimates she understands but this time repeats 'two-thirty' back to me, in English, so I'm forced to accept this as real proof of comprehension, whether or not she knows what it means.

As I leave the building, ducking through the small door, I realize I haven't yet established what I owe for my room. I decide that no matter what I will leave a hundred pounds in lire in the room, just in case after having discussed the issue I'm forced to accept her hospitality or the sum she asks for is not sufficient for the kindness she's shown.

It is hot on the streets. It may be morning but the air is already heavy and humid. Above me the long slat of sky is cloudless and blue. I head towards the Spanish Quarter. My guidebook says it is quintessentially Neapolitan and therefore must be approached with caution. When I get there I am surprised to find the streets are narrower still than those in the old city. Many of the buildings are propped up by wood scaffolding erected after the 1980 earthquake. But what is most astonishing is that it quite literally backs up onto one of the most expensive shopping streets in Naples. The division of rich and poor is a footstep. The disparity is shocking. I am walking into a slum via a retail paradise. Louisa warned me not to appear too nosy. You're looking at how people live now, not a thousand years ago. I pretend I'm heading somewhere or at least try to look as though I know where I'm going.

Like yesterday, I take little detail in. I'm not a natural anthropologist. I don't think I'm particularly observant. What I am after is a deeper impression – what it feels like to live here, to grow up here, to spend a lifetime here. Something experiential. There is almost a nineteenth-century feel to its poverty – it's an old-world inner city, without regeneration or gentrification. Sneaking the occasional glance through the open double doors of the *bassi* I sometimes see three, four generations crammed into one room – a small, sparse room, with divans lining the walls, table in the middle, a cooker, a fridge in the rear; the few feet of street directly outside their front door stands in for every other room a family might need. Mothers, fathers, grandparents, children, babies all spill out and sit along the wall on old chairs, olive-oil cans, a bench made out of bricks and a plank of scaffolding. Above them, rigged out across the street, washing flutters gently like an arrangement of paddle fans, cooling them off. Everywhere I look there is glare from clean laundry – shirts, vests, underwear as bright white as any commercial detergent might implausibly promise. Unlike in the old city, these streets are flooded with sunlight, refracted and intensified by the collages of drying clothes. The whole place feels rock dry, as if the sun has bleached out all of the colour and sucked out all the moisture of the physical material that exists here.

After an hour I start to wander back down the hill. Before I hit Via Roma I come across a *basso* converted into a small pizzeria. I peer inside. Six small tables, a counter and an oven. A man appears from a back door. He is about my age. He waves me in. He has a friendly face and a Tintin quiff, created, it seems, by running his sleeve up over his forehead to wipe off the sweat. He looks hassled, as if the restaurant is busy and he is working away at full stretch in a hot kitchen. His apron, however, is spotlessly clean. He gestures for me to sit down. I am offered a choice between a *marinara* and a *margherita* pizza. There are no other choices. I opt for the *marinara*. The guidebook says the pizza was invented in Naples and the *marinara* was the first and is still considered the best.

While the pizza is baked I am offered *caffè*, Coke, beer, a cigarette, things I don't understand. I order a litre of water – *frizzante* – and drink it quickly. The chef comes and sits at the table with me but doesn't appear to want to talk. He lights a cigarette, rolls his lighter back and forth along his thigh, looking thoughtful. I sit back, cross my legs at the ankles, feeling hungrier than I have in days.

The pizza, when it arrives, is long: an attenuated oval shape. It is crisp, a little burnt around the edge, the tomato sauce bubbling and popping. It looks like the crater of a volcano. I pull it into four quarters, take one quarter, fold it in two and begin to eat. The chef obviously approves, nodding to me. He then disappears into the back and returns with a jug of red wine and two glasses. He pours us both some wine. He drinks while I eat. The conversation that passes between us is little more than grunting noises indicating how much we are enjoying our little repast. It is as though neither of us can quite believe how easy life is – to be sitting in the cool shade on a beautiful hot day drinking flavoursome red wine and eating pizza; my friend has accepted the last quarter of my pizza. I want to ask him what he knows about the *pentito* trial, to get an ordinary Neapolitan's view, but the preamble of do you speak English, etc., tires me out before I even start. Besides, there is something manfully satisfying in the silence between us.

I check my watch. I have about an hour before I should head back. I am tempted to stay where I am but I promised Alessandro I'd have a look at his old place of work, the Castel Capuano. I ask for the *conto*. The chef and I shake hands and I duck out of the place onto the parched paving stones, watery in the early afternoon heat. I head towards the port. I want to see the Bay of Naples up close, the long reach of the Sorrentine peninsula and Capri out in the bay itself.

The dock is busy. Tourist buses line the car park, hordes of Americans wander around with their particular brand of arrogance, ignorance and lousy dress sense. I skirt them with the same dread as they have of the Neapolitans. The biggest of the docked boats is bound for Palermo, Sicily. I wish I were boarding that, heading there, instead of back to London. I scan the line of passengers readying to board for gangster types; I figure a boat from Naples to Sicily must convey its fair share of mobsters. I wonder what kind of relationship the two organizations have. It is always the Mafia one thinks of when organized crime is mentioned, always Sicily, never Naples or the Camorra. Is that because they are less powerful? Less international? Or is it simply because of *The Godfather?* If I was the Camorra I'd be pissed off.

I sit down for ten minutes and watch the ferries and hydrofoils heading off to Capri, Sorrento, Ischia. I had originally wanted to visit Sorrento – it may be like Tunbridge Wells now, yet during the nineteenth century you could run into Wagner, Nietzsche, Ruskin, the Brownings. It replaced Naples as the important southern stop on the Grand Tour. Only a few years before Naples had been the most fashionable and popular city in Europe, with Goethe in its thrall, Nelson and Lady Hamilton in love, Casanova prowling, Shelley in despair. My guidebook informs me that it has yet to recover its popularity. I am overcome with an evangelical desire to spread the word. Naples is the city to visit. Forget Florence, Rome. This is the place to come if you want an authentic Italian experience, a city that has retained its history, and not through preservation or restoration, but by a kind of human energy that flows through its streets, uniting its past and its present. Unlike other great historical cities that have died because their greatest age has passed, Naples remains a living city, and this is primarily because for every Neapolitan *now* is the great age, simply, modestly, life-affirmingly.

I check my watch again. I am running late, but I decide I'll be one of those super-confident travellers who ignore the two-hour check-in time and arrive only half an hour before their flight and miss all the queues, the sitting around, the interminable PA announcements. As a rule I'm early, so I reckon I'm owed a late arrival. I head off at a clip towards Alessandro's old place of work.

As I approach I am instantly aware that the surrounding neighbourhood is the most dangerous I have encountered so far. The streets are dirtier; the buildings, suddenly modern, are rundown; the shops are empty. There are a couple of small, semi-derelict, porn cinemas. The ubiquitous film and political posters covering every wall are sprayed with graffiti or torn down; shreds litter the street. There is something edgy in the air. The groups of young men standing around are larger; the men themselves are more shiftless, less contented. And they stare harder. Their interest in me is not just neighbourhood curiosity, amusement at the lone tourist; it is watchful, territorial, threatening. One small gang spread themselves out across the pavement as I approach, forcing me to step out into the street. As I pass, a cigarette is flicked at my feet. The movement is quick, just a snap of the wrist, but it is hostile, provocative. There is a small burst of embers around my ankles. I flinch but do not break my stride. Don't look scared, I say to myself, look directly ahead and turn off at the first opportunity. Alessandro could have warned me, I think to myself when I have returned to the safety of the shadows of the old city.

By the time I reach the old Tribunale, I do not have much time to look around. It is like most of Naples' great buildings, grand, imposing, solid, without flourish or conceit, the perfect place to dispense justice with moral certitude while still retaining a sense of human theatre. I am envious of such a place of work, and as I jog back to Signora Maldini's my mind turns to tomorrow and the small prefabs behind Middlesex Hospital that will be my office and consulting rooms. I imagine them in the rain, the hard, grey rain of London, windows darkened by its chemical residue; inside so cold and damp the Calor-gas heaters will have to be on most of the year; the carpet worn down to its underlay; and chairs – both analyst's and analysand's – made from grey moulded plastic with one leg inevitably fractionally shorter than the others causing a permanent, irritating wobble. How can anyone summon the will to quit their addiction going there for help? Where's the psychological ergonomics, the clinical feng shui? Where, in point of fact, is the commitment to cure, when the place is no more than a Portaloo?

I am musing on this depressing prospect when I bump into Massimo, my life-saving cab-driver from my first night, sitting on the bonnet of his taxi just outside Signora Maldini's. He greets me like an old friend, pressing his muscular hand over my forehead and saying, *'La febbre, febbre, quarantena per signor. Presto, presto.'*

I struggle free and force a smile. I am pleased to see him, but his grip is alarmingly firm.

'Massimo. *Grazie, grazie* . . . for bringing me here.' I point. 'Signora Maldini's.' And once again the inscrutable expression; it is as though he has no idea to whom I'm referring. But he must do, he brought me here and now he has returned as I am about to leave. Informed by Signora Maldini, I assume. I shake my head incredulously and give him a manful whack on the back to show my appreciation.

I am not surprised to find Signora Maldini is out; she clearly didn't understand when I was leaving. I am relieved but a little sad. I don't have time for goodbyes, and certainly not to argue over the price of my room. I leave nearly all my lire on the table with a scribbled note: *'Arrivederci e molto, molto grazie, love Jim xxx.'* I pack quickly and dash down the stairs. Massimo is already in the car, engine running.

From the moment we pull out onto Via Mezzocannone we are embedded in traffic. It's worse than when I arrived. It takes us twenty minutes to reach Piazza Garibaldi. Massimo is chatty, quite unlike when we first met. I understand little, although I presume it's about football. Besides, I am becoming concerned about the time. If the traffic doesn't break my flight will leave before I'm even close to the airport. I lean over the passenger seat and tap my watch trying to impress the urgency upon Massimo, but all he does is laugh. I am beginning to think he has no intention of getting me to the airport on time; two gaps in front of us have appeared that any self-respecting Italian driver would have exploited. I am sweating again. It is pouring from me. I debate whether to bail out and thread through the traffic on foot, flag another taxi on the other side of the piazza, where the traffic looks more free-flowing, but decide it would be an act of betrayal – four days ago this man saved me from god knows what fate.

It takes another fifteen minutes to nudge our way round Piazza Garibaldi and into the freer traffic. I don't dare look at my watch. A 737 roars over us – it is close, we are close. Massimo snakes through the traffic with ease, his body leaning with each lane change. I rock from side to side in the back. A large sign over the road directs the traffic into the airport. First Departures, then Arrivals. Two slip roads to the left. I can see them approaching. We drive straight past. I sit forward, screaming in English, 'What are you doing? We've missed the . . .' Massimo just points ahead, unfazed. Once again thoughts of kidnapping enter my head. Has my acquaintance with Alessandro put a price on my head? Am I worth something now?

Eventually we take a left. A hard left. The tyres skid and I'm thrown across the seat. We are in the short-stay car park. It leads directly to the terminal. To our left cabs and cars are backed up along the regular access road. I risk checking the time. Five minutes before departure. I can still make it – there's no way the plane's leaving exactly on time, they never do. I pull out my last two ten-thousand-lire notes ready to hand them over. We come to an abrupt stop about twenty yards from the terminal, only parked cars and a small wall between us and the entrance. Massimo is out of the car, opening my door. I don't have time for this nonsense. I leap out, dragging my bag behind me and I shove the money directly into his hand. He doesn't bother to count it or even look at it. He grabs me instead. Like I'm his son. He grabs me and presses kisses to my cheeks. But that's not all. He wants to look at me! He holds me at arm's length, his massive *paesano* hands gripping the tops of my arms. He must feel a bond with me after rescuing me, delivering me to Signora Maldini's. And if I'm honest, despite the extreme urgency, I am touched by this. But now I must go. I say, '*Arrivederci e molto, molto, molto grazie*, Massimo,' and rip away. I hurdle the wall and bolt into the airport. The signs are as much a blur to me as when I arrived. I scan for airline logos, brand colours. When I reach the check-in there is another late traveller before me. I line up, taking deep breaths. As he moves away I step up and hand over my ticket. The girl looks at my ticket, at me, shakes her head. 'The plane is gone.'

'The plane's gone?'

'Yes, *signor*.'

I look at my watch. It's two minutes past its departure time.

'It left two minutes ago,' she says.

'But they're never on time!' I insist. 'They're always delayed.'

'Sorry, *signor*. If you go to that desk they can book you on the next available flight.'

I look around. Usually in these situations I will resort to arguing with the nearest official under the perverse belief that simple logic or impressive rhetorical skills can change, alter, reverse the situation: the plane won't have left; it is delayed; I'm not late; I can go home, etc. But I don't bother. I cross the concourse to the airline desk where I am told that the next available free seat is on Tuesday. I can of course pay *again* and fly home tomorrow. Either way I will be late for my new job. I sit on my bag to think. I have no cash, my credit card is almost at its limit, every penny in my bank account is reserved for direct debits, standing orders and any other electronically convenient way to siphon away my money. There is no way I can pay for the flight tomorrow and stay another night. I'll have to leave on Tuesday. Another two days in Naples – fate has finally colluded with me. All I will have to do is call my new work tomorrow, apologize and explain, and arrange to start on Wednesday or even next week.

The bureau de change hands me three hundred thousand lire. I am charged twenty pounds to alter my reservation. I then buy a phone card and call my answerphone. I change the outgoing message, apprising any caller of my situation just in case I am unable to speak to anyone at the clinic tomorrow. I have been sick. I am stuck in Naples. I will be back on Tuesday night. I apologize for any inconvenience. That done, I wander out of the airport feeling markedly different from the invalid who dragged himself to the taxi rank three nights ago. Even so, I am confronted with the same image, Massimo standing by the open passenger door of his taxi like a limo-driver. I throw my hands up in a gesture of mock surprise – the inevitability of it somehow no surprise. He mirrors the gesture, then motions me into the back seat. Nothing is said – nothing, that is, that I understand – and I am taken directly back to Signora Maldini's, slipping through congested traffic with the ease of a car made of mercury.

Walking up to the apartment I start to think there is something very dream-like about all this – this apartment, Massimo and Signora Maldini, a beautiful girl from my past, her husband, the *pentito* – maybe I haven't awakened from my delirium and have merely plunged into a semi-coherent Naples narrative made up of hundreds of tiny details picked up about the place throughout my life. What do you do when you think you might be in a dream knowing full well you're not, but you'd like to rule out the possibility? Pinch yourself? It seems silly, a cliché, but I do it anyway. I tug sharply at the skin on the back of my hand. I feel pain. It leaves a red mark. A light love bite. I am still on the stairs. This is not a dream.

There is no answer at the apartment. I look over the railings down onto the lemon-and-lime courtyard. Signora Maldini is sitting in a deck chair next to an older lady sitting on a straight-backed chair. I didn't notice them when I walked in. I call out.

'Signor Jim!' Signora Maldini calls up, a little surprised, but then pulls a key from the front pocket of her housecoat and waves it at me.

When I join her she introduces me to the older woman beside her. '*Mia madre,*' she says.

I say, '*Buon giorno, signora.*' We shake hands. Her hand is tiny, dry, like a chicken's foot.

'*Caffè?*' Signora Maldini asks me as usual.

I decline and take the long key she is holding out to me.

'*Grazie*,' I say.

The first thing I notice inside the apartment is that the money and note are gone. I am glad; it makes whatever arrangement we have more formal. I dump my stuff back in my room. The bed remains unmade from the morning. I step out on the balcony. The family opposite are out. I fetch the chair from beside the bed. I have to settle the chair half inside the room because the balcony is too shallow. I rock back and press my feet into the railings for balance. I am finally on holiday, I say to myself, relaxing in my room after arriving from the airport, ready to plan what I will do. I have the luxury of having got most of the tourist things out of the way on my last visit. There are still the big attractions – Capri and Pompeii – Disney Naples. But I decide they are too touristy for such a visitor as me. I made that mistake last time; I have been given a second chance and I want to do something more original.

Louisa said she was free tomorrow; I will call her and ask her to show me around. Then I remember her suggestion: go and see Alessandro at work. That's precisely the kind of authentic Neapolitan experience I am after. Nine Camorra soldiers on trial for murder on the evidence of this one man, this charismatic *collaboratore*. I right my chair. The newspaper is still on the bed. I take another look at Giacomo Sonino. I wonder whether he'll be quite so menacing, so foppishly cocky in court? I pull Alessandro's card out of my wallet.

The telephone is halfway down the hall. After what seems like a hundred rings I get an answerphone. Louisa's voice. The message is in Italian – charmingly sing-song, delightfully lilting, a touch overdone for her own amusement. After the beep I explain what has happened and ask if it will be possible to visit the court tomorrow. I am very clear that if it's a problem I will understand.

On my way out I try to explain to Signora Maldini that I'm expecting a call and I think she invites me to dinner with her mother. It is all so confusing we both eventually throw our hands in the air.

This is my first long wander in the city as a well man. I walk aimlessly. Doing exactly as I please. I stop for a beer in the sun, have a bowl of pasta and clams in a small restaurant, stand at the bar of a café for a quick espresso, buy an English newspaper and read it sitting on a bench in a tiny piazza while the sun goes down. Two, three hours idyllically spent.

When I return home Signora Maldini is watching television. She has a glass of wine on the table next to her, a cigarette burning in the ashtray. I am about to try to discover whether Louisa has called when she looks up at me and says, 'Alessandro Mascagni *ha telefonato*.'

During all my brief exchanges with Signora Maldini I have been completely unable to tell how she feels by the expression on her face. Now it is perfectly clear. Suspicion. What am I doing receiving telephone calls from the president of the court of murder? She looks at me disapprovingly, as if I am fraternizing with the wrong side in a war. I try to disarm her with a smile but she just shakes her head, muttering. I walk down the hall to the phone and call Louisa. It rings for ever and I expect the answermachine, but then Louisa is there. She sounds gleefully pleased that I missed my plane. I ask her if it's appropriate to ask Alessandro this favour.

'It's completely fine. He likes you, I told you,' she says.

'I'm flattered,' I say, and although I am, I am partly being sarcastic, a little disappointed that apart from her playfulness I do not sense any flirtation from her.

'Hold on,' she says, 'I'll just get him.'

The phone clunks down on a table and I hear in the distance a piano being played, then interrupted. After a minute Alessandro's on the line.

'Hello, Jim. I am very happy you stay in Naples.'

'Was that you playing the piano?' I ask.

'Ah,' he says – it is just a short intake of breath but it seems to say: to play the piano is a melancholy passion, a necessary tonic for a weary soul such as mine.

I love this guy, I think. He then proceeds to give me instructions about meeting him in the morning. His court is in the Centro

Direzionale, the Directional Centre, he translates. He tells me what tram to take, where to get off and where precisely to wait for him. He apologizes for not picking me up but it's an official car and it's not allowed. At least, not on work days, I assume.

I ask, 'Are you sure this is OK?' wanting further reassurance.

'It is OK. I am president,' he says chuckling. And then Louisa is back on the phone. 'Why don't you come and stay with us tomorrow night?'

I'm not sure whether to accept; I have grown quite attached to my strange set-up with Signora Maldini, even with her sudden coolness towards me.

'I'll discuss it with my landlady,' I say evasively.

'But you'll come for dinner?' she asks.

'Can you cook?'

'I'm married to an Italian,' she says mock-dumbly.

'OK then,' I say.

'You know, once you're here, I won't let you leave . . .'

It is not clear whether she is just being charming, utterly certain of her fidelity, or all of a sudden flirting with me. I say nothing in response.

'I'll see you tomorrow then,' she says. Then after another confirmation from me she cheerfully rings off, 'Ciao.'

I walk back into the front room and join Signora Maldini at the table. She offers me some wine. I accept and she scuttles off into the kitchen for a glass.

The wine is coarse, powerful. True Grit, dubbed into Italian, is on the television. The voice given to John Wayne I think I recognize as Neapolitan. It sounds less generically Italian than the others. Deep, crunchy. Glen Campbell sounds ridiculous, hysterical, camp. The girl, tomboyish, feisty and irritating in English, is sexier in Italian. I wonder whether Signora Maldini was a looker when she was younger. That lopsided beehive is definitely a hint of lost glamour. We smile at one another; her expression remains mystifyingly neutral. We both turn back to the TV. When the film finishes, she applauds.

I stand and say, *'Buona notte . . .'* and head off to my room.

The first thing I notice is that the newspaper is gone. I am oddly put out. I wanted to keep it as a souvenir. I go back out to the living room to ask Signora Maldini if she still has it. She is in the kitchen rinsing the glasses.

'Giornale?' I say and point back to the bedroom.

The disapproving look returns. She mutters to herself as she places the glasses on the drainer and pushes past me in the doorway. She bends over a magazine rack by the TV. Rather than hand the paper to me, she throws it on the table. She looks so insulted I almost expect her to spit. I don't know the word for 'sorry' so I say, *'Mi scusi,'* hoping it will placate her. She shrugs and sits back down. I look at the newspaper on the table, the picture of Sonino folded over in the middle, just his lean handsome face and pistol-shaped hand visible below the headline. I am forced to think Signora Maldini must have some kind of connection to this front-page story to react in such a way. Maybe she knew one of the victims of the gang, hence her disgust. Maybe she knows one of the gang themselves, hence her anger. Maybe she even knows Il Pentito himself, hence her disgust and anger. Or perhaps she just has a pathological hatred of saving old newspapers – it is impossible to tell. But whatever it is I still want the newspaper, so I pick it up off the table and slot it under my arm. There is no reaction. I say goodnight once again, but this time I bend down and plant a kiss on Signora Maldini's forehead. My sudden intimacy takes us both by surprise. I step back and, putting together my most complex sentence yet in Italian, say, *'Molto grazie per . . . tutti . . . cosa.'*

I expect her regular response, *'Prego,'* but instead she places her hands together in the prayer position and with a stern expression, sterner than usual, waves them at me. I have no idea what she is trying to tell me. It could range from 'Don't thank me, I was only doing what anyone would do' to 'If I'd known you were a friend of Judge Mascagni I would have let you die'. I realize there is no point trying to trick her into revealing the truth, she is far too

67

professionally poker-faced for that, but I do decide that it might be wise to accept Louisa's invitation and spend my last night in Naples with the Mascagnis.

crime

I

I am meeting Alessandro outside the Palazzo di Giustizia at nine. The tram, during the rush hour, is packed to sub-continental levels. After a few stops I am so jammed in the middle I am not sure that a) I will recognize where I am to get off (I cannot see out of the window sufficiently well to see the landmarks I have been told to look out for), and b) even if I manage that, I doubt I'll be able to push my way through to the door and alight. I spend the thirty hot, slow minutes jostling for a position close to the door. I say *'mi scusi'* and *'permesso'* countless times. No one wants to move, and my whispered, apologetic entreaties are greeted with hard stares. I begin to wonder whether I am in fact jostling for position with other people heading for the court, other people attending the Il Pentito trial. And if so, what is their purpose there?

I look around me. Faces are dark, moody. The men irascible, the women watchful. I am with a fairly rum bunch. It is easy to imagine they are all part of an extended Camorra family, all riding to court to support those members of their clan wrongfully accused. It feels like finding yourself on a train with a group of football fans – you regard yourself as neutral, but then you also know there is no such thing if they decide to ask you who you support. There is a 'with us or against us' atmosphere on this tram. And the truth is I'm not neutral; I am aligned with the opposition. Each time the tram stops and people get off who I have previously decided are related to people who stay on, I visibly, audibly breathe a sigh of relief. By the time we reach my stop the tram is only half full and the Family has been replaced by ordinary Neapolitans going to work.

The Centro Direzionale is a mile beyond the central railway station. It is a newly built complex of stunted skyscrapers. It looks like a purpose-built financial district – all glass and angular steel, with the requisite municipally commissioned over-sized sculpture in the centre of the piazza. The Palazzo di Giustizia is the first building on the left. It appears to be in three sections, the third still under construction. It is surrounded by a high metal fence and is heavily guarded. There is no sign of the damage caused by the Camorra bomb. I find the entrance – a narrow gap in the fence – and wait for Alessandro. Opposite me is Poggioreale, Naples' prison. It is vast and the twentieth-century security measures do little to bring it out of the medieval. I can almost feel the damp, the dirt, the darkness. I assume that because of the Italian belief in family prisoners are jailed locally and not dispersed around the country. I am probably wrong.

Alessandro approaches. He is wearing a dark-blue suit, white shirt, dark-blue tie. I am again struck by how handsome he is. He is looking even more youthful today; the casual clothes from Saturday were a little less forgiving of his age. He greets me with his hands thrust out to me; it is another two-handed shake.

'Jim. Welcome. Welcome to my work.' He laughs. 'Even if you do not understand Italian it will be very, very interesting.'

'I am looking forward to it,' I say a little awkwardly. I feel I am imposing, that this is too big a favour to ask of a man I hardly know. Alessandro gives me no reason to believe this. Whatever his reservations on Saturday night, they have gone. He leads me through the entrance with his hand on my back, past the guards, through the metal detectors; nobody questions my presence. The building inside is cavernous; the walls a municipal cream; the floor a dark-grey rubber. It is cold – air-conditioning. Alessandro complains about this. He says Mediterranean buildings should have windows. We ride an escalator to the next level.

'Where would you like to sit?' he asks as we glide upwards. 'You can come in with the journalists or in the public gallery.'

I don't say anything but try to look as though I am happy with what's easiest.

'For you it will be more interesting in the public gallery. It is there the families come to watch the trial.' He seems keen I experience something beyond auditing the courtroom proceedings.

'OK then,' I say a little anxiously.

'It is number twelve. Up there.' He points to the next level. 'It is best you go up on your own.' He smiles. 'You do not want the families seeing you with me.'

I laugh nervously.

'Did you visit the old Tribunale?' he asks.

'Yes,' I say, 'it is very beautiful.'

'Ah . . .' he says ruefully. I'm beginning to suspect he uses this sound to express a whole range of emotions from pleasurable regret to an acceptance of hardship and the certainty of human folly.

'This court, it is horrible. There is no ambience. I feel like a man who works in a factory.'

Do I detect vanity, or is he simply saying that it is dangerous to encourage conveyor-belt justice? I have to say I am a little pleased, after my feelings of inadequacy when comparing his former work-place to my future one, that this place, although it's on a much larger scale with pretensions of modernist design and functionality, is not a lot different, at least in atmosphere, from my Portaloo.

Alessandro tells me that he must go and that the trial will start in about half an hour. We shake hands. I am about to walk to the escalator when he calls me back.

'I have a message from Louisa. To meet her at the café near the Post Office.' He studies my face to see whether I understand this message, as if it is unusually cryptic.

'Certainly,' I say obligingly. 'What time?'

'The trial will finish at twelve. I must then do other work so I cannot follow you . . . accompany you. She will meet you at one o'clock.'

I nod; then ask, 'How come the trial finishes so early?'

'I have other work,' he repeats enigmatically, but then adds with a broad smile, 'but two hours will be enough for you.'

I take the escalator up to the second floor and look for courtroom twelve. It is at the end of a series of six courts. Ramps lead up from the main floor to each entrance. I pull at the doors – locked. I am the only person around. Occasionally a clerk or lawyer walks past on their way somewhere else. This trial is clearly not the hot ticket I imagined it to be. I don't quite know what I had expected, probably a throng of people, press, family, the curious like me, all arriving early, desperate for a seat.

An old man in a grey caretaker's uniform appears. He moves slowly from one court to the next, unlocking each set of doors. When he has gone I walk up the ramp and enter the public gallery. The first thing I notice is the thick wall of bullet-proof glass dividing it from the courtroom. 'Great,' I say out loud – Alessandro has sent me to sit with the assassins. I should have joined the journalists.

The gallery itself is steep with twenty rows of tiered seating. I walk down the centre aisle to get a closer look at the courtroom below. It is high and narrow, floor, walls, ceiling all wood-panelled. It is like a gymnasium, functional, cold, lacking in atmosphere. At the far end is the bench, with twelve chairs lined up behind, all plastic except for the one in the centre, which is high-backed and leather and I presume Alessandro's. Before it is a microphone on a small stand. Mounted on the wall above is: *La Legge è Uguale per Tutti* which I translate as meaning everyone is equal under the law. Facing the bench there are two rows of paired desks disappearing under the public gallery. The Italian flag is draped from the left-hand wall like a flaccid towel hung on a hook.

Opposite the flag is the cage. It is larger than I expected: ten feet tall, running along the middle third of the right-hand wall. The bars are thick, black, shiny. Inside there is a bench and a doorway that I expect leads into some sort of holding cell. Despite the courtroom's lack of atmosphere the cage is unsettling. It is the focus of the room, and even when empty it is quite plain that this place deals in dangerous people.

At the far end of the courtroom there is an open door that leads into a busy corridor. A number of men, mostly my age, walk in. The lawyers I presume. Some wear designer suits, their black hair sleek. The others, mostly older, are more dishevelled, suits stained, hair unkempt. Briefcases, files and bundles are set on the desks. From beneath the public gallery five policemen appear. They wear ill-fitting blue uniforms, loose white patent-leather belts with holsters, and caps, either a size too big or too small, and therefore worn at jaunty angles. But there is nothing jaunty in their manner. They look bored, restive, irritated. They lean against the wall opposite the cage. There is no acknowledgement of the lawyers.

After a minute or so one of the younger lawyers walks up to the cage, casually grips a bar and calls in. Nothing happens for a moment or two, then two young men step into the cage; they all shake hands through the bars. The prisoners are trim and youthful, in jeans and shirts. They are not smart, but then neither are they scruffy. They could be dressed to meet a girl, to go to football. They're both smoking – cigarettes turned inwards, hidden in their palms. Another young man appears from the holding-cell door and walks to the end of the cage nearest me. He looks around the courtroom for his lawyer and, after he spots him, calls out. Within a few seconds the cage is full and surrounded by lawyers. It is clear now who is prosecution and who is defence; the more dishevelled have remained at their desks. The discussions taking place through the bars look casual; there is no desperation or anger from inside the cage. All nine prisoners appear calm, relaxed. As do their lawyers. The only difference between those outside the cage and those inside is the quality of their coolness. Inside it is the subtle braggadocio of young men who are pleased with themselves but are too bored to swagger; outside it is the affected intellectual superiority of young men who want, for purposes of courtroom theatre and personal vanity, to show a similar indifference to the law as those they are representing. I am more interested in the real thing. I'm not sure it goes much beyond gangster mystique but these men fascinate me. I don't even know whether they are guilty of planting the car bombs killing three innocent people, but from where I am standing they *look* like Camorra soldiers, a gang of local kids born, attracted or seduced into this life. They look like friends, old comrades, neighbourhood buddies, unconditionally bonded because the streets they could walk along were circumscribed by other streets they couldn't walk along. Share that and you don't have to like one another to be close. That's what I can see: nine young men at ease with their imposed physical proximity because for all their lives they have been standing around together, talking, drinking, smoking, taking up no more space than the cage they are now held in.

I walk back up the steep steps and take a seat in the back row. Behind me the doors open and two young women walk in. They cast a quick glance at me and then make their way to the glass partition. They shuffle along the front row until they are facing the end of the cage and rap on the glass. All nine men look up, instantly breaking off discussions with their lawyers. All wave, but two make their way to the near end of the cage to be as close as possible to the women. They smile and gesture to one another. From their expressions one would think that the only thing that divides them is a glass window and not a ten-month trial for murder with the prospect of life imprisonment. Then one of them spots me. Elbows his pal. Their women are suddenly of little interest as they try to figure out who I am, what I'm doing there. They don't confer or point, but I sense their interest in my presence is strong. A wave of fear passes through me, and even in this electronically regulated temperature I break out into a sweat. I look away, stare into the middle distance, try to appear self-amused, unfazed and content to be where I am.

The door behind me opens again and more people come in. I don't look round. I want to avoid eye contact with anyone. I hear more rapping on the glass partition. I then sense a slow-moving presence beside me. I sneak a look. It is an old woman making her way down the stairs. Each step she takes is careful to the point of dainty. She is sideways on and turned away from me so I can't see her face. Her grey hair is pulled tightly back into a bun. She is wearing a black dress. Below her hemline, her calves are flabby and veined; her ankles bulge around her shoes. She is in some pain as she moves, but is clearly determined to get to the bottom rather than take a seat near the door. As she passes me I quickly glance over to the corner – it is now packed with wives and girlfriends, like groupies crammed around a stage door. All nine prisoners have dispensed with their lawyers and are assembled in the near end of the cage. They are like a group of young soldiers packed in a train ready to leave, using up every last moment they have to smile, wave, signal something meaningful to their girls before being shipped off to war.

When the old woman reaches the bottom she places her hand against the glass. At first I think it is to balance herself, to catch her breath before she shuffles along the first row to join the younger women in the corner, but she remains where she is, her palm pressed flat to the window as if she's taking an oath. The nine switch their attention away from their women. Their expressions change; there are no waves or smiles. For the first time they appear to fully understand the gravity of their situation. The women cast sideways glances along the front row. Even the lawyers stop what they are doing and look up. This woman is important and I suspect not because she's a respected legal reformer. She must be some kind of Camorra matriarch. Head of a family. Her frailty means nothing; her power is palpable and extensive. She only sits down once everyone has acknowledged her presence. The nine and their women return to their silent communications.

I am being looked at again. As each of the nine notices me I am subject to hard stares, dark eyes squinting, pulling focus to make me out, who I am. The curiosity is clear on every face – my presence is troubling them. I am the only observer unconnected with them and it is making them suspicious and me uneasy. I am relieved when the doors open and two policemen step in. As with their counterparts in the courtroom below, their uniforms do not inspire respect or authority, so they use sullen, irritable expressions instead. They call over to the huddle of women in the corner and order them to sit down. Their hands rest on the butts of their pistols. The women look over to the old woman, who without turning around nods for them to obey. They slowly disperse around the gallery.

One of the men in the cage, angered by this sudden and premature interruption, locks his gaze onto the policemen and placing his fingers under his chin, flicks them sharply in their direction. It is a contemptuous and dismissive gesture, and for the first time this morning I sense the explosive hostility in these men.

The policemen leave. I am inclined to follow them. It was a nice idea Alessandro suggesting I sit up here, local colour and all that, but I doubt he realizes how menacing these guys are when they are staring at you without the protection of the court. This is a trial about betrayal – it's not surprising they're going to be deeply suspicious of a strange face peering down on them from among their wives and families. And suspicious as they are it's unlikely they'll conclude that I'm just an English bloke who has wandered in – an intrepid tourist doing a bit of imaginative sight-seeing.

The wives and girlfriends show no interest in me. Even when I'm looked at, it's an idle stare, their minds elsewhere. I am finding it hard not to stare back. They are extraordinary-looking women. There really does seem to be a direct correlation between the professional risks of their men and their style choices: the life of a gangster is cheap so the wife of a gangster is cheap. Their foundation is so thickly applied their faces are the colour of terracotta; their Nile-black hair is so tortured with fat orange highlights they all look like Medusa on fire; and their fingers are so weighted down with gold and nail extensions they droop and curl like talons. Every aspect of their appearance has a kind of fleeting flashiness, a superficial brilliance reflecting the short life expectancy of their partners. None of them is unattractive, most are pretty – probably the best-looking girls in the neighbourhood; but they are also hard-looking, hot-tempered, hostile. Only one, the youngest, stands out. She is sitting on her own. With her hair cropped short, wearing jeans and a denim jacket, she looks more like a hoodlum herself – a tomboy from 1950s America.

Below us a line of people files into the courtroom. They all wear silk sashes across their chests, the three colours of the Italian flag. They are followed by a young man in a black gown. He is followed, a few steps behind, by Alessandro. His youthfulness is gone. The black gown ages him. He looks venerable, serious, wise. The sash-wearers all take their places behind the long desk, with Alessandro in the middle. He remains standing. Everyone who was previously sitting has stood. The nine line the cage, hands gripping the bars, their knuckles protruding like dark-pink rosebuds. Above their knuckles a sequence of impressive noses sticks out between the bars.

Alessandro slowly scans the courtroom. He appears distracted, irritable. He then says 'Buon giorno,' and sits down, opening the large file he has brought in with him. Everyone except the nine takes their seats and readies themselves for the start of the proceedings. The women break off conversations and face forwards. The gallery seats about a hundred with plenty of standing room. There are thirteen of us. If there is any apprehension, worry, anxiety up here there is little atmosphere to conduct it.

On the floor of the court two defence lawyers have stepped forward and are addressing Alessandro. He sits forward attentively, his fiercely intelligent eyes locked on them. Apart from Alessandro and a man I take to be his deputy there are ten others sitting behind the desk. They must be jurors of some kind. From their demeanour they don't look like legal professionals, but more like the wives of the accused and the accused themselves – they appear less interested than either in what is being said. I decide it is pointless struggling to make sense of exactly what's going on, all I can do is watch and hope to understand the general drift, and wait for something dramatic to happen. Most of the nine have now sat down on the bench at the rear of the cage. A couple of them, towards this end, surreptitiously smoke. I assume from their lack of interest that the subject being discussed is a point of procedure and this is something that happens a lot. But then one of the nine, the one situated nearest Alessandro, calls out. It doesn't sound insulting or rude, but there is something frustrated about it. There are a few cheers from the nine. Without looking at the cage, to the source of this outburst,

Alessandro slams his palm down on the bench and booms, *'Silenzio!'* He then instructs the two lawyers to continue. As they make their case, two clerks wheel in a television on a tall stand. There is some confusion as to where they should leave it; there isn't a plug socket near the spot where the screen will be visible to everyone. The two clerks look around helplessly. Finally, after directions from Alessandro, they place it directly opposite the cage. This means everyone on the right of the court has to move or lean round to see the screen. If I want to see, I am also going to have to move. I wait until the four girls sitting in my half of the gallery cross to the other side and cross with them. They don't take any notice of me, but as I sit down I am aware of another one of the nine following me with his eyes. I ignore him and stare at the television. What I see is a white room, a desk, two men – one man sitting behind the desk, the other a few feet to one side, almost out of frame. Although the image isn't that clear from up here, I recognize the one behind the desk as Giacomo Sonino. He must be giving his evidence by video-relay from a safe house. I am disappointed; I had desperately wanted to see this man for real. I look down at the nine. How do they feel, their accuser being excused from appearing in person? Another example of his cowardice? They don't seem to care. Not one of them is even looking at the television.

I turn my attention to Alessandro. He is still listening to argument from the same two lawyers. He is beginning to look bored and shifts in his seat. Whenever the lawyers begin to talk over one another he raises his hand to silence one and points to the other to continue. Each gesture is instantly obeyed. I had expected the general behaviour to be more like the Italian parliament – noisy, hot-tempered, volatile; emotions before reason; histrionics over decorum – but I sense Alessandro's impressive presence keeps these things in check.

There is another outburst from the cage. The same prisoner. This time his frustration is even more apparent. He thrusts his arm through the bars, and with his finger pointed, jabs in the direction of the television.

'*Silenzio!*' Alessandro demands and slams his palm down on the desk again.

A couple of the policemen push themselves from the wall; but they fall back the moment the prisoner retracts his arm.

Alessandro taps the end of the microphone in front of him with two fingers. Dull thuds echo around the court. He then addresses the television. I have no idea what he says but the man sitting adjacent to the table shuffles himself forward in his seat so he is completely inside the frame. They start to discuss something. There is a couple of seconds' delay between them. It takes them a few exchanges to adjust to this and they have to repeat themselves a few times. I really want to understand what is being said. In the courtroom lawyers butt in now and again. Alessandro holds his hand up, signalling for them to be quiet. Hands are thrown in the air with impatience. Emotions are beginning to show. Unable to control himself the argumentative member of the nine shouts out again. I recognize the name Sonino. For the first time Alessandro turns to face him. I expect a serious admonishment but instead his response is calm, almost placating. The prisoner reluctantly takes a seat on the bench. I can see he is wound-up, angry. Alessandro says, '*Grazie*, Signor Savarese,' then swivels back to face the television.

I turn my attention to Sonino. He is very still. I cannot work out whether he is concentrating hard on what's being said or is just in a daze. From where I am he could be a dead man propped up in a chair – he certainly doesn't exude any of the charisma, the elegance, the languid menace of his front-page photo.

Alessandro moves closer to the microphone. His voice is low, his articulation certain, his delivery deadly serious – he wants everyone to understand that this is a fundamentally important question that no one must misinterpret. Nobody moves. Even the restless members of the nine at the near end of the cage, drawing hard on their cigarettes, concentrate on the courtroom silence soon to be broken with Sonino's first words. There is a long pause. Alessandro repeats the question – the same deliberate words, the same focused gravity. The whole courtroom strains forward. I think for a second that the audio-link has been lost and Alessandro is speaking into a void, but then, barely audible, another voice is heard. I am expecting a voice similar to Alessandro's, a voice of confidence, of certainty, perhaps darker; but all I hear, all the court hears, is a distant, feeble, 'Sì.'

The response in the courtroom is deafening. Protests are volleyed at Alessandro from all the defence lawyers, almost scrambling over their desks to reach the bench, every one of them losing their designer cool. The nine grab the bars of the cage and shake wildly, but the bars are so solidly fixed they merely shake themselves like toddlers lacking the strength to rock their cot. The women around me leap to their feet, shout and curse. One runs down to the front and hammers on the glass. None of this appears to bother Alessandro who is leaning to his right, shielding the mike with his hand, and conferring with his junior. When they finish Alessandro holds his left hand up as if about to take an oath himself. It is a modest gesture compared to slamming his hand down on the table, but it has the same effect of silencing the court instantly. Everyone is waiting for something important from him. His ruling at this point will be an indication of his thinking thus far and each side will have a sense of how well their case is going. I sit forward.

With a natural instinct for the dramatic, Alessandro refuses to lower his hand even though the courtroom is silent. Instead he starts to make notes with his other hand. The nine are now more restless than ever and for the first time behave like caged animals, prowling along the bars, walking tight figures of eight in their small space. Their indifference has vanished. They want some action. The jurors, as ever, are expressionless. I glance over to the television. Sonino is on his feet, arms drawn into his body, locked straight, cuffed at the wrists. He looks like he is urinating with both hands. He shuffles sideways from behind the desk. From his restricted movements it is obvious his ankles are manacled. This explains his reluctance to move earlier. He shuffles out of shot.

Finally Alessandro speaks. It is only a few words, ending with a warm '*buon giorno*'. And that's it. Session over. I expect another outburst all around the courtroom but there is no reaction whatsoever. Was I misreading the situation, the expectant expressions, inventing suspense where there was none? I cannot think what Alessandro could have said to defuse such levels of frustration.

The lawyers are quick to their feet. The nine mill about in the cage; some disappear through the door into the holding cells. Most light up. For the first time Alessandro looks up in my direction. To any impartial observer it is no more than a passing glance around the public gallery. But I know he's looking for me. I check my watch. The session has lasted forty-five minutes. I am not sure what to do: stay here and see if he comes up, or go and wait where we parted earlier or just leave. The wives and girlfriends all pile back into the corner and wave at their men. They exchange some final signals – mostly requests for cigarettes. I notice the tomboy is communicating with the most argumentative of the nine. Girlfriend or sister, I wonder. On their way out all the women stop before the old woman. Some bend down and kiss her forehead, others her hand. It is respectful, dutiful, ritual. Only the tomboy seems keen to help her, but she is waved away. As the women pass me a few check me out, but it's no more than curiosity. The tomboy smiles. I grin back. This is not a place of human warmth.

Below Alessandro is standing, slotting papers he has just been handed into his file. There is another call from the cage. It is the same guy. At first I think he is trying to grab the attention of his lawyer, but no – he wants Alessandro. Alessandro turns to the cage. I expect him just to be looking over out of curiosity but instead he says, 'Sì, Signor Savarese?'

I do not understand what they are saying, but it seems to be a perfectly amiable exchange, like two colleagues in an office, one preparing to leave while the other is forced to stay late. It is a parting chat. This is the most surprising thing that's happened all morning. A judge chatting with the accused. They end it with an informal 'ciao' and the guy, raising his hand up through the bars, gives Alessandro a friendly 'see you soon' wave. I try to get a closer look at him but he disappears through the door.

The courtroom is now empty. The white room on the television is empty. In the public gallery there is only the old woman and me. I want to slip out before she makes her slow ascent towards the door but I realize offering to help her is a better idea; she is clearly very powerful and if she knows I'm just a tourist then any concerns over my identity raised by the nine can be set straight. I wait until she stands and then walk down.

'*Signora?*' I say.

She looks up at me. This is the first time I've seen her face. She is old – very old. Her brown face is so heavily and deeply lined it's like tree bark, the hard vertical grooves splitting around her powerful nose. The sun has aged her; she could be sixty or a hundred. She is the first Neapolitan I have seen with blue eyes. They are small, bright circles. Marbles lodged in a tree trunk.

I cannot think how to phrase my offer of help. I hold out my hand, hoping the gesture will be enough to convey my meaning.

I am expecting a stern refusal, but she says, '*Si, signor,*' and holds out her arm. We take each step slowly. Her backbone is almost serpentine. We do not speak until we have left the courtroom when she makes an effort to straighten up and look at me.

'*Turista,*' I say rather absurdly in response to her examination of me.

'*Americano?*' she asks.

I am quick to set her right. 'No, no. *Inglese.*' She sits down on the bench.

'*Grazie, signor,*' she says, holding out her hand and smiling a weak, meek smile.

'*Prego,*' I say and shake her hand gently.

We part with polite glances and nods. On the floor below I find a seat near where I parted from Alessandro earlier and wait. I give him half an hour, then leave.

The late-morning weather is oppressively hot. I walk to the tram stop and wait. I have a couple of hours before I am due to meet Louisa. I don't have time to go to Capodimonte to see the Michelangelo and Caravaggio. I decide instead to visit the Palazzo

Reale where they have an exhibition about the Bourbons of Naples.

The tram is very busy and immediately my imagination starts to work on my fellow passengers. This time, though, I am not just riding with members of a Camorra family; they are riding with me because they're interested to know who I am – the courtroom stranger. Young men dressed identically to the nine stare at me. I am scrutinized without shame, without a flicker of warmth in their dark eyes. I try to swivel away from their gaze, push myself closer to the door. They do not move. They know I'm not going anywhere fast. Not in this packed tram, this stifling heat.

By the time I get to my stop and shove my way off the tram I am convinced I am being followed. The one guy I hoped wouldn't get off with me has done so. I pretend not to notice and cross the street. He crosses with me. I tell myself I am being ridiculous, there is no way my presence in court would require a tail. After I have taken a couple of corners I glance back to prove to myself that there is nothing to worry about. But he's still there, thirty yards away, watching me from beneath his fringe as he lowers his head to light a cigarette.

I need a plan. There are two ways to the Palazzo Reale: the quick way, taking the major streets, or the scenic route through the old city. The second will determine fairly quickly whether this guy is really following me – there is an almost infinite variety of streets I can take.

I set off along Corso Umberto and turn right sharply into Via Mezzocannone. I look over my shoulder. Still there, wearing sunglasses now. This is already more than coincidence. I turn left into the narrow streets of the old city; at least here it is so busy I don't fear bold attack. I take lefts then rights, heading for Via Santa Maria la Nova. But every time I think I've lost him, he appears again, keeping the same perfectly ambiguous distance. It's like he is aimlessly meandering. But I know he has an aim – to keep me just within his sight. My route has been contrived to prove this. I must now face reality; I pick up speed. The thing to do is get to the Palazzo Reale as soon as possible and hole up there until it is time to meet Louisa, then explain to her what has happened and hope some protection is afforded me until I leave tomorrow. I weave quickly down Via Santa Maria la Nova. I check my watch. Admonish myself. Anyone would think I am in a perfectly innocent hurry. That is my plan. I know I'm being tailed but I don't want him to know I know. I don't want to force a precipitate action on his part. Crossing Via Monteoliveto towards the Post Office adrenalin provides me with enough road rhythm to make it through the traffic swiftly.

Halfway up the steps beside the Post Office I risk another look behind me; I have a clear view about sixty yards up Via Santa Maria la Nova. I can't see him, but then he could be obscured by the sudden crowd of Neapolitans taking their lunch break. I run to the top of the steps and scan the whole area. He's not there. This does not reassure me, however. What I think is that he's taken some alternative route, guessing my objective, and is looking to cut me off somewhere unexpected. But then I have to admit that, even with Neapolitan clairvoyance, him knowing I was heading for the Bourbon exhibition at the Palazzo Reale is stretching credibility. I relax a little, wipe the sweat from my brow and the back of my neck. Was I really being followed I wonder, or is paranoia the inevitable result of any contact with organized crime? Does any association at all with this world make you suspicious about any unusual event or detail? Is this how Alessandro *feels*? What about Louisa? How come she was bowling along so casually when I met her the other day? Surely she's a prime target for kidnapping. Maybe there was a bodyguard and I didn't notice. Certainly the driver of their official car sat outside the restaurant on Saturday night.

My god, it just didn't occur to me to examine the implications of getting even peripherally close to this kind of thing. Someone could have warned me. There was I thinking it was all so fascinating: Il Pentito, the Camorra, car bombs and murder, when really it's fucked-up stuff, seriously fucked-up – dangerous, mortally danger-ous. Like the Mafia, the real Mafia. They don't mess about. They're not reasonable men. Merciful. Compassionate. They kill people.

Judges, politicians, civilians, anybody who interferes. My amateur paranoia and suspicion is nothing compared to theirs. Theirs is a way of life. A professional requirement for survival. What was I thinking? Sitting up there in the public gallery giving nine men locked in a cage something to think about. Giving them a conundrum they can't work out. Nine men betrayed, on trial for murder. How do I know one of those many signals passing between them and their women didn't include: find out who this guy is? I mean they weren't going to ask Alessandro, were they? Who's the guy, Presidente? And even if they did, I instantly become an object of mistrust. These guys have two enemies – other gangsters and the law. Cheers Louisa. I may not have been the ideal boyfriend during those two short months but there was no need to have me killed. OK, slow down. No one's going to kill you. Don't be ridiculous. By tomorrow night you'll be back in London and by Wednesday morning back to fraternizing with the homeless, the addicted, the dispossessed, a warm and friendly bunch of people compared to these Neapolitan mobsters . . .

I cross Piazza Matteotti and walk down Via Miguel Cervantes towards the Bourbon Palace. I keep a lookout for my friend, but as my fear begins to recede I start to look forward to meeting Louisa. The prospect of spending a whole afternoon with her makes me a little light-headed, daydreamy. Symptoms I recognize. And if they don't always lead to love, they always lead dangerously close to it. I must ignore them, I tell myself – as I must also ignore any flicker of sexual tension between us that might have survived these last ten years. Yet simply the anticipation of seeing her shortens my breath and makes my heart pound twice as hard as being followed by the Camorra. I decide there is little point in denying it or indulging it – I'll be gone in a day.

The exhibition is a bit of a bore. I am unfamiliar with most of the grandees. Don Carlos, the first Bourbon king of the Two Sicilies, doesn't look half Spanish, half French – he looks more like an English private-schoolmaster, immensely keen on cricket. His son Ferdinand, apparently crude, rude and boisterous, looks fey, fragile and sensitive. I try to learn something but my mind is on Louisa. I glance at my watch every minute hoping ten have passed. I leave after half an hour and sit outside. I lean back against a low wall, the business of the harbour audible below, and with a hand shading my eyes watch the few tourists amble to and from the Palazzo Reale to the church of San Francesco di Paola. After a while the heavy heat forces my eyes closed. I cannot resist dozing. I awake with a start, as a group of tourists trample over me for a view of the bay. I am disorientated – dreaming of Louisa back when I first met her. A party girl, resistant to charm, attention. Lovelier than any girl I'd ever met.

I look at my watch but the face disappears in the sun's glare. I am almost blinded by the reflection. I shake the light from my eyes. Two bright discs float before me. I can vaguely make out the hands – one-ten. I'm late. I leap to my feet pushing aside everyone in my way.

Naples is not a city you can run in. No one anticipates, or even understands, such pedestrian speed, so it feels like the pavements are full of immovable objects. At one point I receive the chin flick from a man I brush past. In this context it is an overly aggressive gesture. I only see it because I stop to apologize. I decide to have a go at a little Neapolitan clairvoyance myself. I place my hands together in the prayer position and shake them. What I am trying to convey to him is this: a man only runs this fast when he's late to meet a beautiful woman. I don't know whether he understands, but he looks less pissed off.

I arrive at the café out of breath, damp all over and in excruciating pain, after attempting to take the steps next to the Post Office three at a time; I slipped and almost drove my spine up through my head. Louisa is not here. For a moment I think I might have missed her, but then I remember the whole reason for meeting at a café is so you can sit down and wait. I sit down and wait. Order an espresso from the waiter who seems to recognize me, because although I am on my own he raises two fingers and says, 'Due?'

I shake my head. 'Uno, per favore.'

Louisa arrives moments later, the strap of her satchel slung across her body, separating her small breasts, the satchel itself bumping against her left hip as she walks. She is smiling, beaming.

I stand and we kiss on each cheek, during which Louisa says, 'Buon giorno, Jim. Come va?' with breathless intimacy.

I am keen to reciprocate the Italian greeting but find I am too embarrassed, so I say, 'Fine. You?'

'Me? Oh, I'm fine. A little exhausted.' She sits down and pulls her satchel over her head and dumps it underneath the table. She then calls to the waiter for a cappuccino.

'So how was the trial? Did you enjoy it? Isn't Alessandro great? Silenzio!' she mimics and slaps the table with her hand. Everyone at the café is startled and looks around. 'Did he get cross all the time?'

'Not really.'

'That's unusual. Where did you sit?'

'In the public gallery. Everyone kept looking at me. It was quite unnerving . . .'

'Was it full of wives and girlfriends?'

'Not really full, but I was the only man. There was this old woman . . .'

'Was she tiny, frail?' she interrupts.

'Very.'

'That's Eugenia Savarese. She controls the Forcella Quarter. Right at the other end of Spaccanapoli. Women run the Camorra now; all the men are in prison. They're apparently worse than the men, so Alessandro says. One of her grandsons would have been in the cage today – Lorenzo Savarese.'

'I helped her up the stairs at the end,' I say.

'That was nice of you. One day you might need her to return the favour.' She pulls a mock grimace.

I don't let on how deep my paranoia goes; instead I ask what I hope seems like an innocent question. 'Does it matter that I was there . . . because I was thinking . . . surely it looks a bit suspicious some anonymous person turning up to watch?'

'I don't think Alessandro would have suggested it if he thought you were in any danger. He's not stupid.'

I am quietly relieved. 'I tell you what I thought was the most amazing part. Right at the end one of the guys in the cage started chatting to Alessandro. That would never happen in England.'

'Everything is more informal in Naples. I also think most people trust Alessandro. Even the Camorra. One, he's Neapolitan. Two, he accepts the Neapolitan dialect in his court. And three, he's not corrupt. The one thing the Camorra like more than a corrupt judge is an incorruptible one. They're big on honour these people. They are used to going to prison so they accept it as long as it's fair.' She pauses, yawning. 'Sorry, I'm tired. Late night. What about Sonino, the *pentito* – what was he like?'

'He was on the television. I couldn't really make him out. But he looked weak.'

'So he hasn't made an appearance yet. Today was supposed to be the day. Were there ructions?'

'Something was going on.'

'I bet there was.'

Our coffees arrive and Louisa asks me what I'd like to do this afternoon.

'I thought I'd leave it up to you,' I say. 'You're the expert.'

'Well, I thought we'd have some lunch first and then I'll show you some of those little secret places most tourists don't find.'

'Sounds great,' I say, and knock back my espresso.

Louisa sips her steaming cappuccino. Tiny beads of perspiration dot her forehead; stray strands of her marble-black hair fall loosely around her face. I stare at her, entranced.

'What are you looking at?' she asks, a little put out.

'Oh, nothing, sorry . . .' I say, pretending I was in an unfocused reverie.

'I hate being stared at. The Italians do it all the time.'

'I'm sorry.'

'That's OK,' she says, and then adds, 'Alessandro really likes you.'

I suspect she is reminding me of her situation, the person between us. Our past isn't in contention for her affections.

'I like him,' I say.

'But he thinks you're wasting your time as a counsellor. Don't be insulted. He thinks that about everyone unless they are really happy with what they're doing in life. It's a Neapolitan thing.'

'So it's not about the job itself?'

'Yes and no. He'll never admit it but he has prejudices. He hates weakness. And addiction is a weakness in his eyes. Oh, he'll say it's all society's fault and all that. But deep down . . . he thinks people should be able to control themselves. He's so self-controlled. For a Neapolitan.' She pauses for a moment, thinking, then adds, 'But that's probably fear, isn't it? He is worried that if he lets himself go . . . you know?'

Louisa looks directly at me. She appears to be asking me about something specific, about something that's been troubling her. I decide it's not a good idea to discuss her and her husband in any way that could be perceived as critical, however well intentioned.

'Any man as remarkable as Alessandro will have oddities,' I say neutrally.

'I suppose,' she says with equal neutrality; then adds, 'Come on, let's go. I'll take you to a nice little *trat* near where you're staying.'

We head up Via Santa Maria la Nova and I ask Louisa about her parents, whom I met once. Her mother looked like Audrey Hepburn and her father like Henry Fonda. She says she has little contact with them: a phone call once a month, lunch in London when they're over there. They've been to Naples once. Stayed in Sorrento.

'They disapproved of me marrying Alessandro. My dad hates Europeans and my mum said I should marry a man taller than myself.'

'Is Alessandro shorter?' I ask.

'Same height. It's so superficial that attitude.' She is peeved by her parents' narrow-mindedness.

'I'm not sure I could marry a woman taller than me,' I say.

'I know, but she'd be a freak, wouldn't she?'

I laugh and trip up on a loose paving stone. Walking with Louisa is like trying to keep up with a keen student striding to her next lecture; for all her natural elegance, with her satchel slung across her black silk shirt and her long legs protruding from her short, black, A-line skirt, she is coltish and almost a little geeky.

I am about to ask her to slow down when we arrive at the *trattoria*. Louisa pushes her way through a curtain of coloured plastic beads and greets two elderly waiters by name, kissing them both, her long, slender fingers clasping their bony shoulders. We are shown to a table at the back, next to the kitchen.

Once seated, Louisa leans back on her chair and with a little arch of her neck calls into the kitchen, *'Buon giorno*, Don Ottavio, *come va?'*

A disembodied voice answers, *'Buon giorno*, Louisa, *come va?'*

There is a brief exchange in Italian before a man appears, wiping his hands on his apron. He is small, about fifty, and sweating profusely; his short hair appears to be soaked in olive oil; there are four perfect black curls across his forehead. He gestures to Louisa to introduce me. I stand and we shake hands. He looks me over. I cannot tell whether I meet with his approval. He says something to Louisa, clearly about me, and she laughs. He then turns back to me and says something else.

'He's saying it is an honour to have you here. Whatever you choose he will make specially for you.'

'Grazie, signor,' I say.

'Call him Don Ottavio.'

'Grazie, Don Ottavio.'

He smiles and returns to his kitchen. I take my seat and grab a lump of bread from the basket just placed on the table. The crust is hard, snapping between my teeth, the bread itself is light and porous, a dry honeycomb texture; the combination is perfection.

'I know them quite well here,' Louisa says. 'I eat here most days I'm at the university. I eat and read. It's very pleasant.'

'I can imagine.'

There is a written menu so I choose without Louisa's help. I settle on *penne all'amatriciana*. Louisa has the same. We order a small *caraffa* of wine. When I call it a 'carafe' Louisa says, 'You're not in Pizza Express now.'

I ask her about her Italian, her fluency.

'I'm not fluent fluent,' she says, 'but two years is a long time. This isn't like Milan. Not everyone speaks English. I took some lessons at first, but I picked it up quite quickly. How do you think I'm managing to do a degree?'

'You're doing a degree?' I say with too much surprise.

'No one's more shocked than I am. That's Alessandro for you. No use trying to get away with a few courses. Besides it takes about seven years here, and the exams are oral like I told you – so why worry?'

'And the degree is in Italian history?'

'I suppose,' she says.

'You suppose?'

'It's something like that.'

'Are you enjoying it?' I ask, wondering whether or not to bring up her utter lack of interest in anything remotely academic, intellectual or otherwise when I first knew her.

'It's all right. Everyone spends a lot of time arguing in the lectures. There are so many students. You should come. The auditoriums are full. Packed to the rafters. I think sometimes any more hot air and the place will blow.'

'Do you have many friends?' I am pleased with this avuncular question in my quest for a strictly platonic friendship.

'Not really.' She doesn't seem bothered by this.

'Why not?'

'I don't know. The boys are troublesome. Girls . . . they don't like me. Well, it's not that they don't like me . . . it's just they're quite fiery here and . . .' She stops, mulling over whether to give me the full story.

'Were you a bad girl?' I ask provocatively.

'No,' she says crossly. 'God, I always get the blame. If you want to know, there's this professor. He's only thirty-five. He's very charming, very handsome. He loves the opera. Alessandro hates the opera. The San Carlo is a big deal here. I like to go and he takes me. Anyway, these girls found out and that was it. God, you should have been there. There's this little piazza near the university building. We were screaming at each other. They were calling me *puttana, sgualdrina*. All because of this professor. By the end of it I was in tears. I had to call Alessandro at work and tell him to come and get me.'

'What did he say?'

'Nothing.'

'Nothing?'

'He thinks the opera is bourgeois.' She shrugs.

'Inappropriate reaction to the situation,' I say psychotherapeutically.

'I know. But he does care, really. You know that saying, he's old enough to be your father. Well it's rubbish, I mean, when you're in love. But sometimes I think being married to me must feel like having a teenage daughter . . .'

'You're twenty-seven.'

'I said "feel like" not "is like". Sorting out problems like jealousies over university professors and cat-fights with a load of girls . . .'

'I see what you mean.'

Our food arrives. While we eat Louisa tells me how she met Alessandro – it was very romantic apparently. They met in a bookshop in London. Louisa was sheltering from the rain; certainly not buying a book. Alessandro thought she worked there. 'Ha!' she exclaims, remembering the absurdity; she was actually working in Nicole Farhi in New Bond Street. She helped him find a book anyway. He'd written the author's name down from the radio. She worked out that he'd got 'j' and 'g' mixed up. He left and she knew he'd come back to ask her out, so she ended up spending all afternoon and all the following day hanging around in the bookshop. He didn't turn up until five minutes before closing. He took her to Quo Vadis.

'What was the book?' I ask. 'The one he was looking for.'

Louisa looks at me with a mixture of astonishment and consternation. 'God, you boys with your irrelevant details.'

'Important information, you mean,' I say defensively.

'How?' she asks, a little irritably.

'Don't you mean "why"?' I cannot resist being difficult.

'No, I mean "how is it important?"'

'No, you don't. You mean "why is it important to know what book he was buying?"'

'I think I know what I mean,' she says sharply.

We don't speak for a minute, then Louisa leans forward and whispers, 'Oh no, our first row.'

I don't know what to make of this. I decide to smile and ignore it, but she continues, 'Didn't we use to get at each other like that – you know back then?'

I remain silent.

'Don't tell me you don't remember?' She is being insistent – she wants me to join in this little game, this flirtation.

I say, 'I think it was my fault. Too uptight.'

'I quite liked it. The difficult type – always a big turn-on.'

This is getting dangerous. Our relationship consisted of little but bickering and sex. There is little conversational mileage in the former.

'You *are* being tight-lipped,' she says with a smile.

I remain so.

'Are you still angry at the way it finished?'

I decide it will be easy to control this conversation if I say something rather than let her continue to interrogate me.

'Please. If you don't mind I don't want to talk about it.'

She looks a little affronted but quickly recovers. 'You're right. It's ten years ago and I'm married.'

'Yes, you are,' I say with a strained smile.

'What about you?' she asks.

'What about me?'

'Are you with anyone?'

'I was. For quite a while. It ended a year ago.'

'No one since?'

'Not really.'

'There are a lot of lovely women in Naples. Great bodies. I can't help staring. They're all hips, bums and tits. Lovely olive skin. And pretty, so pretty . . .'

'You should have seen the women who turned up today,' I say, keen to shift the focus of conversation away from Louisa's descriptions of Neapolitan women, a subject as frustrating, if not more so, as hearing her edge ever closer to mentioning our sex life together ten years ago. Because what might seem like harmless appreciation of female beauty, coming from Louisa, is charged with the potential for erotic adventure. I don't know what it is about her – there are no contrived gestures to subvert the innocence of what she's saying; she's not licking her lips, sucking her fingers, playing with the large pepper pot between us on the table. There aren't even subtler signals, just something emanates from within her that makes me believe that while she's saying all this her imagination is indulging in every conceivable erotic thought. That even though the subject is simply the loveliness of Neapolitan women, somewhere in her imagination she's being fucked. By Alessandro, by me, by one of these women, by all of us. I pour us out some more wine and knock mine back.

'Sometimes you just need a hit of something,' I say.

Louisa pushes her plate away and searches in her satchel for cigarettes. 'Sometimes you just do,' she agrees.

After lunch I am given Louisa's tour of secret Naples. First I am taken to the church of San Gregorio Armeno, a Benedictine convent. The entrance is via the street with the little clay figures. I do not have time to ask Louisa about this bizarre phenomenon before I am arrested by the spectacular interior of the church. It is almost Byzantine in its ornamentation and the air looks gilded with the reflection of sun's rays fragmented and refracted from the gold ceiling. We are not alone; other tourists, a long line of Italian schoolchildren, surround us. Not so secret, I say to Louisa. I mustn't doubt her, she says, and grabs my hand and leads me out of the church and around the corner to large iron gates. She rings a bell. A woman appears at the top of the steps that lead down from the side of the church to the gates. She is not a nun. She looks more like a poor Neapolitan housewife. She approaches us, gesticulating, cursing, 'Madonna mia, mamma mia,' waving us away. Louisa remains where she is, still holding my hand. When the woman reaches the gates she looks us both up and down, clearly disgusted by our temerity. Louisa says something I don't understand. Instantly they begin to argue; Louisa uses the whole range of Neapolitan gestures to aid her argument. It is hostile, intense – they could be arguing over a man for all the passion, lack of restraint. I try to pull away but Louisa pulls me back. I wait beside her quietly. Eventually the woman throws her hands in the air. Louisa smiles. The gates are unlocked. The woman retreats.

'It happens every time. The place is supposed to be open to the public but it never is. I just wear her down.' Louisa leads me in by the hand. We pull the gate shut and walk up the steps and through an arch into a beautiful cloistered garden. Louisa drops my hand.

We sit down on a stone bench in the shade of an orange tree. In the centre of the garden there is a fountain bordered by prancing seahorses. Behind it are two figures; Jesus and the Samarian Woman, Louisa informs me. From where we are sitting these graceful statues seem to be walking among the orange trees. Louisa counts her cigarettes and decides she can smoke. I stretch my legs out and cross them at the ankles. The air is miraculously cool around us and the noise of the city seems far away. This is an urban oasis, perfumed with citrus, sheltered by boughs, defended from the city's chaos by high, ancient walls. I am just about to doze off when Louisa elbows me and says it is time to go.

Back on the street with the little clay figures Louisa explains what they are. It's a Christmas tradition in Naples to have a nativity scene in your house made up of all these tiny little figures. The presepe, it's called. People come from all over Italy to buy them. Leading up to Christmas the street is packed for days, so much so the police have to rope off the surrounding streets. I point out they're not just religious figures, there are some men in suits. Modern figures. Laurel and Hardy even. Occasionally if a personality touches the country's imagination they get made into a little model, I am told.

'And do they get placed in the nativity scene?' I ask.

'I don't know – we're not allowed to have one,' Louisa says ruefully, adding, 'I'm lucky if I can persuade Aless to recognize Christmas at all.'

'He's a man of strong convictions.'

'He usually gives in.'

'So he's without principles, then?'

'He loves me, that's all . . .'

I had meant it to be a joke yet Louisa seemed to want to make sure I understood how loved she is – truly, and not just as a trophy wife.

We cut across Via dei Tribunali and then head down a very narrow alley to another church.

Louisa tells me we are here to see the little icon of the crucifixion that supposedly addressed St Thomas Aquinas when he was living in the monastery next door. The painting is indeed small, hung over an altar at the end of the many chapels leading off the main transept. A knee-high railing and gate prevent us from entering the chapel. From where we are standing, twelve feet or so away, the image is vague, dark – a banal medieval crucifixion scene. Louisa pushes open the little gate.

'What are you doing?' I say in a concerned whisper, peering around for someone to stop us.

'Don't worry,' she says, and proceeds towards the end of the chapel. I follow her nervously. We have to lean up over the altar to see the painting more closely. Our bodies, turned inwards, touch.

'What did it say to Thomas Aquinas?' I ask, modulating the tone of my voice to give my enquiry the appropriate solemnity.

'Christ asked him what he wanted. He'd grant him anything.'

'What did he say?'

'"Nothing, if not you,"' Louisa quotes thoughtfully, and then adds, 'He was very religious, you know.'

I refrain from saying 'I know that'. Instead I look at Louisa peering closely at the painting. Her pale face glows in the almost miraculous light emanating from the picture. It is as though a soft bulb has been placed behind the canvas, diffusing all the colours into a pool of light into which Louisa has dipped her face. The experience isn't as profound as Aquinas's I'm sure, but it's very moving nonetheless.

Would Alessandro understand the psychology of a man who would kill for a woman like Louisa?

I turn back to the painting. I find myself answering Christ's question in exactly the same way – except I'm referring to Louisa. I try to stop myself but it quickly becomes a prayer echoing inside me. I turn to Louisa and say it, 'Nothing, if not you.'

'That's what he said,' she says and for some inexplicable reason gives me a quick kiss on the cheek.

We leave the church and double back along Via dei Tribunali. I am perplexed by her spontaneous show of affection. I want to pull her into a narrow, dark street and take her in my arms. I want to kiss her passionately, ridiculously so – like film lovers, fantasy lovers, dream lovers. But instead, as we cross Via Duomo, I look up towards the cathedral and I say, 'I like Duomos. The Santa Maria del Fiore in Florence is my favourite building.'

I am ignored. Despite being English, from the Home Counties, Louisa has adopted the Neapolitan habit of regarding the rest of Italy as irrelevant.

We come to a stop by a mass of scaffolding fixed to high iron railings, behind which is a plain but imposing façade of grey-black stone with a great iron door. The place has an impenetrable feel. It is like a giant vault. 'Another church?' I say.

Louisa tells me to wait by the gates and disappears down a side street. She is gone a full five minutes, during which time I am almost shredded by a Vespa that careens past me trying to clear a group of schoolchildren without stopping. When Louisa reappears she is with an old man, his dark face and hands as gnarled as it is possible to be while still recognizable as flesh and not tortured bronze. He is carrying a set of keys on a large ring; he looks like a medieval jailer. He unlocks the gates and then the great doors. He pushes them open for us. After handing Louisa the keys, he disappears. We step inside and Louisa locks the doors behind us. We are in a bright, octagonal nave, divided into eight small altars, each hosting a large altarpiece. High above us, through windows set in an octagonal dome, sunbeams strike through the air with such direct and palpable intensity they are like golden spears thrown down onto the marble floor.

'This is part of an important old Neapolitan charity called the Pio Monte della Misericordia.' Louisa pronounces the Italian with an accent so plaintive it accords with the misery in the name. I say this and she says *misericordia* means mercy, pity, not misery. She points to the huge painting before us over the central altar.

'*The Seven Acts of Mercy*,' she says. 'Caravaggio.'

I am amazed. 'I love Caravaggio. I have a small reproduction of this in a book.'

There are no pews, just five untidy rows of wooden chairs. We sit down facing the poorly lit painting.

'How come we were let in?' I whisper.

'Just like the cloister, it's supposed to be open to the public but it never is. You can make an appointment if you're desperate. I made friends with the old guy the first time I came. Now, if he's around and in a good mood he'll open it up for me. The painting is in all the guidebooks, but no one actually gets to see it. You're very lucky.'

'I am,' I say, confirming it to myself.

'I can't be doing with all those floaty, floaty Renaissance painters. All those Botticelli. This guy . . . he was a punk.'

'With talent,' I add.

'You know what I mean . . .' she says, not particularly interested in my qualifier. She then adds, 'This is where you'll find me when I'm feeling low. Providing, that is, I'm allowed in. It's hard in Naples to feel really alone. Even at home. It's Aless's family home. He's lived there all his life. So even though it can get quite lonely there, I never really feel alone. That's why I come here.'

There is no hint of indulgent soulfulness. She is merely explaining to me that one of the negatives of living in such a city and being married to such a man requires her to find a place of retreat, a place that is nominally hers. It is not important that it is a small chapel with a huge Caravaggio. It could have been anywhere. I take her hand. It is the hand of friendship because for the first time I feel close to her without the frustration of desire.

'I'm glad you brought me here,' I say, watching her in profile absently chewing her lip.

She remains quiet for a moment before saying, 'Enough melancholy,' and gently removes her hand from mine.

I realize taking her hand was a mistake. I am crushed by the quickness with which she has withdrawn it. I regard it as a clear indication of her indifferent feeling for me, and that all the subtle and playful intimacies we have shared over the past two days mean nothing. I feel sick. Humiliated. Stupid. I am curt when I refuse to accompany her to return the keys. She seems not to notice. When she reappears all traces of her sombre mood are gone and she locks her arm in mine. As we launch once more along Spaccanapoli she asks me whether I've enjoyed her secret tour of Naples. I feel her pull me closer. She wants an effusive response, to be told she has chosen well and been an excellent guide.

I say, 'I've had a wonderful time.'

'You've also learned how we do things in Naples.'

'What do you mean?' I ask.

'There are three ways to conduct business here. The cloister: you can always get what you want if you're prepared to argue for long enough. The private chapel with the painting: it's only wrong if someone says it is. The Pio Monte della Misericordia: you can open any door if you know people in the right places. See, I'm not just a pretty face any more.' Her clutch is now tight as we thread through the early-evening crowds. We look like lovers.

'Now we need to get some shopping,' she announces.

As we head towards a small neighbourhood of shops at the bottom of the hill, Louisa points out the interesting aspects of modern Neapolitan life. The bootleg-CD sellers. The homeless with their blankets of junk spread out below the ancient buildings. The young boys, *scugnizzi* Louisa calls them, standing around in small groups, moodily smoking.

She says, 'Anywhere else they'd look horrible, scuzzy, but here, with their dark hair, dark skin, dark eyes, they look as if they know something. Something we don't. I've watched them. Boys as young as eight, sometimes, sitting on a step staring out. As pretty as can be, but no angels. I think they're sexual younger here. The way they look at women. Even little boys. As though they know exactly what they'd do given half a chance. I tell you, it shouldn't be, but it's quite sexy being looked at like that.'

'Eight years old?'

'Maybe not that young, but fifteen, something like that. These boys just exude something.'

'You weren't so different yourself.'

'I was as sexy as a Neapolitan boy? I like that.' She then nudges me and asks, 'Fish or meat?'

'Sorry?' I ask.

'Tonight. Fish or meat. What do you want? Do you like fish?'

'Yes.'

'Fish then. Follow me.'

We enter a small busy street that appears to be one long fish market. In the blinding sunlight the fish, displayed in shallow boxes and arranged in tiers running along the length of the street, shimmer like a million silver coins at the bottom of a fountain. From an oblique angle they look like the individual scales of a giant sea-serpent's tail undulating below the water's surface.

'I'm going to bake the fish and serve it *alla napoletana*. It's a compromise.'

'Between what and what?'

'Tradition and not frying the fish.'

'What goes with it?'

'It's a kind of stew of tomatoes, capers, black olives, pine nuts. It's supposed to have raisins as well, but I don't like them.'

'Sounds fabulous.'

'Now all we need is to decide on the fish. It's supposed to be cod, but it's hardly exotic when you're English, is it?'

We decide on sea bass. It's gutted before us on a black slab of marble. We buy some clams for the pasta. I've never tasted clams like these before, I am told. We buy the rest of the food on a parallel street. The tomatoes, I'm assured, are the best in the world because they're grown on the side of Vesuvius. She pops an olive from a barrel into my mouth.

By the time we've finished we have three heavy bags. There is some debate about how Louisa's going to get home because I choose this moment to inform her of my decision to accept her invitation to stay with her and Alessandro, and that I will therefore need to collect my things. The debate ends in a call to Alfredo, their driver. It is another forbidden use of the car. He will be ten minutes.

We sit on a wall and wait; the bags sit between our feet. Louisa rests her head on my shoulder wearily. 'Do you mind?' she asks. 'Of course not,' I say. She nestles in my neck. Her eyes are closed. I feel a powerful urge to speak, but I am worried some insane declaration of love might shoot out – some impassioned, un-reasoned, irrational suggestion that she leave with me tomorrow, that we start over where we left off ten years ago. I force myself to stay silent. I feel it, though. Deeply. My body thrums with the possibility of her – the precise pleasure of seeing her face every day, her body every night. My imagination is strong and I cannot help but yield. I rest my head against hers, close my eyes and dream, while all around I hear the guttural whispers of the people of Naples shopping under a burning hot sun.

2

I am unsure how I shall deal with my departure. Certainly I owe Signora Maldini more money, but how much will be difficult to ascertain. My inclination is to work out what I'll need for tonight and tomorrow and bung her the rest; overpay rather than underpay. Outside the front door I can hear the TV is on. I unlock the door slowly so Signora Maldini isn't taken by surprise. However, when I walk in it is me who is surprised. I almost don't recognize the woman standing by the kitchen door. Gone are the housecoat, the black dress, the puckered flat shoes – all replaced by a smart new blue dress, tied at the waist with a patent leather belt, and new high heels. But that's not all: her hair, the leaning beehive, has been carefully recentred on her head and given extra volume. She is also wearing a little make-up, a string of pearls around her neck, and some gold bracelets on one wrist. She is looking quite glamorous. I can tell she is delighted with her new outfit. She quite unexpectedly gives me a twirl and says, 'Grazie, signor.' She is thanking me for her makeover. I say, 'Bella, bella, signora.' My compliment elicits a little coy smile – the joy in her new clothes supplanting her usual inscrutability. I try to make an Italianate noise to express that she's been caught out and that her cover is blown. I think she understands because she cannot resist a giggle. She goes into the kitchen and I hear the now familiar sounds of caffè being prepared.

I will be unable to leave tonight, I realize. I spent an age this morning explaining to her I was leaving at four tomorrow and if I pack and go now, after our little bonding session, she'll be hurt and I don't want that. Plus, I like my room here. I'd miss waking up to the family opposite arguing over breakfast, the thump of footballs below, the gossip resonating up and down the washing lines as if the street is a giant stringed instrument.

Signora Maldini brings out the *caffè* and sits down. She pushes the little cup over the table and then lights a cigarette. We don't talk. We both turn and face the television. It is a game show of some sort and every now and then Signora Maldini calls out. I presume she's answering a question. Whenever she gets the answer right she claps; when she gets it wrong she calls out *Gesù* or *Madonna mia* and shakes her head. I look over and shake my head in support. I feel for the first time that Signora Maldini and I are friends.

At seven-thirty I have a quick cold shower. I then dress in the cleanest of my clothes. Crumpled and unshaven, I am now borderline vagrant in appearance. I am a preposterous-looking dinner guest for a judge and his wife. I shuffle into my shoes without socks. My shoes are so old the leather is soft and supple and I barely notice I have them on. I fold a few thousand lire and pocket them with my long key. For some reason I feel a little native. Like a Neapolitan.

Strolling towards Via Monteoliveto to catch a cab I realize I haven't felt better in months, years even. It doesn't matter how shit my life is – right now it isn't. It hasn't been all day. It won't be tomorrow. I stop. I am going home tomorrow. I say it aloud to myself: 'Tomorrow I am going home.' But I know I'm not. I have known it all day. Why go home to certain misery when I can be, at least temporarily, happy here? I stick my hands out before me as if to literally weigh up my options. Happiness here, misery there. I try to be fair in assessing their particular weight imagined in the palms of my hands. Happiness, although constituently lighter, is more bountiful, and the scales tip that way. As for the new job, counselling is now in the past. And at last I know I've finally drawn a line in the sand as straight as Spaccanapoli divides Naples. My new life begins here. Now. From this moment. All I have to do is write to the charity, stop my direct debits and standing orders and I can stay for a month at least. I don't know why I didn't do this weeks ago when I first quit my job.

I decide to walk to Louisa's. Too much adrenalin is flowing through me to catch a cab. My muscles flex with involuntary excitement. I am a victor over something. I should punch the air. I feel like running, skipping even. Long bouncing strides. I have the weightlessness of a child, the unbounded energy. I am tempted to try it down wide Via Roma but I sense my body will resist me. Existential freedom does not rid the body of its inhibitions.

I decide to cut up through the Spanish Quarter. I shouldn't – it's dangerous at this time of night. But my confidence is high. From the moment I leave the brilliantly lit Via Roma I am plunged into umber darkness. There are no streetlamps. The only source of light is the low sodium glare from the *bassi* or the occasional flicker of an obsolete neon sign. Even the sounds of the night seem suppressed by the darkness; all I hear is a dog barking, a tin can kicked, voices close by but unseen, TVs and radios all echoing through the warm still air. The neighbourhood feels empty, but then as I peer into the open doors of the *bassi* I see whole families sitting around tables; bowls of pasta, jugs of wine, bottles of water, loaves of bread spread out in front of them, their arms a nest of reaching, pouring, pass-ing. Suddenly the place seems full of life. With access to books in English and an Italian equivalent of Radio 3, this is just how I'd like to live – in Epicurean simplicity. Primary needs satisfied: shelter, food, company, music. And for privacy I could persuade someone somewhere to let me sit in a private chapel.

Instinct takes me to Louisa's neighbourhood and a cab takes me the rest of the way. I push open the big iron gates and run up the terracotta steps. One of the big front doors opens just as I arrive at the top. Louisa ushers me in with an order to be quiet, her long slender finger pressed to her lips. I can hear the piano being played. I am led into the large kitchen. Pots and pans hang from a central rectangular bracket over a massive wooden table. There are three large work surfaces, all worn away from years of use. The stove is also large, with circles of blue flames burning below wrought-iron hot plates, upon which three large pans sit with ample room. It is a kitchen for a professional. There is nothing delicate or fancy. A man's kitchen. Louisa doesn't look out of place, but she doesn't look particularly in control either.

She whispers, 'He came in late. He has to play for an hour. I tell you, trying to cook and be really quiet in this kitchen is impossible.' It is only now she kisses me: a quick, formal peck on each cheek. 'Sorry, I must seem so rude. Let me get you a drink.'

She pours some white wine into two of the three tall wineglasses at the ready on the kitchen table.

I whisper, 'Is that why you answered the door before I knocked?'

She nods and sips her wine, her nose disappearing into the bowl of the glass like a child's into a beaker. The piano is faint – two rooms away, I judge. I back up to the door, open it a little. Chopin. A nocturne. Well played. I close the door.

'Not bad,' I whisper.

'It's Chopin,' Louisa tells me.

'I know,' I say.

'I only know because that's all he plays. He's obsessed. I find it a bit overwrought most of the time.'

'It is,' I say.

Louisa approaches me, her glass held to her chest. 'Did you have a nice day with me today?'

'Very,' I say as warmly as I can. I then remember my decision to stay another month. I want to announce it simply, hoping Louisa's reaction, whatever it might be, will not affect me. I say, 'Actually, I've decided to stay in Naples a little longer.'

'Really?' she says, clearly pleased but stifling her reaction for fear of disturbing her husband. 'That's great. How long?'

'A few weeks.'

'A few weeks? What about your new job?'

'I don't want to do that kind of work any more.'

She looks concerned by this, covering her mouth with her hand as if she has said or heard something terrible. 'It wasn't Alessandro, was it? What he said? He shouldn't have interfered.'

'It wasn't Alessandro,' I say.

'Sometimes I think people just do what he says because he's a judge.'

'Jim, I order you to change your life!' I say, badly mimicking Alessandro's unhewn-marble accent.

'Sssh,' Louisa says, eyes wide.

The piano stops.

'Now we're in for it.'

The door opens and Alessandro appears. He is silent and stares at us both. He doesn't seem to recognize either of us. He then scans the kitchen: the table top, the work surfaces, the stove top, his intense eyes searching for something, a discrepancy in the detail, something that will give away whatever it is his intuition has told him has occurred here in his absence. He then looks back to Louisa and me. His face breaks into a smile.

'Jim, welcome.' He steps forward and my hand is once again enveloped by his massive paws. 'I have been playing the piano. I must . . . to relax. Louisa is very quiet. Like a mouse. So when I heard the noise, I knew you were here.'

'You play well,' I say. 'Chopin, wasn't it?'

'It is pretty music. But also profound. I like the . . . how do you say . . .' He looks over to Louisa for help.

'Detail, intricacy, complexity . . .' she reels off.

'Very good,' he says. 'Yes, all those things. And the beauty. Played well. Do you like Chopin?'

I am tempted to lie. But instead I rather lamely say, 'Yes and no.'

'Do you like classical music? Or are you like Louisa and her friends?' He might as well be talking about a daughter.

'No, I like classical music. But I find Chopin too fussy, too often lacking delicacy. Which I think was what he was after.'

Alessandro appears to take this in and assesses it. I sense he thinks I have a point. 'But for me, after a day at work, he is perfect,' he says a little dismissively.

'I can see that,' I say.

Alessandro pours himself some wine and leans against the table.

'Thank you very much for this morning,' I say.

'Ah, yes. This morning. I had forgotten. Did you find it interest-

ing? I am like the director, no? Like the director of the orchestra.'
He waves his finger in front of him as though conducting.

I am invited to sit down. Louisa directs where I should sit with
her eyes. I walk round the table and take a seat. She sits opposite
me after setting three clean wineglasses out and placing two opened
bottles of red wine on the table. It seems it will be Alessandro who
will serve the food. He opens one of the large pans on the stove
and sticks his face into the rising steam.

'*Perfetto*, Louisa, *perfetto*.'

Louisa looks at me proudly. He takes out three bowls from the
cupboard and dishes out the pasta and clams. He grates some
Parmesan on top and hands us a bowl each. He then hands round
forks and spoons. It is very informal. Louisa stands and fetches
some bread. 'He always forgets something.'

We all eat ravenously. Following Alessandro's lead, every now
and then I grind a little black pepper, crush a little sea salt, shave
off a little more Parmesan, or drizzle some extra olive oil over the
pasta – each addition shifting the emphasis of flavour.

While we eat Louisa informs Alessandro of my plans to stay –
plans that are greeted with hearty approval; he regards a month in
Naples as the minimum length for any serious stay. The subject of
conversation then turns to the trial. I do not instigate it. Alessandro
wants to talk about his day at work and I imagine the conversation
wouldn't differ much if I wasn't there. The basic problem facing the
prosecution, Alessandro explains, is that Sonino's lawyer is trying to
delay his client's appearance in court in order to force an acquittal,
because, under Italian civil-rights law, if the accused is on remand
beyond a certain amount of time the case is dismissed; the accused
in this case are the nine he is testifying against and there are only two
weeks to go. After weeks of legal wrangling Sonino was due to
appear today, but then the court was told he was sick. A doctor's
report was requested. He was certified healthy, if a little under-
nourished. He will be in court tomorrow, I am assured. Alessandro
is taking it for granted that now I am staying I will want to come
and watch again. I am advised to be there early, as it will be busy.

'Busier than today?' I ask.

He nods his impressive head. 'Today they knew before the court Sonino would not be there. Tomorrow will be different.' He then asks me how it was in the public gallery.

'Unsettling,' I say.

Alessandro looks to Louisa for help. 'Unsettling? I don't know this.'

'*Inquietante*,' she says.

'Ah,' he says. 'Louisa tells me Eugenia Savarese was there. She is a very powerful woman. I have known her many years.'

I am struck by this but I refrain from asking what he means precisely by 'knowing' her, because I don't want him to think I'm only interested in his relationship with the Camorra rather than his work as a judge.

'I helped her up the stairs,' I say.

'That was very kind,' he says.

I am tempted to ask whether or not my presence in the public gallery placed me in any danger, but as it was his suggestion it might seem rude, so instead I ask him about the member of the nine who seemed the most disgruntled, the one he spoke to at the end of the session. Lorenzo Savarese. Eugenia's grandson. Alessandro tells me he was second-in-command of Camorra Moderna, Sonino's right-hand man. Sonino was, and some say still is, *capo di tutti capi* – the boss of all bosses. I am told Savarese is very violent but also intelligent, something he, Savarese, is only learning about himself during this trial. I sense this is an important discovery for Alessandro in his search for the psychology of the man. I ask about Sonino but Alessandro holds his hand up to stop me, very much like he did when silencing the court this morning. I shrink back.

'I will tell you,' he says, 'but first I must serve the fish.' He stands and walks over to the oven. He opens the door, letting out a huge waft of heat, and with his hand squeezed into an oven glove removes the fish wrapped in tin foil and laid out on a baking tray like sleeping spacemen. Meanwhile Louisa collects up our bowls and dumps them in the large, deep rectangular sink; she sits straight back down as though even this might be an infringement of the demarcation of duties. Alessandro sets the fish down on the table. He then returns to the stove, removes the lid of another of the pans which are bubbling away and leans over it.

'*Perfetto*, Louisa, *perfetto*,' he repeats, his nostrils flaring to gather in more aroma. He then carries the pan to the table. I sneak a look in while he hands the plates around. It is a tomato sauce with all the ingredients Louisa bought earlier. Alessandro sits back down and grabs himself a wrapped fish and dumps it on his plate. Louisa does likewise, and I follow suit. We then ladle the sauce over the fish. The flesh of the sea bass is indeed *perfetto*, firm and succulent. The sauce is equally good – light, aromatic, yet without any particular ingredient overpowering or distorting the flavour of the fish. I compliment Louisa effusively, saying I haven't eaten this well in a long time.

'And all cooked in silence,' she says, glaring at her husband.

Alessandro lays his knife down and reaches across the table to his wife. He doesn't touch her but the gesture, the reaching, is unmistakably a signal of love, of his adoration, even of his inability to love her enough. Louisa remains quite still, yet with a tiny lift of her eyebrows lets him know it is only because she loves him that he can be so demanding. It is a touching moment. I raise my glass. Alessandro is quick to raise his.

'To what?' he says.

'To Louisa,' I say.

Louisa looks a little puzzled. 'Me?'

Alessandro is also unsure why I have chosen his wife for this honour, but he soon realizes. It is through her we are all here, it is she who has brought us all together, cooked this wonderful meal; and for both she should be toasted. Alessandro is pleased with this. We all clink glasses. Alessandro then decides it is his turn to propose a toast.

'To your visit in Naples,' he says.

We raise our glasses. Alessandro then looks at Louisa, keen for her to propose something so we are all equal in these celebrations.

She thinks about it and then looking at me says, 'To our new friend.'

I nod modestly and say, 'Thank you.' Then glancing over at Alessandro I add, 'To my new friends.'

'It's my toast,' Louisa says a little sharply, then repeats firmly, 'To our new friend.' Alessandro echoes her.

We return our glasses to the table and continue to eat. I am about to prompt Alessandro to tell me more about Giacomo Sonino when, after two large slugs of wine, he begins without my encouragement.

I am told that for the last ten years Giacomo Sonino has been the most feared man in Naples. As *capo di tutti capi* of the Camorra Moderna, he was responsible for 90 per cent of all criminal activity in the city and beyond: murder, smuggling, prostitution, drug-trafficking, protection, even street robbery. His gang filled the vacuum when the war between the Nuova Camorra Organizzata and the Nuova Famiglia ended in the late 1980s. Sonino recruited ad hoc any young men he could impress and manipulate. And in Naples there are many such young men. There were few blood ties in this gang. Loyalty was produced by violent initiation, the code of silence – *omertà* – and the Sonino mythology. This mythology consisted of a university education (almost unheard of in southern-Italian organized crime); a predilection for writing poetry (here he is less unusual); but most importantly his being endowed with a kind of immortality after surviving a knife attack by three men. Alessandro explains that since the Neapolitans are so susceptible to superstition being 'lucky' is the most powerful attribute a person can have.

'Is any of this true?' I ask.

'He has many scars.'

'So why has he become a *pentito*?'

'He has killed many people.'

'How many people?'

'Ten.'

I am shocked that this does not shock me. 'How old is he?' I ask.

'Thirty-three.' I am more shocked by this. Not that he is thirty-three and has killed ten people but simply that he is younger than me.

'So what does he get for becoming a *pentito*?'

'If they convict, a new identity,' he says. I sense Alessandro's disgust with the system and the deals it does, as well as a tacit acceptance that these deals are the only way to convict these people.

I try another angle. 'Why would Sonino delay testifying if that means the nine go free and he doesn't?'

'He has much power even in prison.'

'Then why is he turning *pentito*?'

'He is a complicated man. But he hates Savarese. Savarese connects.' Here Alessandro presses the knuckles of his hands together. 'Savarese connects with the people. You understand. Like the old Camorra. He looks after you. He has honour, they say.'

'What do you think?'

It was a stupid question. I am offered only the praying gesture for an answer. I change tack. 'Who do you think will win?' I mean between Sonino and Savarese, forgetting the actual contest here is between the Camorra and the law.

Here Alessandro sighs and shakes his head.

'It is not so easy, Jim. This trial is not so easy.'

I am then told about the *pentiti de camorra* debacle of the early 1980s. Even though he wasn't involved, the memory wearies him. After the anti-Mafia law made belonging to a criminal organization a crime in itself – it was the only way to reach the *intoccabili*, 'the untouchables': those so high up they no longer committed the crimes – there were suddenly tens of *pentiti* accusing thousands of their fellow *camorristi*. It was decided to prosecute everyone together, one trial – the *maxi-processo*. It lasted three years and was almost solely based on the *pentiti* testifying that each of the defendants 'belonged' in some way to the Camorra.

'That was it?' I ask, incredulous.

Alessandro's gesture – pressing the fingers of one hand together and shaking the hand close to his chest – explicitly tells me what a nonsense he thought it all was. He then goes on to tell me almost all were convicted initially, but that almost all were then released on appeal. The testimony of the *pentiti* was so weak it collapsed under the harsher scrutiny of appeal.

'This is why this trial is so important, Jim. This is why it is important to understand Sonino. If he tells us the truth and we convict, we will not be embarrassed again.'

'I thought these men were accused of a car bombing?'

'There is only Sonino's testimony,' he says.

I ask, 'What's the chance of securing a conviction based solely on that?'

'Conviction is easy,' Alessandro says a little impatiently. 'It is making it . . .'

'. . . Stick,' interjects Louisa almost before her husband has begun the search or appeal for the word.

'It is my job as president to find out the truth. The other judges in the *maxi-processo* . . . they wanted to convict. It was very bad. I do not blame the *pentiti*. I blame the judges. They were not strong with the testimony.'

Louisa says, 'This is why it's taking so long.'

'Down to the wire,' I say.

Louisa nods.

I sense Alessandro has become irritated. This trial is wearing him down. Law and justice have become secondary to damage limitation and redeeming the justice system for an earlier fuck-up, a fuck-up he himself wouldn't have made because he would have striven for the truth not convictions in the beginning. It seems the *maxi-processo* damaged the fight against the Camorra because it discredited both the Justice Department and the whole notion of the *pentiti* – because this was the first time so many members of the Camorra had broken the *omertà*; tens had done so, including five or six heavyweight figures. If it had been handled correctly the one insuperable barrier in fighting this kind of criminal organization, the code of silence, would have been permanently compromised –

a potential death blow to the whole culture itself. As it was, the defendants were acquitted and the *pentiti* thrown in jail. It had cost millions; a new courtroom had been built; it was a national news event. It was a major fuck-up.

We have finished our food and pushed our plates to the middle of the table. I am full, and so it seems is Alessandro. We both pat our stomachs. He turns to me.

'So, Jim, you will leave counselling?'

I am not sure I mentioned this part of my plan to him. This unnerves me. But I answer the question affirmatively.

'What will you do?' he asks keenly.

I look at Louisa. Walking here I was happy not to know; now I feel that to say so will look aimless. However, I don't have to answer because Louisa supplies me with a get-out. Standing up and piling the plates together she says, 'If you could choose anything. Anything in the world . . .'

I look at Alessandro; he doesn't have a problem with this approach.

'Be a great violinist,' I say.

'Ah,' Alessandro sighs, fully appreciating the aspiration. 'The violin I think is the most sensual and the most intellectual of instruments. You know in Italy we have always made the best violins?'

'I know,' I say.

He then asks, 'Do you play?'

I shake my head ruefully.

'Ah,' he says, but this time it is not so much a sigh as a clipped inhalation, suggesting that if I don't play now it is probably not something I should think seriously about as a career.

I laugh at the remarkable duality of this man – both romantic and practical, and able to express both aspects of himself with a simple utterance.

'What else might you do? Go into politics?'

I have no idea why he suggests this unless the original confusion over my job has stuck in the complexities of his mind and he has mistakenly logged away political counsellor as a potential career choice; either that or he suggests this to every man in need of direction in life.

'No. But I have often thought I'd like to make cheese.'

'Really?' Alessandro responds enthusiastically.

'Yes,' I say rather timidly, having said it partly because it's true and partly because of the absurdity; I didn't expect such a reaction.

'Why?' he asks.

I don't really have an answer except I was once told I had a good palate for cheese and I love the stuff; so this is what I say.

Alessandro nods and studies my face. I think he's looking for cheese-making qualities in me. As he does Louisa places before us a plate with what I take to be a slice of pie of some sort and a perfectly round scoop of pure white ice cream.

'As if by magic. Cheese,' she says.

'Cheese?'

'Did you know mozzarella is from Naples?' Alessandro says. 'The best.'

I shake my head. 'What is this?' I ask pointing at the pie.

'Wild asparagus,' Louisa says.

'Jesus,' I say, quite glad my appetite has returned.

I am invited to taste the mozzarella. Alessandro is keen to know my opinion after I have confessed to a career choice in cheese. I cut a thick slice from the ball. It is so soft, so creamy, so moist, yet with such textural delicacy, I am unable to articulate my appreciation; I just make the noises it inspires.

Alessandro looks pleased and then says, 'I love Stilton. Wonderful.' I wait for more, a comparison between English and Italian cheeses – cheese as cultural metaphor, but that is it. I guess that even though he finds cheese-making an interesting and possibly suitable occupation for the next half of my life, he has little to say on the subject besides asking my opinion of his native cheese and telling me his preference among my country's.

★

We spend the next half hour picking at rum baba and drinking grappa. As on Saturday night Alessandro becomes less and less involved and appears to drift into a contented reverie. Louisa and I talk about my plans for the next few weeks, my decision to stay at Signora Maldini's. I decide to risk another appearance at the court, so we make arrangements to meet tomorrow. All through our conversation Louisa holds Alessandro's hand laid on the table in front of him, absently flicking his thick fingers so that they thump down on the wood. There is something potent about the difference between their fingers – hers white and slender, his dark and thick. It is as if they embody what is so attractive about the opposite sex – the extraordinary variation in such physical similarity. I can imagine their individual thrill in this difference when lying naked in bed together. It must be key to their sexual appeal. A kind of peasant–princess thing. I am certain their sex is good.

It is now eleven and I figure it is time to leave; Alessandro has a big day ahead of him. I am ushered out by both husband and wife with an invitation to their house in Sorrento at the weekend. I am told it is cooler there. There is a lemon grove. I will love it, they both assure me.

Out on the porch, Alessandro asks me how I'm getting home. I say I will walk.

'My driver will take you,' he says, and picks up a portable phone off the table inside the door. He whispers something and I hear an engine start below. We reconfirm Sorrento at the weekend and Alessandro jokes he will wave to me tomorrow in the public gallery. He is most amused by my anxious expression. We all kiss and I walk quickly down the terracotta steps. At the gate I wave goodbye one last time. Standing in the doorway, Louisa with her arms folded, Alessandro with his arm around her as if keeping her warm, they look like a suburban couple seeing off their guest on a chilly autumn night. The car pulls up. I climb in. As we pull away I remember sitting in this car with Louisa and Alessandro two nights ago and feeling despairingly like a man approaching middle age without much to show for the first half of his life, whereas now, quite in contrast, I feel like my life is just beginning.

3

When I reach the third level of the Palazzo di Giustizia, which yesterday was cavernously empty, there is a large throng of people surrounding the entrance to the public gallery. Standing before it are two armed policemen. They are being shouted at, clearly insulted. A number of the women I saw yesterday are amid the crowd. Despite this scene being like my initial expectations my anxiety is quick to return. These people are roused and angry. What if they decide to take their frustrations out on the stranger amongst them? I cannot see Eugenia Savarese. Perhaps she might speak up for me, return the favour offered to her yesterday.

I join the back of the crowd. A little way in front of me is the tomboy. She is very pretty and stands out among this homogeneous crowd. She seems to have deliberately subverted the traditional look of the Neapolitan woman with boyishness, while at the same time appropriated and feminized the classic appearance of the young Neapolitan male. She reminds me of some black-and-white image of a girl from an Italian or Hispanic neighbourhood in 1950s New York. Looking around the crowd she sees me. I smile. She smiles back but it is quick, nervy. She is apprehensive. I look away. I do not want to invite contact.

The doors open and the two policemen stand either side to filter people through. Everyone is asked a question before being let in. The answers are spat out. It is doubtful I will understand what I am asked. But then it is also doubtful there will be any room left in the public gallery by the time I get to the doors. I consider turning back, but there are now people amassed behind me all pushing forward, so I am stuck. When I am nearer the entrance I notice that the answer to the police's question determines which side of the public gallery they direct you to. Are they splitting up rival families, gangs? If so, where will I go? I really don't belong here, I realize. I am annoyed with Alessandro. He should have insisted this time I sit with the journalists.

After five minutes' pushing and shoving I find myself next in line. Before me is a little old man; he is arguing with the police. He is not being aggressive but is insistently trying to explain something. The officers ignore him and just repeat over and over the same question they have asked everyone. The crowd behind me are now shouting, hectoring them impatiently. It feels like it is me holding them up. I am hot, panicky. Finally one of the policemen pushes the old man to the side. I step up promptly. The question is fired at me. I say, *'Non capito. Inglese.'* I try to look disarmingly innocent. The question is asked again; it is irrelevant to them that I do not understand. This time I just say, *'Turista.'* They look at me dumbly, irritably; they have had enough for today without this. Now would be the perfect moment to leave, to step to the side with the old man. But then, from inside the public gallery, the girl appears, explains something to the police officers which includes me being *inglese*; the rest I don't understand. The policemen look at both of us suspiciously and then shrug insolently. The girl waves me in. I step forward hesitantly – I haven't been directed to a particular side. The girl then reaches for my hand and pulls me in. I pass from the frustrated energy building up outside the public gallery to the clamour and anger enclosed within. This was a mistake. A big mistake. I am now trapped in a room full of people almost vibrating with anxiety. There is no way out – a packed crowd at the door, reinforced glass between gallery and courtroom. And now I realize most of the seats are taken and I'm going to have to jam myself somewhere in the middle of a row. I don't want to sit where I'm not welcome. I want somewhere neutral. Below in the cage all nine are crushed together communicating with the public gallery. My first thought is that Savarese is looking directly at me hand in hand with his girlfriend/sister. I stiffen and she quickly releases me and runs down the steps to the glass wall. I know not to follow – she has got me in and that's it. I take a seat halfway along the fourth row down. Each decision I take traps me further. My heart begins to pound – pounds so powerfully that for a second I think I can feel the first tremor of an earthquake shaking the building. I try to take deep breaths without alerting those around me that I am trying to control my fear.

The courtroom itself is full of policemen, four times as many as yesterday. They stand around in groups chatting or singly leaning indolently against the walls. I count fifteen of them, all as young as the defendants, with interchangeable moody Italian looks. The lawyers are more animated than yesterday, crossing from desk to desk, forming huddles, talking into mobile phones, sending assistants out of the room. There is no television. The long bench is vacant. In the public gallery I only now notice a policeman is posted in each of the four corners. In England they would be sentinel-like, but here they smoke and slouch lugubriously, indifferent to their duty and barely concealing their irritation towards anyone whose behaviour requires them to act as police-men. I sense that for a Neapolitan being a policeman is a difficult occupation, and that for some it is as much a betrayal of the general culture as turning *pentito* is to the criminal world.

I decide I can't look to them for protection if anything goes wrong. I scan the court for Eugenia Savarese, whom I have now elected as my protectress. I can't see her, but then almost everyone is standing and either shouting through the glass to the cage or across the gallery at one another. There is real animosity. It seems I was right: we were being split up at the door into factions, camps. Which means, whichever way you look at it, I am aligned with someone. I try to locate faces from yesterday. They are all on the other side. Surely the public gallery hasn't been divided between supporters of the nine and Sonino; if that were the case there would be calls of *Vendetta! Vendetta!* As it is, everyone is fractionally less impassioned, at least in Italian terms, behaving more like rowing neighbours than vengeful, murderous *famiglia*.

Alessandro enters the courtroom followed by his deputy and the jurors. He looks up for a moment. I try not to make eye contact.

The lawyers take their seats and the nine spread out more evenly in their cage. It is this that finally calms down the gallery. Alessandro swings his microphone towards him. He taps it. Dull thuds echo in the court and in the gallery.

'*Buon giorno a tutti,*' he says cordially.

Immediately there is a flurry of questions from the lawyers, falling over themselves to approach the bench. Alessandro answers each of them patiently. Everyone is straining forward to make out what is being said. There is a shout from the cage. I don't catch who it is and there is no response from Alessandro. It is quickly followed by a family member standing up and shouting out from up here. The policeman nearest steps forward. He is abused from every corner of the gallery. He sneers, backs away; a hand resting on his white-leather holster. Excitement is beginning to replace my fear. I am aware I am watching something quite special. Nothing has happened, yet the atmosphere up here is intense. I sense a mob energy. I can feel myself succumbing to it, becoming part of it. My independence is falling away. I am choosing a side. The nine. I recognize some of them. I even know the name of their captain, so to speak, the enigmatic Lorenzo Savarese. I don't regard the judicial system as the opposition; I have allegiances there. But I am finding my original attraction to Sonino has been replaced by a kind of knee-jerk disgust at his betrayal. I want him discredited. As these people become more real to me, so the way in which they choose to live their lives is becoming more real, and for the first time their rules and codes resonate inside me. And it must be deeply frustrating when a man you have known, a man who has led you, a man who has confessed to ten murders, is then willing and permitted to testify against you. It's not surprising then that I'm taking sides. I'm rooting for those who accept that their crimes have no new value once they have been arrested.

Down in the courtroom a chair and microphone are being placed before the bench. I presume this is where Sonino will sit to be interviewed by Alessandro. It is bizarre that in such a new court-room they don't have a box or a fixed place for the witness. There are shouts from the cage. I think they are insisting that they are able to see Sonino clearly – his face. Alessandro raises his hand to silence them, then issues an order that the chair must be moved. Comments about this resound round the public gallery. From their expressions I can tell they are pleased by this and expect Sonino to crack when confronted with all nine staring at him as he gives his testimony.

Then Sonino is led in. He is surrounded by seven policemen. The place erupts. The cage, which yesterday seemed so immovable, vibrates wildly as the nine shake the bars with ferocity. Up here I fear the glass separating us from the courtroom will shatter with the shrieking of the families. The reaction of the police is swift: in the court they line up in front of the cage; up here they take out their batons. We are ordered to be silent or leave. The gallery quickly quietens.

I look down at Alessandro. He looks relaxed, leaning back in his chair, talking to his deputy. Judging from his manner the conversation could be about anything from Napoli beating Lazio at the weekend to the wonderful fish cooked by his wife last night.

The guards form a semi-circle behind Sonino. It is my first clear look at Il Pentito. He is tall – extravagantly tall for a Neapolitan. He is wearing a black suit, a white shirt, a dark tie. He looks very thin. His black hair is greasy and untidy. He lowers himself into the chair slowly; he seems unable to sit upright and leans heavily on the arms of the chair, slumped forward. Betrayal seems to have exhausted him. It is clear that his decision to testify against his friends has taken its toll. Until now I have only considered the cost of betrayal on the betrayed, yet it is clear from Sonino's condition that the act itself can be equally damaging to the betrayer. He has been wrecked by it. Whether or not the decision is cowardly, the process, actually saying the words, listing the names, has been as terrible as having the very same information extracted by torture. Sonino looks like a man who has undergone days, weeks, months of torture. He is barely able to sit in the chair, so collapsed is his body. He is like a flaccid rag-doll of a man, empty of spirit.

I am angry. He is too weak to be interviewed under these conditions. I look to Alessandro. I didn't expect this of him. A man of such integrity must surely understand that to examine a man in this state is as morally suspect as it is legally inexpedient. He's going to fall into the same trap as the previous *pentiti* trial. Sonino's testimony will not stick – whatever he says. Notwithstanding accusations of unfairness and civil-rights violations, if he decides later to retract or deny anything, he merely has to say he was unable to withstand the pressure of the prosecution to reach a conviction. I lean forward in my seat. And as I do something remarkable happens. From his collapsed position Sonino starts to shift in his chair. With slow measured movements, he raises his head from his chest, straightens his long slumped body, leans back in his chair and makes direct eye contact with the nine. I realize quickly this is not a stunt, some planned theatrical metamorphosis from crushed penitent to defiant *camorrista*. It has just taken Sonino, in his weakened condition, a few minutes to work out where he is and remember who he is, and for his vanity, a far more powerful force than any sense of shame, to return him to something like his former self – the gangster dandy. It has required a monumental act of strength and the strain is evident on his face, but then the desire not to appear beaten in front of these men is essential. Disdain, contempt, languorous superiority is what he feels, and he wishes to express it. My previous concern needs amending. Almost every impression I have about this trial needs amending every few minutes.

The nine are now very angry, climbing the cage like crazed primates, apart from Savarese that is, who clearly isn't going to be manipulated by Sonino, and sits at the back of the cage, cigarette held in the palm of his hand. He doesn't even flinch with the others flailing around in front of him. In the courtroom police move in and shove hands and arms back through the bars, but they are struck and pushed away; hats fly off their heads and land on the courtroom floor like frisbees. They draw their sticks from their belts and start to jab, forcing the nine to the back of the cage. The gallery is enraged. Firstly they scream at the police down in the court, then at Alessandro, then at the *carabinieri* up here.

I am the only one still seated. The factions are now apparent. I am, as I thought, on the Sonino side. Not in the middle of them, but close enough. Association by proximity. The arguments and insults fly over the central aisle in two distinct registers – the women invoke dark and terrible curses on the other women, and the men outline what the family of a *pentito* must expect when they no longer have any honour. I can tell all this without understanding a word of what is said – intonation tells me everything. I am trying not to look at anyone. The situation is both frightening and comic, but increasingly more frightening. The *carabinieri* have given up trying to bring order and I sense real danger. Fear swells in my stomach. I am imprisoned by people wound up by passions that need release, expression. I am an obvious target, for both sides. The stranger. I am sure that it only needs one person to ask who I am, to attract everyone's attention, and all the anger will be focused on me. I try to tell myself nothing bad can happen, but I don't believe it. I could be stabbed right now and who'd notice, my screams merely melding into other screams, my prone body screened from the police by the paroxysmal insanity of the crowd?

I hear Alessandro call out *'Silenzio!'* and slam his palm down on his desk. The sound booms from the speakers like approaching thunder. There is little if any reduction in the noise level. Alessandro then resorts to shouting his command for silence and smashing his fist on the desk repeatedly. It is pointless: things have gone too far. Below I can just make out Sonino through the wall of *carabinieri*. There is a faint mocking smile on his face; he is enjoying his impact on the proceedings, the pandemonium he has caused. After another attempt at silencing the court Alessandro stands, swiping away the folds of his robe. I can just make out his voice, hoarse and strained. Pressing his knuckles into the bench he leans forward. Lawyers lean back as if his presence is bearing down on them. He then points at the cage, his powerful arm locked by his fury. A moment later the cage is swamped with police forcing the nine back into the holding cell. This causes a fresh wave of anger in the gallery. Family members, women I recognize, rush down and bash on the glass. Alessandro then points up to the gallery, and with a flick of his hand indicates we are to be removed. This is met with jeers, abuse, obscene gestures.

The *carabinieri* shout orders to leave. No one moves. I, however, am happy to comply, and with polite '*mi scusis*' and '*grazies*' begin to shuffle to the aisle. This attracts everyone's attention. Those I pass are pissed off and show it, giving me the flick. I am pushed, jostled. One or two men purposely stand in my way, so I am forced to show my fear and deference and change direction. Both sides of the aisle stare at me. I am being given no way out. I look for the girl, for help, but I cannot see her. I climb over two rows. I am shouted at, cursed. I am three seats from the centre aisle and they are all occupied by women. I take my chances and push past them. I am helped on my way with a shove. I fall over and have to claw myself the last couple of feet. Embarrassment takes over from fear. I am red and shaking. The doors are opened for me by a policeman, who seems more amused by my ordeal than concerned for my safety.

Outside the gallery all is calm. A couple of security guards seem vaguely interested in my sudden appearance but they soon return to their conversation. I walk quickly to the escalator.

When I leave the court building I am unprepared for the sun, and the sudden heat and glare make me reel. I lean against a wall to catch my breath and calm down. That was tense, I say to myself – more to convince myself that it's in the past than to sum it up. A big fucking mistake is how I would sum it up.

Other gallery members start to exit the building. I turn away, not wanting to be recognized. Catching the tram back to the centre of the city is not an option, so I quickly cut across the Centro Direzionale in the opposite direction from the main road. I stride purposefully without looking back. I am halfway across the main piazza when I hear footsteps behind me, running. I turn quickly, but ready myself to back away, to bolt if necessary. But it is the girl. She stops before me; digs her hands deep into the pockets of her jeans.

'What do you want?' I say abruptly, rudely.

'*Inglese?*' she says with a softly burnished Neapolitan accent.

I am caught between the desire to be friendly and a wish not to become further involved with anyone or anything to do with the trial, especially someone clearly bonded in some way to Lorenzo Savarese. My instincts tell me to walk away. But instead I say, 'Do you speak English?'

She nods. I look around. Are we being watched? Is this some kind of trap? A large concrete sculpture screens us from the crowd leaving the court.

'Do you speak English well?' I ask, hoping she won't understand and we can part company easily, without insult.

'For ten years at school,' she says, a little defiantly.

'What do you want?'

'What are you doing here?' she asks me.

Has she been sent to find out? Once again I have two options: if I lie and tell her I read about the trial in the newspaper and decided to have a look for myself there is the chance my connection with Alessandro is already known and I will give them a real reason to be suspicious. Yet if I tell the truth: I am a friend of President Mascagni and they don't already know – Lord knows what that might mean. For some reason I choose the first option – I lie.

The girl listens patiently as I list the chronology of events that brought me here: my illness, Massimo, the newspaper, the picture of Sonino, missing my plane.

She then says, 'You don't have . . . like this in United Kingdom?'

I don't notice any dissimulation on her part and I calculate my connection to Alessandro is not known.

'Not really,' I say. 'Occasionally.'

She really is very pretty. Full-figured in her denim. A nascent Neapolitan beauty.

'I am with my *famiglia*,' she says.

It is hard to credit how innocently she says this. *I am with my famiglia*. She could be telling me with whom she is on holiday, so throwaway is the manner in which it is said. But in this context it cannot be anything less than a warning, and is probably an out-and-out threat. I am beginning to regret my decision to stay in Naples. I look at my watch. I still have time to make the plane this afternoon. I am just about to make this my excuse when the girl spins around. A woman some way off is calling her.

'Giovanna.'

I take this opportunity to say goodbye and walk away, but instead of turning and walking away herself, the girl follows me – walks into me, in fact – knocking me off balance for a moment. It is like a shove a bully might give a kid in the playground – all shoulder and elbow. My reaction is a disabling mixture of surprise and fear. Another threat? An intimation of the physical violence I face? I want to ask her, but by the time I recover myself she is halfway to the courthouse. To her *famiglia*.

4

On my way back into the centre of the city I buy a newspaper with a picture of Sonino on the front. It must have been taken this morning: he is wearing the same black suit. My plan for the rest of the day – that is if I can stop looking over my shoulder and criss-crossing Naples to lose invisible assailants – is to have lunch in the restaurant Louisa took me to yesterday (I am half hoping she will be there so I can tell her about my terrible morning and be comforted), then buy some stationery somewhere and go back to my room to write letters and make some calls. To fully appreciate my freedom here I must sort out my life back there.

The restaurant is busy; Louisa is not there. I am recognized by the waiter and greeted warmly. Don Ottavio is notified of my presence and he appears in the kitchen doorway. We shake hands. I am sitting at the same table as yesterday. It seems to be reserved for regulars. I order my food from the list of specials chalked up on a small blackboard hanging over a garish painting of the Last Supper with famous Neapolitans in place of the twelve disciples. I recognize only Sophia Loren and Caruso. I spread the newspaper over the table and try to read. I always expect Italian to be easy to decipher, full of recognizable Latin words, but its similarity to English tends to end with nouns so even though it is clear what the piece is about, the detail, the opinion, the angle is a mystery. I persevere, however, only looking up when the beaded curtain is disturbed by a customer coming or going, hoping it will be Louisa.

The pasta is good. The sausages and *friarielli* are great. I drink a whole litre of water. When I'm finished I cannot refrain from slapping my stomach and saying, 'This is the life,' but I feel pretty stupid after doing so. The bill, which thankfully is written down on a piece of paper, converts to about five pounds. I lean back in my chair to pull money out of my front pocket and as I do a small flyer, folded in two, appears in my hand. I open it. CyberDante, a cybercafé in Piazza Bellini. Advertising Internet rates. I turn it over. There is a message, or rather a time, scribbled on the back: *6 hour.* I can't think where it has come from; did I pick it up absently somewhere? Was I handed it on the street? Did Louisa give it to me for some reason and I don't remember? I place it on the table in front of me while I sort through my lire to pay the bill. Then I realize: *she* must have given it to me – Giovanna. That was what the shove was all about. A pickpocketing trick – big push: you don't feel a hand in your pocket. Jesus, I say to myself, instantly shaken with a mixture of terror and excitement. I know this is something I should ignore, yet at the same time wasn't this exactly what I hoped for when I decided to come to Naples? But then this is not a date being arranged. You don't use such clandestine means of communication, not even in Naples. The only reason she could possibly want to meet is to warn me about something. Be careful, the family doesn't like strangers watching their loved ones suffer. The humiliation of the cage. Of betrayal. You were lucky today but don't turn up again.

I leave the restaurant wondering whether I should talk it over with Alessandro. I know I should but something in me doesn't want to be counselled against it. Besides, if Giovanna is indeed trying to warn me of something wouldn't it be foolish not to find out what? Plus, she took such precautions to hide the fact she wanted to meet me, she must have selected a place where there is little danger in us being seen together, so what is there to be afraid of? I am aware I'm talking myself into meeting her. Because if I followed the real logic, her precautions imply danger; not lack of it. But this logic is not persuasive. What is persuasive is Louisa is married and I am alone. What is persuasive is that dressed in denim and looking like a gang member from New York in the 1950s Giovanna is as sexy as Louisa. What is persuasive is that I need some kind of excitement in my life. Finally, what is persuasive is I am amassing arguments to go rather than not go, and years of experience in this very particular personality disorder tells me that I'm going whether it's the right thing to do or not. I look at the card again. *6 hour*. I decide to check the place out.

When I arrive at Piazza Bellini I try not to appear too furtive, but I don't want to stride into CyberDante until I am certain it is what it says it is and not some store front hiding a Camorra hangout. It seems unlikely, right next to two of Naples' few street cafés. The door is open and I go in. The first room is like a wide hallway, with a long bar running along one side. Behind the bar a young man reads a newspaper; he looks up as I walk in. He returns to his paper before I can say or do anything. At the far end of the bar three steps lead up to a dark back room where screensavers float about on computer monitors. There appears to be no one back there. As usual in Naples the only natural light comes from the door. The place is windowless and, with no other door, a cul de sac. Perfect for a hit. No escape. But then outside the piazza is very busy with tourists drinking cappuccinos under vast yellow sun shades. A smart place to meet me, I decide. I leave after a cursory nod to the guy behind the bar; I notice he is reading the same paper I bought earlier.

I head back to my room for a siesta. I feel as exhausted as Sonino looked. I also need to find a local launderette. I fear if I ask Signora Maldini she'll offer to wash my clothes, which I don't want. The apartment is empty when I arrive back and I take the opportunity to wash my T-shirts and underwear in the sink with a powder I take to be detergent. I wash them thoroughly, knowing full well that hanging out to dry on my balcony they will be competing in whiteness with the rest of the street's clothes. I then have a long cool shower and lie down on the bed. I debate whether to call Louisa and tell her about Giovanna, just in case something happens to me. But it occurs to me the last thing Alessandro needs is to be informed by his wife that I've met up with a member of a Camorra family without consulting him. He has made it very clear he is currently in the process of redeeming the entire Neapolitan justice system. The last thing he wants is me dragged into court during the appeal and asked, Were you spending time with President Mascagni and his family while also fraternizing with Giovanna, Lorenzo, sister or girlfriend of Savarese, a defendant in the trial over which he was presiding? Yes, your honour. Conviction unsafe. The accused are acquitted. The prospect doesn't bear thinking about. I therefore conclude the best thing for all involved is for me not to fraternize with Giovanna at all rather than choose not to tell Louisa about it. But this is not what I do. At five-forty-five I start the short walk to Piazza Bellini.

The streets are busy. Vespas snake past me. Arguments flare outside shops. Cars impatiently nudge their way through pedestrians strolling home from work. I am forced against walls, into doorways. By the time I reach the piazza and enter CyberDante I am almost relieved to be somewhere quiet. Like this afternoon, it's empty. I look around for Giovanna. She is not here. It is a different guy working behind the bar. I order a beer and he tells me in broken English that he's been to New York. He thinks I'm American. I don't bother to correct him. He says he likes basketball. I nod; big basketball nation the Italians. I keep looking through the doorway and across the piazza. I want to be ready for her – calm and in control. I don't want to appear scared, as if I'm only here for information.

She approaches, skipping around the central statue and over the grass verges mazed around it. She looks relaxed, unguarded – there are no quick peripheral glances; she's either sure she's not being followed or knows she is. I step back from the bar and check for myself. I don't see anything suspicious.

She steps in and says, 'Buon giorno, inglese.'

I detect a hint of playfulness, of sarcasm in her greeting. It knocks me as off-balance as her shove this afternoon.

The guy behind the bar says, 'Buon giorno, Giovanna,' and pushes over a form for her to sign. She signs with her left hand.

'Do you want a drink?' I ask, unable to think of anything else to say.

She shakes her head, but then changes her mind. 'Coca.'

A bottle is opened and a glass is filled. She picks the glass off the bar and walks towards the back room and the computers. '*Inglese,*' she calls at the top of the steps. I follow her.

I sit next to her and watch as she picks up her emails. She scrolls through each message swiftly, laughing now and again; she deletes some, saves others. There is nothing anxious in her manner, little that would suggest she is the bearer of bad news. Then without turning to me she says, 'My name is Giovanna. You?'

'My name is Jim,' I say.

She nods. 'Why are you there . . . at the court?' she asks again.

Is she giving me another chance to tell the truth knowing I lied earlier?

'I told you, I read about it in the paper,' I say, deciding that changing your story is always the worst thing to do.

She turns to face me. 'Do you understand Italian?'

'No. I just wanted to have a look.'

'But you came two times?' She is now staring at me, her brown eyes meltingly warm; her look is hypnotic rather than intense.

'I wanted to see Il Pentito,' I say honestly.

She takes this in, then says, 'My brother is in the cage.'

I try to look surprised but I don't think I'm very convincing.

I ask, 'Why did you ask me to come here?' I try to smile. I don't want this to be purely about my welfare. I want her to be here because she is curious about me.

She turns back to the computer and, with her hand over the mouse, moves the cursor around the screen aimlessly.

'Giovanna?'

Again without looking at me, she says, 'People want to know who . . .' She points at me.

If I've been pretending, hoping, this meeting was about something else, then I have been set straight. In an instant my stomach sinks to some primordial place at the bottom of my being, a place that understands human brutality is as present as mercy in this world. I clench my buttocks fearing I might shit myself.

'Who do they think I am?' I ask, the tremor in my voice audible.

She shrugs.

'Who do you think I am?' I ask.

Giovanna just continues to follow the cursor as it roams around the computer screen. Her complexion is caramel brown, without a hint of the green in olive skin. Her short black hair is without a natural highlight.

'I'm not going to come again . . . to the trial . . . to court,' I say.

'That is good,' she says and turns to me. 'Napoli is very dangerous.'

What she doesn't say is, 'Napoli is very dangerous *for you*.' Which is something, but I still need to ask her whether this is what she means. I ask why she planted the flyer in my pocket in such a way.

'When in the morning I help you. My *famiglia* say . . . you . . .' She stops. I can see she is struggling for the right words, but she settles on a general negative. '*Famiglia* say, bad man . . .'

'Bad man?' I say. 'I'm a good man.' I sound ridiculous, trying to convince this beautiful young girl of the quality of my soul.

She shrugs.

'Giovanna, tell me, has coming to the court to watch the trial placed me in any danger?'

She thinks for a while – too long. She then asks, 'You do not come again?'

'No,' I say firmly.

She shakes her head. But this is not enough for me. I need certainty. She must say it. I rephrase the question. 'If I don't come again I'm not in danger, but coming again I might be?' It's too complicated a construction for her to understand. I try another way. 'Is that why you're here? To warn me not to come again?'

She looks at me searchingly. I sense something else is on her mind.

'What is it?' I ask.

Her big eyes narrow. 'Jim,' she says, for the first time calling me by name. She trails off and she looks away.

'What is it, Giovanna?' I am not here just to be warned away. Experience tells me there is something else on her mind. She is suddenly pensive. Her eyes focus inward. What I'm not sure about is whether I want to know what it is. But I press her nonetheless.

'Giovanna, is everything all right?'

For a moment I think she is going to respond, but she then says, 'I go now,' and jumps up from her seat. She walks out. My calls to wait are ignored. By the time I reach the door she is halfway across the piazza. The caution she took to avoid us being seen together prevents me from following her. I watch her disappear up Via Santa Maria di Costantinopoli. I look back at the guy behind the bar; he is smiling.

'Does she come here often?' I ask.

His smile fades.

I repeat, 'Does she come in here often?' I am stern – I want a precise answer.

He holds up two fingers. 'Two time . . . *settimana* . . .'

'*Grazie*,' I say.

'*Prego*,' he says a little irritably.

I leave CyberDante and take a seat in the café next door. I order beer and pizza. My situation is now clear. If I don't go back to the court, everything will be fine; if I do, I risk trouble. I wasn't going back; I don't want to go back; I won't go back – everything will be fine. I am glad I didn't get Alessandro involved. It was unnecessary and would have complicated our relationship.

My beer and pizza arrive and I eat and drink while watching a group of young Neapolitans assemble on the other side of the piazza. Fifteen, sixteen years old, they all shout and giggle – the girls' voices a chorale of youthful coquetry, the boys' growl hoarse from bravado. Some push their Vespas, some scoot them, some ride them down the slope – good-looking boys on the back reaching forwards to steer, while their good-looking girlfriends sit coolly in front of them in Capri pants and sunglasses, long, dark hair tumbling over their shoulders. Y2K teenagers and they look like 1950s Italian film stars.

I wonder whether Giovanna has such fun. Is such carefree behaviour acceptable for the children of the Camorra? I doubt it.

Then what do I know? Giovanna might have dashed off to meet a gang of her friends and be sitting on a Vespa right now, discussing the latest gossip surrounding Luna Pop, the current Italian boy band. But I doubt that also. She is too watchful, too preoccupied with darker thoughts. Underneath the hoodlum sassiness, the sexy boyishness, I detected loneliness, anxiety, fear. She reminds me of patients I have had: young people stubbornly uncomplaining in their horrendous circumstances yet unable to avoid communicating their feelings, eyes full of hurt, panic. But even if that is the case with Giovanna, what can I do about it? I can hardly offer her counselling. What would I say: association with organized crime is a bad lifestyle choice? Hardly helpful. I don't know of a thera-peutic model for such circumstances. Self-ostracism is the only way. Which is tough in Italy when you add to its tradition of family the hugely complex issues of growing up in a criminal world which is more like a secret society. Not for me. There are experts in this. Deprogrammers. Cult specialists. But then I'm not sure how they'd deal with an entity like the Camorra. It might be an interesting area of research if it didn't involve splitting up families whose members almost always include one or two professional killers.

5

Louisa says, 'Watch this,' and presses ice from an ice tray into two tumblers. She then pours over plenty of gin, followed by some tonic, after which she pushes open the French windows, walks out into the garden and plucks from the nearest tree a lemon. On returning to the kitchen she places the lemon on a large, worn chopping board and chops it in two with a large knife. She then takes a smaller knife and finely cuts two thin slices and drops them into the glasses. There is a sharp fizz and the flesh of the lemon disappears, leaving only a pale yellow ring of rind floating above the ice.

'Taste it,' she says. 'The lemon is so young and fresh it just liquefies.'

I sip – it is cold, sharp, heady. '*Perfetto*,' I say and walk out into the garden. Louisa follows me, slipping her arm through mine. Her physical ease with me is reassuring. She is a confident, charming wife with her special guest. She is declaring a discreet intimacy. I am a much-loved brother visiting after a long absence. And this relationship allows for such warmth, such proximity. But that is all.

We walk in silence through the lemon grove, our drinks clutched to our chests. The night is warm. There is a light, citrus breeze. The air is completely different here from Naples – fresh and cleansing. We are a mile or so above the main villages that make up Sorrento. I am almost overcome by the wonder of such a beautiful setting. The house – a big old square block with peeling lime-green paint and tall shuttered windows – has an unaffected, simple majesty. The front of the house looks over the sea, west to the islands of Ischia and Procida, where, Louisa tells me, the sun sets not prosaically into the sea but mysteriously behind the island – its home for the night. The house itself is full of robust nineteenth-century furniture with almost no hint of modernity except for an audiophile stereo, jagged columns of CDs and racks of LPs. The garden is an orchard of ancient trees, every one as uniquely gnarled as the old men and women I see sitting outside the *bassi* in Naples, men and women whose skin looks a thousand years old and as sun-dried as the bark of these lemon trees. Beyond the garden an olive grove rises to a set of rocks, which then rise further to become a high cliff; the other side descends to the Amalfi coast. From where Louisa and I are standing there is no sign of human intervention – not a telegraph pole, aerial, road. If it didn't have such connotations of sexual transgression I would suggest to Louisa we were in Eden. Instead I say, 'I can see why Alessandro loves it here.'

'We both do,' she says, sipping her drink. 'It's like heaven on earth.'

We return to the house and sit on a cast-iron bench in the last of the sun. Making herself comfortable, Louisa slips off her sandals, stretches her legs out, hitches her skirt up her thighs, flicks the straps of her top from her shoulders, raises her face skyward and closes her eyes. She wants as much body area as possible exposed to the sun. I slip off my shoes.

Without turning to me or opening her eyes, she says, 'We must see about getting you some new clothes next week.'

'I don't think my budget will stretch to an Italian wardrobe,' I say, looking down at the old jeans and T-shirt I am wearing.

'My treat,' Louisa says. 'It was me after all that persuaded you to stay longer.'

I am shocked by this interpretation of my decision.

'I doubt Alessandro will be very pleased. You buying me clothes.'

'Oh, he doesn't care. Anyway he doesn't have to know.'

'I don't think that's such a good idea.'

Louisa doesn't respond but stands up and says a little tersely, 'I should prepare the dinner.'

As she passes me I grab her hand.

'Louisa,' I say looking up into her dark face, silhouetted by the sun. 'You still are . . . really are . . .' I pause, faltering, not sure quite what I want to say.

'What?' she says flatly.

'Nothing,' I say. It is pointless to tell her I still find her irresistible, but resist her I must. It's cheap. But then, for the first time, just for a moment, I sense my feelings for her, my attraction to her, are not irrelevant. Before removing her hand she strokes my palm with a finger. It is a signal as clear to me as a handshake between Free-masons. It is sexually wistful. The familial intimacy we acted out only moments ago in the lemon grove has been transformed into some kind of promise. She pulls away and enters the kitchen.

I am left alone in Eden with my gin and tonic and my unwanted knowledge. I finish my drink staring out amongst the lemon trees, watching the night grow dim and the garden shrink into the shadows. A car pulls up. Doors open and close. I hear the low rasp of Alessandro's voice echoing like the low rumbling of Vesuvius. Louisa responds in Italian – quick, agile sentences. I decide to stay where I am and not disturb them. Music is turned on. I am suddenly bathed in light; Alessandro has switched on an outside light. He approaches me, his arms, as usual, wide open in welcome.

'You are in the dark,' he says. 'Dark thoughts?' He laughs heartily.

I stand. 'Not at all.' We shake hands, kiss.

'How do you like my house?' he asks, looking over it himself, evidently proud.

'Beautiful,' I say.

'Ah,' he says – this time as an expression of concordance with my appreciation. I have good taste, he is saying. He has in his hand a remote control, which he aims inside the house and turns up the volume of the stereo.

'I will join you,' he says. 'But we must be quiet.' He sits down next to me on the bench.

Louisa brings out more drinks, and then fetches a chair for herself.

'We missed the sunset,' she says to me under her breath so as not to disturb her husband's enjoyment of the music.

139

'Next time,' I whisper.

Alessandro ignores us. He is transported by Bach, pristinely played on the piano, sharp as the citrus breeze. The only other sounds around are the clicking and buzzing of insects and the occasional chink of ice in our glasses. We all stare out into the garden, almost surreal in the artificial light. I am present at a ritual. Friday nights in Sorrento. The garden. Piano music. Contemplation. A habit entirely due to Alessandro, but who would dissent from such a civilizing activity? I look at Louisa; she seems content. Alessandro scratches his ear thoughtfully. I find I am more intrigued with the subject of his thoughts than the opportunity of communing with my own. Is he thinking about work, his wife, the music, or some stray idea inspired by the music? Whatever it is I can see it being turned over in his mind. His face is heavy, grey, patrician. There is an expression of benign power, superior intelligence, human dignity. His broad chest expands as he breathes. Then, anticipating by a bar or so the end of the music, he sighs – it is deep, long, complete. Something cathartic has occurred. His face, hitherto animated by inner discourse, finally relaxes. Turning to me with his hand melodramatically placed over his heart, he says, *'La musica è fondamentale per l'anima, no?'* So taken is he with the moment he has forgotten to speak English.

'Assolutamente,' I say, comprehending the gist of his question.

'Ah, *italiano? Bene, bene.'*

We all stand in unison as if asked to rise by a conductor.

While Louisa prepares the dinner Alessandro and I move into the library. It is more overstocked than the one in his Naples home. He points out his English books. Mostly politics, philosophy, history. There is the odd novel: Orwell, Greene, Huxley. There is some poetry: Coleridge, Shelley, Auden. I am invited to look around as he sits at his desk and piles up some papers. There are many books in French.

'You speak French?' I ask.

He nods.

'Any other languages?'

'A little German. A little Russian. But not to read. To find directions.' He laughs.

I come across a large volume of Walt Whitman, battered from reading.

'You like Whitman?' I ask.

As expected, Alessandro places his hands together in the prayer position and waves them at me.

'Not many people do these days,' I say, by way of an excuse. 'I love him. I read him when I can't sleep. It's like taking a walk across America – it tires you out.'

Alessandro smiles at this. 'Please,' he says and gestures for me to sit down and to read. At first I think I'm merely to indulge myself but I then realize I am expected to read aloud. Alessandro absently scratches his closely cut beard; I hear a faint crackle.

'Please,' he repeats, with his hand still aimed at the chair, 'read.'

I sit down and I flick through the book. I stop randomly at 'Starting from Paumanok'. I read silently through the first few lines. It is Whitman at his most vast – the wandering democrat, the American Christ, first great urban prophet. I begin hesitantly. At first the tremor in my voice is audible and I stumble over almost every word. But I soon settle and find myself carried along on Whitman's undulations. Now and again I look up at Alessandro but he continues to read his papers, leaning back in his large leather chair. I sense he is listening, however. Though I am not *not* enjoying myself, the situation is so bizarre I am very relieved when I hear Louisa open the door and steal in. I must look and sound ridiculous and I feel myself blushing. But as I only have a page to go I soldier on, lowering my voice for the last two lines, saying them directly to Louisa:

O hand in hand – O wholesome pleasure – O one more desirer and
   lover!
O to haste firm holding – to haste, haste on with me.

When I look up Alessandro is staring at me. At first I think he's angry with me for serenading his wife, but then a smile breaks over his face.

'*Bravo*, Jim. Wonderful. Wonderful. I ask Louisa to read to me but she says no.'

'I sound stupid,' she says. 'I like it when Alessandro reads to me, though.'

'I read Petrarch. Love poems. I am not a communist any more. I am a romantic.'

He is pleased with this and laughs loudly, but for the first time there is something forced in his manner – his gregariousness is not entirely genuine. I am not sure I wasn't correct when I sensed irritation in the manner I finished off the poem. Coveting a man's wife in that man's presence is after all very rude.

We eat dinner – grilled vegetables and Sorrento sausages – discussing the euro. Alessandro has no sentimental attachment to the lira. Louisa says she prefers different currencies. She thinks it's part of visiting other countries, working out the money. I say I'm fairly confident Britain will never join the euro if it's left to a referendum. Alessandro asks how I will vote. I say pro-euro, but not for any ideological reasons, just because I loathe a certain kind of reactionary patriotism.

'Are you not proud to be British?' Alessandro asks.

'I'm not embarrassed about it,' I say honestly.

'Ah, very good,' he says, laughing; then pushes me. 'But not proud?'

'It's hard to say. My interest is primarily artistic and barring Shakespeare we fall very short of most other comparable European countries.'

'Are you not proud of Tony Blair?'

It is a joke, I know, so I laugh, but nevertheless I know he wants a serious answer. 'He's a practising Christian, you know. I want to know what a good Christian would make of his party's policies on immigration?'

'Did you vote for Blair?' Alessandro asks.

'I did,' I say.

He nods thoughtfully. He then asks me why I think there has never been a successful communist movement in the United Kingdom.

'We are not idealists,' I say, aware we talked about national characteristics when we first met.

'So Marx was wrong . . . saying you would be the first to have a communist revolution?'

'Clearly, because we haven't had one.'

Alessandro regards this answer as facetious and waves his closed hand in front of his chest.

'I'm sorry,' I say. 'His reading of the situation was based on the effect of the industrial revolution on a kind of abstract populace. He wasn't a psychologist, I guess.' As I say this I wonder how much of this I actually know and how much I am making it up, hoping to impress Louisa. I then add as an afterthought, 'I don't think we have much time for radicals or charismatics.'

Alessandro takes this in with a gentle nod of his head before asking, 'What do you think starts revolutions?'

'Intellectual vanity.' I don't know whether I believe it, but it follows my current train of thought.

'Is that all?'

'No. There is youth, passion, sentimentality.'

'You don't think oppression, poverty, hunger are important?'

'Only in that they provide reasons for the ideologists to indulge their intellectual vanity.'

'What about Eastern Europe?'

'I think you'd agree it's not revolution when market capitalism is the goal.'

Until this point Alessandro has been deadly serious, his small eyes fixed on me, tempting me to impress or slip up – something to keep him amused. But now he laughs. 'Neapolitans are not natural revolutionaries, Jim. We are like England here. But the reason is very different. We enjoy life too much. Even the poor

143

have everything they need for happiness. Food, wine, love, football. The weather is good. In Herculaneum they have excavated a library. Many scrolls by Philodemus. A disciple of Epicurus. Neapolitans are natural Epicureans. The best. We enjoy simple pleasures. It is hard to be political when you are satisfied with little. It is hard to be political when the land is abundant, the weather is good and the people are warm.'

'But you are political . . .' I say.

'I am Neapolitan, Jim.'

'Which means?'

'I am political because it makes me happy. If it made me unhappy, I would not be so.'

'I see . . . I think.'

'We are a mysterious people,' he says obliquely.

Louisa says, 'I don't think I could live anywhere else now. I met a woman recently. A twin. From Milan. Her sister still lived there. They both suffered from high blood pressure. But the one who lived here . . . hers was almost completely normal. That's Naples for you.'

'I am really eighty-three years old,' Alessandro says, laughing. '*And* I only look half my age.'

'Not quite half,' Louisa says smiling.

Staring at me, Alessandro says, 'You should stay in Naples – life takes longer to live.'

After dinner we clear the table and wash up together. We are a commune of three. Alessandro with his thick arms in the sink, me drying, Louisa slotting the dishes away. We amuse ourselves with twenty questions – famous people. Once we're finished Alessandro suggests we go for a walk. We leave by the back door and take a path that veers off to the right; it is narrow and rocky. We stop at the top of an incline and find ourselves on a little promontory overlooking the Bay of Naples – Naples itself a long cushion of light in the distance. Louisa adopts her usual position, arms folded, leaning against her husband; he wraps his arm around her. I stand a little way away.

'Down there, Jim, Odysseus sailed.' It is a proud statement. And I realize it is the night for classical references.

'And over there,' he points directly to Naples, 'Parthenope killed herself because of him. Parthenope was the first name of Napoli.'

I nod gravely. To our left Sorrento looks like a fairground – a circumscribed pattern of light. Behind us there is nothing but mountain blackness leading up to the blue night.

We return to the house via a different route, which includes the road but from which we can hear the sea below us crashing against the cliffs. I can taste the salt in the air. Alessandro is telling me rather crossly that the English press dismiss Sorrento these days because it's crowded with tourists, cars, souvenir shops, etc., forgetting its historical significance. It was a favourite place for many of Europe's intellectuals. Tomorrow he will give me the tour he says. 'It is very important,' he says. I hear Louisa chuckle.

'I'd like that,' I say.

Back at the house I am offered a nightcap, but have to decline. The night air has knocked me out and I am straining to keep my eyes open. I say goodnight and Alessandro and I shake hands. Louisa accompanies me to my room. She wants to check I have everything I need, she says.

At the door she says, 'It's so nice having you here. I know Aless is enjoying it.'

I say, 'I think he thinks I'm a lightweight.' I expect a disclaimer from her or a denial on Alessandro's behalf, but she merely lingers in the doorway.

'I'm waiting for a kiss,' she says.

Her demands are becoming more and more teasing, more and more provocative. I kiss her on the cheek.

'Goodnight,' she says lightly.

'Goodnight, Louisa,' I say seriously.

I watch her tiptoe down the hallway because below the melancholy melody of a Chopin mazurka has begun.

6

As I awake I'm struck by how soft the sunlight is across my face. There is no glare or heat; it's just a gentle, almost downy warmth, rousing me from sleep. The room itself is golden, as if the light has been diffused through the lemon grove outside my window. It is nine o'clock. I cannot hear any sound from the rest of the house. I am unsure what to do: wait to be woken by Louisa or just go downstairs and make myself some breakfast. I decide to make myself at home. It's the weekend – they should be free to sleep in if they want to.

In the kitchen, coffee percolating, I am suddenly ravenous. I tear at some dry bread left over from last night. I look around for something more appetizing. I find some salami and pecorino in the fridge. I cut thick slices of each. I pick some fresh basil from the garden. I make a sandwich, drizzling olive oil over the bread to moisten it. I sit on a bench at the front of the house, looking over the light-blue sea, Ischia hazy in the far distance. The sun is brighter now and I am forced to squint. I hear movement behind me. I turn and see Alessandro in pyjamas and dressing gown – both look expensive.

'*Buon giorno*, Jim.'

'*Buon giorno*, Alessandro.'

'Louisa has a headache,' he informs me. 'She apologizes.'

I sense this is not the truth. 'Is she OK?' I ask.

'Only a headache,' he says. 'We will go into Sorrento without her.'

He doesn't sound enthusiastic about this but then it's Saturday morning, maybe he needs time to warm up.

'Do you want some coffee?' I ask. 'I've just made some.'

There is no response to my offer.

'Are we going now?' I ask.

Again no response. He looks at me. 'I will change.'

We leave the house in silence and head towards Sorrento. It is about twenty minutes to the town. The outskirts are a little shabby, but as we approach Piazza Tasso it starts to look more like a holiday town. Tour coaches line the streets, cafés are full of tourists, small souvenir stalls are filled with crap.

Storekeepers and vendors greet Alessandro. He clasps each of them in his two-handed handshake, kisses some, others not. I am introduced to those he kisses. I smile, shake hands, look awkward when I'm addressed in Italian. I feel like a timid son with his embarrassingly extrovert father. At a news-stand Alessandro buys *Il Mattino, Corriere della Sera, Il Manifesto, Herald Tribune* and the *Guardian Weekly*.

'Five newspapers,' I say, dumbly.

'I like the *Guardian Weekly*,' he says, 'the American journalists. Do you read the *Guardian?*'

'It's the newspaper I buy,' I say.

'We will share,' he says.

We cut through the centre of the town, stopping off at a café for an espresso. Alessandro drinks his in one gulp. I do the same. We then walk through some winding streets to a tiny piazza overlooking the sea. Only a stucco balustrade divides us from a sheer drop of over two hundred feet to the rocks. Alessandro settles himself on a bench a few feet away. He starts with *Corriere della Sera*. I sit on the balustrade and stare out over the ocean. It is a translucent blue; each wave, undulating without surf or spray, looks like the facet of an exquisitely cut sapphire.

After five minutes of deep reverie, I join Alessandro on the bench and ask whether I might try the *Guardian Weekly*.

'Please,' he says without looking up from the piece he's reading.

I read fitfully, never finishing an article. I am on the last page before Alessandro has finished the front page of his newspaper. I simply haven't mastered the pace of life yet. It is ten o'clock and there is nothing else to do but sit in the dappled shade with the

Mediterranean below, and read a newspaper. There is nothing I'd rather be doing, but I'm still unable to settle. I fold the newspaper and place it on the bench between Alessandro and me. Alessandro turns over the front page of *Corriere della Sera*. It's a precise movement, arms opened wide to avoid creasing and crumpling, then an experienced snap of the wrists to fold the main section back so he is faced with an immaculate second page. During this he turns to me and asks casually, 'Back in England you were Louisa's lover?'

I don't detect any menace in his voice. I don't think I've been brought here to be interrogated.

'Not really,' I say; then add, 'A long time ago.'

'How long ago?' he asks.

'Ten years.'

'Were you in love with her?'

'I thought I was.'

'Then you were,' he says philosophically. He then looks at me directly. 'Louisa is a very wonderful woman. I am very happy.'

'I see that,' I say. I'm not quite sure what he wants from this conversation; I can't imagine it is reassurance that I'm not looking to take his wife away.

'When I was younger I refused to marry. I was an idealist. I was proud of my transparency. Not only as a judge. As a man. Love is like fog. Women are a fog. I knew that. But times have changed. The world is different. We lost. I am forced to relax. I sometimes ask myself what would have happened twenty years ago with Louisa. I was stronger then.'

I am not sure quite what he is trying to express, but he seems to be confiding in me rather than warding me off.

He continues. 'I am fifty-three. Louisa is not yet thirty. She is strong *now*.'

Rather naively I had thought his age wouldn't trouble him. I say firmly, 'Age has nothing to do with it. You are an extraordinary man – that doesn't diminish with age.'

'Ah,' he says – this time as a kind of rueful thank you.

He then asks me, 'Do you think Louisa wants children?'

I don't know what to say. Even though I have suspected this might be an issue, I am surprised by his directness, implying I have knowledge of, and an intimacy with, his wife on this delicate and personal subject. I don't know the answer.

He says, 'She says it is my decision.'

'Do you want children?'

'I say, no . . .'

'But you don't know?'

'We have a good life. It is a terrible world. I do not know how Louisa feels. It is a difficult situation.'

What strikes me about our conversation is not only that it should be taking place between Alessandro and Louisa but that it is Alessandro's age that prevents this – he doesn't know how to talk to his wife, and this troubles him greatly. This is why any suspicion of an affair between me and Louisa is irrelevant – it is nothing in comparison to the damage not being able to understand her will do to their relationship. Alessandro recognizes this and has chosen to elicit my help rather than display meaningless jealousy or possessiveness.

I say unhelpfully, 'You should talk to her . . .'

Alessandro looks at me sternly. 'I am talking to you.'

'I'm sorry,' I say. 'You're right.'

He grabs my shoulder with his powerful hand. 'No, *I* am sorry. You are a good man – my friend.'

From the way in which he says this, I am not sure whether he means 'you are a good man, my friend', using the designation as a term of comradeship, or 'you're a good man. *My* friend', which has both definitive and possessive connotations. I reach my hand to my shoulder and touch his hand. I want to say something but nothing useful comes to mind.

After a moment Alessandro withdraws his hand and goes back to his newspaper, but then unexpectedly returns to the subject with which he began this conversation, asking me, 'Did she love you?'

This is a courtroom tactic. He has asked the most important

question as if it is merely an afterthought, a throwaway enquiry, little more than curiosity. I am rattled by this calculated approach. It makes a mockery of our friendship.

'No. I don't think so,' I say non-committally.

Alessandro responds with a nod but doesn't divert his eyes from the newspaper.

We head home after about an hour. We walk a circuitous route taking in all Sorrento's literary landmarks: the hotel where Ibsen wrote *Ghosts*, built on the birthplace of Tasso, Sorrento's most famous son; the retreats of the Russian exiles Maxim Gorky and Isaak Babel. Alessandro returns to something like his old self and we talk animatedly. I tell him I'm particularly interested in going to Ravello where Richard Wagner wrote much of *Parsifal*. Alessandro regards me suspiciously. It seems the one clear expression on a Neapolitan's face is suspicion; it was equally so with Signora Maldini's when she found out I knew Alessandro. I explain that my love of Wagner is not a sign of neo-fascist tendencies. My tone is sharp, irritable. Alessandro laughs.

'I love Wagner. You love Wagner. Louisa hates Wagner. Tomorrow we shall go to Ravello!'

When we arrive home Louisa is out of bed but not dressed. She greets us both grumpily. She has on a diaphanous robe, hanging open; underneath she is still in her pyjamas. She is a picture of lazy languor. Of effortless domestic elegance. Even her irritability is becoming in such attire. Alessandro addresses her in Italian and she snaps back at him. I feel awkward so I excuse myself and head out to the garden, stopping off at the library for the Walt Whitman.

From the garden, I can hear the whispered strains of an argument. In Italian. Alessandro is trying to placate Louisa about something. She is angry, irresistibly angry. Nothing he says subdues her. I hear a door slam. Louisa appears. 'I'm sorry. We're arguing.'

'Really?' I say.

'He really can be a prig.'

'Is it my being here?'

'You? Why do you think it's got anything to do with you?' she says curtly.

'I don't. I'm just wondering.'

'Well, don't.'

'There's no need to snap at me,' I say, and return to my book.

Louisa backs away and disappears inside. All is quiet for half an hour and I read *Song of Myself* twice. Then I wander off into the lemon grove. Everywhere I look little lizards cling in diagonal stillness on tree trunks. I pick a lemon. It feels like a living ball. I walk along tossing it in the air, catching it, spinning it on my palm. If I hold it up to the sun it disappears in the light. I make a deep gash in the skin with my fingernail and prise it apart. I dip my tongue into the flesh. It is so sharp my taste buds seethe. I grimace from the sensation. I hear Alessandro and Louisa approach. I turn. Hand in hand, they dip beneath the branches. Louisa says they've made up. Alessandro apologizes. He looks both embarrassed and content to be open about their row. Louisa feigns a smile. She takes the lemon from my hand and bites into it. It is a rebellious, defiant gesture. The sharpness makes her shiver.

'Strong,' she says.

Back at the house a pot of *caffè* is waiting for us and Alessandro pours us all a cup.

'We will not be at the court on Monday, Jim. Did Louisa tell you?'

'Is there a problem?' I ask.

'I must interview Sonino in prison.'

'Really? Why?'

'After last week it is important we have his testimony.'

'Is this normal?'

'Not normal but not exceptional. We run out of time soon.'

'Will you make it?' I ask.

'It is not a race,' Alessandro says flatly.

'You just said you are running out of time.'

'I must do what I can.'

'So if it's not finished, what happens?'

'I have told you,' he says irritably.

Freedom for the accused. Power in prison for the *pentito*. All because the trial time is delimited by law.

'I remember,' I say.

Alessandro knocks back his coffee. 'Would you like to come along?'

'Where?'

'To the prison. There will be many observers. I thought you might find it interesting.'

My first impulse is to explain everything that has happened: the mistake to sit in the public gallery, the scrutiny of the nine, their families, Giovanna Savarese's warning. But as usual I don't; I ask with dissembling curiosity, 'Who will be there?'

'Me and my deputy. Sonino's lawyer. Defence lawyers. A clerk. Reporters. A doctor. Others . . .' he says with a wave of his hand.

'Thank you for the invitation, but I don't think it would be right . . .'

Alessandro looks at me directly. 'But I say it is right.'

I cannot work out whether he's angry that I have questioned his authority or he's trying to reassure me.

'It's very kind of you, Alessandro, but I don't really understand what's going on.' I look at Louisa for assistance, support – surely she recognizes the subtle insistence in my voice and will come to my rescue. She doesn't say anything, evidently not wanting to get involved in a discussion between her husband and me.

Alessandro continues, 'It will be very interesting. Sonino is a fascinating man.'

'That's true,' I say, unable to argue with this particular point.

'Then it's decided. You will come.' Alessandro raises his hand to silence any argument I might have. I am a little taken aback by both his insistence and the imperious gesture to shut me up. I look at Louisa. Alessandro notices. 'Jim. For a psychologist it will be a very interesting situation.' His smile is forced, embarrassed; as a judge he expects to get his own way and this often carries over into regular life where he is required to be more flexible. His embarrassment puts me under extra pressure not to make my case further. I try one last way to wriggle out.

'I have to say, Alessandro, I did feel quite a lot of intimidation in the public gallery last week. It wasn't a pleasant experience.'

His embarrassment vanishes and he bursts into laughter. 'Is this why you don't want to come? Do not worry. You will be with me. The president. I will look after you.'

Louisa looks at her husband crossly. 'Don't laugh at him. I'm sure it's very frightening . . .'

Not wishing to be the object of disagreement between them, I say, 'That's all right, Louisa. I'm a natural paranoid. I spent most of last week thinking someone was following me.'

Double-taking to make sure he has heard correctly, Alessandro roars, 'Like in the movies.' He looks around furtively, as if being spied upon.

His laughter is infectious and I blurt out, 'I thought I was going to be murdered just for watching the trial.'

This kills us.

'You thought a *camorrista* was going to get you, ha, ha, ha.'

'In the back streets of Naples. Ha, ha, ha.'

Louisa stands up, tutting, and walks inside the house. Alessandro and I try to control ourselves, but every time we look at one another we burst out into fresh laughter. The feeling of friendship we experienced the first time we met has finally managed to overcome the propriety of our manners, the disparity of our positions – the fifteen or so years between us have become more like our shared age.

Louisa steps outside. 'Where do you want to eat lunch? Here? Or the kitchen?'

Alessandro asks me. I say I don't mind. He leans back and says, 'We do not mind.' More laughter.

'I'll bring it out then,' Louisa says dully.

Lunch is much the same as my breakfast: salami, pecorino, but with fresh bread and chilled white wine. Louisa cheers up a little after a few drinks. That is until Alessandro suggests she takes me swimming which she flatly refuses to do. He shrugs at me.

After lunch I am quite glad to be ordered to my room for a siesta. I close the curtains and lie on the bed. I listen as Alessandro and Louisa retire. They seem to be talking more amicably. I strain to work out what is being said. But then the whispering is replaced by grunting. They are having sex. I try not to listen but it's impossible. From the sound Alessandro is making I picture his heavy weight above her. Louisa is quieter, only the occasional sigh interrupting her husband's chain of powerful grunts. It is over quickly. Alessandro's orgasm is neat. A breathy submission to the moment. There is silence for a minute or so and then Louisa starts to come; the sound she makes is restrained, concentrated, and she peaks in gasps. I remember this – she said it was a way of controlling her orgasm, prolonging it.

I turn on my side, away from the door, from the direction of their room.

I am not envious. I am not aroused. But I do think back to fucking Louisa myself. I can't help it. There was something so agile, so physically trim in the way she undressed. It was designed for maximum sexual appeal without resorting to erotic cliché. She'd kneel on the bed with her legs slightly apart, yank off her top, un-ping her bra, flip onto her back, raise her arse, shove her jeans from her hips, grab them at the feet and pull them off – completely naked in one almost unbroken movement. It was winter so she left her socks on. She'd then disappear under the duvet with a swiftness all but denying me a clear sight of her nudity.

Body-shy, she'd say dishonestly and then flash me, whipping the duvet up and down as though she was covered by some great wing.

Lying next to her, a slender thing with slender hands roaming over me, demanding constant kissing, with her own quick, thirsty pecks over my chest. The way she guided me in slowly, gently, breathlessly sighing. It was . . . a precise pleasure. For her, for me.

She was ardently in charge for the first few moments and then . . .

I wake up. Louisa is standing over me. She is wearing her diaphanous gown; this time she is naked underneath, her body a discreet light beneath the fabric. I am dreaming, I am sure. But no. She says, 'Alessandro's in the shower. I'm sorry about before, really. Do you forgive me?'

I say, 'I do,' and without restraint I reach for her.

She backs away; my hand clasps the air. 'I knew you would,' she says and is gone.

Later that evening Alessandro is in an expansive mood and decides we will play a game. My first thought is: chess. But, as usual, I am wrong. He disappears into the house and returns with a familiar red-and-white box.

'Monopoly. A communist's favourite game,' he says.

'Is it the Italian version? Is there an Italian version?' I ask.

Louisa says, 'No. It's London. That's what Aless likes so much about it.'

Alessandro sets the board out on the small table we used for lunch.

'You like Monopoly?' he asks.

'Certainly,' I say.

'You have to play to win,' Louisa informs me.

'You mean no messing around?' I say.

'We take Monopoly very seriously in this house.'

'Who usually wins?' I ask.

'It depends how long the game lasts. I have more stamina,' Louisa says, 'but Alessandro is more ruthless.'

'And no partnerships,' Alessandro states seriously.

He sorts the money, the property cards, chance and community chest. We do not squabble over our representative pieces. I am the hat, Louisa the boot, Alessandro the ship; he is also the banker. He chuckles to himself as he arranges all the money before him. Then, with elbows on his knees, chin resting on his fists, he studies the board as though we *are* playing chess and his concentration must not waver from beginning to end. I am more relaxed, sitting back, waiting until the first trip around the board is complete and we can start buying some property. Louisa seems happy, with no trace of her earlier crankiness. I am trying to forget the image of her in my room, her veiled, dreamlike nakedness.

Within half an hour all the property is bought and we are evenly matched. Louisa has Mayfair and Park Lane. Alessandro is pleased with Whitechapel and Old Kent Road; but then he also has all the greens and the yellows. I have red and orange, and the stations. The utilities are divided between Louisa and me. There is little cross-board chat, our communication limited to phatic groans and squeals as our luck ebbs and flows. Louisa and Alessandro are equally gleeful of their individual successes. I don't detect any partisanship.

My strategy is to build big and quickly and force the others into rapid bankruptcy; however, Alessandro already has a house on every one of his properties and is preventing me from accruing enough money to accomplish this. We spend the next half an hour handing money back and forth. As usual we are spending most of our time praying we don't land on Louisa's heavily built-up Mayfair and Park Lane; she may not have much else but landing on her all but wipes us out. It's an old trick but a good one. Alessandro and I are almost euphoric when the roll of the dice allows us to leap them. Louisa merely smiles; she is playing a waiting game.

A partnership, which was strictly forbidden at the start, is forming and Alessandro and I decide to make a deal. We will bail each other out if we land on Mayfair or Park Lane. This makes Louisa livid. It's against the rules, she says, and then warns me: Alessandro is not to be trusted. I make him swear that if he lands there first and I come to the rescue he will return the favour. He assures me that he can be trusted and to prove it to me opens a good bottle of single malt, which will be shared by us as a symbol of our deal. Louisa shakes her head. Alessandro is outraged by her low opinion of his loyalty. She has played with him before, she reminds him. He laughs; he likes her mockery. During the last two rounds he has amassed some serious money; Louisa and I have landed on his property with every move while he's avoided ours with slippery convenience. He embarks on a massive project of hotel building.

I am most definitely losing. The game is now between husband and wife. I could offer my meagre holdings to Louisa to shore up her portfolio but I'm already tied up with Alessandro and he might be offended. I will wait to be approached. Next time round the board I will have to mortgage my property just to stay in the game. Alessandro seems to have forgotten our partnership. I lean over to Louisa. Help, I say. No deals, she says. Alessandro grins. My next two turns lose me the reds to Louisa and I am sent to prison. It is a relief. I decide to miss my next three turns, maybe a string of bad rolls for either of my opponents will even things up.

No such luck. They consolidate. The board is covered now in red hotels like an outbreak of acne. It is almost stalemate between them. Whoever takes my stations from me will win. They are awaiting my release. I watch Alessandro land on Park Lane, smugly pay up, then, after Louisa's go (visiting me in jail), roll a double one and land on Mayfair. It's all over. Hotels are ripped from the board like unwanted radishes from a salad. His properties are wastelands. I emerge from prison back in the game. The energy around the board is heavily depleted, however. Alessandro's massive loss has taken its toll on all of us. Louisa is clearly the winner. It will take some nimble luck for Alessandro to avoid ignominious bankruptcy, and I'm just small-time. We throw in our hands. Alessandro congratulates Louisa by leaning over and kissing her on the cheek. Spontaneously I do the same. During the game Alessandro and I have polished off almost three-quarters of a bottle of Scotch. As I stand and stretch I suddenly realize how drunk I am. The night air, seemingly banished from the intense atmosphere of our game, hits me and I wobble. 'Time for bed,' I say.

'You go up,' Louisa says. 'I'll clear up here.'

'Are you sure?'

'Are you capable of helping me?'

'I don't think so.'

I wish them both goodnight. Alessandro, having realized he is as drunk as I am, just waves. Louisa looks at us both with mild amusement. Look at you two, she is thinking, beaten at Monopoly, too drunk to function – a right pair.

Sunday we recover. A lazy day – lazier. Our trip to Ravello must be postponed. Headaches; hangovers. Alessandro promises me we will go before I leave Italy. We drive down to a small dock underneath a high cliff east of Sorrento and have lunch. It is my treat, I say, and Alessandro graciously accepts. After lunch we stop off at friends'. A couple; academics, in charge of the papyrus scrolls from Herculaneum at Naples University. Their apartment is full of artefacts from sites they have excavated throughout their lives. It is a mini museum. I wander around while they talk. The small statues, busts, fragments make a deeper impression on me away from an orthodox museum setting; I am allowed to touch them. And it is precisely this additional tactile element that deepens the experience. I am then given an English translation of the scrolls that my hosts have been looking for. I'm not really up to reading a classic text but I thank them and cast my eyes over it while at the same time watching and listening to Alessandro and his friends talking. Alessandro is clearly a different type of conversationalist in his native tongue. He talks at speed, intensely, alert, employing the whole range of Neapolitan gestures. He is like a passionate university student high on ideas. Louisa and I are flaking out, whereas he is sitting on the edge of his chair, whisky in hand, showing no sign of last night's stupefaction. Once again I feel lightweight in comparison.

It is late afternoon by the time we return to the house. Closing up takes some time with Alessandro insisting every window, door, appliance is checked.

It is stifling in the car as we drive back to Naples. The sirocco, the hot wind from the North African desert, is the reason, I am told. It is unbearable; dry, dusty, heavy, suffocating. Even so, Alessandro prefers the windows down to the air conditioning. We pass the coastal towns that make up greater Naples, illegal building encroaching ever higher up the fecund slopes of Vesuvius. Alessandro tells me that here, in the *paesi vesuviani*, the Camorra run everything. There is almost no legitimate business left. It is one of the most socially deprived areas in the whole of Western Europe. Without hope of any investment as long as it's controlled by the Camorra. To me it looks like the outskirts of every Mediterranean town: small unfinished apartment blocks line the road like three-dimensional geometric husks; arid, unploughed fields; long, low greenhouses with torn polythene covers blowing in the hot breeze.

We do not pass through the residential districts, but I can see they are made up of cheap modern housing, densely packed. Only the soft burnished light of the afternoon sun differentiates these areas from the deep gloom and grimness of similar places on the outskirts of Glasgow or Berlin.

'But it is a complicated situation,' Alessandro continues. 'Without the Camorra many people would suffer more. But what country, what rich country, relies on organized crime for its welfare programme?'

'Will the Camorra ever be beaten?' I ask. I realize it is a ridiculous question given his last statement.

'Ah,' he says – this one denoting the absurdity of it all, his weariness at fighting the absurdity.

Back in Naples I am taken all the way to Signora Maldini's alley. I am not sure this is such a good idea. Should I really be seen around here with Alessandro? I look around for Camorra spies. Alessandro tells me where we are to meet in the morning. I want to make one final protest but there is no room for compromise in his instructions. I will need my passport, he says finally. Louisa, twisting round in her seat, says she will be free all day Wednesday: do I want to go shopping? She winks and smiles. I agree, adding under my breath: if I live that long. We arrange to meet in the usual place. We all climb out of the car and kiss. I thank them both for a wonderful weekend.

As I duck in through the small door I see Signora Maldini sitting in the lemon-and-lime courtyard with her mother. We all call, 'Buona sera,' and I am beckoned over.

'Vo' magna cu' nuje . . .' Signora Maldini says brightly.

I shrug, smile.

'Mangiare . . .' she adds, 'spaghetti,' and points at me and then back and forward to her mother and herself.

I am being invited to eat, I realize. I am too tired and hung over to go out, so I accept. I look at my watch. Six-thirty. It is inconceivable they'll eat before nine. Time for a nap. I press my hands together and place them to the side of my face. The international gesture of sleep I hope, and not an invitation or even insult of some kind. Signora Maldini and her mother both look up me, the same inscrutable expression. If I try to work out what they're both thinking, I'll faint, so I excuse myself with a grazie and a ciao and make the long climb up to the apartment and my bed.

7

We drive in silence to the high-security prison near Salerno where Giacomo Sonino is being held. I sit in the back beside Alessandro. He tells me I am *giornalista*, if asked. After that he reads papers the whole way. I feel very out of place: awkward, scruffy, unofficial. There is something unnerving about Alessandro's seriousness. Once again I am forced to contemplate the complex nature of his job. Today he is going to interview a self-confessed killer who is testifying against nine of his comrades, testifying that they murdered seven people: four rival gang members and three innocent members of the public. This is not a normal occupation. It's a job about truth – moral truth. Whatever the crazy behaviour of the families, whatever the informality of Italian or Neapolitan court procedure, whatever the socio-political leanings of the judge, Alessandro's task is to make sure that the facts of the events that led to the death of seven people are disclosed, that there is a complete account from which the law can then do its work. The rest – the sentencing, the appeals, all the legal wrangling – can be left to the refined mechanism of centuries of civil jurisprudence. Anyone can do that. But not everyone can conduct a trial in which all participants are intent on maintaining their 'honour', ensuring their *omertà* is uncompromised, while at the same time trying to destroy these things in their opponent. This trial and trials like this are about will. Gangster will against moral will.

My faith in Alessandro's honesty, his incorruptibility, is absolute. I trust him instinctively. There is almost a moral beauty about him. It is the quality that gives him his handsomeness. It is probably why Louisa fell in love with him. I wonder what Sonino makes of him? It is clear the nine aren't as automatically contemptuous of him as one might expect. And what about the lawyers? Surely they would prefer a judge with weaknesses – susceptible to manipulation. Arrogant, preening, vainglorious. Aspects they can exploit. I realize now how much of the subtlety of the courtroom drama I have missed. I am looking forward to today. To observe close-up. We will all be in the same room, Alessandro says. The white room.

It is like a film set. In the centre of the room are a table, two chairs, two cameras. There are lights mounted high on tall tripods. Cables run out of the room, secured to the floor with gaffer tape. As soon as he walks in Alessandro is irritated – it's too contrived, too movie-like. We are not the first to arrive. Lawyers, reporters, miscellaneous others stand in the corridor, milling about. We are constantly counted. I show my passport twice to police officers. My name, addresses (Napoli, London) are noted down in a log. The room itself is large. The walls are whitewashed brick. The floor is linoleum. There are no windows. It looks like it was once a dormitory or ward – a cafeteria, perhaps. I recognize people from the courtroom back in Naples: clerks and lawyers. No one is interested in me. Sonino is nowhere to be seen. A young man approaches Alessandro and asks him to sit in one of the chairs. He then positions himself behind the camera opposite and adjusts the framing. When he is satisfied he moves to a spotlight and adjusts that. Alessandro stands but is asked to sit back down. I sense he wants to abandon this now before it becomes something it's not.

I keep out of the way by tucking myself into the one corner with a clear view of the chair in which Sonino will sit. I am occasionally spoken to, but I just shrug and say, 'Giornalista, inglese,' and am left alone. Alessandro is finally allowed to stand. His deputy has arrived. They confer. Alessandro looks at his watch. No one seems to be in charge. The director seems to be the only person in the place who knows what he is doing. He is looking around the room for something. He has a finger across his lips indicating active thought, practical thinking, a problem to solve. He looks at me. Fixes on me. 'Tu,' he says and points. Yeah right, I think, and remain where I am, pretending not to notice. He calls me again. Alessandro looks round. I shrug. The director approaches. '*Inglese, non capito,*' I say. He isn't deterred; he grabs at my arms and pulls me towards the centre of the room. I am forced to submit if I don't want to make a scene. He directs me to Sonino's chair. I have been selected as his stand-in because I am tall. I protest lamely. Alessandro laughs. But then he doesn't realize there is a very definite possibility the video images are already being relayed to the courtroom and right now nine *camorristi*, already deeply suspicious about my existence, are looking directly at me and wondering why I have now appeared in the room at the high-security prison from which their accuser will testify. I ask the director whether the cameras are running; I figure his youth and profession mean he will speak some English. He looks at me blankly.

'Are the cameras running?' I repeat. 'Are they on?' I point.

'We are not filming,' he says rather archly.

Clearly his failure to become the next Fellini or Pasolini has given him attitude issues. I stand, but like Alessandro I am ordered to sit back down.

When he is finally finished I ask once again, 'Just tell me, can the pictures be seen in the court?'

With almost perverse haughtiness, he says, 'Who are you?'

I grab his arm firmly and pull him to me. 'Tell me, can they see the pictures in the courtroom?'

'No, no,' he says and shakes his head, unsettled by my behaviour.

Alessandro comes over. 'Is everything OK?'

'Everything is fine,' I say, and let go of the director's arm and return to my corner.

Prison officers bring in more chairs, quickly appropriated. Someone, perhaps noticing I came in with Alessandro, passes one to me over the heads of others. Everyone is now seated, waiting, expectant. An older man in a business suit enters and walks directly up to Alessandro. They shake hands. There is an exchange of information, voices low. They could be two politicians doing a deal, outlining reciprocal benefits with professional swiftness, clarity, precision. Everyone is silent as they speak. The man then leaves and

Alessandro turns and says something that indicates that they are about to start. He takes his seat with his back to us, unpacks his files and spreads papers out before him. He taps the microphone on the desk in front of him. There is no boom. He calls to the director, who places a pair of headphones on. Alessandro speaks into the microphone. He is given the thumbs up.

Surrounded by five police officers, Sonino is led in. He is wearing the same black suit, white shirt, dark tie; everything is creased, as if it has all been bundled up in a ball and used as a pillow. He drags his feet. His wrists are pressed together with handcuffs. I wonder what surprises he has in store for us today. Even in his emaciated state his presence fills the room. As with all charismatics it is hard to define what gives him such specialness, but in this instance it is as if he stands in some sort of relief to the rest of us. We are shallow forms; he is rich in detail. Most people are hazy, we discern them slowly. But Sonino is strikingly instant. We are forced to take notice of him, even hunched over, inwardly collapsed, knees caved in, dragging his feet.

Before sitting down he scans the room. There are dark, heavy bags under his eyes. For a moment I am looked at directly. I force myself not to lower my eyes.

Shrugging off his guards, Sonino pulls the chair back from the table and sits down. He slouches: it is partly weakness, partly ironic insolence – a pose. Alessandro doesn't look up. The director is forced to adjust the angle and focus of the camera; my participation was pointless. He then crosses from one camera to the other pressing buttons; red lights come on. Filming has begun. Alessandro raises his head and greets Sonino politely. He orders his handcuffs to be removed. Sonino doesn't show any sign of gratitude.

Alessandro is in no hurry to begin. He studies his papers, calls over his deputy, whispers to him over his shoulder. Sonino is unconcerned, motionless in his chair. I don't think this is part of some psychological battle. If it is, we are going to be here a long time. After another minute or so Alessandro speaks. He asks Sonino to confirm his name. Sonino leans forward a little, as if straining to hear. Alessandro repeats the question. Sonino answers in the affirmative. Alessandro then asks another question, in which I recognize the word Camorra. Sonino again answers, 'Si.' Alessandro then reads out a list of names. Nine of them. Sonino looks over Alessandro's shoulder to the camera facing him; he stares into it as if he can see straight through the lens into the courtroom and into the cage. Without averting his eyes, he confirms for the record that the nine accused were members of his gang the Camorra Moderna.

There is a strange tension in the room. The minimalism of the exchange gives the proceedings an intense, concentrated quality. It is more like a play by Beckett or Pinter – more an absurdist two-hander than a judicial encounter. It is often said that great theatre shouldn't require the spoken language to be understood. That's true here. The brinkmanship between Alessandro and Sonino is as clear to me as to the other observers. Alessandro is leading Sonino through his own statement. He is making him underscore every detail of his previous testimony so there is no confusion when he later begins to test it in relation to the defendants' versions. Every time Sonino says 'si' he moves into greater conflict with those he's accused. And Sonino knows specificity is risky – it can be disproved so much more easily than generalizations, allusion, insinuation. But then he is hoping it will rattle the defence because it is precisely the opposite tactic of the *pentiti* in the 1980s, when almost nothing of substance was said, yielding little but Camorra hierarchies, hedges and insults.

The questions become more detailed. I recognize dates, places – places in Naples I know. Sonino clarifies, corrects, fine-tunes. He does so without pausing. His mind is quick, as if physical exhaustion has intensified his cognition like some eastern mystic. I watch him closely, elbows on my knees, chin resting in cupped palms. Many of my patients are gifted liars, disguising continued addiction with clever dissimulation; often as much self-deception as the desire to fool me. I want to know whether behind all this complexity of information Sonino is hiding something. I suspect this is Alessandro's fear: the whole *pentito* enterprise is about something else entirely. Maybe others are involved. Higher up. There is higher. If not in the Camorra, then the Sicilian Mafia, the American Mafia. Maybe he's been ordered to do this. Turn *pentito* and negotiate a deal for a new identity (what organization wouldn't want a man like Sonino), while at the same time taking the heat off themselves by having a bunch of lesser *camorristi* banged up for the street warfare which has stretched the tolerance of even the Neapolitans. Whether or not this is a plausible scenario I have no idea.

A recess is called. Sonino doesn't move; he waits for the handcuffs to be replaced. He is given a cigarette. Alessandro stands and confers with his deputy. He is brought an espresso and knocks it back. I cannot tell what he's thinking. He is just stern-faced, concentrating. Sonino smokes with his head lowered, his chin almost to his chest. The director checks his cameras. Apart from a little whispering between lawyers, between journalists, no one talks. We are like an audience during the scene-changes of a play – we do not want the spell broken. Alessandro sits back down, rubs his face and takes a deep breath. Sonino looks up and stares at Alessandro from beneath lowered brows. His eyes are dark but without warmth. His cigarette is taken away, pinched out of his fingers, and he is uncuffed. I sense the break is to allow Alessandro to gather himself before he begins a different line of questioning. When he begins I recognize words like *omicidio, assassino, morte*. Sonino is having to verify his own criminal activity. He doesn't falter. His stare is constant, his smile mocking. He knows that whatever he confesses, however horrific the details, it is of limited importance compared to his testimony against the nine, because he has only killed other gangsters whereas the car bombs killed innocent people. This is part of the reason for his blatant enjoyment. Whatever the state of his pathology he is not as bad, as stupid, as *sinful* as the nine – all goons who did not understand the higher value that society places on the life of a citizen compared to that of a criminal, a mistake he hasn't made, ensuring that society will always want to convict other killers fractionally more than him. He is clearheaded in the economics of murder.

But then there is another reason for his pleasure. He knows his murders are myth-making. Since no one really cares about his victims, the particulars of the killing become the primary focus. The level of barbarity, the style of the brutality. They are folkloric in their ability to spellbind without producing moral outrage. So as Alessandro reads out his crimes Sonino responds keenly – yes, I did those things – then shrugs them off. He is both proud and dismissive. Although I can't be sure from where I am sitting, Alessandro doesn't seem to react to any of this and just continues to read out the next section from his file, the point of his pen pressed to the page to mark his place. He is being as methodical as possible, reducing any susceptibility he might feel to Sonino's perverse charm. Occasionally he requires greater elucidation. Only then is there direct eye contact; Alessandro fleetingly raising his eyes as if to say, please, more detail. After which he lowers his head to make the necessary notes.

It is one o'clock. The session is finished. The guards who have been stationed along the wall recuff Sonino, help him to his feet and lead him away. At the door he shakes them off him. They do not retaliate in any way. The room quickly empties. I am left with Alessandro, his deputy, the director and one other person I don't know. I am unsure what to do. Alessandro remains seated; he pops the top of his pen on and presses it down with his thumb. He is deep in thought.

'What happens now?' I say.

Alessandro turns. 'Now?' he asks looking a little distracted. 'Now we eat.'

Lunch is prison-canteen food served in a small office. Pasta and beans. I eat with the bowl on my knees. It's good, cooked with fresh ingredients, olive oil. Alessandro and his deputy sit at the desk across from each other. They chat, laugh. I do not understand a word. After a while Alessandro asks me what I thought.

'It's hard to tell,' I say.

'Did you understand what was happening?'

'A little. The second hour you were talking about his crimes?'

Alessandro nods. 'One time he says he killed a man who had sex with the widow of his brother. He cut his head off. At the time we thought the murderer was a doctor, a *chirurgo*. You know – who performs the operations . . .'

'Surgeon.'

'Yes, surgeon. Sonino says he practised for six months cutting heads off rabbits. He wanted us to think it was a *chirurgo*. A surgeon.'

No wonder he was looking so pleased with himself. The persistence of such vengeful impulses. To teach himself amateur surgery to avoid capture.

'What else did he do?' I ask morbidly.

Alessandro laughs. 'He eats . . . he bites . . .' He confers with his deputy, who shakes his head.

'What is the past tense of "he bites out his tongue"?' Alessandro asks me.

'He bit out his tongue, but I get the picture,' I say.

'He then killed him a week later,' Alessandro adds.

'How?'

'He *says* he stabbed him one hundred times,' stressing the conjectural tone of the statement.

'Is there some doubt?' I ask.

'The coroner's report says between sixty and seventy times.'

'I see how that's a problem.'

'You do?' Alessandro is interested in my instinct here.

'Sonino doesn't approximate. He is precise. He is patient. One hundred is a number that requires time, determination. Seventy is a frenzied attack.'

'We must read the original report again. Speak to the coroner. It is probably nothing.' Alessandro throws his hands in the air. Probably nothing, but they must establish the facts.

'What happens now?'

'This afternoon we continue.'

I finish my pasta and beans and accept the offer of *caffè* from Alessandro, who leaves the room to fetch it. I remain with his deputy. We smile at each other. He's not much older than me.

Even though he aspires to a little glamour – he holds his cigarette high, nonchalantly – he lacks the presence of Alessandro. He seems like a capable apprentice who will eventually work somewhere else, where the work is less demanding. If I were a deputy judge in Naples I would want his job. Alessandro returns with the coffee. He hands me mine, and we knock them back together. It is time to return to the white room.

I do not go straight to my corner but instead remain with Alessandro in the centre of the room, perched on the side of the table. We laugh about our game of Monopoly, promising each other one of us will beat Louisa next time. Foolishly I do not pay attention to the director, circling the table with his camera. I'm aware he's there, out of the corner of my eye, but for some reason I think he's just being pretentious, a pantomime film director. It is only when Alessandro says with a big smile, 'Look, Jim, you are a movie star,' that I realize the camera is on the both of us, we are framed together, reflected in the black mirror of the lens. A two-shot. And the red recording light is on. I want to shout STOP! Cover the lens with my hand. But it's too late. For all those in the courtroom back in Naples intrigued by my identity, it is now clear: I am someone who knows the judge well – well enough to chat to him between sessions of one of the most important trials in his life. After telling Giovanna twice I am merely an inquisitive tourist.

'Fuck,' I exclaim.

The director smirks – this is his little revenge for me grabbing him earlier.

'What is the matter?' Alessandro asks.

'Nothing,' I say; then add, 'I just don't think it's particularly wise to be seen here, talking to you. These are paranoid, desperate people. Aren't they going to wonder who I am?'

'You worry too much,' Alessandro says, patting me on the shoulder and laughing.

Maybe I am worrying needlessly. Who will be paying attention to a courtroom TV at the end of lunch, when nothing important is happening, the 'actors' not in their place? I relax a little, but decide this trial is knocking years off my life.

My corner seat is taken so I opt for a place that will allow me an equal view of both protagonists. From this angle they will face each other like chess masters.

Sonino is brought back in. He sits back down, this time pulling the chair forward and resting his arms on the table. Alessandro is forced to move his files a little; he spreads them out laterally across the desk. The director adjusts his camera for the second time.

During this session Sonino is shown photos. I can't see them clearly, but most are mug shots. Some are of murder scenes. Black and white shots of dead men lying slumped in corners, over steering wheels, over dinner – the splattered black blood becoming a motif. Sonino explains what he knows. He occasionally picks up the photos laid before him and studies them more closely. I don't think the killings are his work. He looks at them with disdain, contempt. These men are butchers, not surgeons. Amateurs. Sonino then says something that makes Alessandro laugh. A joke? At the expense of the dead? About the killer? I don't know. But everyone gets it except me. It does, however, prove one of my earlier theories: there is a categorical difference between criminal victim and innocent victim, because I doubt Alessandro would countenance a joke about the latter. This is further substantiated by a new set of photos, which appear to be from the car bombings. I can see bodies, parts of bodies, lying in the street. There are cars burning, engulfed in black flames, smoke. Sonino tries another joke but this time, and for the first time today, Alessandro slaps his hand down on the table and orders *silenzio*. Despite his close proximity, Sonino doesn't flinch; he doesn't even blink.

Alessandro continues to lay photographs before him. What Alessandro is after is proof that Sonino not only knew of the plan to plant the bombs but also knew when, where and how. They are discussing the logistics of such an operation, both of them gesturing with their hands, drawing diagrams in the air, leading each other through the streets of Naples. For a moment they are no longer judge and *pentito*, no longer in a prison, but have become two ordinary guys in a bar discussing the best way to get from Via Roma to the Stadio San Paolo. The session ends with Sonino demonstrating an explosion with his hands and mimicking a muted blast noise. It is not a joke or an attempt at cheap theatrics – he is merely explaining a particular detail. The strength of the bomb in relation to the street. The reason it killed so many pedestrians was that the high walls contained the blast and sent debris up and down the street. He then shakes his head. He would not have made such a mistake.

After Sonino has been removed and Alessandro has consulted with a number of people, including his deputy, the man he conferred with just before the interview, we leave. I sit in the front of the car while Alessandro sits in the back with his deputy. I get the feeling his deputy is beginning to find my continued presence irritating. As usual after witnessing these bizarre judicial proceedings I am very tired. Betrayal might be exhausting but so too is paranoia, which I am beginning to feel in similar doses to criminals who have something to be paranoid about – namely betrayal. I wonder whether I am unconsciously looking for a way to empathize – that this is now my natural inclination whenever I witness a psychological condition. I try to edit out the conversation in the back and have a snooze, but Alessandro calls out, 'Is he telling the truth, Jim? What do you think?'

I am half expecting the question. I don't think I've been used – why would I be, I'm no expert – but Alessandro is too smart to forget that I have experience working with complex people.

Without turning around I say, 'He's a tricky fellow.'

I hear Alessandro chuckle. 'What else?' he says.

'Probably insane.'

Alessandro laughs again. 'Your professional opinion?' he jokingly asks.

'My professional opinion would include a total lack of ego boundaries based on intuitive understanding of his own specialness.'

Alessandro translates this to his deputy. They both laugh.

'What I want to know, Jim. Is his betrayal real?'

'You mean, is this whole thing somehow a set-up?'

'Yes.'

'I was wondering about that.'

'What did you think?'

'That I have no idea. I think it's impossible for an English person to try to second-guess a Neapolitan. We are two entirely different creatures. An English person's sense of right and wrong is rigid. Irrespective of what is right, the point is fixed and the two sides are unambiguous. I would say Neapolitan morality is a movable feast.'

'You think this based on what?'

'Intuition. I certainly don't have experience of it.'

'You are a courageous man,' he says, and resumes his conversation with his deputy.

I'm not sure what he means by this last statement. I cannot tell whether he is offended by my comparison.

We arrive in Naples and I am dropped off in Piazza Garibaldi. We don't kiss or shake hands. I hop out in the middle of traffic.

I walk slowly back to Signora Maldini's via Spaccanapoli. The sun is about to set and I am waiting to see whether the light will flood down in the same miraculous way as on my first evening up and about in Naples. I feel in the mood for a mystical experience. Concentrating on the mind of Giacomo Sonino all day has depressed me a little. He may be fascinating but there is always the fear of contamination from such powerful personalities. I am thinking this when I am suddenly enveloped in light. I am further along the street so it arrived more quickly than last time. I am forced to stand still and wait for it to pass. It's so bright I can't even see my feet.

When the world returns to shadow it takes a long time for my eyes to shake off the multiple images I have of everything I look at. For a second I worry that I might have done some permanent damage.

By the time I can see clearly again I'm on the corner of Piazza Bellini. I am not sure why I am here – my destination was the apartment. I sit down at a table and order a beer. I try to convince myself that this was my reason. A beer at the end of a long day. But I know in reality I am hoping Giovanna will pass on her way to or from the cybercafé. I tell myself I need to see her because I want reassurance that my presence in the prison wasn't noticed, but I am perfectly aware I am here because of an undifferentiated desire to see her again – by which I mean I cannot pinpoint what part of me desires it, the fearful or the lustful, I merely have the feeling.

I wait for half an hour and then decide to leave her a note. I borrow a pen from the waiter and on a napkin I write: *Giovanna. CyberDante. Wednesday. 7.* Compared to her note it is positively verbose. I leave it with the guy at the cybercafé. He reads it, I suppose not wanting the place used as some drop-off point for the Camorra. He then folds it up and places it under the bar. I walk back to the apartment. Signora Maldini isn't around but there is a message by the phone that Louisa has called. I am too tired to call back. I sit down in the living room, turn on the TV and search for a local news programme. Before I've checked all the channels Signora Maldini opens the door. I am pleased to see her, and even more pleased that her hair is once again tilting. As she enters she gives it an unceremonious shove up. It sways, totters almost, but then settles back to its gravity-defying lopsidedness. There is something oddly reassuring in its Tower-of-Pisa lean, and I decide with almost native superstition that as long as Signora Maldini's hair is just this side of collapse all will be well with the world, my world.

sex

I

I have arranged to meet Louisa on the dock, at the ticket office below the Castel Nuovo. The sun is high, white, in a translucent blue sky. Naples is a different city without shadows. It appears in the disguise of a holiday destination – bright and welcoming. I know, however, that the shadows are there, only a street away. Before me the bay is blue with Capri a hazy rock perched on the horizon. I sit on a bench and wait. Last night when I called, Louisa said, 'For shopping there is only Capri. It is paradise, darling.' She was affecting a high Sloane accent, playing up for Alessandro, whom I could hear grumbling: 'Jim doesn't want to go to Capri – *inferno borghese*.' I laughed, but I don't think he was trying to be funny. Louisa said, 'Don't worry, Jim, you'll love it.'

On the other side of the port, a huge luxury liner is docked. I cannot quite believe its size – more: I can't quite *accept* its size. It is like a special effect in a movie. Its vastness is disturbing. It is just too big to float. It is like the Chrysler Building turned on its side. I want to walk over and stand directly beneath it, feeling the crush of its shadow, but a cab pulls up and Louisa climbs out.

We buy tickets for the ferry rather than the hydrofoil. It takes longer, Louisa says, but it's so much more civilized. She slots her arm in mine as we wait on the dock for the boat to arrive. I point out the liner. They're here all the time. Mediterranean cruises. The passengers disembark, walk the hundred yards to catch the boat for Capri. And that's about as much as they see of Naples.

'Bourgeois inferno,' I say.

'He can be such a bore.'

I remain quiet.

She continues, 'He loves Sorrento but hates Capri. I think that's a bit hypocritical.'

'I have no idea.'

'You'll see,' she says and squeezes herself closer to me. She smells fresh, light, crisply clean, straight from the shower. Her hair is faintly damp. She is wearing blue linen trousers, gently flared, and a white linen vest. A bright white bra strap is visible over her lightly tanned shoulder. Her sunglasses are big.

The small Capri ferry docks and we embark with natives and tourists. We find a seat at the prow. From the moment we leave the port and enter the Bay of Naples the breeze cools us down. It's the first time in two weeks I've been anything less than hot. Louisa's arms are covered in goose pimples. I want to wrap my arm around her like a lover, like her husband. She leans forward on the bow and her vest rides up, exposing the small of her back. I want to run my finger up the faint relief of her delicate spine. She is covered in a film of perspiration.

'Are you hot?' I ask.

'I was baking. I'm all right now.'

I want to kiss her; I don't know why – why here. Perhaps, now we have left Naples, the shadow of Alessandro has receded and for the first time I feel Louisa is more mine than his. I sense Louisa knows, feels something similar. She is looking up at me invitingly. I decide to play her at her own game.

'I'm not going to kiss you,' I say.

'I should think not; I'm a married woman,' she says.

I shouldn't play games; I'm no good at them. Her response crushes me. I laugh it off, change the subject.

'Your husband was very impressive on Monday.'

'He was completely exhausted when he came home. Played the piano and went straight to bed.'

'Is he feeling the pressure?'

'It's hard to tell. The Italian system is so complicated, I'm not even sure what he needs from Sonino.'

'Enough to convince him and the jury the nine were involved,' I say without actually knowing whether this is the case. Maybe there is something else, something more arcane in Italian law.

Alessandro did tell me that witnesses don't have to swear they're telling the truth – which must make everything much more problematic, doubtful.

I lean forward on the bow and stare out towards Capri. Louisa rests her head on folded arms, looking at me sideways, a little mournfully. 'I know I keep saying it but I'm really happy you decided to stay.'

'I'm very happy I'm staying,' I say.

This is followed by a short pause. She then says, 'You are my friend, aren't you?' She squints a little afterwards and then smiles sweetly. She wants it to seem like a harmless question, no more than a girlishly coy enquiry, but it is clear she is asking something more. Of course it might be no more than: 'I like you as my friend, please don't make a pass', but I don't think it's that. She is saying, 'Having a friend has made me realize how lonely I was before.'

I say, 'Of course I am,' and push away the stray strands of hair that have blown across her face. She curls them behind her ear, only for the wind to loosen them again.

We are now approaching Capri. The boat heads for the tiny harbour at the bottom of the valley formed by the two small mountains that make up the island. The town of Capri itself is located higher up the valley, a white stucco saddle slung between the two peaks. A funicular railway runs between harbour and town like a trouser zip. The small port looks quaint, welcoming; but touristy, very different from the city we have left behind. I look back. Naples is vague, sun-hazy, vast and thinly spread for miles. There is nothing to suggest its internal darkness, its heavy beauty.

We leave the boat and head straight for the funicular. We stand with a large group of tourists waiting for the next carriage to descend. I feel like I'm queuing for a popular ride in a theme park. I have never actually done that, but I imagine this is how it feels. When the carriage arrives we elbow our way in; Louisa, regarding herself as a native, refuses to be jostled out of a space by Americans. I push myself in behind her.

'The funicular is the worst thing about Capri. You think it's going to be one of the nicest but it's like getting on the tube.'

We travel up in silence. Pressed to a window I marvel at the beauty of the place. The sky is high and blue, the ocean blue and clear, the island lush and bright. Everything I look at has a material translucency, a clarity I have never seen before. Each aspect – house, villa, tree, palm, flower, rock, stone – seems uniquely distinct, as if pure air, open sunlight and mirroring ocean suffuse everything with extra life. The whole place feels not quite real, but at the same time more real than anywhere else. It has prelapsarian vividness. I feel like I am on an island-Eden experiencing a kind of original relationship with the world. I turn to Louisa and say, 'This place is quite something.'

'I know,' she says. 'It's beautiful.'

I stare at her face. She too seems suffused with extra vividness. The impossibly soft down on her cheek glistens; her eyes seem variegated with a million blues; her lips poised between the thought of a kiss and the kiss itself. We hit the top of the funicular with a jolt and Louisa wobbles and falls against me. I steady her, my hands on her hips. It is the moment for a kiss. But we are pushed apart by other tourists trying to be the first to disembark.

The town centre is like a film set before the set designers have added the dirt for authenticity. The stucco walls are unblemished white, the cobbles and terracotta tiles glassy. A little convertible electric-powered cab passes us. It's like a golf cart. And typically full of Americans.

We sit down at a café and order cappuccinos. Sensing my dismay at the cheesiness of the place, Louisa says, 'You have to ignore all this. We're here for the shops.'

'What do you want to get?' I ask, my head following ancient Italian women, dressed as jaunty sailors, with faces lined by the sun and rigid with make-up, clutching four, five, six bags each.

'We're not here for me,' Louisa says. 'We're looking for you.'

'Louisa,' I say sternly, 'I haven't got the money to spare and you're not buying me clothes.'

'Why not?' she says, openly puzzled.

'Why *not*?'

'Yes, why not?'

'Because it doesn't feel right.'

'What doesn't?'

'You buying me clothes.'

'Why not?'

'Because I say so.'

'You need new clothes.'

'Possibly.'

She is looking at me with imploring eyes. 'I want to do this. Just regard it as a thank you. For staying in Naples and keeping me company.'

I am forced to relent. 'But I get to choose what we buy.'

Louisa shakes her head. 'No way. What's the point in that?' she says playfully.

'I thought the point was to buy me some new clothes.'

'No, the point was for me to buy you new clothes.'

'Then I have to decline.'

'You can't.'

'Why not?'

'Because you've already agreed.'

'When?'

'A moment ago. You said, "I get to choose what to buy" .'

'That's not an agreement, that's a condition.'

'But you agreed to accept them, right? And your original argument was me buying them. You're shifting the goalposts and it's not fair.'

'*I'm* not fair?'

'Look, you know I'm going to get my own way. And if you're worried about Alessandro – I've already told him.'

This really annoys me.

'I told him we were going to Capri and if we saw anything you liked I'd buy it for you as a present.'

There is something in the manner in which she says it that makes it entirely acceptable in a way I could not foresee.

'There's nothing wrong with that, is there?' she asks, genuinely looking for approval.

'No, I suppose not. It just sounds a bit odd, telling your husband you're off to buy clothes for another man.'

'Put like that of course it does. But that's not what I said.'

'I know that now.'

'So it's settled?'

'Do I have a choice?'

'Not really.'

She promises me nothing too ridiculous, but adds I'd be surprised what I can carry off. I grimace. I am told not to worry – she's an expert.

At first I refuse even to enter the shops. Though tempted by the quality of each item in the window it's still too great a leap to see myself wearing them. I like clothes, and when I've found something I like I have now and again spent more money than I should, but here nothing is under two hundred pounds, which is too much for a gift. Louisa warned me not to look at the price tags, that everything's expensive, you can't avoid that in a place like this so I should just accept it and get on with it. I am finally persuaded to enter Dolce & Gabbana.

With a look of deep concentration, Louisa picks from the few trousers on the rack those she wants me to try, at first holding them against me and stepping back for a fuller view. The selection is quickly narrowed from three down to one.

'Here,' she says. 'See what you think?'

They are light cotton, dark grey, loose, untapered, almost slightly flared. Exchanging them for my jeans is like being clothed in air. I marvel at the fit, the line, the sheer perfection of them. Even with my old T-shirt on I am a changed man.

Louisa calls, 'How are they?'

'Good,' I say, too embarrassed to exit the cubicle.

'Can I come in?' And before I answer she pushes her way in with slender fingers curled over the top of the door.

'Wow, they look great. Better than I thought. But let's not make any snap decisions . . .'

'You're joking. I'm not going to find anything nicer than these . . .'

'Jim, we are just getting our eye in.'

'Louisa, please. I can only take so much.'

We continue on our way, ducking in anywhere that takes Louisa's fancy. Mostly I let her test things against me, but slowly I become more compliant and agree to try more extravagant items on. In Versace Louisa selects a suit which looks like my parents' bedroom when they went for the disastrous 'paradise at sunset' wallpaper. I am shocked by how unridiculous it looks on, and think if I had somewhere to wear it, some surplus cash, I might consider buying it myself. The only thing which really deters me is a spontaneous image of myself wearing it lying in a coffin. Louisa loves it, but agrees we're after something a little more functional. The shirt we settle on – Armani – is white, fitted, which Louisa says complements my shape, and even though the material is thickish it is airy and cool due to the almost imperceptible tiny diamond pattern stitched in. It is somewhere around the 250 pound mark, even allowing for a strong pound. I put up a bit of a battle but my vanity doesn't push it.

'It's going to be very embarrassing thanking Alessandro if he knows how much this costs,' I say.

'He can afford it. Anyway he's a communist. Redistribution of cash and all that.'

'I don't think they had this in mind.'

'Really, you don't need to mention it. He won't be interested.'

'But it would be rude not to.'

'It's up to you.'

After another hour we return, as I knew we would, and buy the first pair of trousers I tried on. Louisa refuses to tell me how much they cost. I am keen to wear my new clothes now but Louisa tells me to wait until tonight.

'Tonight?' I ask uncertainly.

'Alessandro said to invite you to dinner.'

'I can't,' I say apologetically.

We have just stepped out of the shop, each of us with a bag.

'Why?' Louisa asks.

'I have to meet someone.'

Louisa is unhappy with this. Her mournful look returns. However, she says, 'It's good you're meeting people.' Then, as if the thought has only just occurred to her, she asks, 'It's not a girl, is it?'

'It is. Very beautiful. But too young for me,' I say.

Louisa reacts badly to this, replying sharply, 'They're all beautiful here, that's no great shakes.'

Her blue eyes cool down. It is not so much jealousy as the reflex of possessiveness. I feel I need to reassure her. You're still my number one girl, or something equally ridiculous. But then she's married and Giovanna *is* too young for me – so why should I? Besides, it's not even a date. It's a summit. Was I seen in the court by the nine, by their families? And if so, what does that mean? My fear may have diminished over the last couple of days, but I cannot forget her saying, 'People want to know who you are,' and the explicit warning not to be seen again.

'It's just someone I met at a café near where I am. I do spend an awful lot of evenings on my own, Louisa.'

If she cares, she doesn't show it. We enter the main square. She flounces into a chair by an empty table and requests a menu from the waiter.

'I'm hungry. Lunch is on you.'

'Don't be a child, Louisa.'

'Aren't you hungry?'

'I want to sort this out.'

'There's nothing to sort out.'

'I think there is.'

'Well, I don't. I invited you to dinner. You can't make it. That's it. End of conversation.'

'So we sit here in silence?'

She shrugs.

'Louisa, I can't cancel it. But I'll make it just a quick drink. I can be with you by nine at the latest.' It is a compromise. Besides I have no idea whether Giovanna will turn up at all. I am expecting Louisa to protest, now I have made this concession, but instead a smile appears. 'Nine is fine,' she says. 'And you must wear your new clothes.'

'You don't mind me wearing them to see Giovanna?' I say teasingly.

She ignores me. Giovanna has been overcome, she is no longer important. This irritates me. Suddenly all that is elegant, warm, generous about Louisa becomes hard, mean, cold.

'Did you hear what I said?' I say impatiently.

'Yes,' she says flatly. 'And of course I don't mind you wearing your new clothes to see this girl – they're your clothes.' Her smile is forced.

I feel like saying, 'No wonder you have so few friends if this is the way you behave.'

We order our food without further communication. Louisa opens her cigarette packet and tugs one out without her usual counting tic. She takes a long drag. This is followed by a long exhale – a smoky sigh. She places her hand over mine.

'I'm sorry, Jim. I like to have you all to myself. It may seem selfish, I know.'

'It is selfish,' I retort.

Keeping her hand where it is, she continues, 'Please, I don't want you to think like that. I hate being thought of as selfish. If there is a downside to the way I look – and I'm not one of these people who think being attractive is some kind of burden – but people jumping to conclusions whenever you act a certain way, it's not fair. We're all selfish, we all like our own way. It's not something different if you're pretty, it just looks worse or something. I know people think I must be horrible sometimes . . . I mean I might be if I was a model or an actress or something, but that would be because I was a model or an actress, but I'm not . . .' Once again, she subtly

185

changes tack. 'You know, I am trying very hard at my course. I find it very difficult . . . it doesn't come naturally to me . . .'

I hear a touch of self-pity in her voice, special pleading for such perseverance, hardship. But I sense what she wants is for someone to be proud of her, and Alessandro I imagine takes for granted her level of effort and is failing to appreciate her commitment, or at least articulate it. Plus, I feel she wants me to show some pride in her because I remember what she was once like, how little inclination, indeed, how little aptitude she showed for such things.

'I'm very impressed by what you're doing,' I say, trying not to sound condescending. 'It's hard enough, but in another language . . .'

She nods, pleased by this. It's right to be impressed.

We are now back on firmer ground. Louisa removes her hand from mine. Our food arrives.

Before she begins to eat, she says, 'You understand me.' It is a simple declaration, not a compliment or flattery, and not open for contradiction.

However, I say, 'I'm not sure about that.'

Louisa nods. 'It's nice to be understood. To feel understood. I think it's quite rare. I mean for most people, not just me. I understand Alessandro but he –' Her sentence finishes abruptly. I want to explain his seeming lack of understanding as more a generational thing, a reluctance to express understanding rather than actual ignorance, but I don't want to bring up their age difference or act like some kind of expert on their marriage. 'I'm sure he does,' is all I say.

It is three o'clock by the time we board the ferry back to Naples. It is a fresh and breezy journey. Louisa slips her sandals off and puts her feet up on the bow. I remember her feet from before, slender, sinewy, sexy. The sun has browned them a little, a dirty caramel. It gives them an erotic quality; I don't know why. I take off my shoes and put my feet up next to hers – they are white, almost reflective in the sun. Compared to hers they are grotesque, lacking anything erotic.

Louisa says, 'They're big 'uns.' And knocks one with the side of her foot, adding, 'You should have been a policeman.'

I am tempted to say, 'You know what they say about a man with big feet,' but refrain, realizing she knows whether it's true in my case – or rather, that she knows it isn't particularly true in my case. I withdraw them from the sunlight. We sit in silence as Naples draws closer.

When we part at the port Louisa wishes me a pleasant evening with *that girl* and makes a sound somewhere between a purr and a growl.

I say, 'I will, but I'll be thinking only of you.'

'I hope so,' she says, adding, 'I'm all you should think about.' It is said gaily, with a wide smile and a little of the breathlessness of love. She is acting out a scene: we are falling in love, but she is married; I am off to meet another woman as I must, but she wants to feel secure in my devotion. As she should be in reality. There has been such little passion in my life that my resolve not to love her is melting away, and the more she play-acts, the more I feel for real.

As we kiss goodbye I rest my hand on her hip and she presses herself to me. Her acting has even fooled herself for a moment. My instinct is to take advantage, to continue with this ritual I know so well: move my hand to her back, pull her closer to me, exploit the moment. I know she will momentarily respond; but my good sense gently guides her away and I raise my arm to hail a cab. Louisa says nothing, but remains close to me. A cab pulls up and I open the door.

As she slides in the back she looks up at me and says, 'Do you remember what it was like?'

I stare down at her with a look of admonishment, of serious censure. She cannot refer to our sexual past – it permits too much into our friendship.

'I know you do,' she says, 'I can tell every time you look at me. A woman knows when she is desired. I mean, *really* desired.'

I cannot think of what to say, so I close the cab door with a gentle push. From the open window, I hear Louisa give her address in imperious Italian and then in an instant she's gone, sucked into the slipstream of Neapolitan traffic.

2

If she is coming, she is late. It's twenty minutes past the appointed time. I am standing in the arched entrance to CyberDante, a beer in my hand. I am wearing my new clothes. I am transformed by them. I now look like a wealthy man on vacation, taking it easy, content to pass the time under the sun, relaxed, without a care, as free of stress and strain as the fit of his clothes. I feel contentedly Mediterranean, not a native entirely but certainly not a Northerner – a man over whom drizzle and clouds hang. If there is a greater sense of the voluptuousness of life here it is because there is little reason for inwardness – certain death to the sensuous – and more reason for the body to delight in its own vivacity. The sun and the proximity of the sea change everything. Even hidden away in this doorway, in the heart of the old city, I feel like a man strolling along a sunny beach. If I crane my neck and look upwards there is the sun, and if the noise of the traffic subsided for a single second, I could, with sharp ears, hear the waves lapping against the docks. It is my guess that, despite the grime and darkness and noise, these two constants are the most powerful influences on the Neapolitan character; certainly I can feel them altering me.

I am deep in my reverie when a Vespa pulls up, startling me. It is Giovanna. *'Presto,'* she says. *'Presto.'*

I do not move. For a second I don't even know what she is asking.

'Inglese!' she says sharply and snaps her head back to the empty seat behind her. *'Presto!'*

I finally obey, and within seconds we've circled the piazza, weaved through a staggered line of cars stalled in the road and are on the main road heading up towards Capodimonte and the hills surrounding the city. It is a precarious ride and I am not sure where to hold on, Giovanna zipping slinkily in and out of the traffic. At first I think that if she doesn't want us to be seen together in public, this is a strange way to go about it, but as I look around I notice we are just one of a hundred identical Vespas shooting around Naples – we are indistinguishably part of a horde. I begin to feel quite exhilarated. Young. My new clothes flap in the terrific breeze we are whipping up.

Leaving the last vestiges of the city, the road clears before us and we sail along. We are travelling at quite a clip now – passing olive groves, fields of citrus trees, vineyards. For a second I wonder whether I'm being delivered to some isolated place, for assassination perhaps, but my feeling of exhilaration has banished my usual fearfulness. I look behind me: Naples is below us – a vast amphitheatre slipping into the bay.

We continue for a few miles, out beyond the city, before stopping on the side of a narrow road, arched with trees. Falling from the branches, the light is golden and green. I slip off the back of the scooter and Giovanna kicks down the stand and rocks the Vespa onto it. I look out beyond the trees to a knit of vineyards rising up the banks of a shallow valley. It is dusk. The light is smoky.

I am led off the road into an aisle of vines. Blue-black grapes hang heavily, succulently. I cannot imagine where we are going. Giovanna's pace lacks urgency, which reassures me. I ask in a half-shout, half-whisper, 'Giovanna, where are we going?' She doesn't answer. I keep following. After about five minutes we reach a building made of grey, crumbling stone. It is almost derelict; the roof tiles are broken and slipping, the wooden shutters in the windows are split or busted. The entrance is a stable door. Giovanna pushes the top half open, and then gently kicks the lower half open and walks in. I remain outside. I feel faintly ridiculous standing here in my brand-new Capri clothing. I brush the dust whipped up by the wheels of the bike off my trouser legs.

A match is struck and I step forward to look inside. An orange glow spreads across the back wall. Giovanna is holding a small plate with a candle in the centre; she beckons me in. Built into the floor there are two brick circles about ten feet wide with large plugholes in the centre. Around the walls old barrels are piled up, wood rotting, rings rusted. Thin pipes, once systematically bracketed along the walls, hang down like some large but delicate skeleton collapsing in on itself. I expect to be able to smell the residue of the wine once made here, but there is nothing. There are a couple of benches. A small table. Debris has been swept into the corner.

Giovanna moves around lighting more candles. We are slowly bathed in a diffuse, flickering light, each flame dancing seductively in the many competing breezes wafting in from the chinks in the walls, windows, roof.

I lean against the small table. Giovanna sits down on the edge of one of the benches.

'Who are you?' she asks, staring up at me, her eyes dark and deep.

'I'm no one,' I say wishing to sound enigmatic, but it sounds more pretentiously existential, so I add, 'just a tourist.'

'You are no one, just a tourist, but you are at the court and then at the prison.'

I don't say anything, just shift my weight from one buttock to the other.

She asks again, 'Who are you?'

For some reason, instead of explaining and dropping to my knees to beg for understanding, forgiveness, I say, 'Who wants to know?' I hear my voice crack, my anxiety is audible.

Not interested in answering any of my questions, Giovanna shuffles back on the bench, propping herself against the bare stone wall. 'In court you were on television with *il presidente*. Mascagni. It is not good. My brother he is very angry. My grandmother.'

There is no need to ask who her grandmother is, I know. Specifics are not important; all I need to know is I have angered two powerful, protective, vengeful people.

'Why did you bring me here?' I ask.

'I must tell them who you are . . .' There is something a little imploring about the way she says this. I am beginning to suspect she has not been sent to extract this information, she hasn't been ordered to interrogate me. She is here, I am here, because she wants, for some reason, to clear this up herself. Whether or not it is for my sake I don't know.

I explain. 'Giovanna, there's nothing going on. There's no mystery. I know President Mascagni's wife. She is English. A friend. When we met he invited me to the court. He thought I'd find it interesting, that's all. I really was just there as a tourist. You must believe me.'

'At the prison. It is not possible.' She wants to believe me but cannot.

'He arranged it. I promise. There were lots of people there. Reporters . . .'

She places her hand across her chest, just below her neck, spread around it like a necklace – she is thinking.

After a moment she says, 'Wife . . . *Lei è bella, no?*' I understand this and concur.

From the bench Giovanna stares over the grape-treading circles out through the open door into the dusk. It is now quite cosy in here, its dereliction transformed into homeliness by the contrast of the warm light to the night outside.

'You do not understand Napoli,' she says evenly, almost thoughtfully. 'You to be careful to mix with the wrong people.'

'I know that now,' I say.

'You stay away?'

'Definitely. You can promise your family.'

She nods three times: taking this in, weighing it up, accepting it. She smiles for the first time tonight, for the first since we met. It reveals her age; but it also reminds me of how lovely she is. I shift on the table, look around the room. It hasn't been used in years, decades even. Every piece of metal is covered in thick rust.

'How long you stay in Naples, before you go back?' she asks.

There doesn't seem anything behind this question, so I tell her my plans as they stand. A month; basically when my money runs out. Longer if I can.

'You like Napoli?' she asks a little moodily.

'Yes,' I say with enthusiasm; then add, 'You are very lucky.'

'I am not lucky,' she says shaking her head. 'It is a prison for me.'
She pushes herself off the bench and stands. 'This is where I come
to dream I am no longer prisoner.' There is a hint of soulfulness
here, also revealing her age.

I look around. 'What do you do here?' I ask.

'Nothing. Sleep. Sometimes . . .' She mimes drawing or writing
in the air before her.

I look around again; there is little sign of anything creative
happening here. Giovanna follows my eyes as I scan the walls.

'What do you look for?' she asks.

'Nothing,' I say, a little embarrassed.

'You cannot work in a prison,' she says with sudden vehemence.
'It is impossible.'

'I am sorry,' I say.

Giovanna approaches me. Her body is accentuated by the
shadows, the dimness, roughness and unsubtlety of the candlelight.
She leans against the table next to me.

Recovering herself she asks, 'Where do you live in United Kingdom? London?'

'Yes.' I am expecting her to ask me about it – cursory, almost
polite questions, the way one does about a city, but instead she
twists her torso and looks up at me and says, 'It is where I want to
go. I will help you here and then you help me there.'

Not one fraction of me has been expecting this. It is more of a
surprise than her sudden appearance on the Vespa earlier, our first
encounter outside the court, finding her note slipped into my
pocket.

'I don't understand,' I say.

She stands before me, her hands in the prayer position, but
this is not a request for clairvoyance, it's a genuine plea for help.
Even her explicit 'favour for a favour' tactic was devoid of any
threat. I have been brought here, to her secret place, to negotiate
an escape plan.

'Why do you need my help?' I ask.

'*Inglese*,' she says, recovering something of her earlier, more wilful demeanour. 'I do not have money, no *passaporto*. They . . . never to let me. I am girl. You do not understand. I must stay with *famiglia*. My brother will go to prison. My grandmother she will die. I must stay.'

'And do what?' I ask with alarm.

'Look after my *famiglia*.'

I have to remind myself this is an old-world culture, with old-world sensibilities, and on top of that there are the deep bonds of loyalty created by the kind of life they lead to contend with, so it's no use saying, 'Do what *you* want to do,' and leaving it at that. So instead I say, 'I wouldn't know how to help you. Besides, they'll come and look for you . . .'

'I do not care,' she says defiantly.

'I do,' I say. 'You're young. What do you think they'll do to me?'

'I have helped you already. My brother want to kill you.' And with melodramatic flair she slashes a finger across her throat.

It has been a long time coming, this verification of all my fears. And in an instant all breath leaves my body, bursting from my mouth like a pneumatic spring; my legs give way and I buckle over. I only remain upright because Giovanna catches me, clutches me around the chest and pushes me back on the table. She hands me a small bottle of water. I drink. It is sparkling and the bubbles fire off in my mouth; the release of oxygen makes me light-headed. It takes a little time before I can say, 'What do you mean, he wants to kill me?'

Giovanna still has hold of my arm. 'These are bad times. People are . . . *paranoico*. You understand?'

I pull myself away and sit down on the bench. 'But why kill someone just because you don't recognize them in court?'

'You lie. *Turista*, you say, and then we see you in the prison with Mascagni. My brother . . . killed.' She motions behind her – he has killed before, she is saying.

'Does he still want to kill me?'

She shrugs, then says, 'I will tell. I will explain. But you must help me.' The quid pro quo of this deal is now much more persuasive.

'I don't see how. I'm using up all the money I have in the world. I might not even have a flat when I go back . . .' I pause, then thinking out loud I say, 'Maybe Alessandro will help?' I look to Giovanna.

Giovanna stiffens. 'No. No Mascagni.'

'Why? He might be able to help you.'

'No. *Prometti!* No Mascagni. Me and you.' She points back and forth. '*Per favore, inglese . . .*'

'OK. I promise,' hoping it's more just fear of what he represents than anything else. 'I need some air,' I say. I stand just outside the doorway in a dim cone of light. 'I'm supposed to be on holiday.' I say this as much to myself as to Giovanna.

'You are in Napoli,' she says, reminding me that this is a place which offers more than sun and baroque architecture.

I laugh wryly. Can this be so ordinary an experience here? I turn around to Giovanna. She is leaning against the splintering doorframe, arms folded. There is something fatalistic in her manner now: we have passed a certain point and things must be done. There is now an intimacy between us. Our predicament is providing a shortcut to it. I can feel myself wanting her. To connect with her somehow. To be passionate and with that assuage our fears, our loneliness, our confusion. I cannot tell whether Giovanna desires anything similar. Even if she does I doubt whether she will be able to tell it apart from all the other emotions she must be feeling. I look at her body through blue denim and white T-shirt. Her sexuality is youthful and supple. Mine is old and aches. We are very different.

'Look, Giovanna, if I agree, I want to know I'm in no danger. No danger at all. I want assurances.'

Giovanna steps towards me. 'I tell you. You are in no danger.'

'How do you know?' I ask.

'My grandmother,' she says solidly. Her faith in her grandmother's influence is so complete it is mesmerizing. It is as though the authority of her grandmother to guarantee my safety is transmitted through to her. I understand now how some people locked up in prison can remain so powerful.

'Is this because I helped her up the steps?' I ask.

Giovanna nods. The nod is firm and I understand that this little service has earned me one reprieve but no more.

'What are you going to do?' Giovanna asks.

'I don't know. I need to think about it.'

'*Grazie,*' she says and smiles. She then steps forward and rising on her toes kisses me gently on the cheek.

'We must go now,' she says.

'When will I see you again?' I ask. I'm not sure whether that comes from suddenly being kissed or because we are now joined in this pact.

'I will find you,' she says. 'We must . . . secret.'

But I have a better idea. Hiding the fact that we see one another is mad. Deception is the worst possible tactic with these people. We are bound to be discovered at some point and then how do we explain ourselves? Why not just become friends? Openly. Meet in the cybercafé, have pizza together. She must be allowed friends.

I say this. Giovanna looks at me sceptically, then says, 'You will have *cena* with *mia famiglia?*'

It is a joke; there is a rare smile. But I push it. I realize I need to meet these people, whoever they are. I need to meet them because I need them to know who I am. I don't want to be misconstrued. When they learn that I really am a tourist who happened to bump into an old girlfriend who happens to be married to a judge who happens to be presiding over the trial, and I'm *not* an informer, a spy, an enemy – then there will be no need to distrust me, which means I will no longer have to be fearful of them. I experience the sense of relief in advance. My stomach unwinds like spaghetti freed from itself by olive oil. My objective here is to be honest and therefore trusted.

This is what I tell myself. But then, I have to accept my fascination with these people runs almost as deep as my fear of them. I've met many types of people in my job, most of them wretched in one way or another: hard-drug users, criminal drug users, dealer drug users, alcoholics, abusive alcoholics, victims of abuse, the list goes on. But these people are of a different type altogether – people whose lives have been marked out by fate before they are born, whose ways of behaving and terms of business – *human business* – have been circumscribed by a perverse tradition. People for whom each act of personhood, at whatever age, is never a choice of self-improvement or self-abasement but simply about what level of gain, power and criminal activity is possible before you are killed.

Unless you are like Giovanna, who knows the only way to break from this is to break away completely.

'Giovanna, I can't help you if I'm scared. If I'm in danger myself.'

She looks at me. She doesn't want to understand anything that might be a refusal to help.

'Giovanna, we need to do something to build some trust.'

She looks down at the dry earth for a moment and then back up at me – she is listening now.

'I want to meet your grandmother again. Explain who I am. It'll make everything so much easier.'

She untangles my English in her head, staring beyond me, out into the night.

'It will mean we can meet and talk openly. I promise you it's a good idea. It gives us so many more options . . .' I know this is the case, but I also know it releases me from Giovanna's threats.

'It is not possible,' she says, but I can tell she is beginning to see the sense. And I am beginning to realize that she will be led by me if she can trust that I understand and am willing to help.

I do not say anything more. To try to persuade her would be in bad faith. This is as much, if not more, about me as it is about her. But then I add, 'It will make it easier to get you out . . .' I don't know why I say it. I only partly believe it. Naples is teaching me: survival is not about being straightforward. My stomach immediately rewinds. It is like cold spaghetti, sticky, tangled, dried out.

She looks up at me and repeats, 'It is not possible.' She goes back inside and the candlelight vanishes, leaving only high, dim starlight. I hear Giovanna shut the door behind her. She passes me. 'Follow.'

I turn. We set off through the vineyard. I cannot see anything around me. The night sky is dark blue. The long curlicue stems of the vines stroke my face. I follow the crunching of Giovanna's footsteps. In the midst of the vines it's so dark there is no light for my eyes to become accustomed to. I trip up. Giovanna stops. Her hand reaches back for mine. She leads me through the darkness. I feel a mixture of excitement – the thrill of her hand – and foolishness at my inability to walk unaided.

When we reach the road, moonlight picks out the Vespa. Giovanna climbs on and I hear the high buzz of the engine and the hard beams of the headlight shoot up the road.

'On,' Giovanna instructs.

I climb on. Giovanna blindly reaches behind to me, pulls at my arms and wraps them around her waist.

'It is not possible,' I hear her say again.

3

Last night at dinner Alessandro insisted my expedition for today should be Capodimonte. 'Wonderful; very important,' he said, a big, powerful hand on my shoulder. It was an awkward evening. I was late. Louisa was grumpy, assuming I'd rather extend my time with Giovanna than be early to spend longer with her. Remaining silent throughout dinner she refused to rescue me from the unbroken intensity of Alessandro's conversation. I was unable to concentrate, looking for an ideal moment when I could tell them, guilt-free, of Giovanna's request. It didn't come. As the evening progressed I was less and less able to look directly at Alessandro whenever he fixed me with his serious eyes. As I was leaving he turned to Louisa and said he thought I was unhappy – it must be homesickness, or love . . . There was a pause before his big laugh. I tried to make the heat an excuse, but I knew that that was my moment and I'd missed it. I could so easily have said, 'Look, something has happened,' and explained. But I didn't; in that moment all I could see and hear was Giovanna stiffening at the mention of Alessandro's name and saying, *No. No Mascagni.*

In my guidebook Capodimonte is described as Charles III's hunting lodge but it is more like a hilltop palace. Like most other Neapolitan architecture it is without flourish or ostentation, relying instead on its monumental size to amaze. It is now the home of Naples' art collection.

I have come mainly for the Caravaggio, but I'm in just the right mood for a long and aimless wander through the seven centuries of painting. Although I cannot forget my promise to Giovanna or rid myself of my feelings of guilt towards Alessandro, I am still able to relax enough to enjoy those paintings I like and study those that the guidebook tells me are important in the history of art.

The long galleries are busy with tourists, and even though I see the same faces from room to room, no one looks as if they are following me. I leave after a second stroll through the medieval section and sit in the gardens overlooking the city; I am not accompanied by anyone sinister. I relax enough to doze under the high palm fronds. After about half an hour I hear English voices behind me. I open my eyes and look over my shoulder. A young couple in their mid twenties have settled a few yards away; he has two cameras and is fiddling with lens and film; she is sketching the view before us, the panoramic slope of Naples down to the bay. We smile. I am tempted to introduce myself, make conversation, tell them of my experiences, but I fear they might think I'm strange. I do feel a little strange. I've been here for two weeks now, and there have been days when I hardly speak at all, and if I do it is slow, pidgin Italian or simplistic, stilted English. Even with Louisa – the only person with whom I get to speak normally – our sudden intimacy affects how we talk to one another, making it seem oddly private, a secret language almost.

I turn around and say 'hi' to the English couple. They say 'hi' back but do not make any other gesture towards further conversation. I lie back down and close my eyes.

Then the girl calls out, 'Are you staying in Naples?'

I twist around to face them, wishing I hadn't said anything now. She repeats her question.

I pause before answering. I am tempted to tell them exactly what has happened since I arrived, from sickness to meeting the sister of a Camorra killer. But instead I say, 'I live here.' I want to be thought of as more than a tourist. I don't want them to think we're the same.

'Really?' she says. 'Where?'

I can tell the truth here. 'In the Centro storico . . . the old town.'

'Wow. We're staying in Sorrento. I wish we'd been a bit more brave, actually. Naples seems so . . . so exciting.'

Without looking up from his camera her partner says, 'We were warned against staying in Naples.'

I don't say anything. Perhaps they were right to be warned off.

'Is it dangerous?' he asks.

'It's a myth,' I hear myself saying, but I'm not really listening.

'It always is,' he says, wiping the lens of his camera with a tiny soft green cloth.

What would they think if I told them what was happening to me? Would they believe me? Probably not.

'How long have you lived here?' the girl asks, smiling broadly.

I turn weeks into years. 'Two years.'

'What do you do here?'

I have to think for a moment. Teaching English as a foreign language comes to mind, but I decide on something a little more unique to the city. 'I work at the university. I'm studying the papyrus scrolls from Herculaneum.'

The girl elbows her boyfriend to pay attention. He elbows back, saying, 'Jules! Careful. My camera.'

Jules rolls her eyes for me to see. 'What are they about?' she then asks.

'What are they about? A lot of things. How to live mainly.'

She takes this in. 'What language are they in?'

'Greek. Ancient Greek.'

'And you can read that?'

I give a quick nod; it doesn't seem such a big lie as saying yes.

'Wow,' she says for the second time. 'What do they say?'

'They say you should try and live simply: food, shelter, company.'

'Sounds a bit boring.'

'I hadn't finished,' I say, and add my own, 'You also need love and danger.'

'Really?' She's much more excited by this. 'Is this why you live in Naples? Are you in love?' She is keen that I practise what I preach.

I laugh. 'I only learned this when I came here. But I suppose, yes, I am still here for those reasons . . .'

The boyfriend looks up, eyebrows raised. 'What's so dangerous?'

Good question. 'Nothing really,' I say. 'It's just an atmosphere thing.'

'Are you in love with an Italian girl?' Jules asks.

I laugh. 'No. She's English.'

She's a little disappointed by this, so I add, 'But she's married.'

The boyfriend ignores this and stands, aiming his camera directly at Vesuvius. He then shunts forty-five degrees right, adjusts his lens, then another forty-five degrees, followed by another focus adjustment. He's trying to cover the whole area from Vesuvius to Chiaia in three contiguous photos, and he's checking where the framing for each will begin and end. The girl returns to her drawing, then looks down at me.

'That's danger as well, I suppose,' she says after a while. 'Phil and I are married. I would consider it very dangerous to have an affair.'

Phil begins his triptych of the Bay of Naples; the girl and I halt our conversation so as not to disturb his concentration, his aim. When he is done he breaks the camera apart like it's a weapon.

'I didn't say I was having an affair,' I say. 'So I think the only danger here is my heart being broken.'

'What other danger could there be?' Phil asks.

Another good question from Phil.

'Her husband is a judge and Naples is a complicated place,' I say.

Phil is much more interested in the zip on his camera bag, which isn't working, than my understanding of the internal workings of Naples. He asks Jules for help. She opens it immediately, dumps it on his lap. He starts to reassemble his camera from parts inside the bag – it looks remarkably similar to the version he's just dismantled. He stands.

'I'm going to have a wander,' he says. Jules looks up at him, shielding her eyes from the sun. 'I won't be long,' he says.

Jules and I are alone. She tells me she and Phil have been married for two years. They work in the same call centre in Bracknell. He's mad about photography. She does an art class. Their life is a bit boring, she admits, but she can't think how it could be more interesting without disrupting the things she likes about it: namely her friends, their cat . . . She searches to lengthen her list but her thoughts elide into a sigh. She says she wants kids, but not yet. Part of her would like to live somewhere exciting before she does but she doesn't think Phil wants to. They've got a killer mortgage. This is their first holiday since getting married.

'Why Naples?' I ask.

'I thought it'd be romantic.'

'Is it?' I ask.

'S'pose,' she says with a smile.

Phil returns saying he got some good ones of Vesuvius, and it's time they got going. Jules packs away her coloured pencils and stands, brushing herself down. We say goodbye. Jules tells me to be careful, and I promise I will. She tears the leaf of paper from her pad and hands it down to me. It's the picture she's been sketching whilst we've been chatting. 'Keep it,' she says, 'it might be worth something one day.' I say, 'Thank you.' The bay looks like a pond, Capri a sleeping camel, Vesuvius an egg cup. I lay it on the grass beside me.

'And be careful,' she says, holding Phil by the arm, who is clearly keen to get away. 'Don't get your heart broken. Find yourself a nice Italian girl.'

I smile and say, 'I'll try.'

The bus ride back to the centre of the city is slow, hot, cramped. I want to sleep, but nodding off on a Neapolitan bus doesn't seem like a good idea. After ten long minutes I am unable to resist and my head keeps dropping. Only the straining of my neck when my chin hits my chest jolts me back to consciousness. I feel self-conscious. I try resting my face on my palm and digging my elbow into my ribs; at least it looks like I know what I'm doing. I fall asleep instantly. I dream of Louisa. She tells me off for falling asleep on a crowded bus, then lifts up my face with both hands and smothers me in kisses. I am passive, revelling in her kissing me.

The bus stops and I am jostled into wakefulness. We are at Piazza Dante. I am last out and I head for a bench in the shadow of a great palm. The air is thick and dirty with heat. It feels like Africa or the

Middle East. I am too exhausted to walk all the way back to Signora Maldini's, so I make my way to Piazza Bellini for a coffee and a beer. As usual there are few people around, despite the piazza being the only real spot for tourists to eat and drink alfresco. I slump in a chair, drop my head and close my eyes. I hear a waiter approach. I open my eyes and look up. It is Giovanna. Her face is in silhouette, hazy and diffuse. My pleasure in seeing her is not mirrored in her expression.

She hands me a piece of paper and says, 'But if they know you to help me . . . *capito?*' Her gesture is a finger slicing across the throat.

I do not have enough time to respond before she retreats across the piazza to her Vespa and is gone.

I open the note. *Come. 7 hour. 4 Via San Gennaro. Please, to understand, I must leave.*

It is a reluctant invitation. But I sense she can now see the advantages. Less reason for them to be suspicious about me; no longer any need to meet in secret; any escape plan can be implemented more quickly. All my reasons, yet part of me now regrets making them so convincing. The idea seemed right at the time. Set up some kind of meeting, start some kind of dialogue, begin some kind of process. It's what I've been trained to do. Develop a relationship, which usually begins with both parties having a face, then a name, followed quickly by more individual aspects: a smile, a laugh, a response in the eyes. All things which reveal the human.

But then this is not just about me, Giovanna, her family. This extends through me to Alessandro, his world, his responsibilities. Yet, Giovanna made me promise not to talk to him. That was a mistake. I've made these promises for over fifteen years and I've never broken one; patient confidentiality is central to everything I've done in the past. In order to help someone they must trust you – *must*. But this is not my role here. I'm on holiday, a tourist. I am not bound by ethics. But then I want to help Giovanna if I can; but I don't know how that is possible. I don't want to betray Alessandro's friendship, but I've promised not to involve him. Who loses most?

Giovanna was adamant I should not involve Alessandro; Alessandro knows nothing about any of this and in a week or so the trial will be over, and he will be in China with Louisa. I look at the note again: *Please, to understand, I must leave.*

If Alessandro and I share something, it is love for Louisa – an emotion forbidden to me. If Giovanna and I share anything, it is the need to escape our lives. This is what drove my decision to go and meet her in the first place. Escape means to live differently, and right now that includes danger. One of the five pillars of life.

So if I go, what should I expect? I realize I have no idea. From the moment I arrived in Naples everything has been impossible to predict. Yet as each day passes I realize that this is just the way the city *feels*; if it really was this way, who could live here? Native Neapolitans and no one else. I doubt a Camorra family is very different from all other families; a life of crime doesn't discount the domestic, the humdrum. The glamour, the myth-making, the romance – that is invented by Hollywood, newspapers, novels. I expect to find nothing more sinister than a powerful grandma lording it over a paranoid and suspicious family, predominantly female, and only Giovanna's fear as the point of difference from the families I used to meet every day in my work.

The address is in Forcella. At the far end of Spaccanapoli. The area is cramped, poor, dirty. Unwelcoming. I have strayed here once before, in search of Alessandro's old place of work, the Castel Capuano. Although I don't quite look the tourist this time, my presence is monitored by the young men sitting along the streets. They slouch in their seats so languorously I think they are going to slide off. But it's a pose, they are posturing – they are provocatively, don't-give-a-fuck relaxed. I criss-cross the streets to avoid them. Their dark eyes under dark brows follow me. I try to demonstrate clearly that I am not lost by displaying the note from Giovanna. I tell myself this is what I meant by a new experience.

I find the street after a couple of wrong turns and one dead end, all of which make my heart beat faster than I would like. It is the narrowest street so far. Not even wide enough for a small car. Laundry is slung lattice-like from window to window. The evening hasn't cooled down even a degree from this afternoon's North African heat. Even so, as I draw near to the address written on the note I shiver. A single shiver across my shoulders and down my back.

The Savarese are not just a local family gone bad, they are at the top of the murderous network of Neapolitan organized crime. For the last two hours I seem to have forgotten this fact, or at least what this means in real terms, and I have been playing out the scene in my imagination: no danger, real danger, but an intense, fascinating, unique experience.

I am surprised to find that no. 4 is a *basso*. I wasn't expecting splendour – there isn't one foot of potential luxury around here – but I had imagined at least an apartment, above street level, away from an opportunist hit or planned attack. But then maybe a *basso* is right. The Camorra is not international big business like the Sicilian Mafia, it is still working class, with a lot of street-level activity: drugs, extortion, protection.

The *basso* number is painted on the wall and therefore I know I have arrived moments before I appear in the open doorway. I'm going to make quite an entrance, poised on the threshold, the dark of dusk behind. I gird myself, or at least that's what I say to myself: gird yourself.

Giovanna is the first person I see, reading a book at the big table in the centre of the room. A woman I vaguely recognize from the court is at a stove. There is no sign of Eugenia Savarese.

Giovanna looks up when I knock dully on the open door. Her expression is serious, her eyes hard. She regrets ever arranging this. She wants me to go away. I try a smile. She swivels in her seat and says something to the woman at the stove. The woman turns, wiping her hands on a small cloth. I am not invited in. I stay where I am, looking down into the room. Narrow beds, four of them, line the walls. Above one bed there are three postcards. One is of the New York skyline. Jammed into the corner is a huge widescreen

TV with the latest computer console balanced on top. I don't imagine Giovanna is a big computer-games player.

Eugenia Savarese appears from behind a screen at the rear of the *basso*. There must be another room back there, a bathroom probably. She seems less frail in these more intimate surroundings. Her face still looks like ancient sun-baked bark. There is something very invitingly tactile about it, as if you could tell something of her character by running your fingers over the deep lines in her skin. She doesn't smile, but her hand welcomes me in. I enter saying, '*Buona sera, buona sera, grazie, grazie.*' Giovanna pulls a chair out from under the table for me and gestures for me to sit down. I have my back to the door. A dangerous place. Giovanna then goes to the small refrigerator and pulls out a bottle of Coca-cola and sets it down in front of me with a glass, after which she slumps back down into her chair like a sulky teenager. The woman, her mother I guess, returns to her cooking. I was right: an ordinary, humdrum family. I relax a little.

Eugenia Savarese addresses me. I don't understand a word. The language doesn't even sound Italian, it is more a cross between an Eastern European language and Arabic: sharp, raspy, angry.

Giovanna looks at me. 'My grandmother want to know . . . you are friend of Presidente Mascagni?' She shrugs – she knows the answer so the question bores her. She returns to her book. It is *Jane Eyre*. I am unaccountably moved.

'Tell her I'm an old friend of Signora Mascagni.'

Giovanna repeats what I said without even looking up from her book.

Eugenia Savarese nods. She also smiles. She finds her granddaughter amusing. Buried in a book, translating for us – she is not old-world Camorra.

I pour the Coke into the glass and drink. I am addressed again. Giovanna interprets. Her grandmother wants to know what I think of Presidente Mascagni. Big question. I think for a moment and then say, 'Charismatic.' I want to avoid specifics. There is no need for a translation. Eugenia nods; studies me. She knows 'charismatic' doesn't particularly suggest allegiance nor is it a judgement on competence or even trustworthiness. I think she likes it as an answer. I feel a bit safer. Our little exchange suggests that she is not a stupid woman and we could talk reasonably if we really had to.

There is a noise behind me. Eyes trained on me now look past me. I swivel round. Two boys stand in the doorway. They look like old-fashioned hoods. Thugs. One knocks me as he enters. The place might be small, but I know it's deliberate. Eugenia does not reprimand him as I'm expecting her to. I stand nervously. I want to seem polite, ready to be introduced, shake hands. Eugenia says my name then 'Mascagni'. The two repeat it back, then look at me. I don't recognize them from the court. Both swing seats from under the table and sit down across from me. Giovanna's brothers, I guess. She got all the beauty, clearly. Both have small eyes, thick lips, big-boned noses. Not twenty-first-century faces. They are twins. Almost identical in appearance, completely opposed in manner. One is sitting like all the young men I saw on my way here, slouching, legs wide open, arms hanging insolently over the back of the chair. But his brother – he is more tightly wound, limbs closed, jaw clenched. He is perturbed by this stranger in his home. He wasn't warned. He doesn't like surprises. He shares an intensity with his older brother Lorenzo.

Giovanna eventually introduces them. Salvatore and Gaetano. '*Miei* brothers.' 'Her stupid, annoying brothers' is the way she says it. Ordinary sibling irritation. Gaetano is the intense one.

I say, '*Ciao.*' I've sat before hundreds of boys their age, but none has ever wriggled on his chair to get comfortable and decided that removing and tabling a gun would be the answer. It is Salvatore and it's obviously done for my benefit. It is a display of power. He is showing off. He is both ridiculous and almost moving in his need for a reaction, and it is this which stops me panicking. He doesn't want to frighten me, he wants to impress me. I nod to show I've seen it, appreciate its meaning. It is a small revolver. A neat piece of hardware with which to threaten and pistol-whip.

Suddenly the room is full of screaming, high, intense, deafening. I look around. It's not Eugenia, it's not the silent woman at the stove, and it's not Giovanna. It's Gaetano, motionless on his chair, looking blindly ahead. The command is, if not clearly, then unmistakably, to remove the gun from the table, from sight. Salvatore jumps up, swipes it away and secretes it back wherever it came from.

It is clear where the power lies between these two. Salvatore's posturing is nothing compared to Gaetano's display. One's a thug, the other obviously a sociopath. That's not a diagnosis, but if I had seen that in a therapeutic situation, I would have instantly advised sectioning him.

The whole episode has made me very uncomfortable indeed and cold sweat runs down my back. I wipe my brow, glug down my Coke. I decide it's probably best to leave and I am about to stand and thank everyone, when Gaetano pulls himself up to the table and lights a cigarette. He performs this simple action with a grand swirl of arms, hands, fingers; an unexpectedly flamboyant movement from such an originally constricted position. I cannot work him out, but then it occurs to me that he is merely trying to mimic Sonino, volatile and threatening, foppish and showy. That must piss the family off. Emulating the enemy. But it helps me. It reminds me he is just a boy.

Gaetano regards me silently for a moment or two and then turns to Giovanna. She is ordered to ask me something. Her lip curls; she doesn't like taking orders from her brothers and goes back to her book. But then Gaetano leans over and grabs her bare upper arm. She tries to shake him free but he begins to squeeze. Her arm blushes around his grip. He repeats his order. A question. To me. He points with his free hand. A jab. Then to her: '*Traduci.*' Translate.

I look to Eugenia. I expect her to stop this, but she just watches as her granddaughter silently resists. I can see Gaetano's fingers pressing in, maximizing the pain rather than the pressure. His nails are long and he concentrates on making them cut in. Blood appears and a slow line runs down her arm. He doesn't stop. There are tears in Giovanna's eyes. Her face is turned to me, away from him.

Unable to stop myself, I say, 'Jesus! Let her go!'

Gaetano quickly releases his grip with a high arc of his arm. Giovanna runs behind the screen and slams a door.

All eyes are on me. 'You were hurting her,' I say, trying not to betray how shocked I am by my intervention.

Gaetano says calmly, '*Mia sorella.*' I detect a smile. It is a precise smile. Not menacing or sarcastic. A smile of fact. His sister. Not my business.

Salvatore is enjoying himself, chuckling almost, absently playing with the joystick on the computer-game console. He likes the way his brother wields power.

Giovanna returns with what looks like a bandage wrapped around her arm. She sits back down defiantly, flashing me a look. She's furious and embarrassed, yet at the same time pleased that I have witnessed the brutality she has to contend with every day, contend with unflinchingly if she is not going to be annihilated completely.

I just don't understand why her grandmother didn't stop it. Maybe she didn't even realize what was going on – too short-sighted or something. But I don't think so. With the older brother in prison, Gaetano is the man of the house and he cannot be countermanded.

Salvatore stands and goes to the refrigerator. As he passes Giovanna he ruffles her hair. She shrugs him off. I don't think his gesture is meant to be mocking, looking to add to her humiliation with a pretend show of affection, tenderness; he wants her to get over it. It's just Gaetano being Gaetano.

I am about to stand and make my exit when Giovanna asks, 'What is your work?'

I wonder: was this the question she was ordered to ask? If so, why is she asking it now? Is it because she has now decided to and therefore it is no longer an order? Or is it because not to ask it at all means trouble later – that she cannot disobey indefinitely?

'Psychotherapist,' I say, realizing that this is when I should have lied about my job. I know this before they've even had a chance to spot the similarity with the Italian and make the translation in their heads.

Even the woman at the stove turns and mutters, 'Psichiatra.' I don't see the point in correcting her. I notice that it is Gaetano who is the most affected by the information. He knows he has most on display and most to hide. He gives me the flick. It is not particularly aggressive: the back of his hand almost stroking the underside of his chin before the snap of the wrist. But it is a signal of disrespect. I decide I don't care about Gaetano, it is Eugenia's reaction that concerns me, how this plays with her old-world Neapolitan superstition. Am I regarded as a kind of mind reader, brainwasher, and therefore dangerous to Giovanna? They must know she has dreams of escape. She must have threatened to leave in moments of despair. A tantrum of ultimatums. I look at Eugenia. It is her job to keep the family together. She is impassive. I know this means nothing. This is not an ordinary family. Ordinary families argue, brothers and sisters kick each other under the table, calm down after parental reprimands. But not this one. This one is vicious, where the power lies with an insane teenager because he is male and cruel. I need to leave because I'm shocked, angry, powerless.

I know the thing to do is withdraw meekly, implying I understand the signals, where the power lies, but that would be too cowardly and cowardly is not the same as fearful, which is what I am right at this moment. And it's a fearfulness very different from all the paranoia I've felt over the past two weeks, different from my reactions to Giovanna's warnings. I am fearful because I have been witness to a level of dysfunction that is beyond my experience and because I now understand unequivocally why Giovanna wants to escape this world. It is not the murders, the kidnapping, extortion and racketeering; it is the lack of love – she will not be loved in this world, not ever. This is her family – grandmother, mother, brothers – and here she is abused.

I stand, look round the room and shake my head. I don't say goodbye.

The moment I'm free of the basso I break into a run. I have to, I need to get away. Ordinary fucking family, I say to myself breathlessly, who was I fucking kidding!

I am halfway along Spaccanapoli before I stop running. My breath is short, shallow. I look back. Moonlight softens enough of the shadows for me to see quite a way. The brothers are nowhere to be seen, just a few shopkeepers packing up, sweeping their narrow doorways. I walk on quickly, flicking my fingers on my thigh. What should I do now? Action has to be taken, I know that much. I should hail a cab and go straight to Louisa's, invite myself to dinner and insist on them hearing the whole story from beginning to end. I'm going to have to imply that it was Alessandro's suggestion that I sit in the public gallery which started all this; he needs to feel responsible. I can then insist whatever we decide to do must be handled sensitively and swiftly . . . and most importantly without Giovanna knowing he is pulling the strings. Yes, I must talk to Alessandro. It is the only sensible thing to do. I can't help Giovanna on my own; it's madness to think I can.

At Piazza del Gesù Nuovo a Vespa sails past me and circles widely, stopping ten feet away at the obelisk in the centre of the square. It is Giovanna. She wrenches the Vespa onto its stand and props herself on the seat. I stop where I am. I can see the blood seeping through the bandage around her arm. For the first time I feel like it's all my fault. I cross over to her. 'Sorry,' is all I can think to say.

'I tell not to come.' This is not said sharply and it is followed by a fatalistic shrug. I sense she doesn't blame me. She then says, 'The woman,' she points behind her. 'That is me.'

'The woman?' I'm not sure who she is referring to.

She mimes hands in sink, washing up. 'That is me.'

I don't understand straightaway, but then I realize she is telling me, if she stays she becomes her mother, the woman at the sink in the *basso*: silent, almost invisible, there to cook, to serve. She wants me to understand her fear is not the physical pain she might suffer at the hands of her brother – *that* she can handle – it's the horrendous eradication of her self that she fears.

211

I do not know how to respond. I want to say I don't need any more convincing but I can't afford to raise her hopes; yet she hasn't repeated her request for help, she hasn't issued any veiled threats. She is just standing there looking at me. I'm probably one of the few people from the outside who have witnessed her life and right now all she wants is to know that I understand. After that I can decide whether or not to help her. I will *want* to help her. She is appealing to me in this way now because she knows about my job. She's appealing to me as a professional.

'I don't know how to help you, Giovanna . . .' I say honestly.

She looks across the piazza to the serrated stone façade of the Gesù Nuovo.

'I do not have money, *passaporto*. In Napoli, the *campagna*, everyone know me.'

This fact is unassailable; her escape has to be far from Naples, out of Italy.

I pause for a moment and then say, 'Let me talk to Signor Mascagni.' I say it pleadingly because I need her to understand that's all I can do.

Her hand leaps to my upper arm, fingernails sink into my skin. 'No Mascagni.' Her eyes are fierce.

'OK, OK,' I say, whipping my arm away.

Giovanna drops her head. She is sorry. She knows to deserve help she must be different from her family and she has just resorted to the same tactic of persuasion as her brother – deliver obedience with pain.

'I am sorry,' she says mournfully. 'They like me.'

I don't understand. I study her face.

She thinks for a second then reverses the sentence, the meaning. 'Me like them. Me become like them.' She shakes her head.

This is another reason she must leave. She cannot become like them, her brothers, her family. But if Lorenzo is convicted, something happens to her brothers and her grandmother dies, she will be expected to take over. Her succession and her responsibilities are taken for granted. A network of warring families will assume this and act accordingly. It seems ridiculous right now, looking at this lovely young woman, but if this happens her life instantly becomes about a different kind of survival, and she will have to take decisions that will change her or kill her. There can be no deferment.

'Giovanna, you must let me think about what to do. I don't have much money and I don't know how to get you a passport. But I promise I will try to help if I can.' I hear myself, my tone of voice, reasonable, sensible, and I know however much it might reassure Giovanna, there is little I can do.

'I will find you,' she says, kicking the Vespa off its stand.

My wave is weary, barely making it above waist height. The Vespa circles the piazza and disappears.

4

'How easy is it to escape a life of crime if you come from one of these Camorra families?'

I ask this matter-of-factly, over a glass of whisky, after my surprise appearance on their doorstep, inviting myself to dinner. Alessandro is sitting at his piano casually playing Chopin. Louisa is sitting in an armchair, legs tucked up under her. I am leaning rather uncomfortably in the curve of the piano like a lounge-bar singer – a crooner.

'It is hard,' is all Alessandro says, watching his hands on the keyboard.

'But some must decide it's not for them and lead different lives . . .'

Alessandro looks up at me. 'Yes. But the families are strong.'

'So how do they do it? Escape?'

'They must leave.'

'Is that difficult?'

'It is difficult to leave your family whoever you are.'

I nod; I see I'm not going to get a flood of information without asking more direct questions.

Louisa says, 'Why are you asking?'

Once again I am confronted with telling the truth or remaining discreet. For the first time I opt for the truth. I leave out all the details and merely say I've been approached for help.

Alessandro stands, takes his whisky glass from the piano and refills it. 'You must not be involved,' he says gravely.

I am surprised that he is not more surprised by my admission. I say nothing.

He stares at me, his small eyes are serious. 'Do you understand, Jim? You must not be involved.'

'I understand. But what do I do?'

'Do nothing.' He is firm.

'But what if they make contact again?'

'You must say you cannot help,' he retorts irritably. He is losing patience with my questions.

'I'm sorry,' I say.

Five minutes ago I would have counted on the praying gesture to follow an apology of any sort, but this is too serious for clairvoyance and he states firmly, 'Do not get involved with this girl, Jim. In any way.'

I didn't say it was a girl. I look at both Alessandro and Louisa quizzically.

'I didn't say it was a girl.'

Alessandro smiles, but there is no warmth. 'It is the Savarese girl. Naples is not an anonymous city.'

I have to think for a second. How does he know this? What does him knowing this mean? I look to Louisa and then back to Alessandro. I can only think that he heard this from courtroom gossip, prisoner to lawyer to judge. And although this might be entirely innocent, I am forced to think about Alessandro in a new way, or rather I'm forced to alter my judgement of him as somehow uncontaminated by the world he works in. And even if it's just courtroom gossip, it means that in principle there can be unofficial communication between Alessandro and the Camorra. I then remember my first day at the trial, Alessandro chatting to Lorenzo Savarese in open court. Surely it's not this that Giovanna is afraid of: if I talk to Alessandro he might tell Lorenzo? Perhaps she doesn't understand where his loyalties will lie. Maybe she doesn't really trust loyalties. Which makes me think about my own behaviour. I should have gone straight to Alessandro the moment she approached me. He is angry because he feels I have been disloyal. He has explained to me how serious and how important this trial is to him. And I risked jeopardizing it. He had to find out through courtroom gossip, something he makes a point of ignoring, but this time was unable to because it was about an English tourist, a friend of his wife, and the sister of one of the accused, the most important of the accused.

If there is a right time to confess that I've just come from her home, it is now, but I don't, I can't. I am stopped by an altogether different fear. Firstly, I don't want to make Alessandro any angrier with me, but more importantly I don't want him to feel any more disappointed in me. I recognize it as a father–son thing, and the absurdity is not lost, but it still stops me saying anything. Instead I try to laugh it off with a 'Well, she's too young for me anyway.' I'm not sure exactly what I say, but it has a hollow ring and nothing is said in reply.

For the first time I feel that I have outstayed my welcome. My apology hasn't solicited any reassuring response, neither of them has offered to refresh my drink and I now feel more like an intruder than a guest. Even Louisa, yesterday more lover than friend, makes no effort to assuage my obvious awkwardness.

'I should go,' I say and head for the door.

'Louisa . . .' Alessandro says, and motions with his eyes that she should see me out. He then offers me his hand, one hand, and says, 'Goodnight.'

In the hallway I whisper, 'Oh god, I'm so sorry. I didn't realize . . . He's really angry, isn't he?'

'He's not angry. He's tired. He feels responsible. And it's not something he really needs right now.'

'Just tell him to forget I said anything.'

'It's not that easy. He doesn't want you to have to deal with this. He wants you to enjoy Naples. It's very important to him.'

'Will he do anything?'

'I don't know, but you won't be bothered any more. Trust me.'

'Louisa, you must tell him not to do anything, please. I promised Giovanna.'

'You promised Giovanna what?' she asks sharply.

'That I wouldn't tell anyone she asked for help.'

'She shouldn't have asked you for help in the first place then.'

She sounds for a moment as though she is more piqued that there is another woman in my life than because of any danger I might be in or any inconvenience it's causing her husband.

'For god's sake, Louisa!' I say. 'Get some perspective.'

She is shocked by this. We both look to the piano-room door. Neither of us wants Alessandro to think we're still talking about it.

'Look. You have been his guest. You are my friend. He will feel it's his duty to sort it out.'

'I shouldn't have said anything.'

Louisa warms up a little. 'Don't worry. It's nothing. It'll be fine. But I do sometimes think we don't realize quite how hard his job is, what he has to contend with.'

'Promise you'll make sure he doesn't do anything.'

'I promise I'll try. But you have to promise you'll keep away from her like he said.'

'Louisa, you don't know what her life is like . . .'

'That's the deal.'

I don't want to promise this. I'm not sure I can. Louisa looks at me hard.

'What?'

'Promise.'

'I promise.'

'Good. Now go home and we'll see you tomorrow for Sorrento. We'll have another game of Monopoly and everything will be forgotten.'

We kiss on the cheek and Louisa lets me hold her tightly, aware of how suddenly alone I feel. There is no sexual undercurrent to this embrace, it is about friendship, caring, safety.

I walk out into the night to the muted sounds of a Chopin nocturne being played. It is brooding, melancholic, not the choice of an angry man. I stop and listen, exhausted and emotional. If I lived in this city, I would need to play the piano, and I'd probably have to play Chopin; who else could produce such emotional intensity without truly troubling the soul?

5

It is five-thirty. The sun is low. The shadow created by the Bellini monument looks like a Giacometti figure lying across the piazza. Louisa is waiting for me, sitting at a table reading a magazine, her hand absently clasping a bottle of beer. I can't see Alessandro around. I watch Louisa check her cigarettes, elect to smoke one.

'I have a surprise for you,' she says as I approach. She lets a lazy plume of smoke out of her mouth. She seems relaxed, back to her old self. I can only hope things are equally relaxed with Alessandro.

'What?' I ask. But before I get an answer I see Louisa's eyes look over my shoulder. I swivel around.

Alessandro, a bundle of files stacked in his arms, is dashing towards us; his official driver has parked the car on the pavement. He is out of breath by the time he reaches us, but far from sounding or appearing old, unfit, he seems youthful and vigorous, his breath-lessness caused by high levels of energy, excitement. Perching on the edge of a chair and dropping his files on the table, he reminds me of a fanatical student between lectures, stopping to discuss some point of Marxist theory – its brilliance, prescience, logic – with other like-minded, if somewhat less passionate, fellow students.

'Everything all right?' I ask, looking for any sign that last night has continued to be a problem.

Alessandro turns. 'I apologize, Jim. But I must go to Rome this evening.' He turns back to Louisa, and for the first time since we've met he speaks to her in Italian while I'm present. The information sounds grave; his tone is ardent. Louisa nods, taking it all in at the speed it's being explained. When he's finished he is on his feet, files gathered up. With his free hand he pats me on the shoulder. 'I will see you tomorrow evening, Jim. Take care of my wife.'

I haven't time to assure him I will before he is halfway to the car.

'What was all that about?' I ask, while ordering a beer from the waiter.

Unfazed by her husband's dramatic entrance and exit, Louisa says, 'It's a long story. But it's very important. It might mean the prime minister has to resign.'

'What's it got to do with Alessandro?' I ask curiously, not realizing his influence reaches to the capital.

'He used to work in Rome. For the government. Anti-Mafia and all that stuff. He's always dashing off when there is a crisis like this. I think that's what he'd love to do: bring the government down.' She laughs.

'It's a right-wing government, right?'

'He hates all government. It can get a bit irritating. Everything, everyone's corrupt.'

'Even the judiciary?'

'He says there are a few good ones. I think because they're like him, against everything.'

My beer arrives; I take a long drink. It's been a very hot day, the sunlit streets scorched dry, the shadows dense with humidity; I have spent most of the day desperate to dive into the sea.

'What's my surprise?' I ask.

'You've got me all to yourself,' she says, surprised I haven't guessed by now.

'Are we still going to Sorrento?'

'God, yes. The city's unbearable like this. We'll go by boat.'

I deny myself the projection of a night of passion and instead ask her about Alessandro and 'my problem'.

'Have you seen her again?' Louisa asks, her manner subtly changing, instantly reminding me of last night when both she and Alessandro seemed suddenly hardened to me.

I am relieved at being able to tell the truth for once. 'No.'

'Then it's fine,' she says abruptly.

'How do you mean "fine"?' I push.

'I mean "fine", Jim. I made him promise. Please, leave it. In Naples it is sometimes best not to ask questions.'

I feel well and truly warned off.

Louisa suggests we have pizza – it's too hot for anything more, she says.

She calls the waiter and orders two *marinaras* along with more beer. She then tells me that she spoke with her mother this morning, who threatened to visit.

'I found out when she wanted to come and said it was then we were going to China,' she says mischievously.

'I forgot you were going to China,' I say.

'Two weeks,' she says without any great enthusiasm.

'I thought you were looking forward to it?'

'I am, sort of. But I can't quite see what we'll do there. You're not really allowed to explore by yourself, and Alessandro will meet all these boring people.'

'Well, it'll be a lot more interesting than my life. However much I resist it, I'll have to go back to London at some point.'

'That's another thing. You won't be here when we get back.'

She's right. I can conceivably last until they go and for some time after that, but not until they return.

Our pizzas arrive and we tear them into four slices. It is only seven-thirty when we have finished eating, the pizza followed by zabaglione.

'What are we going to do now?' I ask.

Louisa smiles. 'I've got a little excursion planned.'

We walk up Via Santa Maria di Costantinopoli past shops full of old prints and photographs of Naples. I am keen to stop and have a browse but Louisa drags me on. Just beyond the Archaeology Museum we sit down at a bus stop. I tell Louisa I could spend days looking at the Apulian vases. She shrugs – chipped pottery is obviously not her thing. A couple of buses pull up before Louisa says, 'This one,' and we board, electing to stand although the bus is almost empty. Ten minutes later we are standing alone on a bridge, with the city below us. I must have crossed this bridge a number of times, with Giovanna on the Vespa, going to Capodimonte, but I don't remember the city falling away like this. Posters tied to the railings prevent me from looking through. Louisa leads me to a door. A lift. Night is falling as we descend.

At the bottom we walk out into a long, busy street. There are hundreds of young Neapolitans hanging out, perched on Vespas, chatting, holding hands, couples clasping each other, groins pressed together. First glance tells me it's a poor area, without even the small tourist or student economy of the old town. The ubiquitous Vespas are older, rustier; none of the clothes, if still stylish, are new.

'Friday night,' Louisa says, elbowing me to look in the direction of two young lovers, slightly separate from their pals, kissing passionately.

'Where are we?' I ask.

'Sanità,' Louisa says. 'Isn't it romantic?'

There *is* something romantic about the place. The walls are high, the air heavy, every shadow inlaid with young people in love. The atmosphere is abundant with their passion, their ardour, trembling in the heat. The whole scene could be the perfectly detailed set of an opera – Verdi in modern dress.

Louisa takes my arm and we walk slowly down the centre of the street. We quickly become indistinguishable from the other courting couples. We are silent, unless Louisa chooses to point something out, which she does merely by saying, 'Over there,' trusting I will instinctively know what she is looking at. I think to myself, if this is the height of my romance with Louisa I will be satisfied, yet I cannot deny that I still want to pull her into the shadows and kiss her with the unhurried and unselfconscious passion of the young Neapolitans around us. I want her pressed against the high walls, pressed to me. I want to feel her thigh rise up my leg as the sheer physical closeness forces our limbs to wrap around our bodies with greater and greater eagerness. I want all this because it is this that is happening around us and I am envious – envious of the multiplicity of sensations being felt compared to the meagreness of ours. I cannot tell what Louisa is thinking but then it was her idea to come here, to bring me here. Perhaps after two years of marriage she wants to remember what it's like to walk arm in arm with someone new through the back streets of Naples on a Friday night. I know as much as she that the thrill of romance is gone for ever once intimacy becomes familiarity. And I also know that as we get older romance is undermined by the rapid route we take to sex. So maybe Louisa is trying to recreate that more innocent time. I certainly feel the delicious desperation of sexual potential I last felt years ago: a girl I want next to me, her arm in my arm, her head on my shoulder – everything still waiting to happen.

I am impressed and grateful. It is an imaginative solution to our situation. We are having a kind of acceptable affair, without the deception, the betrayal, the guilt. I pull Louisa closer to me. She reciprocates with a nudge of her shoulder. A light, warm breeze wraps her hair across her face; she flicks it away.

We must have walked in a circle because we are now back at the lift. We take it up to the bridge, then walk to the bus stop. I pull away a couple of posters and look through the railings to Sanità below.

'There's a lot of love down there,' I say, then add musingly, 'young love . . .'

Louisa joins me, saying, 'We're not old though, just not young like them.'

'I think it's a common misconception about age. Age is not the problem, it's experience. If I had to choose between ridding myself of years or experience, it'd be experience every time.'

'It's different for a woman,' Louisa says evenly, 'but I know what you mean.'

The bus pulls up and we hop on. It takes us all the way down to the port. The air is instantly cooler by the sea. The breeze strong and insistent. Louisa has to pull her hair back to read the timetable.

'We're OK, it's at nine o'clock. We haven't missed it,' she says, then after looking at her watch she glances across the harbour. 'There it is,' she says spotting the dark shape, dully lit, heading towards us.

We sit down on a bench and watch the ferry pull in, a crust of surf in its wake. A small stream of people disembark. We board alone and take a seat in a large, empty cabin. I suddenly feel as young as the lovers in Sanità: the two of us sitting on these basic benches, on a Friday night, in the summer, with nothing really to do but chat, laugh and while away the time. I haven't felt like this for years – not since I was a teenager. The easy enjoyment of hanging out with a friend. And it occurs to me that this is what Louisa has been talking about; it is this that she's going to miss when I'm not here. With nothing to do, no responsibilities, no boundaries or curfews. We are teenage best friends. Right now we could be sitting in a bus stop, on a bench in a park, outside a youth club, on a train, anywhere. It just so happens that we are sitting on a boat crossing from Naples to Sorrento. We stare out of the window over to the dark hump of Vesuvius.

'It's funny living near a volcano,' Louisa says. 'It's not normal, is it? I mean how many people do? I wonder whether it changes you. They say it's why Neapolitan men are so fiery. Radioactivity from the volcano. I don't know whether it's true.'

'It's probably more symbolic than anything else,' I say without much thought.

'That's what I think.'

'But I can see how it might affect you. Just its presence. It's not extinct, is it?'

'Nope. Could blow at any time.'

'What about all the people who live up there?' I point to the high necklace of lights around it.

'Barbecue.'

I laugh out loud.

The high cliffs of Sorrento come into view, sheer and angular. The port is small: a few fishing boats, a luxury yacht.

Sorrento itself is a long walk up steps which rather oddly end in the outside dining area of a restaurant. I think we've come the wrong way but Louisa assures me she knows where she is going.

Tourists are everywhere. English is being spoken by everyone. Louisa and I head for the taxi rank on Piazza Tasso. Louisa spots a driver she knows and calls out to him. We all climb into his gleaming, dent-free taxi. We are at the house in ten minutes. It takes us another five minutes to open it up. We work quickly; I obey orders. When we are finished we head out to the garden with a cold bottle of white wine. We sit opposite each other in the garden chairs. The sea breeze doesn't reach up here, but the night air is so much cooler here than in Naples. The sky is light blue. I offer to put on some music but Louisa says if there is one joy in not having Alessandro around it is not having to listen to classical music.

'Don't you like classical music?' I ask.

'It's all right, but not all the time. I like music you can dance to.'

'I don't suppose Alessandro is a big dancer.'

'He has his moments, but it's very old fashioned.'

Louisa stands and demonstrates. She wiggles her hips with her elbows tucked into her body and shoulders slightly raised, and chugs her arms back and forth like a child pretending to be a train.

'Sexy,' I say.

'But that's me doing it,' she says. 'Alessandro is more suave.'

She sits back down and looks at me. 'Jim? Tomorrow . . . can we go dancing?'

I don't know what to say. Dancing is never very high on my enjoyment agenda.

'Do you know somewhere?'

'There are loads of places. They'll be full of tourists, the music will be dreadful, but let's get really drunk and go anyway. I haven't been dancing for ages. Please, Jim.'

'I'll need to get very drunk.'

'Will you try and kiss me?'

'No,' I say. 'I never make the first move. You should know that.'

There it is. My first direct reference to our sexual past, my first unashamedly provocative response to her unashamed flirtation.

'I don't remember you being so coy, Jim.'

'You kissed me first. Don't deny it.'

'Did I? I don't remember.'

This wounds me. It's said so discardingly. The details of our first kiss not even worth searching her memory for.

We sit in silence. I want to demonstrate how pissed off I am, but I can't think of anything to say or do which won't seem ridiculous. I look at my watch. It's only just past eleven.

'Are you tired?' she asks.

I shake my head. All our teenage intimacy and ease has disappeared. But then there is still plenty happening here that I remember from those years. One moment thinking she likes me, the next being frozen out for no apparent reason. A kind of capricious dismissiveness. I trained myself to ignore it, which was clever because I soon learned it didn't matter. You can't judge a girl on how she plays with your feelings. Ultimately, 'Will you try and kiss me' is heaps more important than any sudden coolness.

'Are you tired?' I ask.

'A little, but Alessandro will phone soon. He'll worry if I don't answer.'

I pour us some more wine and say, 'It really is beautiful here,' for lack of anything else to say.

'Boring more like.' It's said sharply but without petulance.

I am a little taken aback and ask, 'What's the matter?'

She shrugs non-committally.

'Come on,' I urge.

'Nothing,' she says, but then adds, 'It's hardly exciting, is it, my life here? Alessandro has to rush off to Rome. It's exciting for him. It's all new to you. But to me it's . . . I'm nothing more than a Cheshire wife.'

'In paradise.'

'You get used to it.'

'You've got your course.'

'I'm not really interested in it. I'm doing it more for Alessandro than anything else.'

'What do you want to do?' I ask, knowing full well she doesn't know and that's the problem here.

She shrugs again, but this time it's plaintive, resigned.

'It seems we're in the same boat then,' I say trying to add a little empathy to my concern.

Louisa looks over at me. 'I know what you're thinking. You're thinking I need a baby. I don't. I'd like one one day but not now.'

I don't contradict her even though it was not what I was thinking. I have enough therapeutic nous to let her project her thoughts onto me.

'Alessandro doesn't want children. He says he's too old. But then there was that Italian woman who had children in her sixties. If we had one now he'd be seventy when they were fifteen. That's fine. This part of the world, you live a long time. Do you think he should give me a baby, Jim?'

I am no longer a therapist so I decide to say what I feel, which is prompted by watching a small tear drop from her eye and splash into the wine which she has nestled in her lap.

'If I was married to you I'd let you have whatever you wanted.'

She wipes away a second tear with a slender finger – a windscreen wiper across her cheek.

'But you're not married to me,' she says evenly. 'Anyway, it's a horrible world to bring a child into, isn't it?'

It's not an argument that will defeat instinct but it'll do for now. What surprises me is the overwhelming drive I have to fuck Louisa right now, as if a powerful instinct to have children has been awakened in me. It feels entirely different from the more general desire I have for her. And its strength is disconcerting. It wouldn't matter if it was over in a couple of seconds, the point is to come in her – just that.

'What's the matter?' Louisa asks interrupting my thoughts, staring at me.

'How do you mean?' I say, taking a slug of wine to bring me back to my senses.

'You look strange.'

'How so?'

'I don't know. Mad.'

I laugh. 'You make me mad.'

The phone rings. Louisa turns to look inside the house. 'That'll be Alessandro,' she says wearily.

'Aren't you going to get it?'

'Let him wait,' she says, and standing up she yawns, arms stretched wide, back arched, rising onto the balls of her feet. At the top of the yawn she almost topples forward.

'He'll hang up,' I say.

'No he won't.' She places her wineglass carefully on the ground and goes inside.

It is a quick call. A few minutes. Clearly not prolonged by endless whisperings of love or mutual refusals to hang up on one another.

'How is he?' I ask when she returns to me.

'Oh, excited. There is a photo of the finance minister, De Barco, kissing Luciano Graco. He used to be one of the most powerful men in the Camorra. He's dead now. His boat was blown up. There has always been a rumour it was political.'

'What'll happen?'

'Not much. He'll resign and that's it. Nothing changes.'

'Alessandro must find it frustrating.'

'I don't think so. There is something about the Italians – they don't actually want too much change. They might say they do, but they don't. Everything they do, everything they are, is so inter-woven with the way of life – to change one thing is to change it all, to change themselves.'

I am impressed by her analysis of the Italian psyche. 'Maybe you should take a course in psychology,' I say.

'They are a simple people,' she says wistfully.

The night is a little cooler now. It is time for bed. It is not late but the interminable heat throughout the day is exhausting. Louisa leads me through the house, up to the room I occupied last week. In the doorway she wraps my arms around her and rests her head on my shoulders.

'It's nice to have a hug in this big old house.'

I hold her gently, positioning my legs awkwardly so that if I get an erection she cannot feel it.

'Let's have a seriously lazy day tomorrow,' she says quietly.

'OK,' I say.

She pulls herself away and kisses me; it's on the lips, light and quick.

'*Buona notte.*'

'Goodnight,' I say and close the door, not wanting to watch her walk down the hallway to her room.

Louisa is up when I wake. I can hear her downstairs, rattling around. I am tempted to stay where I am and wait for her to come and wake me. But the light is so bright it's giving me a headache. It's going to be a very hot day.

Louisa is sitting at the kitchen table with coffee and *cannoli*. She is wearing white pyjamas and a robe.

'Morning,' she says brightly, and fetches me a cup and a plate.

'So what's on the agenda for our extremely lazy day?' I ask.

'There is only one thing you can do on a day like this.'

'What's that?'

'Go swimming.'

'I don't have a costume,' I say.

'Where we're going, you don't need one.'

My first reaction to this is not what you might expect: a rush of erotic excitement. The sight once again of the body of this beautiful woman, the thrill of her naked proximity, is not my first thought. No. My first reaction is anxiety. My first thought is that when Louisa last saw me naked I was as thin as she is slender, and I was happy with myself and unselfconscious naked. But I no longer have the body of a young man. The change is not great. Yet any impression of natural muscular firmness is gone. I'm on the slow descent to physical atrophy. I have a gut where once I had a stomach. All fat is now obstinate. There is the odd grey hair on my chest.

'You're not shy, are you? I don't remember you being shy,' Louisa says, smiling.

I hold my stomach. 'I'm not as trim as I once was, darling.'

'Don't worry, we'll take big towels to protect our modesty.'

'My modesty *needs* protecting these days. I'm sure you're as lovely as ever.'

'I wouldn't bet on it. It's ten years on for both of us remember.'

'I'd lose a comparison test.'

'Shy and vain. Interesting combination.'

'I'm not vain.'

'Of course you are. You're concerned about how you look. That's vain.'

'Then we're all vain.'

'To me, vanity is when a person cares as much, more even, about what they themselves think than how other people see them.'

'Are you vain?'

'Women can't be vain. We're required to care more about what other people think than ourselves, and if we manage to overcome that and care more about what we think, then that's a virtue, and vanity is not a virtue, is it?' The precision and simplicity of her logic are impressive.

'I suppose not,' I say.

'Anyway, don't worry. I'm married to an old man. You'll look great to me.' Her expression is friendly, warm, not in the least provocative or flirtatious.

'Have you heard from Alessandro this morning?' I ask.

'No. He'll be in meetings all day. He'll call when he's on his way home.'

'Do you think he'll be back today?'

'Maybe. I don't know. Don't you like me all to yourself?'

'You're more dangerous than the Camorra.'

She laughs. 'That's funny. Can I tell Alessandro you said that?'

'I don't think that's a good idea, he might ask what I mean by it.'

'What *do* you mean by it?'

'You know what I mean.'

She mock-glares at me, then lights a cigarette. 'We'll need to buy lunch, water and magazines before we go. I suppose you need factor 100 like me?'

However cutely it's said, the only thing I take out of her exaggeration is that I will have to rub suntan oil over her back. I remember yesterday, crossing the bay on the boat, when for a moment my desire for her fell away as I experienced the purer enjoyment of our friendship. But it was short-lived. Everything since, to a greater or lesser extent, at least for me, has been sexually charged. And it's painful. I realize I want to fuck Louisa, so much so I can barely contain myself.

'Jim?' Louisa disrupts me from my reverie.

'Yes,' I say, drinking cold coffee to bring me back to myself.

'You were doing that mad look again.'

'Sorry. It takes me time to wake up.'

We stop at a small shop in the little town of Meta and buy prosciutto, mozzarella, tomatoes, bread and two big bottles of ice-cold water. At the news-stand Louisa buys Italian *Vogue*, *Harpers*, and I buy the *Herald Tribune* and *Guardian Europe*, and a pen for the crossword. It is all placed in Louisa's massive beach-bag. I am careful that the condensation on the outsides of the bottles of water doesn't smudge my newspapers. Louisa has also packed two bottles of suntan oil: factor 15 and factor 6. The two towels *are* big and rolled up in traditional fashion. We head towards the sea. It is a steep walk. Small, perfectly whitewashed houses shadow us from the high morning sun. Far below us is a little bay, protected by high cliffs, and a beach with huts and a small café. There are a few people sunbathing, a few in the sea.

'We're not going down there, are we?' I ask alarmed. 'We'll be arrested.'

'Wait,' Louisa tells me.

We turn a corner and the whole of the bay becomes visible. Directly across from the beach, separated by a timber jetty, there is a smaller beach, without huts and café – and it's packed. Louisa points. 'Private beach. Public beach.'

We cross the top of the cliff, over the road that zigzags steeply down to the bay. Occasionally the breeze carries up the shouting of the Italians below. Louisa breaks off the road and into dusty scrub. Three feet to my right the drop is sheer and high. The sea at the bottom crashes roughly over large grey rocks. After five minutes or so we start to descend; we angle our bodies against the slope to keep our balance. I take the bag from Louisa. It's heavy and cumbersome, and I lose my footing from time to time. At the bottom we have to pass through a narrow passage of rock. It is the last little test for the intrepid beach explorer. It is a squeeze and again I'm made aware of my extra pounds. On the other side we find ourselves in a tiny cove. Nothing but rocks, big rocks, with large, smooth surfaces. The sea looks relatively calm, the jutting cliffs acting as natural breakers. I step up onto a rock and look down. Clear blue water. Crisp even.

'Do you like it?' Louisa asks.

'It's great.'

Her forehead is covered in sweat. Her hair damp. I wipe my forehead dry with the back of my forearm; Louisa does the same.

'By the time you get here, all you want to do is dive in, right?'

'Right,' I say.

'OK then . . .'

'OK . . .'

Louisa grabs the bag and tiptoes across the rocks to a place she clearly knows well. 'This is the best place.'

I follow. The smooth surface of the rock is square almost, with enough room for two to sunbathe. It is slightly angled down to the sea, facing up to the sun. The occasional strong wave laps at its edge.

Louisa pulls out a towel, snaps it open.

'Hold it like this,' she instructs. I am to hold it against her and look the other way. She will undress and dive in.

'And what about me?'

'I promise I won't look.'

I do as I've been told. I can sense motion from her, arms high as she pulls off her top, a wiggling as she pushes off her skirt.

The whole enterprise is quick and she's in the sea. I drop the towel. Louisa is a few yards out, treading water, looking up at me.

'Cold,' she says excitedly. 'But lovely.'

Despite the transparency of the water, the only clue she is naked is her bare shoulders. My erection is instant.

'In you come.'

I need the water to be cold.

'Turn around then.'

Louisa swivels instantly onto her front and begins to swim out. Her bottom is occasionally just visible. I undress quickly and dive in. The freezing temperature nearly stops my heart. By the time I have recovered Louisa is by my side.

'It's freezing.'

'You'll get used to it.'

We are naked, a foot apart.

We are naked, a foot apart.

We are naked, a foot apart.

The truth of it resounds in unison with the gentle ebb and flow of the waves surrounding us.

'Now what?' I ask, licking the salt water on my lips.

'We swim.' She swivels again and is off, but after a few strokes turns on her back.

I grab hold of the rock and watch. Then I push off in pursuit. I catch up quickly. We are now almost past the cliffs. Out in the Gulf of Naples. The sea is rough, choppy. White surf breaks around us. The current is strong. Louisa places a hand on my shoulder. She wipes her nose. Her hair is flat to her head, stringy across her face. No artifice. No disguise. She is absently beautiful. I am transfixed. I must express it. 'You are . . . just the most . . . incredible . . .'

'Not now, Jim,' she interrupts.

We swim back to the rock and I am instructed to turn around. I face the open sea. I am a man adrift.

'OK, your turn.'

I turn back. Louisa is wrapped in a towel, holding the other towel open for me, looking away. I pull myself up and take the towel from her.

We sit down on the rock. Louisa pulls a magazine from the bag and lays it out in front of her and gingerly turns the pages with damp fingers. I stare out to sea. After a few minutes Louisa takes out the suntan oil and applies it to her legs. I look away when she reaches her thighs.

'Will you do my back?' she asks, tapping my arm with the bottle.

I take it from her and she turns her back to me, loosening the towel so I can apply the oil more easily.

'I'll do you next. You probably need it more than me.'

I feel very self-conscious. I am nervous that I might not be doing this with any particular style, that I'm lacking the erotic touch. As I smooth oil around the sides of her back I can just feel the shape and weight of her breasts.

'Your turn,' Louisa says when she senses she has been adequately covered.

We both spin round. Louisa is very matter-of-fact about the application, slapdash even. I say thank you when she's finished.

We share a bottle of water. It is now lukewarm. Louisa has angled herself so her back faces the sun. She clutches the towel around her. It is not the most relaxed position for sunbathing. She flicks through the magazine contentedly.

'Have you ever been here with Alessandro?'

'He's been here, but it's my place.'

It is the Sorrentine equivalent to the small chapel in Naples.

I apply oil to my feet, ankles, calves and lie down on the hot rock.

'You could be grilled on this rock.'

'I know. If you need respite, you can always sit in the shade over there.' She points at a configuration of rocks facing away from the direction of the sun forming a pool of shade. I grab the *Guardian Europe* and a bottle of water.

Louisa says, 'I'll join you in a bit and we can have some lunch. Take the food with you.'

I tiptoe over the scorching rocks. I hope Louisa is not looking –

I am awkward, unsexy, too English. When I settle in the shade I relax a little; the direct sun was making me faint, Louisa making me nervous. I can just see her from here, hunched over, towel around her, hair falling forward, reading. She is absorbed. I lay the newspaper out in front of me. There is an article on immigration. Most non-Western European immigrants want to go to the UK because it has the best reputation for human rights. France and Germany are known to be too severe in their application of the Refuge Act and Italy doesn't have any policy at all, in the hope, the article says, that the immigrants will just move on. Italy's main problem is the Albanians crossing the Adriatic. But whilst not refusing them entry, they make no attempt to legitimize their asylum status. It is a clever ploy, understanding that people want that legitimacy. A few might be happy to work illegally, but most want security, recognition of their plight, the legal sanction to start their new life.

Sweat drips from my forehead onto the newspaper. To my right I hear Louisa shuffling around. I look over. She is standing up. She waves at me. I wave back. She then removes the towel and is naked. She flaps the towel out to spread it over the rock and lies down, disappearing behind the edge of the rock. During those few seconds, the distance between us did little to obscure her body; the sun's position refusing to cover her with shadow or hide her in silhouette. Her nakedness was clear, precise. My lungs fill with yearning. My cock, caught under the heavy, damp towel, throbs upward. I return to my newspaper, to a piece on Portugal's economy. My aroused state quickly subsides. After twenty minutes or so I call over, 'Your bum'll burn.'

Louisa's head appears. 'We can't have that, can we?'

'No, sir,' I say.

'Are you hungry?' she asks.

'Are you?'

She sits up, her back to me and drags the towel around her. I watch her make her way daintily over the rocks, one hand holding the towel at the tuck, just above her left breast.

I unfold the newspaper and spread out the food: the prosciutto wrapped in greaseproof paper, the mozzarella in a tub, the tomatoes clinging strongly to their thick vine. I break the bread in half.

'Did you bring a knife?' I ask as Louisa makes herself comfortable, cross-legged before me.

'Of course.' She searches at the bottom of her big beach-bag and pulls out a small knife. She then takes the mozzarella out of its tub, shakes it dry over the sand with outstretched hand. It is a glistening, smooth ball of white. It has that innate tactile quality – you just want to knead it. I am faintly envious as Louisa holds it steadily before her and slices it. I wrench the tomatoes free of their vines. It requires a firm tug, and the release is satisfying. Louisa shares out the sliver-thin prosciutto, two slices each. The hardest and least enjoyable job is cutting the bread. The knife is too small, the crust as tough as rind. Inside, however, it is wonderfully porous and tastes like olive oil. We make identical sandwiches, the prosciutto, followed by the cheese, topped off by thick slices of tomato, dextrously cut by Louisa.

We eat in silence. Juice from the mozzarella and the tomatoes, soaking through the bread, runs down our chins and drops onto the newspaper. Sweat drips from our foreheads. The water we drink is now almost hot. We both absently read bits from the newspaper in front of us. Despite the deliciousness of the contents, my favourite part of the meal is the crust on the bread. Like the toughest rind, it has to be pulled apart firmly with hands and teeth. It has a beautifully subtle burnt flavour.

Finished, Louisa wraps up the debris in the newspaper and plonks it in her bag.

'I'm going to sunbathe for a bit longer; then shall we go for a swim and head home? It doesn't do to stay out in this heat too long.'

I nod, still chewing away at my bread.

Louisa makes her way to the rock, and in a swift movement, her back to me, drops the towel, spreads it out, and lies down. This time the position of the sun affects my view. Half her long, slender body is in shadow, the other half is golden, bright and shimmering.

She is mesmeric. I am tempted to join her, lie out naked next to her on the rock. But I remain where I am looking absently at the crossword, writing in the first words that come to mind regardless of whether they fit. I then doodle in any available space. Time drags. It is a strange kind of torture, sitting here, Louisa fifteen feet away. I try to think about Alessandro in Rome, his eyes serious, arguing the case to bring the government down, knowing on Monday he will have to make a decision about the trial: Sonino's testimony, the fate of the nine. Does he have any room in his mental life, I wonder, to worry about how much I desire his wife? What would he think of this situation if he knew about it?

If he trusts her, then I imagine a certain pride. A younger man coveting his wife. But does he trust her? Does he trust me? I suppose in this kind of situation trusting one of the parties is enough. Her betrayal with me needs us both. I ask myself, am I trustworthy when it comes to Alessandro? It's not something I've thought about. Our friendship may be only recent but there is a bond there. He likes me and I like him. And despite the disparity of our ages, experience, achievements, he takes an interest in me with the same honest energy with which he seems to approach everything in his life. So could I fuck this man's wife? Phrased like this the answer is, of course not.

But then, perversely, Louisa is no longer this man's wife. Or even a briefly loved ex-girlfriend of mine. She has become, over these last few weeks, so highly individuated she makes me unsure exactly who I am. Around her everything is just a little less real than she is. Even Alessandro, with his patrician demeanour and occasional judicial irritability, can appear less certain when in her company. She has the unassailable assurance of a person whose mind, body, spirit are in perfect accord with their self-image. Without knowing it, Louisa is who she thinks she is. And compared to the rest of us, that's a psychological coup.

So the question stands: would I make love to Louisa? And the answer is, that's up to her. Or in more clichéd terms, her will is my command. My resistance to her thus far has had little to do with self-control on my part and everything to do with lack of opportunity to succumb. I feel like a husband assuring his wife his fidelity is in fact, based on the fact he's not been offered any chance to corrupt it.

I call over, 'Is it time for a swim?'

Her voice is low, muted, barely audible over the soft splashes of the waves on the rocks.

'I can't hear you.' I stand. It's involuntary, responding to the need to hear her better. But I can now see her, naked, stretched out on the rock. Her body is cream-coloured against the hard grey. Her face is turned away; slowly she looks my way.

'Taking a peek, are we?' she murmurs, as if roused from sleep.

I don't know what to say. But I don't move or look away. The ridge beneath my towel is evident. I try to shift it, pressing it upwards, flat to my stomach. I want her to say something; indeed I want her to want me to reveal it to her. I almost feel a kind of projected pride in what looking at her does to me. I want her to understand that it's an erection of significance, and due to her. It is hers, so to speak. It sounds erotically corny in my head, but I can't deny it's the conversation I'm having with myself.

I drop my towel. My erection springs forward. I pause, and then turn and walk into the sea.

Louisa watches from the rock. She is sitting up, perfectly posed to reveal nothing. I invite her in and turn away. I hear a splash behind me. We swim in silence, avoiding proximity. There is now a strong current pulling out to sea. Part of me wants to give in to it. Drift to Capri, down to Sicily, to North Africa. How long before you die, I wonder. Not long. Drowning is supposed to be an easy death when you give up the struggle: painless and quick, a return to the womb.

Louisa calls over, 'Are you ready to head back?'

'Are you?' I ask. She waves me out of the water.

I heave myself up onto the rock, retrieve my towel and wrap it tightly around my waist. I then stand on the rock holding out Louisa's towel for her, my eyes turned away. I don't give her time to take the towel from me, but instead wrap it around her myself, threading my arms through her arms and fixing it just above her right breast. Despite all the glimpses of nudity, hers and mine, this is the most intimate moment that's passed between us. I am startled by a kiss. It's quick, but firmly on the lips. I don't even have time to respond before Louisa is gathering up our things, shoving them into the beach-bag, informing me there is no need for us to change into our clothes, we can avoid the main road, and we're off, squeezing through the cliff face and climbing up towards the town. The walk back is exhausting – the afternoon heat unrelenting. There is no shade. The earth is rocky and scorched.

We enter the house from the lemon grove. In the kitchen we sit at the table and drink ice-cold water. Louisa's hair is stringy; her lips dry, a little cracked.

'I'm just going to check the answerphone,' she says and hops up, disappearing into the hallway. I hear an electronic-sounding Alessandro, then silence, then Louisa's voice. She and Alessandro are talking. Louisa is matter-of-fact; there are no soft, warm hues to her words. She is not telling Alessandro how much he is missed or loved. She pads back into the kitchen.

'He'll be back tomorrow morning,' she says.

'What's happening?'

She shrugs, then says, 'I think it's siesta time, don't you?'

We head up the stairs and stop at my door.

'I'm just going to have a shower and then I'll come in and see you.'

I hook my finger over the edge of her towel, tight across the top of her chest, and pull her to me. She pulls away, twisting free and stepping back.

'Have a shower,' she repeats.

My shower is short. I wash all the dry salt off my skin. I wash my hair, almost hard from the coarse seawater. I can see the bedroom door from the bathroom. It remains closed. When I turn off the shower I hear Louisa's. I dry myself thoroughly and lie on the bed. It's too hot even for a sheet. I feel self-conscious and adjust my position so my stomach looks flat. My cock is hard and it hurts. Louisa can't be confronted with this. I rip off the sheet and drape it over me, bellowing it for air. The room is bright, too bright. I pull down the blinds. The sun now enters downwards through slats. The blind is like a vast grater and the light is lemon zest shaved into the room.

I hear the shower stop in Louisa's room. I'm half expecting her to decide against taking this any further, the shower reviving her loyalty, responsibility, her good sense. I will not blame her. As much as I want her, my desire is accompanied by anxiety. My stomach is a mixture of the fluttering of butterflies and dragonflies. I grab hold of my cock. I realize nothing can stop me fucking Louisa if that's what she wants. I am not in control of this. The moral issues are irrelevant. Alessandro is irrelevant.

Time passes and Louisa does not appear. I close my eyes; closed eyes increase the coolness in the room. I turn onto my side and press my head into the soft pillow. If she's not coming, I will sleep. All my energy has suddenly seeped away.

I hear Louisa enter. I half open my eyes. She is naked beneath her diaphanous robe. She smiles and with a flick of her hand gestures I should shove over. I shift across the bed and she lies down, backing into me. She pulls my arm around her. There is a sheet and a robe between us. My cock is pressing into her. Louisa moves her hand from her hip and under the sheet. She grabs my cock and moves it. It is not simply practical because her hand lingers there, sexually alert to it. But like me she wants to sleep. We press ourselves closer together. I want her to take off her robe. I tug at it and with a twisting movement wrestle it off her shoulders and arms. I kiss her back once and that's it: we sleep. For me it is light, disembodied; I am present on the bed but not always necessarily myself. I wake often but cannot rouse myself fully. I am constantly aware of Louisa. She is still and silent.

We sleep for two hours. When I wake properly, Louisa is facing me. Staring at me. She smiles and shifts forward for a kiss. Our first kisses are short, tender, slow. Within a few seconds they become more serious – probing, penetrating. We shove sheet and robe away from us. The light is soft, sepia-like. We are clear in our nakedness but not stark. Louisa rolls on top of me, but the position is awkward and I roll her back; she laughs. I climb on top of her. I stare down at her, over her body below me.

'Do you know what you're doing?' I ask.

'Yes,' she says with certainty.

My cock is pointed down at her like the stylus of a record player.

'Open your legs,' I say.

'Wait.' She pushes me off.

I lie on my back; Louisa turns on her side, her hand around my cock.

'Do you know what I used to love most when we had sex before?'

I shake my head. I want her to tell me.

'You used to make me do things to you. Do you remember? God, it made me so horny. Being told what to do. You didn't seem to care how young I was or that I might not have done that stuff.'

'Sorry,' I say.

She squeezes my cock hard. 'Don't say sorry.'

'I'm sorry.'

She squeezes it again. 'I like someone masterful,' she says mockingly.

'Do you want me to tell you what to do now?' I ask, looking for direction, clearly no longer masterful at all.

'I know what to do now.'

She *shunts* herself down the bed and takes my cock in her mouth. Her hair shields her face. I pull it back; hook it over her ear – I want to see her face. She looks up at me. I remove her hand from my cock; her lips fold in and out as her mouth slides up and down. She is kneeling over me, her body at right angles to mine. I rub my thumb across her nipple. It is hard, resilient. I slide my hand down her stomach and between her legs. I hear her breathe out as my fingers press into her. Louisa stops. My fingers are still inside her. I shift my thumb over her clitoris. Her body spasms slightly. One of her hands is holding her stomach. I pull her towards me. Without confusion or direction, she sits astride me and my tongue replaces my thumb. Her taste is rich, bitter, good. I hear her sigh. My tongue flicks in accordance with her sighs. I then bury it inside her, my nose replacing my tongue on her clitoris. She is smooth-walled, slippery, warm. My face is damp, smothered by her. Her hips rock back and forth. I slide out from under her.

'Stay where you are,' I say. She is kneeling, facing the wall.

I move around her on the bed. Her back is lightly tanned, whether from today or from years of cautious sunbathing I don't know. I kiss the back of her neck, her shoulders. I then press my cock between her legs, careful not to enter her. Louisa rubs herself against me. I cup one of her breasts with my hand. My mouth is close to her ear. I can feel her hand between her legs, looking to press my cock inside her.

'Wait,' I say. I pull back and then guide myself inside her, as far as I can go. I stay still as Louisa works herself back and forth in a slow circular motion. When she draws herself up too much, my cock dips out. She says, 'Let's do it straight.'

She lies down and I climb on top of her. She guides me in, raising her bottom to meet me. We fuck, eyes open. Occasionally looking down to where the action is. Either way we are bearing witness to our transgression and this adds to our pleasure. It enables us to imagine what Alessandro would see if he were to walk in. And this turns us on. His ignorance is a turn-on. We fuck harder. We are becoming ruthless. We want extra pleasure because the risk we are taking fucking in his house means we deserve it. And getting away with it means we deserve it.

Louisa groans and arches her back to press down on me. I push in as deeply as I can go. There is no need for movement now. We are as close as we can get. The pleasure is in the strain to stay like this – a fuck suspended.

'Don't come,' she says breathlessly. 'You can't come, you know that?'

I nod. The moment is broken and we slide apart. We take a second to get our breath back.

'I need to be on top to come,' Louisa says then.

'I remember,' I say. 'You want to come now?'

'We don't have to stop just because I come. That's a boy thing.'

She positions herself carefully. She has to grind down on my pelvic bone, her arms reaching to the wall. I just arch up slightly. The sound of her orgasm is freer than last week when she was in the other room with her husband.

Despite what she said, something has ended with her orgasm. I roll her onto her side and fuck her from behind but I can sense the lack of urgency, of fervency. I pull out.

'How do you want to come?' she asks.

'I want to come over you,' I say.

She looks up at me.

'Is that all right?' I ask.

'I want you to.'

I kneel between her legs. But balance is a problem. I kneel astride her.

'Do you want me to do it?' she asks and grabs my cock before I have a chance to respond.

My orgasm is almost instant and the come reaches her hair, splayed out over the pillow. Secondary loads hit her cheek, her breast and across her stomach. The sensation is terrific, electric; I feel it right down to my toes. Louisa wipes her cheek.

'Watching that makes me . . . I don't know. I wish it was inside me. I want you to come inside me.' She shudders.

'That would be a terrible mistake, you said so.'

'I know. I'm being stupid.'

I lie down next to her, my cock jumping with small spasms.

'Are we going to regret this any second?' I ask.

'Regret is silly.'

'What about Alessandro?'

'I wanted to have sex with you. He'll understand.'

I sit bolt upright. 'You're going to tell him!'

Louisa laughs. 'Of course not.'

'Jesus,' I say, dropping back onto the bed.

'Jim. Don't panic. He'll never find out. He trusts me.'

'Then why did you do it?'

'Like I said, I wanted to have sex with you.'

It is evening. We sit outside. The lemon grove sharpens the gentle breeze. We are drinking white wine. Louisa reminds me that I promised to take her dancing. I glare. There is no awkwardness between us. We showered together, kissed, played about. We are having fun in our betrayal. In Alessandro's big house. I am playing his records: Rubinstein playing Chopin. Perverse perhaps, but it is what I am doing. Louisa comes over and sits on my lap, her wineglass held at her chest. Her top is loose. I push it off her shoulder and lean down and take her nipple in my mouth. It hardens. She wraps her arms around me. I move across to the other breast. It is an awkward position but the pleasure overrides that. I stop, replace the straps of her top.

'That's the thing about being with someone new, you just want to do it all the time,' Louisa says, standing up.

She unzips her skirt and it drops to the floor. 'Come on then.' She signals for me to do the same. I stand and drop my trousers, my shorts.

'Sit back down.'

I do as I'm told. Louisa positions herself across me. We fuck. One position. A slow grind. Deep. I have to stop myself coming as she does. It's over quickly. Louisa then pulls herself off me and kneels between my legs. I am in her mouth for a second before I come myself. I withdraw a little shamefully. I should have warned her. Louisa rocks back, picks up her wine and drinks.

We dress. I can smell Louisa on me. The phone rings and she disappears inside. She is gone for a while. I cannot hear anything beyond the Chopin. Alessandro will recognize it and probably approve. I reflect on what I've done. Two weeks and they will be in China and I'll be . . . somewhere, probably home . . . London.

And then I have their annual visits to look forward to, an afternoon with Louisa. Suddenly being back in London doesn't seem so bad, if once a year I can spend an afternoon in bed with Louisa.

Louisa appears, eyebrows raised.

'Well, that was harder than I thought it was going to be. I kept thinking he could sense something. He said he was missing me terribly. More than usual.'

'Did he mention me?' I ask rather selfishly.

'He said at least I wasn't going to be lonely because of you.'

'But you don't think he suspects anything?'

'How do I know?' It's not snappy, but she is uneasy.

'It can end here,' I say, 'and we just forget it ever happened.' It is only as I say this that I realize I'm taking for granted that this will be ongoing, at least while I'm in Naples. I desperately want her to indicate she feels the same.

'I suppose,' she says. 'God, I feel awful.' She clutches her stomach. She looks up at me. 'What about you? Are you all right?'

'I don't know what to think.'

Louisa looks away. 'It's not as though I've slept with anyone new, is it? That would be worse, wouldn't it?'

'I doubt Alessandro would see it like that. He might think sleeping with me is the worst thing in the world. We've all become such good friends.'

'Don't say that. Please.' She looks horrified. 'Maybe we shouldn't do it again. Forget it ever happened, like you said.'

'If that's what you want.'

'What do you want?'

'I'm not answering that.'

She doesn't push me, instead says, 'Anyway, he'll be back tomorrow and it'll be all back to normal. The three of us. He told me to tell you we'll all go to Ravello.'

'Oh good,' I say with little enthusiasm.

We have dinner in a small restaurant in Piano de Sorrento. We both drink our way through the small talk we have adopted to stop us endlessly going on about how we feel, what we should do, etc. By eleven o'clock we are back to normal: just friends, excited, high, having fun. We stroll through the town laughing. Try to blag our way into a private party in a restaurant. Louisa is wonderfully Italianate; I am a little embarrassed. She wants to dance, she says. I shrug whenever I am addressed, finally saying, '*Si, si,*' when I am asked whether I want to dance too. We are let in. It's a family affair. A birthday. Clearly nice lower-middle-class Italians, neither gangsters nor professionals. What is so surprising is that once we're in – and it's taken some tough negotiating by Louisa – we're greeted like old friends. I am hugged and kissed. We are given seats and served food. Dessert. *Cannoli.* I dig in, eyeing the dance floor, which is sparsely populated. Like in England, young girls dance with men who look like their fathers. The music is tinny European pop. Louisa is clearly keen to dance despite this. We are handed a glass of grappa each. I knock mine back. I notice people calling Louisa by her name.

'Do you know them?' I ask.

'No, but they know me. They know Alessandro.'

'Won't they think this is weird – me and you together like this?'

'They'll say we're having a story . . .'

I don't understand and lean closer. 'They'll say what?'

'That's what they say here. Not "they're having an affair", but "*una storia*". We're having a story.'

I'm too drunk to completely get it but I sort of do and quite like that this is how it would be described, how she's describing it.

'Come on, let's dance,' she says, rising from her seat.

I grab her arm. 'I promise I will, but let's wait until we're going to be less conspicuous.'

'Promise?'

'Promise.'

She seems content and sits back down. But it's only a matter of minutes before the dance floor is crowded and we're up. In the meantime I've managed to knock back, much to the surprise of our hosts, three more grappas.

'The Italians aren't big drinkers,' Louisa whispers into my ear as we sway rather uncomfortably to the music.

I sense that Louisa wants to dance rather than dance with me. However, she still wants me there, on the dance floor. I move back and jig as best I can. I tower over the other men. Italian men dance well: good centre of gravity, expressive arms. I don't lack rhythm; I lack the imagination to know what to do with it. Louisa smiles, her face bright with enjoyment. Every now and then she reaches for my hand and we conjoin. Alcohol has done enough to my inhibition to allow for a little sexy dancing when Louisa requires it. I wonder what Alessandro would think of this if he walked in. I wonder what these people think, people who know him. I look around the room. No one is taking any notice. Most are engaged in intense conversation, argument, their hand gestures as elaborate and as expressive as those of the people on the dance floor, more so.

After fifteen minutes or so, I back away from Louisa apologetically and I retire to my seat. She feigns a forlorn look but then closes her eyes and drifts off into the centre of the small dance floor. Various people introduce themselves to me. We laugh at the fact that I'm *inglese*. And don't speak any *italiano*. I'm told time and time again Signora Mascagni is *bella*, *bella*; old men place their fingers to their lips, and with a kiss, kick them away – old-time appreciation for such beauty. I seem to be being congratulated for having such a woman. I am drunk enough to play along, to swell with pride. Tonight she is mine. Alessandro's name is mentioned now and again, but in what context I cannot tell.

Louisa plonks herself down beside me, exhausted. 'That was great.'

'Are we ready to go?'

'Let me just have some water.'

I pour Louisa a glass. She drinks it down.

'Have you had a good day?' she asks as if we'd been to Disneyland or something.

'You could say that.'

'It's been lovely, hasn't it?' And with that she leans forward and kisses me. It's a kiss of drunken passion. And she *is* drunk. Her tongue is thrust into my mouth. She doesn't care who's looking. I pull away.

'Jesus, Louisa, we've got to be careful.'

'Don't kiss me then . . . ever.' Her drunkenness has taken offence.

We stare at one another.

'Scared,' she says. 'I'm not.' She fixes her eyes on me.

I return her look.

'If you don't kiss me now, you'll never fuck me again.' Her expression changes from irritable and petulant to patiently waiting. She wants an answer or some action.

'You're drunk,' I say, looking around. We are being watched. Our standoff is being clearly read by Sorrentine clairvoyance.

'People are looking,' I say, hoping this will bring her to her senses.

'Embarrassed to kiss me in public?'

I don't know what to do because I know to kiss her right now, the way she wants to be kissed, is a big risk – these people know Alessandro. But I can't risk Louisa sticking to her ultimatum if I don't kiss her.

I grab her, kiss her.

There is some applause. This, finally, brings Louisa to her senses. She pushes me away.

'Time we went home,' she says.

We walk home unsteadily. The night air makes us reel. We use each other for support, but this only makes matters worse and we drag each other over. We only begin to sober up as we enter the house. I am sure Alessandro is back, but Louisa is certain he is not. I want to search the house, but am told not to be so stupid. We sit at the kitchen table drinking more water.

'You took a big risk in that restaurant,' I say.

'I don't want to talk about it.' She is firm.

I nod.

Then she says, 'I want to sleep with you tonight but no sex.' There is something regretful in her voice.

'Are you sure that's such a good idea. Alessandro's due back tomorrow morning. What if he arrives early?'

She shoots me the same look as earlier in the restaurant. She doesn't want to be contradicted in this. She knows what she's doing, or rather, what she has to do.

I wish *I* knew.

'He won't,' she says to placate me. 'Anyway, I'll wake up early and move.'

'What if you don't?' We are teenagers and Alessandro has become a parent away for the night.

'We'll leave the blind up and then the light will wake us.'

We make our way upstairs and into my room. Louisa disappears for a minute or two and returns in her pyjamas. We climb into bed and assume the same position as early this afternoon: Louisa backs into me, pulls my arms around her. She arches her head round.

'Kiss me goodnight then.'

I lean up and do so. 'I could be so in love with you, you know?' I say.

'Don't say that, Jim.'

I lay my head back on the pillow. Louisa squeezes my arm, locking herself in more tightly. I respond, pulling her in to me.

'Goodnight, Louisa,' I say.

'Goodnight, lover,' she says dreamily.

The words echo once around my head and I am asleep.

6

I wake at nine, unbothered by the light. Louisa is gone. The white pillow next to me has an imprint of her head, an inverse marble representation of her profile; there are two stray hairs. I get out of bed, pull on my trousers and go and have a look for her. She is in her room. It is dark. She is naked, asleep on her front, facing away, the dark sheet pulled up over her bottom. Her pale back is like a pool of moonlight. I stay in the doorway. My senses are too dulled to hear Alessandro.

'Louisa likes to sleep,' he says, from behind me.

I spin round, the sudden motion making me dizzy.

'Alessandro!'

He laughs. 'I surprise you?'

I look into the room; Louisa is rousing herself. 'Aless?' she calls faintly.

Alessandro passes me and goes into the bedroom and shuts the door. I am frozen, still dizzy. I try to listen. They are speaking Italian; it doesn't sound particularly fraught, accusatory. Louisa then laughs. I go back to my room, close the blinds and lie back down on the bed. That was a horrendous moment and so innocent in comparison to yesterday. I begin to feel sick. I shut my eyes. I will wait until I'm called for. I do not wait long. There is a knock at the door and Alessandro walks in.

'Do you want coffee, Jim? Louisa is a little . . .' He rolls his eyes and his head to signify dizzy, hung over. 'I will make it. Come down when you are ready.' He closes the door gently, appreciating that my state must be similar to his wife's.

I have a quick shower and go downstairs; avoiding him would be more suspicious, I feel. But then what is suspicious in these circumstances? Alessandro has been an eminent judge for god knows how many years, trying to second-guess him is probably a mistake. Whatever happened yesterday – a 24-hour affair – is now over and I must forget about it. Behave as though nothing has happened. We went swimming, to dinner, gatecrashed a party. Jesus. I wonder whether she has told him this. He is bound to ask me what we did last night. Will our stories match up? Alessandro is sitting at the kitchen table, a tiny espresso cup in his paws. There is a cappuccino for me. I sit down opposite him. I feel like vomiting. I am sweating. My heart is pounding. I can hear it.

'Oh, boy,' I say. 'Too much grappa.'

Alessandro laughs. 'You went dancing at Carbone's. Louisa told me.'

Thank god. 'Yes, I think so. A party.'

'Yes, Louisa told me. I will have to call to apologize.' He is smiling, but it is only out of politeness to me.

'I wasn't sure what was going on,' I say.

'It is not your fault.'

'I think Louisa just wanted to go dancing.'

'There are discos.'

'Who were those people?'

Alessandro places the tiny cup on the table and gives me the praying gesture. Who they are is not important, it says. Not to me at least.

I finish my coffee and excuse myself. I need the toilet desperately. I dash up the stairs three at a time, passing Louisa on her way down. I don't have time to stop, discuss, decide on an approach. From inside my bathroom, I hear raised voices. Louisa is snappy, uninterested in the admonishment she is getting from Alessandro, who sounds stern but also frustrated. He wants Louisa to admit what she did was wrong. That's all. Then the whole thing can be forgotten about. The first thing I think is: this is a clever ploy, irritable petulance is not the expected behaviour of an adulterous wife, but then I wonder, is it, though? My psychological training gives me few clues. I now understand why denial is such a seductive choice; in this artificial ignorance we believe we'll behave normally, everything will be as it should be had the transgression not taken place.

I make my way unsteadily downstairs and out into the garden. Alessandro is reading the paper; Louisa, in pyjamas and diaphanous robe, stares ahead, a tall glass of water held in her lap. She looks up at me, smiles warmly, weakly. 'Good morning, Jim.'

'Good morning, Louisa,' I say.

Alessandro folds away his newspaper.

'How was your trip?' I ask him, sitting down.

'It was OK. Everything remains the same. Each time I understand why I hate Rome. They are not animals but men without heart. It is worse.'

'British politics is much less dramatic,' I say.

'You are right. Tomorrow, we have big drama. The final . . . summation of the lawyers.'

'How do you think it will go?'

'For me it will be very boring. I make my notes in English to stop falling asleep.' As he says this he acts out writing and nodding off.

'Then what happens?'

'We make the decision.'

'Who's we?'

'Me, my deputy and the popular judges.'

'The jury?'

'It is the same.'

'So when do you expect the verdict?'

'It must happen Tuesday.'

'That's quick.'

'If you would like to come I can arrange for you to sit with the journalists.'

It seems innocent enough, this invitation, but I know better now.

'Thank you, but no.'

'You will be safe. I think it will be very interesting. I will arrange it.'

A week ago I would have acquiesced, but not now.

'Really, Alessandro, thank you but I don't want to go.'

His expression is hard to decipher; he stares at me, scrutinizing me. My first worry is that I have insulted him as my host, but then I think maybe he's simply unused to such straightforward contradiction, disobedience. Contrary to last week, I am not prepared to be bullied into anything. I wonder whether fucking his wife yesterday has contributed to this. Could I have refused him before that had happened? Indeed, would he have accepted it? He looks perplexed – he senses something beyond a simple refusal of his offer. The standoff between us is palpable.

Louisa looks at us both. 'Aless, it's not so interesting if you can't understand Italian, and look at the trouble he's got himself into . . .'

'When you are ready we will go to Ravello,' Alessandro says, ignoring his wife. He then stands and goes inside.

I lean forward. 'Is everything all right?'

'He's tired, grumpy. He's cross about where we went last night.'

'What's the problem?'

'They are a family he helped recently. They have some land, the Camorra wanted it.'

'And you used that to get us in?'

'Of course not.'

'Still, I can understand why he'd be pissed off.'

'I don't see why, this is a country of favours.'

'Favours are dangerous. Haven't you seen *The Godfather*?'

'Now you're being silly. Anyway, we'd better get ready.'

Louisa leads me in. As we pass the library, Alessandro looks up from his desk. There is no smile; we are merely watched, walking up the stairs together.

Ravello is lushly beautiful, like Capri, but grander. An aristocratic paradise. We walk where Wagner wandered when composing *Parsifal* and I wonder how such a bright and open place could inspire such dark music. Louisa is bored and complains constantly of a headache. After a period of uncomfortable silence, Alessandro and I discuss Italian versus German opera. His preference is for

German – Beethoven's *Fidelio*, unsurprisingly, is his favourite. Verdi is, however, in his blood.

'I understand the deep psychology. It is not just pretty melodies to me.'

'That makes sense,' I say. 'I can't help but love Elgar, however reactionary his music . . .'

'You are not normal for your age. This music is not liked by Italians your age.'

'Rarely in England. It is a lifestyle choice. Few people have the time for this kind of thing. You have to make the time.'

'My father listened only to Neapolitan songs. He was very educated. A judge like me. Very aristocratic. But sentimental.'

'My father is an accountant.'

'Ah . . .' An exhalation that says: a very boring job, we can't expect accountants to love music. He is right.

We have lunch on a terrace overlooking the rocky and jagged coastline of Amalfi. Louisa picks at her food. I eat heartily. Although Alessandro and I have been chatting, when the three of us are together no one speaks. There is no physical contact between husband and wife. This is the first time neither has absently searched for the other's hand, sent messages of love, devotion, understanding. Every time I try to make small talk I am kicked. Louisa doesn't want the awkwardness compounded by my struggle to be polite. Alessandro ignores Louisa, arranges his cutlery, eats vigorously, talks animatedly to the waiter when he checks in with us. Whatever the current state of play here, he will remain dignified.

After lunch we drive down to the sea and Louisa perks up, at one point muscling in between Alessandro and me and threading her arms through ours. Her head rests on Alessandro's shoulder. They talk briefly in Italian. Making up, I hope.

Alessandro wants to look at the small fishing boats docked on the shale.

'I would like a small boat,' he says, 'but the sea makes me sick.' He runs his hands over the brightly painted wood. He avidly questions the fisherman.

Louisa sits down on a concrete slab jutting out of the promenade and stares out to sea. I stand listless midway between her and her husband, desperate to sit down but unwilling to compromise myself further by joining Louisa. The sunlight makes me dizzy and I am still sweating profusely. I can't bear it any longer and join Louisa and sit down.

'Sometimes I hate him,' she says. 'Sometimes I think I really have married my dad.'

'I've met your dad.'

'You know what I mean.'

'We've got to forget what happened and you've got to act and judge him accordingly.'

'Easier said than done. I feel so suffocated. I do love him, but right now I want to be with you.'

'Louisa, that's just wanting a change of scenery. We all want that from time to time.'

'I know, I know. I can't imagine ever leaving him, but I also can't imagine that this is it. For ever.' She pauses, and then says, 'Couldn't you share me?' It's meant to be a joke, but she says it out loud for consideration, a possible solution. Agreement to it would be a quick fix to her big problem.

'We've got a couple more weeks,' is all I can think to say.

We drive back to the house in silence. I feel ridiculous in the back seat, the idiot son. I am happy to be told we're having a late siesta before heading back to Naples. Lying in the lemon light of my room, I am forced to listen to Alessandro and Louisa have sex. It is almost identical to last week's: the grunts, followed by her sigh. I compare it to our sex yesterday and it seems routine, unengaged. It is married sex. There is no depth to Alessandro's grunts; Louisa's moans are physical only – the pleasure is shallow. There is no indication from her that she wants this to last longer than it needs to, that she wants extra pleasure, to prolong anything that feels good. Listening to them sparks only moderate jealousy because I know our fuck yesterday was better and she knows this too. I do not compare well to Alessandro in most things, but for now, with the unusual mixture of newness and familiarity, for Louisa, I am a better fuck than him. I try to resist feeling a rather brutish Italianate pride in this. I resist hating Alessandro for his ignorance of it.

The siesta is short and Louisa calls through the door for me to prepare to leave. The traffic back into Naples is heavy. No plans are made for our next meeting. For no reason I suddenly announce that I might take the boat to Palermo mid-week for a couple of days. I have no intention of going but it provides a topic of conversation: the night boat, Palermo, Sicily and beyond. Alessandro loves Sicily, the country, the food. The people, he says, are not as mysterious as the Neapolitans; they appear so at first, but underneath, no. Sounds like regional prejudice to me. Then he suggests Louisa goes with me. He stares at me in the rear-view mirror as he says it. His eyes are hard. I don't know how to react. I let Louisa respond.

She turns to me and says, 'What do you think, Jim? Or will I cramp your style?'

I look back at Alessandro in the rear-view mirror. 'It's not a definite plan,' I say.

'You must go,' Alessandro insists. 'With Louisa. You can stay at the Grande Albergo e delle Palme. It is where Wagner finished *Parsifal*.'

'It's a great hotel,' Louisa enthuses to me, turned around in her seat.

'It is settled,' he says with a glance at his wife. The same hard eyes.

'I don't know, Alessandro,' I say. 'I haven't made up my mind.'

I sense my refusal to go to the court tomorrow must be overcome with some kind of capitulation. But I resist. We exchange polite prods on the subject without either of us committing ourselves. The subject is then dropped. All the way back to Naples Alessandro continues to study me in the rear-view mirror.

I am very pleased to see Signora Maldini sitting with her mother in the lemon-and-lime courtyard. I feel as though I have been away from home a long time. The emotional journey has been gruelling

255

– desire, yearning, love, sex, contentment, betrayal, guilt, happiness, jealousy, fear and, finally, confusion.

I am invited to a little supper and I accept. Whenever I eat with them, after the initial awkwardness, I find it hugely relaxing. We do not make any effort to speak, and I am expected to enjoy the food, which is not hard. I am always given a little wine. Rustic. Heavy. Just strong enough to soften my body, which I now realize is almost rigid with tension. She always serves linguine; the sauce varies. Tonight it is *genovese* I am told. I am then offered a *secondo piatto*, which they are happy for me to decline; I rarely do. Tonight it is sausages and *friarielli*. Occasionally I've said yes to fried *provola*; a rubbery cheese uncooked, cooked it has the consistency of carpet underlay. It is also without taste.

After dinner I sit and watch a film with the two of them. From what I can tell it's an Italian remake of *Guess Who's Coming to Dinner*. I do not stay to the end because I keep nodding off. I say my goodnights and go up to my room. I tumble into bed. My last thoughts are not of Louisa but of Alessandro. Does he suspect anything? I can now think of a thousand reasons why he should. I am not comfortable with what I've done.

I wake early but cannot get out of bed. It is raining outside. The ambient sound of the streets is of wetness. Everything is awash, soaked. Rain ricocheting off the balcony, the roof. My day is clear. I do not have to get up. I spend the next couple of hours contentedly dozing, listening to the rain, to the cars and Vespas below cutting through the drenched streets, and thinking of Louisa. The phone rings now and again and each time Signora Maldini launches into what sounds very much like a one-sided conversation. I eventually force myself out of bed around lunchtime. I wrap myself in the sheet and open the shutters. The rain has stopped, but heavy drops still fall from the guttering, eaves, balconies, washing lines, clothes. Above, the sky is clear blue, translucent blue, high and pure. I take a deep breath. The freshness of the air energizes me and I decide to go for a walk, find somewhere new for lunch, somewhere down by the sea in Chiaia.

Precisely at the moment I step from the alley into Via Santa Maria la Nova Giovanna pulls up beside me. A blur of blue Vespa and blue denim.

'On, on, *presto*,' she commands. Her voice is hard. She doesn't even look at me.

I do as I am told and we are off – weaving through the narrow streets, spray from the puddles covering my shins. I have to hold onto her as we tear across Piazza Bellini.

'Slow down,' I call to her.

We shoot along Via Santa Maria di Costantinopoli. It is the first straight road and she speeds up. I lean round to tell her to slow down. I reel back, almost losing my balance and slipping off the back. The whole of the left side of her face is smashed in. Her left eye is black, both lower and upper lips swollen. The skin over her cheekbone is split. It's like someone has hit her across the side of the face with a plank of wood.

She knows I've now seen the state she's in but she doesn't react in any way. We don't slow down. My first thought is: this is my fault, and for the rest of the way I keep repeating to myself, this is my fault, this is my fault. What have I done?

We do not pull up alongside the vineyard like last time but plunge down into it until we are not visible from the road. Giovanna drops the Vespa and marches off. I follow. The ground is wet and hard-going. The grapes glisten, drip. I don't say anything until we get to the building, her place of safety. When we get there she flings open the door and goes inside. I wait outside. It is only a moment before she screams – it is a frustrated, frightened, angry, wordless scream. I go inside. She is sitting on one of the benches. It is only now I can see the full extent of the damage. The whole of the left side of her face has been beaten in. She is barely recognizable – all the softness, roundness, loveliness has been obliterated. I do not know what to say; I just stand there.

'Why?' she screams at me. 'Why you go to Mascagni? You tell him I want to leave. Why? He does not care about me.'

'No,' I say desperately. 'I didn't tell him.' I am lying but I made Louisa promise he would not say anything and right at this moment it seems to cancel out the fact I did tell him.

Giovanna starts to cry. She wants to place her face in her hands, but it is too painful. Instead she just drops her head and the tears fall to the floor. She is no longer angry, no longer frustrated or desperate – she is a girl who has been badly beaten up by her family and doesn't know where to turn.

'Who did this to you?' I ask, but it's a stupid question. I saw her blood let just for refusing to translate a question; whatever information has reached Gaetano about her plan to leave is ample excuse for this kind of beating.

'I'm sorry, Giovanna. I didn't even mention your name. I just wanted advice. To help you. I am completely out of my depth here.' I shake my head at the horror I've caused. I sit down beside her on the bench, fully expecting her to scream at me to get away, but she just turns her face away.

She tentatively flicks a tear from the tip of her nose.

'Giovanna, I promise I will help you.' I say this quietly but intently. It is a pledge.

There is no reaction. I repeat myself. 'Listen to me. I will help you. I will think of something.' I cannot think what, but that can come later, the important thing now is that Giovanna believes me.

After another period of silence, I place my hand on her shoulder and I say, 'Giovanna, you must believe me when I tell you I didn't realize this would happen and I'm sure Alessandro didn't want this.'

She spins round. 'You are fool.' She spins back.

It takes me almost five minutes to coax her round. Everything I say is ignored. Every time I go to lay my hand on her shoulder she shrugs it off.

Eventually she turns and says fatalistically, 'Tomorrow, at the trial, they will be free. My older brother. Then my *famiglia* will be strongest in Napoli.'

'You don't want your brother to be free?'

She studies my face. 'My brother is killer. This is nothing.' She points at her face. 'If he finds out I try to leave he will kill me, kill you.'

The beating has worked. Gaetano has done his job. She now understands completely that her family will never allow her to go. This fact is brutally marked on her face. This is the clarity of their censure.

I say again, 'I'm going to help you.'

One plan occurs to me: I buy her a train ticket to France. They don't check passports any more. She could be in Paris by tonight; she'd be free. But then where would she go, how would she live? I could give her all my money but that would only last a few days.

No, she must go to London. My flat and my friends are there. She will be safe and looked after. It's the least I can do now.

I say, 'I need to think of a way of getting you to London.'

Giovanna finally gives in to her unhappiness and melts into me, weeping. Her whole body vibrates with sobs. I hold her tightly, I hold her powerfully – that is, I hold her with the determination that I will make sure she will be all right.

We stay like this for a long time. I know it is important for her to feel, to trust my constancy. After ten minutes or so, she pulls herself free, wipes her eyes, shuddering at the tenderness caused by the bruising. For some reason I lean forward and kiss her on the forehead. She smiles weakly.

'We will work this out,' I say. 'But it's going to take time. Where will you go?'

'I will go home. I must go home. They will not hurt me more. I have promised not to see you.'

This is the first time I have been explicitly mentioned as part of this situation, my position confirmed – I am the one helping her. I now know I am in danger of a similar beating myself. Why shouldn't I be warned the same way? My fear of this transmutes into anger with Alessandro. Why did he meddle?

I say gently, 'Tell me, did Alessandro actually speak to your family?'

For the first time Giovanna adopts one of the quintessential Neapolitan gestures – praying: she is reminding me in Naples things are not done so directly. Alessandro isn't a headmaster calling up the parent of a naughty child. Negotiations are not so straightforward and above board.

I say, 'We'll need to meet again soon. Tomorrow. Is that OK?'

Giovanna searches my eyes for something. I stay still to allow her the time to locate what it is she wants.

'I will find you,' she says.

We walk out into the sun. The ground is now hard underfoot; the grapes and vine leaves are dry. We stand facing one another. When we were last here, there was a sense of mutual adventure, the collusion of escape, movie-like almost, sexual; but now it's all real – real because a beautiful young girl has had the side of her face caved in and real because I have to do something about it. For the first time since arriving here I must make decisions and act on them. No more of this holiday fantasy of being followed by the Camorra, of being befriended by the charismatic Alessandro, of being in love with Louisa – there is only one thing that is important now, one thing that is real, and that is Giovanna.

When I get back to Signora Maldini's I call Louisa. I ask her to meet me. Now. I don't tell her what it's about. I ask her to come here. She says I sound strange, then says she thinks she's persuaded Alessandro to abandon the idea of sending us to Palermo, adding that he's being strange too, what's happening to the men in my life? I say I don't have time for that. See you in an hour. I hang up but immediately call back: meet me at the café, at the end of my road. She agrees, asking, what's the urgency? I say, I'll tell you when I see you. She then asks, we'll we go back to your place after? It takes me a second to understand what she's talking about but then my thoughts collapse into a single memory of Louisa in bed next to me. Yes, I say automatically and hang up again and go into my room. I start to pace. I am aware I'm doing it and feel vaguely self-conscious but cannot stop; every time I sit on the bed I find myself standing up again and on the move. I am deciding what to tell Louisa about Giovanna and what I need from her in terms of help. I also need to find out how much information she can give me on what exactly Alessandro did that led to Giovanna's beating. I realize this will not be easy because from whichever angle I approach it I am accusing him.

I leave early. I am at the café before her. I order a double espresso. I knock it back. The world spins before me. Louisa appears. A still image in the centre of a spinning world. She sits down. She is all smiles, and in precise relief to the blurred background. She leans over the table and kisses me. To any observer it is a quick peck on the lips, but I feel the extra pressure and push she gives it. It is full of the promise of sex. Of fucking. She pulls out her cigarettes, counts them, tots up where she is on her daily quota, then lights up.

'Smoking is terrible when you know you might be doing lots of kissing later.' I am told this as though it's a piece of good advice I might want to hang on to.

I cannot decide how to begin asking her about Alessandro and what he might have done to cause Giovanna's beating, so instead I ask her about Palermo.

'I don't know what's got into him. For most of last night he was talking about it. We can see this, that. If we organize our programme well we can go here, there, some other place. There is the beach at Mondello.'

'But you've talked him out of it?'

'I became moody, petulant – on purpose. He decided I was being ungrateful and didn't deserve to go.'

'Doesn't sound like talking him out of it.'

'I know how to handle him. He needs diverting and then he forgets.'

I decide not to push. Louisa lays her hand over mine. 'It would have been lovely, though, wouldn't it?'

I smile. But I need to move on. 'I want to ask you something, Louisa.' My tone and expression are deadly serious.

'What?' she says intrigued.

I suddenly don't know. I don't have a question. All I have is Giovanna's voice echoing in my head, *He does not care about me.* I can only ask about Alessandro. She has implicated him.

'Louisa, tell me did you really make Alessandro promise not to help me out with that girl?' The stress in my question does not imply simple curiosity; I am after information.

She looks at me, squinting. She wants to know where this is going. 'I made him promise.'

I rub my face with my hands anxiously.

'What is it?' she asks, pulling my hands from my face.

'I saw her today and she's been really badly beaten up. Really badly. And she blames me for telling Alessandro.' I brace myself for a defence of her husband, denials and dismissals and an attack on the trustworthiness of Giovanna, but instead she just looks shocked. It is a while before she recovers herself. 'I don't know what to say. I know he was very angry.'

'So he did do something?'

'I don't know.'

'She says he did.'

'Then he did.'

'Then what I want to know is whether Alessandro knew what was going to happen or if it's all just been a terrible mistake.'

Louisa snaps at me. 'Of course he knew what he was doing. He just didn't care.'

It is my turn to be shocked. She's talking about the ex-communist, the judge-psychologist who 'must understand', the big-hearted Alessandro Mascagni, her husband.

'Are you sure?' I say.

She nods. And in that one moment Louisa completes her betrayal. Not having absolute belief in his moral integrity does this.

After a moment or so Louisa asks, 'Is she really badly hurt?'

almost hoping I will amend my description and everything will seem less terrible.

'I've never seen anything like it and I've seen some fucked-up people . . .'

'What are you going to do?'

'I don't know.' I'm not sure how wise it is to tell her I've decided to help Giovanna, so I say, 'I don't know whether she wants my help or not now.' This is my second lie of the day.

'I've got money. I can get money if that's what you need.'

I take Louisa's hands in mine, lean forward and kiss her. 'I have to be careful. If they can do that to a member of their own family imagine what they would do to me.'

'Maybe you should go home, go back to England now . . .' As much as it's a suggestion based entirely on her caring for me, I am crushed. I don't want her to want me to go.

'If I leave now . . . what's going to happen to her?'

'Well, I don't know, do I? I'm just trying to help.' She is frustrated. She pulls a cigarette out of the packet without counting.

'Don't you worry,' I say. 'Everything will be all right.'

'How can you say that? I'm married to a monster.'

'There's no need to be melodramatic. You must see this in context. He thought he was doing me a favour. He'd be horrified if he actually knew what has happened. The important thing is we don't tell him about any of this. As far as he's concerned she's been warned off and she's stayed away.'

Louisa has been nodding all the way through my attempt to reassure her, keen to believe me. 'You're right,' she says.

We stand. Louisa throws a few thousand lire onto the table.

'What do you want to do now?' I ask.

'I want you to make love to me, Jim.'

I take her hand and we walk up Via Santa Maria la Nova. I can feel nervous energy pulsing through Louisa. I know this because my senses, for the first time in a long time, feel razor-sharp. I was like this for years in my job. I'd only have to sit in the same room as a patient and I could tell what stage of breakdown they were at. It was a physical thing. A vibe thing. They'd be vibrating with distress and I'd pick it up like some human Geiger counter. It's how I'd know where to start, how urgent the situation was. How vulnerable, how volatile, how desperate. And I am picking this all up from Louisa. If she could manage her adultery, she can't manage this.

Until we meet Signora Maldini on the stairs it hasn't occurred to me that we might bump into her and what that might mean. Her disapproval is evident. I push Louisa past her. We are surrounded by enemies, I think. Nowhere is safe.

When we are inside the apartment I say, 'I can't remember whether she knows who you are?'

'Of course she does,' Louisa says irritably. 'All Naples knows who I am. They all read *Corriere del Mezzogiorno*. There was a time when Alessandro and I were in it every week.'

'Why do you think she looked so pissed off?'

'Because she's old world and even if we sit here drinking coffee, we're breaking all kinds of rules.'

'Let's go. Let's go now. Catch her up going down the stairs. I don't want to piss her off. We'll get a hotel.' I see the idea appeals to Louisa. 'Please. I like it here and I want to feel welcome.'

We reach Signora Maldini just in front of the small wooden door. I wave a few notes of lire at her, as though we'd only returned for more money. She glances at me before looking Louisa up and down. It is good we did this, I think. I can tell through all her inscrutability that she's impressed by Louisa. A famous person in her house. A few weeks ago I wouldn't have been able to tell the difference between the disapproving stare we were greeted with on our way up and the approving one she now grants us on our way out. I kiss her quickly on the forehead, and we duck out before her.

We wander the centre of Naples looking for a hotel. It is mid afternoon and even the most dense shadows are stifling. At first Louisa is keen to check us into one of the exclusive palaces on the waterfront in Chiaia, the hotels of film stars and presidents. But then she says she's been to so many functions there, she's bound to be recognized and blackmailed. It's said straight and I have to look directly at her to see she's joking. We settle, rather perversely, for the Jolly Hotel, the skyscraper monstrosity in the centre.

Louisa checks us in. I stand behind her, looking around for anyone who might be watching us. It's now not just the Camorra we have to be worried about. What does Alessandro suspect, and what will he do to prove or disprove it? I remember his hard eyes studying me in the rear-view mirror – what did he think he could read on my face? What was he looking for?

Louisa shakes the card key at me and I hustle her into an elevator. The elevator is empty and we start to kiss. Roaming kisses. Lips, face, neck. My hand is quickly between her legs. I feel desperate; Louisa responds. The bell rings. We are at the sixteenth floor. Louisa straightens herself as the doors open. I follow her to the room. It is plusher than I expected. We close the curtains and turn on lamps hurriedly. The sound of Naples, uninterrupted everywhere, does not reach us here. We undress. We start to fuck. Concentrate on its purpose. We want a lot out of it. Alessandro obliterated, Giovanna obliterated, Naples obliterated. Guilt, responsibility, duty obliterated. I take control. I move Louisa around. She is pliant, willing.

'I want to come inside you.' I don't know why I say it and I don't examine its meaning.

Louisa gets up from the bed and tugs open the mini-bar and pulls out a bottle of water. She drinks half and then hands it to me. She says, 'Don't say anything, just do it.'

She lies beneath me, guides me in. All the aggression, desperation has gone. This is slow, deliberate. We look at one another. Louisa places her hand between her legs.

'I want to make sure I come at the same time.'

I push in deep, pull out fully; repeat. Long, slow strokes. It's not long before the desire to orgasm is irresistible.

'I'm going to come.'

I sense Louisa's hand vibrate beneath me. I look down. I hear her start to moan. I cannot wait any longer. My whole body releases into her. I tremble from my toes upwards. Louisa comes directly after me. Her fingernails dig into my back as her body contracts. I slump down on her, my face buried in the pillow. Louisa pushes me off. Again we lie side by side. What seemed essential only moments ago now seems pointless; with all our urges withering, our earlier desperation seems ridiculous, foolish even. I feel empty, lost, anxious. But then Louisa decides to nestle into my shoulder. She shoves my arm up, ducks under and pulls it tightly around her. Instantly, what seemed pointless now seems essential again, and nothing we have done ridiculous or foolish. I feel full, present, calm.

We sleep for two hours. When I awake Louisa is dressing. Gripping her watchstrap in her teeth, she uses two hands to pull the zip up on her skirt, then she shimmies to make it hang right. She wraps the watch round her wrist, fastens it, shakes her arm to shunt the watch into the correct place. She is braless today. I scoot to the end of the bed, pull her to me and placing my hands on her hips I take one nipple into my mouth, then the other. My stomach fills with desire. I throw myself back. Louisa slips on her shirt, fastening the buttons nimbly with one hand.

'I have to go,' she says. 'What are you going to do now?'

'I don't know,' I say. 'Figure out if there is any way I can help Giovanna, I suppose.'

'Remember, I have money.'

I nod. 'When will I see you again?'

'Tomorrow, of course.'

'Where? I don't want to come back here again.'

'Come to me then. Alessandro will be in court all day.'

'Verdict day.'

'I think he'll know tonight, but they'll have to go through the motions.'

'Giovanna is petrified they'll be released.'

266

'I'm not surprised. Her brother is an animal.'

'Alessandro seems to think he's learned something over these past two years.'

'Alessandro thinks he's intelligent. Which means, if only he hadn't been so deprived he might have been a lawyer or something. The state is to blame. Poor Lorenzo Savarese.'

'I can't work him out. Either he cares or he doesn't.'

'Don't be so naive, Jim. He cares when he wants to. Like us all.'

Something about Louisa's statement makes me pull the crumpled sheet over me.

'Anyway, let's speak later. Is there anything you want me to find out?' She says this with a touch too much seriousness, as if we're kids playing at this.

'No,' I say. 'We don't want to make him suspicious.'

'What of . . . that we're lovers or that Giovanna's approached you again?'

'Oh no, you can tell him we're lovers,' I say. It's half funny – flat funny. We snort rather than laugh.

We don't speak again until I see her to the door and I say, 'I'm crazy about you. Sometimes I think I don't care what happens to me because I can't have you. You'll never feel that way about me, will you?' It's a rhetorical question tacked onto a pointless confession.

Louisa smiles. 'You're too dramatic. You always were. Everything will be fine.'

The door closes. I sit at the desk with a beer from the mini-bar. I start to doodle on the hotel notepaper. I look out of the window, across the city. I try to form words unconsciously. Automatic-writing. A technique used mainly with the traumatized. But I need inspiration. It's pointless borrowing money from Louisa because anything she does will leave some kind of paper trail right back to Alessandro and he can't be relied upon. I need to formulate a plan which doesn't include Louisa.

There's my travel insurance. It covers me and a partner. Tickets and temporary travel documents in twenty-four hours. Surely they can't make all the necessary checks in that time. We make up a name. Giovanna gets on the plane and she's gone. And if they want to check – what will they find? But what if we need proof of who she is before they issue the documents? Everything's been stolen – we have nothing and she's got to get back to London – it's imperative. Why? A personal matter. Is it life or death? Yes, in fact it is. No lie there. OK. But can they do this in Naples? Will we need something from the police stating we reported the robbery? That's too dangerous for Giovanna. What about Louisa? They'll probably recognize her. This is not going to work. I need someone anonymous. I need that girl I met at Capodimonte. What was her name? Jules. She'd do it. Needs a bit of excitement in her life. But what are the chances of running into her again?

I give up and lie back down on the bed. If only the British weren't so fucking obsessed with passports she could just train it to Paris and get the Eurostar. No border checks between Italy and France. But she'd never get through at Waterloo. I turn on the TV and flick through the channels to BBC World. The news in English. I take some comfort in the familiar, but soon scan the channels for local news. I wait fifteen minutes not understanding anything before they appear – the nine. Mugshots of them all posted up on the screen in three rows of three. I haven't been able to see them so clearly before. Ordinary boys most of them, all a little older than Gaetano and Salvatore, but essentially no different. Need a shave, a wash. Photos probably taken after a few days in custody, giving them an authentic criminal look. Good for propaganda. Savarese doesn't look so different from the rest; the intelligence is there, a confidence the other eight faces lack, yet he doesn't have the instant appeal of Sonino. His old-world Camorra credibility is not visible. The picture then cuts to the newsreader. I hear Alessandro's name mentioned, followed by Sonino and Savarese. The rest is lost on me. The tone is serious not sensational. I don't think anything final has happened. I guess I should call later and find out. The news is followed by the weather report. From what I can tell storm clouds are amassed over the Bay of Naples.

7

I am in my room pacing again. I want to call Louisa, find out what
Alessandro knows. What does he think will happen tomorrow? Has
the fate of the nine already been decided? A weekend ago this
would have been simple – I'd just call. I'd ask him myself. But not
now – now everything is loaded with sex and violence. I can't call
him because I've fucked his wife. I don't want to call him because
he fucked up Giovanna's face. I laugh out loud. I am on my terrace.
The family opposite are having dinner. They all turn. My laugh, so
filled with irony, echoes up and down the street. I need to go out,
walk, eat, drink.

I head to the pizza place I discovered a few days after I arrived.
It was in the Spanish Quarter. I am not as alert to my surroundings
as I should be – my measure of danger has changed: I now know
what is really dangerous, and these streets don't compare. I might
get robbed, yes, but I will not get my face bashed in. I will not be
killed. Besides, after almost three weeks here I no longer have the
manner of a tourist – I am looking for a place to eat and do so with
impatience. Every *basso* I pass with a little light flooding onto the
street I take to be the place, but each is occupied by the usual three
or four generations of a family digging into bowls of pasta. Is this
what the Savarese home looks like most nights? I begin to think there
was no restaurant and I merely mistook someone's home and sat
down and was given pizza and wine. But then I stumble upon it,
tucked away on a narrow, downward street, just above Via Roma.

Unlike last time, it is very busy. The pizza man with his Tintin
quiff is hard at it. He looks likes a fencer poised for combat. One
hand held high spins a pizza base, while in the other hand a long
wooden spatula is deftly prodded into the oven to place a finished
pizza deep into the heat.

I take a seat at the only free table. It takes me a moment to realize I'm being asked to call out my order. There is no time for table service. I order a *marinara, acqua minerale, birra*. Everything arrives together and I eat and drink. The beer calms me and things slowly begin to seem less desperate, or at least less unsolvable. Will and money are all it will take. Will most of all. Especially with these people. This place is run by the victory of will: having the will to kill more people than others. Will without mercy. I'm not sure I can compete. My last real act of immorality was having sex with another woman while I had a girlfriend. My only real act of brutality was punching the guy she then slept with when she found what I'd done. Not really a qualification for a face-off with the Camorra. That said, I still think it can be done. But then I realize I'm hoping for latent reason in the Savarese family. They beat Giovanna up because they think she wants to leave and they want to use fear to stop her; I can understand how their kind of mentality decides to deal with it this way. But then once she's gone, when the opportunity to control her is no longer there, surely they will realize that what she's done is for the best, at least for her. I'm not convinced. Why will they succumb to reason just because they have lost the ability to control? I decide there is no point in trying to second-guess what these people will do over and above acts of violence and vengeance. I imagine their memory is as deep as their sense of honour and they will not forget or accept her defection just because she is not present.

These cul-de-sacs of thought are making me claustrophobic and I want to be back out on the streets. I dump a pile of lire on the table and leave. I cross over Via Roma and walk down to the dock. The air is cooler there. I find a bench and lie down. Above me there is a single cloud, pure white, pillowy, shadowless. It looks lost, as if it's strayed from a flock of clouds. It doesn't move. It is paralysed, suspended disconsolately. I crane my head to look for any more clouds, but there is nothing, not even way out to sea or hanging over Vesuvius. Earlier storms were forecast. Is it worth forecasting anything in this part of the world?

Over by the ferry-port ticket office there is a long bank of public phones. If I call Alessandro, will he tell me anything? Is he allowed to? It's doubtful. I'm not sure even what information I'm after. Will anything change if Lorenzo is freed tomorrow? Yes. Everything will change. But I only realize this now, asking the question. I can out-wit Gaetano. Lorenzo is an experienced killer. I don't stand a chance.

'He won't say anything,' is the first thing Louisa says when I ask if she knows anything.

'Can you tell anything by his mood?'

'He's tired, that's all.'

'You haven't mentioned anything we talked about, have you?'

'He asked me whether I'd seen you and whether you'd been bothered by that girl. I don't think there was anything in it. I know there wasn't. He's expecting you to come here tomorrow to hear all about the case. I don't think he suspects anything – you know, *anything*.'

Louisa is whispering by this point, sounding so extraordinarily conspiratorial that if Alessandro walked in on her he'd be bound to suspect something.

'Stop whispering,' I say.

'So you'll come tomorrow night, then? That's great,' she says brightly.

'Talk about overcompensating.'

'What do you expect me to do?'

'Behave normally.'

'OK. I'll try. Have you decided what to do about the girl?'

'Not so loud – he'll hear.'

'You told me to talk normally.'

'Not about her . . . Jesus.'

'Alessandro's in his study, working, he can't hear a thing . . .'

I then hear Alessandro's voice. 'Is that Jim? Invite him, Louisa.' It is an order, firm and unfriendly.

I do not even wait for Louisa's reaction. I say, 'I'm coming right over,' and I hang up.

★

Alessandro and I sit either side of the big oak table. Louisa is attending to the food. We study each other. He might think I am at a disadvantage here: he is older, wiser, adept in reading the inner thoughts of a mysterious people. But I am experienced in this too. This little face-off is nothing new to me. Plus I've never had the luxury of the security of a court, a police force, rank; it's always been just me and my patients – nervy, angry, confused. My antennae are acutely sensitive to shifts of inner thoughts.

Louisa serves the pasta and squid. Clearly Alessandro's tradition of serving the food himself is not always followed.

I'm not hungry, so I pick aimlessly, moving the food around my plate. Little is said. Alessandro does not bring up the trial. I cannot bring myself to ask about it. The ramifications of a failure to convict are too great and I don't trust myself not to bring up Giovanna and accuse Alessandro. Louisa tries to make small talk but quickly gives up as neither husband nor lover responds. The only subject that receives any comment from all of us is China. How long is the Great Wall? We don't know. Very long, probably. I then remember it can be seen from space; it's one of three things that can. We try to name the others. I know one but don't say so at first because I want the subject to distract us for as long as possible. Finally I say: a landfill in New Jersey. It's not deemed funny or interesting. The third eludes us, but then we're not really trying very hard. Tonight is not about guessing what can be viewed on earth from outer space; it's about guessing what each of us is thinking, the content of our inner space, and whether this can be viewed on our faces.

For myself, I am not trying particularly hard to hide my thoughts. Or rather I'm not trying to hide the fact that my mood is serious, which means I am not looking to appease Alessandro, who clearly thinks his moods come first. I have been invited round to entertain him – he is tired and wants to be amused by a little intellectual banter in English. I am not so easily manipulated these days. He tries to talk about Northern Ireland; Britain as a haven for nineteenth-century proto-communists; why America has produced the best twentieth-century poets in the English language. I don't have a great deal to say about the first two, but I am very interested in the third and have to resist being drawn. Shamefully I can't. Alessandro has outwitted me. He has recognized I have a certain intellectual vanity and that not speaking about a subject where I have an opinion is tantamount to admitting to having no opinion at all. All he had to do was search around for a subject I cared about, or where I thought my opinion was original in any way, and my capacity to resist would both fail me and highlight a weakness in me. I remember Louisa saying, 'Alessandro hates weakness.' And I realize that whereas once he looked for reasons to like me, he's now looking for reasons not to. This upsets me before it pisses me off. But still I rattle off my ideas. I can sense Alessandro is far less interested in them than he might have been an hour or so ago; his entertainment for the evening has changed – getting me to talk was his fun for tonight. That was his battle with me.

I turn to Louisa and say, 'When are we seeing each other next?' I take her by surprise. I take myself by surprise. But then if Alessandro wants to play games, I will too. I turn to him and smile.

His small eyes are hard. My smile is not returned. I sense he knows. Not that Louisa and I are having an affair, but that I have decided to make it plain that I can, at least in a small way, compete for her attention.

'My wife has her university and we must make plans for China,' he says coldly.

I nod thoughtfully. These are things to consider. And then I say, 'What about Palermo? Is that still on?'

My question is directed solely at Alessandro, but Louisa interjects. 'I don't really have time, Jim. I'd love to go, but . . .' She is warning me off this course of conversation.

'Palermo is wonderful, Jim, but Louisa is busy. You must go.'

'I'm not sure,' I say.

'It is your decision,' Alessandro says, and then stands, brushing the crumbs from his lap to the floor. 'I am tired. Tomorrow two years' work is finished . . .' His expression gives nothing away except that two years have passed. He sighs deeply and says, 'Every day Camorra, Camorra. A crime of passion, Jim. It would break the *monotonia . . .'*

It is a threat of criminal beauty, so much so I don't even know whether it's a threat at all and not just an expression of weariness and a desire for change. But I can tell Alessandro reads my reaction perfectly. I tense up, look to Louisa, at my wineglass. He then swaps his gaze from me to Louisa and then back. Instinct is telling him to search our faces. I try to break his line of thought by wishing him good luck for tomorrow.

He sighs and says, 'It is not luck, Jim. The outcome will be determined by how Neapolitans want to serve their justice. By themselves or through the law.'

'So they're going to go free?' It's meant to suggest I know there is a corrupt underbelly here from which even his courtroom is not safe. I can tell he is irritated by this.

'Jim, you do not understand.' He then turns without saying goodnight.

Louisa glares at me the moment he is gone. I look away, play with my glass on the table, rolling the base in circles, watching the wine smoothly alter its level in the bowl.

'You're just asking for trouble,' she says quietly.

'What trouble? I'm just getting a bit sick of his imperious manner. Just because he's a fucking judge.'

'Careful. He's still my husband.'

I ignore this and say, 'When am I going to see you next?'

'Don't know. I don't know what to do. Do you think he knows?'

I realize I don't know what I think and right now I am too tired to care. 'When am I going to see you next?' I repeat.

'I said I don't know. But you should be careful tomorrow. Naples has been quiet while all this has been going on and if they get released . . .' She shrugs.

I think for a moment. 'Maybe I should stay here with you?'

'I don't think that's a good idea.'

'Why not? Alessandro invited me . . .'

'Don't be obtuse, Jim. That was before we fucked each other.'

'But he doesn't know that.'

'I do. I do,' she says bitterly, then adds, 'Before you came everything was fine.'

I am crushed. 'I think I'd better go,' I say.

We pause at the front door. I want to kiss her; I want more to be kissed back. But instead I whisper, 'I'm sorry, Louisa. I didn't mean to mess everything up.' It takes control to say this, but I understand what she said is true and I am sorry.

Her face is red, her eyes rimmed with tears. 'I didn't think everything would get so complicated.'

I don't say anything.

She continues, 'I feel so old. Old and tired. I feel like I want to sleep for a week. And all because of sex.' She sighs at the absurdity. She opens the front door for me. We kiss politely, habitually, on the cheek. No arrangements or promises are made. I am outside and the door is closed behind me.

death

I

Signora Maldini and I sit perched on the edge of our seats in front of the television. We have been like this for at least half an hour. To look at us we might well be watching a penalty shoot-out between England and Italy in the World Cup final. Our faces stare, crease, concentrate, anticipate. The cameras cut from Alessandro to the nine to Sonino, back in the white room, in prison clothes, cuffed. Whoever is in charge of the broadcast-edit lingers on Sonino. He is a lone figure, expressionless. He is like an attenuated image of a man on death row: a highly stylized Hollywood representation or, perhaps more accurately, a Francis Bacon depiction of a killer. There is a languid otherworldliness to him which at the same time exposes his interior. Despite the other scenarios on offer – a packed courtroom, nine young men desperate to know their fate – Sonino's singularity in the white room is the most powerful.

Alessandro is making some kind of statement. He is reading from notes. I do not understand and his face doesn't give anything away. The nine, however, are at their most animated. Savarese is the least nervy. He stares out across the court, his fingers opening and closing around the bars. He wants this finished. This is the clearest view I've yet had of him. Resemblance to his sister is small. He lacks all her youth and softness. And unlike the twins, he is hard and circumspect, a man not a boy. He is not particularly good-looking, but the latent intelligence that has seduced Alessandro is present on his face. It makes him look more honest than the rest of the nine. It suggests reason. Calculation rather than blind greed. Is this the quality which Sonino hates, Savarese's unmanufactured complexity, more powerful in its way than his own myth-making and manipulation of charisma?

Every now and then I turn to Signora Maldini and say, 'What's happening?' She doesn't break her stare from the television. I cannot tell what her interest in the case is. I take it that all Neapolitans are watching at this present moment. If it's continually made the front pages, and this part of the proceedings has been televised live, then it's big news. I get up, walk into the bedroom and onto the balcony. The family opposite are sitting as we are: eyes fixed on the screen. I walk back and retake my position. Alessandro has now been speaking for over an hour. I notice Signora Maldini edge fractionally forward. This is it, I say to myself. The camera pans the line of faces in the cage. Alessandro's voice takes on a more declamatory tone. Is he now reading the verdict, I wonder. I imagine I will recognize the Italian for 'innocent'; I am less sure about 'guilty'. I am taking it for granted these terms are used. I should have asked Alessandro last night. The camera is now on him. He is holding a piece of paper. He addresses the court without even a momentary glance at the nine. This is good, I think. Signora Maldini inches ever forward, her hands lightly covering her mouth. She has even fractionally angled herself away from the TV, as though wanting to make sure she doesn't miss a thing – unconsciously aiming her best ear. But then I'm doing the same thing and I don't understand anything. I expect uproar no matter what the verdict. I am slightly irritated I can't be there myself, but then the public gallery is liable to combust. We haven't yet had a shot of the families. I expect we will once the verdict has been given. I wonder whether Giovanna is there.

Something is said which makes Signora Maldini gasp, stand up and stride into the kitchen, rasping '*Madonna mia, mamma mia,*' followed by a long litany of I don't know what in Italian. The verdict has been given and it is not good according to Signora Maldini. But what is it? The camera is obstructed by bodies; Sonino merely rises from his seat and shuffles, ankles braced, out of frame. When the camera does focus on the cage all I can see is a crush of bodies. Alessandro has already left the court.

'What's happened?' I ask pointlessly, knowing full well Signora Maldini's non-existent English won't suddenly, miraculously, be able to provide me with the information I need. But then Neapolitan sign language isn't built on nothing. She tucks the back of her fingers below her chin and flicks them away with proud and haughty disgust, saying just two words, '*Savarese innocente.*'

It's a sublime moment. The gesture is full of deep Neapolitan significance – violently dismissive, yet rich with vengeance; and the words are delivered with such impressively strong irony, it is as if '*innocente*' actually means irredeemable guilt.

Savarese is to go free then. I don't know quite what to think. I find I am squinting, trying to bring this information into the equation as if I've never thought about the possibility before, what it means. But I know what it means. Helping Giovanna must also include getting out myself. We must leave together. And soon. I wait a few more moments in front of the television to see whether they will be immediately released – all nine flooding out onto the streets, into the bosom of their *famiglia*. But the pictures revert from the courtroom to the studio where a discussion ensues. The only word I understand is '*drammatico*'. You're right there, I say to myself.

Signora Maldini returns from the kitchen and plonks down a cup of espresso on the table. Her mood hasn't improved. At least I know which side she's on, or rather I know she's not on the Savarese side; her actual allegiance could be anywhere from belief in justice to support for Sonino. But that doesn't matter to me now. I'm debating whether or not to call Louisa. I don't care how she views our affair now. I call; engaged. I wait five minutes, try again – engaged. I begin to pace. Signora Maldini watches me. I try Louisa once more, and when it's still engaged I decide to go out. I feel like my head is going to explode. Louisa's warning to stay inside today twists through my brain but I ignore it. I'm propelled by something beyond myself. It is only when I've left the building that I know what. Giovanna is going to arrive here at this spot any minute and she can't afford to wait. I must be ready for her.

I do not venture out of the alley. I don't want to stand in full view. I just lean against the wall. There is no need to look around – she will be here and moments later we will be gone, blending in with the other traffic and heading out of the city. I have decided what we will do. Train to Paris, Eurostar to England. I then have to convince passport control that she's my wife or girlfriend, that she's been attacked, lost everything, she wanted to come straight home, can you blame her – look at what those animals did. Pray they believe me. If not we'll just have to return to Paris and I'll have to think of something else. At least she'll be free of Naples.

The Vespa pulls up and I'm on. I wrap my arms around her waist. We weave through the pedestrians as if on a slalom course. What is astonishing is that this doesn't make us particularly conspicuous. We are just like other young couples desperate to get somewhere, urgency a matter of youth rather than necessity.

When we arrive at the winery we don't go in, but stand opposite each other on the patch of ground before it. It is just past midday. The sun is directly above us, a hazy white disc, blazingly diffuse. Giovanna's face is healing. Where it was caved in, roundness is returning, softness resurfacing. Beauty is pressing through the bruises. Her age means healing is quick and she will soon be back to normal. What do I say at passport control?

Our meeting is brief. She must get back. There is a party. For their release. Her brothers. Will I help her? Yes, I say. When? I say tomorrow, then the next day. Then Friday. Then I don't know. I have to think. I'm thinking of Louisa. She cannot stay with Alessandro; she will decide to be with me. You'll be safe soon, I assure her. I hold her. She stares up at me. She pushes up. To kiss me. Our lips meet. I do not pull away immediately. I can feel her preparing to give in to me. It is a decision she has made, if that's what I want, if that's what it takes. I slide from her lips to her cheek, to the patches of dry, congealed blood. There is a crackle. Her cheek feels as though it is covered an inch deep in foundation. It is like make-up on the dead. She winces away. We stare at each other. I can see and sense Giovanna's fear. It is complex, shifting, intense. There is a charge working its way through her. She is feeling it physically, all over her body. I am feeling it, on my skin, my hands, my lips. Our proximity is transforming our fear into desire. It seems like the only reasonable expression of all the unreason around us. Giovanna stares up at me, crosses her hands to the hem of her white T-shirt. It is a determined movement, a peeling away. I grab her hands, stop her.

'We should go back now,' I say.

She looks up at me, her hands still gripping her T-shirt, but now they are twisting the material, wringing it. I sense she doesn't know what to do next, what to say. I grab her hand. It is my turn to lead her through the vineyard.

Back in the apartment I call Louisa. I tell her I am leaving soon; she'll be free of me. She bursts into tears. I am told I can't leave her. She is sorry for what she said. I say I want to see her now.

'You can't . . . Jim, don't make me. Please.'

'When's Alessandro coming home?'

'I don't know. Later. He says we're all going out to dinner. I'm to call you. I'm frightened, Jim.'

'I'm coming over,' I say and hang up.

I take the stairs three at a time. Something of Giovanna's urgency of flight has transmuted into an urgency for sex. I have to see Louisa, fuck her. I run along Via Santa Maria la Nova. I am breathless and drenched in sweat. I fall into a cab. I want the driver to be Massimo because I want to cry suddenly and I want him to rescue me again. I feel almost schizophrenic. I love Louisa but I must help Giovanna. I am being split apart. Love and responsibility. One involuntary, the other a necessity. I call out Louisa's address. The cab turns sharply left and heads up a narrow street.

Louisa lets me in. I don't know why but I am pissed off that she is dressed. She leads me upstairs into a small guest room. A single bed.

The first thing I say is, 'Take your clothes off.'

She looks directly at me.

I repeat myself, 'Take your clothes off.'

They drop to the floor. I push her onto the bed, open her legs and bury my face. I hear her say my name. There is something pathetic, tragic in the sound. I stand up and undress, our eyes fixed on each other. Louisa shuffles forward and takes my cock in her mouth. It is her turn for desperation. I start to collapse inside.

Louisa pulls away. 'What do you want me to do now?'

I don't know. I don't say anything. I just pull her up and turn her around. I press myself in. She arches forward, groans. Presses back. I know I cannot last long in this position. I don't care. It is the release I want. Not pleasure. I come. It is a dead sensation. I back away. I do not feel anything. I know I cannot have what I want, which is to remain in Naples as Louisa's lover. For Alessandro to disappear. Then to become her husband. To live with her here and in Sorrento. To live happily ever after under the hot sun amid lemon groves, Vespa hordes and gangsters.

'I love you, Louisa,' I say ruefully.

She stands awkwardly before me, arms crossed over her chest. 'You're very special to me.'

'But you don't love me.'

'Would it change anything?'

'I'd feel loved.'

'You are loved.'

I feel worse because it doesn't change anything, and anyway, I'm not sure I believe it.

'I must go. I have arrangements to make.'

'What arrangements?'

'To get Giovanna out.'

'Do you need anything from me?' she says dully.

'Yes. Enough money for tickets to Paris, then to London. More. I don't even know how I'm going to get her into England.'

'When do you need it by?'

'I don't know – tomorrow. She's desperate now her brother's out.'

'Are you going to meet us later?' Louisa asks, changing the subject, I notice.

'I don't know.'

'Please, for my sake. You're leaving me behind, remember.' It is bribery that I'm unable to resist.

I agree but add, 'Why don't you come with us? You know that's what I want.'

Louisa looks at me and shakes her head. 'I'm not going to leave him, Jim. I love him.'

I feel foolish, stupid, naive. Of course she isn't going to leave him for me. I stand silent and still for a minute, taking this in – the certainty. I can tell my silence unnerves Louisa. She doesn't want the tragedy of this played out in front of her. She doesn't want a display of my feelings, the truth of them. Before now she has managed to ignore this, or at least to pretend it was all part of the game we were playing. Love as part of my lust. Driving it. She gives me a squeeze and says, 'You make me crazy.'

For a second we're not surrounded by betrayal and danger but simply a couple struggling with an imbalance of feeling and wondering how to deal with it, both knowing that without some kind of emotional equality it cannot last. But this is a pointless struggle because we are surrounded by betrayal and danger, and Louisa is married, so it cannot last, whatever we feel. I push her away.

'Louisa, I won't change my mind, not now, tomorrow, not in London.'

'But will you come back for me?' It's a teasing, testing question. She is testing her hold over me. And I realize it's the only game she knows.

My frustration breaks, and breaks hard. 'What the fuck do you want from me, Louisa? You say you won't leave him and now you want to know whether I'll come back for you. It's not the time for stupid games, people are in danger. I'm in danger. Tell me what you want from me.'

It is her turn to break. She drops to the bed, crying, 'I don't know. I don't know. I don't know.' Each repeat more helpless than the one before. I don't know what to say. I realize for the first time she doesn't have a clue what she's doing. Every shift in response to me has been an attempt to fix herself somewhere, to locate what she feels by trying it out: anger, coldness, distance, denial, desire – gradations of all, mixtures of many.

She looks up, her index fingers brushing away the tears before her eyes like little windscreen wipers. 'Please leave, Jim, I'll be all right. He could be back any minute.'

She smiles. It is a mockery of a smile. Desperate and pathetic. But she holds on to it in the hope I will accept that she is OK and that she can cope without me right now. She doesn't want us to be caught together here. She can't cope with that.

I make her reassure me.

'I'll see you tonight and tomorrow I'll get you the money. Everything's going to be fine. I promise.' She begins to dress with her back to me.

I leave and have to force myself at every step not to turn back. Outside on the road I am only seconds from the house before Alessandro's car appears, sleek, dark-windowed, ominous. I press myself against a white stucco wall hoping to be no more visible than a relief of a person against a bright background, a shallow form. The car turns smoothly into the driveway.

2

As we sit down to dinner Alessandro is exuberant. There is something madly ecstatic about his mood. I am his best friend again, it seems. Louisa is quiet, smiling in support, but her heart is not in it. The restaurant is packed. The young waiter is attentive, with a hundred sideways glances at Louisa. Alessandro is the object of sideways glances from the other diners. It is always like this at the end of a big trial, I am told.

'I am big celebrity,' he says. 'Like film star.'

Alessandro fixes his stare on me. I think I see something hard, dark in his eyes, but his smile is so broad I choose to ignore this. I have no other choice.

Alessandro ignores my questions about the outcome of the trial until we have finished our *primi piatti* and he has ordered our *secondi piatti*, which as before requires a trip into the kitchen.

'He's in a good mood,' I say, half-questioningly.

'Like I said last night: he's acting weirdly,' Louisa says dully. 'Can we meet tomorrow?'

I nod.

'At the café. I'll come straight from college. Twelve o'clock. I'll bring money. I wish you were taking me.'

This last statement is made just as Alessandro returns from the kitchen. My stomach contracts, my heartbeat quickens.

'You know how I feel,' I say.

Alessandro sits down. Looks at Louisa, me. He knows he's just interrupted something. His expression doesn't reveal this, but his strong, tough hands twitch nervously. He then turns to me and tells me in one long breath that I make his wife very happy and when I leave she will be very sad – he will not be enough for her any more . . .

Louisa and I make our first mistake – we don't look at one another. It's not much but I can tell Alessandro takes something from this. He smiles to himself – it's a closed smile. His eyes are inward-looking and cold.

Louisa breaks the silence. 'Tell Jim about the trial. He's dying to know why they were all set free.'

Alessandro refocuses his gaze on me.

'We decided not to believe Sonino.'

It is as simple as that.

'Are you annoyed?' I ask.

'I would rather they went free now than the Court of Appeal contradict the verdict.'

'But do you think the nine were guilty?' I ask.

'Of course. But my opinion is not important. I am a judge. The prosecutor . . . it is his job to prove to the court they are guilty.'

I remind him of our first conversation in this restaurant when he said that he must have the truth, not just the truth of the court. He must be satisfied.

The dead smile returns. He leans forward in his chair, reaches over the table with his strong, tough hands and grips my wrists.

'Jim, I must be satisfied of guilt. Guilt.' He then pauses and effortlessly tightens his grip around my wrists. 'Innocence . . . none of us is innocent.'

Just as his grip becomes painful he pulls away. The motion of his body causes his chair to rock back unsteadily. He only manages to balance himself with the aid of a nimble waiter tipping him forward and Louisa grabbing his big shoulder. He is angry; the momentary lack of control embarrasses him. I am to blame, he thinks. I am having this kind of effect on his life in other ways.

He stares at me. 'Savarese's sister has been attacked.'

I do not avert my eyes but my throat tightens. This is where I learn exactly how all these people know one another.

'Her boyfriend,' Alessandro continues, 'he is a very brave man.'

It doesn't take a therapist of genius to know I have now been cast as the boyfriend and that Alessandro is getting some kind of

288

perverse kick out of it. His gaze is hard, penetrating. He wants to read my reaction on its deepest level. I look at Louisa. She seems small. Next to her husband in this mood she is like a little girl.

I try not to give him anything. 'How did you hear about this?' I ask.

Alessandro laughs. My question had the intonation of cross-examination. He is amused that I could be thinking of taking him on.

'Her brother's lawyers,' he says.

'And what did they say?' I ask, making it clear I understand a game is being played.

'The boyfriend is a mystery,' he says coolly, followed by a little laugh.

'Really?' I say sarcastically.

Alessandro doesn't like this. He snorts. 'But they will find him. There are not so many foolish people in Naples.'

Something is becoming very clear to me. Alessandro's proximity to the Camorra is not measured by their closeness in the courtroom but by their shared understanding of Neapolitan codes of conduct. It seems you are a Neapolitan first, criminal or judge second. I am not even sure Alessandro is entirely aware of this; he may well be as much a victim as Giovanna. I look at him sympathetically for a moment. But then I realize all these systems of communication are being used against me.

I decide to cut through the codes.

'We both know someone in her family beat her. Why pretend otherwise?'

'Jim, I tell you what I know.' He drinks a little wine. 'More importantly, how do *you* know?'

I look at Louisa. Her expression says, don't push it.

'I know, Alessandro, because she told me. And now I'm going to try to help her. And you should help me to do this.' I say all this evenly, without releasing my gaze from his small eyes. I'm trying to make his moral obligation simple.

The hands come together in the praying gesture, accompanied

by a slight shake of the head. I am being censured. He will tell me what he chooses to tell me, he will help me if he chooses to, but right now he has no more to say.

He turns to Louisa. 'What do you think?'

Louisa stays silent. She knows this is not about Giovanna; this is about me and her. 'I think we should help them,' she says flatly.

'Help Giovanna Savarese or help Jim? We can only help one.'

It takes a second to comprehend what has been said. The choice Louisa has been offered. I am the first to react.

'Excuse me, Alessandro . . .' I say incredulously.

His hand raps down on the table and he cries, *'Silenzio!'* The whole restaurant jumps and then falls silent.

'Alessandro,' Louisa whispers, 'what are you doing?'

'I am asking you. You choose . . .'

'I won't,' she says firmly. 'You're being silly. Calm down.'

Alessandro checks himself, holds his hand out in front of himself as if signalling a lawyer to cease speaking for the moment. He then broadens his thick shoulders and draws in a deep breath. 'Jim, you make love to my wife, no? You are my friend. You tell me what to do.'

I don't know what to say. I'm not sure what has been asked. Have I made love to his wife? Am I his friend? Does he actually want some kind of guidance on what to do if the truth is what it is?

'Jim?' he repeats. 'Answer me . . .'

Insulting his intelligence with lies is out of the question. With years of testimony, of courtroom faces, of lies, half-lies, half-truths, cover-ups and denials – the truth, if it's not clear to him by now, will be evident the moment I open my mouth.

So I say nothing and instead bring my hands together in the prayer position and gently shake them. I am saying: 'If I am your friend, don't ask me whether I've fucked your wife.'

It may be the Neapolitan way, but I am not Neapolitan. And something tells me I have made a very big mistake.

Alessandro leans back in his chair and looks over his shoulder towards the back of the restaurant.

'Limoncello, per favore.'

He then stares straight at me. His small eyes, usually so bright, are now tight grey balls. 'Jim, you are a foolish man.'

The ice-cold *limoncelli* are placed before us on the table. Alessandro knocks his back and then stands.

'Louisa!' he calls down at her.

She stands. She is just about to say something to me but Alessandro grabs her arm. I stand, my chair rocking back. My instinct is to pull her from him, but I keep my hands by my side and stare at him in disgust. He dismisses my expression with a wave of his hand. He lets Louisa go.

I am not expecting a parting gesture, a handshake or a kiss. I know that as far as Alessandro is concerned our friendship is over and we will not be seeing each other again.

I offer my hand anyway. It is ignored. Louisa offers her hand. I clasp it, and in our own obvious way we try some clairvoyance: we have to meet, have to – it's not ending like this. Louisa is pulled away.

Once again we are father, daughter, boyfriend. Louisa and I have just been told we can't see one another again by the incontrovertible force of parenthood. But this time I know it's final. The obtuse rebellion of adolescents in love will not overcome here. We are not obtuse adolescents. And I am not sufficiently loved. Loved yes, but of the three of us I have the smallest share. Louisa turns in the doorway. Her look confirms this. A swell of loneliness, fear, desperation rises in my stomach and I have to stop myself from throwing up.

3

I am aroused from sleepless delirium by the phone, its sound breaking my wide-eyed stare into my room's total blackness. The heat of the night is so oppressive I have to press through it just to get out of bed. I am covered in a film of sweat. The telephone continues to ring. I do not know where I am in the room. Slowly the tall frame of the window, highlighted by a faint moon, orientates me. I leave my room and make my way along the hallway. I fumble for the phone. Louisa. Whispering.

'Jim. Listen to me. You must leave.'

'What's happened . . .' I say – it's not a question, it just spills out.

'Whatever your association with us, with Alessandro, however it's helped, it's not there any more.'

It takes me a moment to untangle her meaning, but doing so allows my brain to find a gear. 'How do you know?'

'I just know. In the car he kept going on about you and me. I expected him to be silent. I expected him never to say your name again. But he was furious. I've never seen him like that.'

'What did you say?'

'Nothing. That's the point. He doesn't care what I think. He doesn't seem to care about what really happened. I don't even know what he thinks happened. It's something else. It's something else.'

'What?'

'I don't know, I don't know. It's like he's compromised in some way. Maybe he has helped you. And now . . .'

'And now what?'

'You fucked me . . .'

'But you said he doesn't actually think that.'

'I said he doesn't seem to care what really happened. That's different. It's worse.'

I begin to understand. Something is stopping Alessandro from obeying his instinct to corroborate before condemning.

'I'm going to get you some money tomorrow.'

I am about to ask where we should meet and another hundred questions when I hear Alessandro's voice calling out Louisa's name and the phone goes dead. Every bead of sweat covering my body is sucked back into my skin. Jesus, Jesus, Jesus, I say through clenched teeth.

I stare at the stretching rectangle of light that is dawn moving dimly across my floor. My watch sits on the chair. If I concentrate I am able to alter my perception of the speed of the second hand and slow it down – so much so that each sweep lasts a full breath of my body, which is now so slow I imagine it is possible to slip past sleep and into death. Helplessness has exhausted me. For hours since the phone call it seems my mind has been full of pretty pictures of Louisa – hazy home movies, full of colour, sunlight, joy. I want the pretty pictures to be real and this horror to be inside my mind. I want to magic this, as my mother might have said – magic the world that way round. But it is only when I drift into a half-sleep that Louisa and I are vividly elsewhere, in love and happy. As morning approaches I fall into a deep and dreamless sleep.

Lorenzo Savarese is in my room. Standing there. In the centre. At the edge of the rectangle of sunlight obliquely shining across the floor. This is not a dream. I sit up, push myself into the corner of the bed, into the corner of the room, my hands pressed into the mattress. I want to disappear into the wall. But I feel pressed out. Resisted. I am scared. Am I going to die? It's a question I ask.

Savarese is motionless, staring at me, down at me. Scrutinizing. His face is plumper than I remember. I recognize Giovanna's eyes. They are deep brown and warm; not the eyes of a killer. He is not frightening. Not preternaturally frightening like Sonino. Not standing there, regarding me with his warm eyes. He is in a dark suit, black shirt. His hands are in his pockets.

'What do you want?' I ask.

There is no response. It is as if the sound of my voice doesn't even carry across the room.

How did he get in and past Signora Maldini? I look to the bedroom door. It's closed. I cannot hear the television, radio, Signora Maldini on the phone. What time is it? My watch says seven-twenty.

I say again, 'What do you want?'

Nothing.

I am naked under the sheet. I look to my clothes thrown over a chair. I want to be dressed to deal with this. Savarese's gaze never breaks from me, wherever I look.

I cannot think of anything new to say, so I repeat myself, 'What do you want?' But this time I add, '*Turista*,' and point to myself. We both know this is ridiculous. He doesn't even have to express it. The clairvoyance again. I'm not a fucking tourist any more. Haven't been for weeks. Claiming it makes me look pathetic, cowardly. There is not a single movement of muscle in his face and I know this is exactly what he thinks. But then he knows exactly who I am and what I do. This isn't a getting to know one another session; he's here to take action. He isn't interested in any promises on my part. There can be no special pleading here. Mercy is not part of the Camorra currency. Nothing I can do will influence his thinking. He's probably had people begging for their life plenty of times and remained unmoved; it's not an emotional thing. But then this is – this is about his sister.

And then I realize. This is why he's here, why I'm not dead yet, killed anonymously in the street. Savarese doesn't know what to think about this situation. Somewhere deep inside himself he knows he should let his sister go. I doubt he's even aware of it, but whatever faint voice is corrupting his usually straight thinking is telling him this isn't just straightforward business: killing a guy who wants to help his sister. It's not as straightforward as the vengeance he must now exact after spending two years in prison, betrayed by Sonino. Not as straightforward as going to war to regain his territory and to re-establish his power base. All that is clear to him. Necessary. Necessary for him. But not for his sister. Is this what Alessandro meant about his latent intelligence? He's beginning to see past the ineluctability of this life?

I don't have time to decide because in that second Savarese strides across the room, pulls a gun from his trousers and slams me across the head with it. His face is tense. The draw of the gun, the palming of it, is determined and seamless. The impact is sudden and immense. A white light of pain consumes me. For a moment I am a thousand white sheets billowing in the wind.

Signora Maldini's face is pressed close to mine, her thumb pulling open one of my eyes – she thinks I'm dead. I can hear her, way off in the distance, saying, 'Mamma mia – è morto, morto.'

I cannot move. My body feels broken. I can taste blood. I feel like my lungs have collapsed. The pain sucks away all my energy. I want to move, but I remain motionless. I try desperately, concentratedly, to raise my arm, to touch my head, the wound. How bad is it? What it feels like is . . . oil paint clogged with brush hair. What it is . . . is open flesh, congealing blood, my matted hair. I reel from the pain. I hear myself cry out. I look at my hand. Each fingertip is dabbed with a perfect red circle. Glistening.

I sense something pressing at my lips. It is Signora Maldini with a glass. She tips brandy into me. Only drops. She is muttering but the strength it requires to understand her takes away from all the strength I need to make sense of what's happened to me. I remember Savarese. I remember being hit. But it's not the facts that I am after; it's the consequences. What does this all mean?

I heave myself up and, with the aid of Signora Maldini, shuffle to the edge of the bed. Despite the immense pain, my thoughts are becoming more focused. What to do is clear. I have to leave. I have to leave now. I will be killed if I don't. I've been given a chance and I must take it. Savarese is giving me a chance. I wanted to help his sister and for that he will allow me one last opportunity to save myself. That is his deal. Leniency because of kindness – the good of my motivation abstracted from the situation and then traded against his instinct to kill.

I am sick. It comes quickly from my stomach – a fluid passage. With my head slung down, it falls from my mouth to the floor. Signora Maldini skips back. I do not move, react, apologize. I just let my stomach spasm, emptying its contents.

Signora Maldini leaves and returns with newspapers. She spreads them out over the floor between my legs. One sheet has the mug shots of the nine. Savarese, the leader, as always, top left. I lift my foot and press my heel into the pictures and into the vomit. I feel a warm slush break through the paper. When I remove my foot they have become one disintegrating grey mass.

I look up at Signora Maldini. 'Thank you,' I say. I attempt to stand and she offers her arm as support. I am naked but I don't care. I say, 'Bathroom,' and point. She keeps hold of my arm, her tiny grip barely noticeable, as I make my way slowly out of my room. It's only at the door, when I cannot see both hallway walls, that I realize I am blind in one eye. The realization makes me list over. It's only Signora Maldini's cantilevering that keeps me upright; I rest against the doorjamb for a moment for my eye to adjust.

Once I'm in the bathroom I grip the sink and stare at myself in the mirror. My face is like a Picasso painting. I am recognizably human, but the place where I was hit is a flat surface, angled away from my forehead – a cubist addition to an otherwise ordinary face. It is as though a slice of my forehead has been removed and pasted further up my head. It is viciously red.

My left eye socket is black, swollen shut and creased with blood. The side of my face is streaked with dried blood, pink and powdery. I want to cry, but shock and its yield of adrenalin are stopping me. I want to cry because I hardly recognize myself. I want to cry because my face and head were powerless against Savarese's decision to hurt me badly. I want to cry because there is a break in me, from my eyebrow up into my hair. I want to cry because I can't defend myself when this is possible – when gunmetal can open me up like this.

I gently raise my hand to my head, but the reflection and blind eye make me miscalculate distance, position. The concentration makes me dizzy. Taking sharp shallow breaths, I feel the wound. The pain is excruciating and I swoon. My legs weaken, my body drops. I have to swing with the fall and hope momentum and a modicum of strength in my arms will be enough to position me back upright. I almost faint. I give up. I run the cold tap and wash my face, carefully avoiding the upper left side. I then fill the basin with lukewarm water. I must clean the wound and sterilize it. I call Signora Maldini and ask for the brandy. She brings me the bottle.

I dip my head into the water. I do not know how I am able to remain conscious, the pain is so vast. The water turns opaque with blood. I brace myself, press my waist to the sink, grip the edge with my hand. Now the brandy. I reach for the bottle. I estimate where the damage starts at the top of my head and pour. For a second I feel nothing, and then I collapse. It's like my body is sliced in half by an axe buried into the original cut, as if that was just a first marker, a provisional strike for position. I cry out. Signora Maldini is by my side, on her knees. I reach for her, her hand. Gradually the acute pain subsides and I can sit myself up on the toilet. Dark drops of brandy run down my chest, my legs. My closed eye stings and spasms deep in its socket. Signora Maldini moves back to the doorway. What does she think has happened, I wonder. She didn't see me come in last night, so presumably she thinks it happened yesterday. Does she think I fell over drunk? Does she think I was mugged? There is little point in trying to explain. What would she think if she knew? Lorenzo Savarese in her apartment. I need support and sympathy right now, not fear and condemnation. I smile weakly. She shuts the door and I start to cry. I sit upright on the toilet, with outstretched arms pressed against the walls to keep myself balanced. I don't know what to do. I am frightened and I want this to end. I just want this to end.

4

I dress slowly, taking each movement gently, as anything sudden makes my head swim. It's like my brain is filled with blood and each time I move it floods my skull. I can taste blood at the back of my throat. Swallowing is difficult, I don't know why, and even when I do manage to swallow, it is followed by a coughing fit that brings up the rancid, searing taste of vomit. It's worse than the blood.

When I leave my room Signora Maldini is sitting at the round table, smoking. Her hair leans nonchalantly, but I can tell she is perturbed. She looks up at me, focusing on the wound, which is now clean, free of matted hair, congealed blood. It looks like a burn – white and pink flesh melted around a jagged ridge where the skin is still open. A scab is forming thinly over it. It looks like the result of a high-impact car crash, my head cracking down on the steering wheel.

I know I owe Signora Maldini an explanation, but all I could say that she would understand is a list of names: a judge, his wife, killers, relatives of killers, all accompanied by sign language absurdly describing the attack, ending with a finger dragged across the throat after pointing to myself and then off into the distance. I know what I mean: if I don't go they will kill me.

I sit down opposite her and take a cigarette. First one in ten years. I light it, drag, let the nicotine swim inside my head. It makes me sick and light-headed, but at the same time it makes me feel good, dulling the pain.

I finish the cigarette and call Louisa. I assume Alessandro will be at work. There is no answer. I sit back down. I tap Signora Maldini's lighter nervously on the table. I need to get out. I can't sit here waiting for things to happen. I've been given my warning. No one's going to repeat it for fun. Right now I'm as safe as I've ever been. I check I have lira coins so I can call Louisa from a public phone.

Out in the sunlight, standing on the threshold of the alley and Via Santa Maria la Nova I realize I have no plan, no direction, no time-line; all I know is I'm leaving today. I cut up Via Santa Chiara to Piazza Bellini. Waiters and waitresses are setting out the tables and chairs, erecting the heavy shades. I want to stop, eat something, but I keep on walking. I head up Via Costantinopoli. Part of me is hoping Giovanna will appear and that she will see why it is now impossible for me to help her, but I am fairly certain she has received a similar warning herself and therefore understands that we have been defeated. I must leave; she must stay.

I stop at a phone, call Louisa. Still no answer. I begin to worry about where she might be, what has happened to her. Maybe she's getting the money she promised? A pointless risk now. I have just enough for a ticket home for myself; I don't need the extra. But then if she gets it maybe she can give it to Giovanna when all this calms down. More, perhaps. Enough to start a new life. She can even give her my address, send her to me. With these thoughts I realize how much Giovanna's fate is on my mind, how much I care what happens to her. I am leaving her behind when I promised to help. This brings on an entirely new sensation of nausea. I have to stop and rest against a wall. I don't want to leave her, but they will kill me if I help her. She will live. There are better ways, where we both survive. This makes me feel better – the rationale is undeniable. I look for another phone and try Louisa again.

Alessandro picks up, '*Pronto.*'

I don't say anything. Alessandro repeats, '*Pronto.*'

My head pounds. 'It's Jim. I want to say goodbye to Louisa.' I want to sound confident, certain, but the tremor in my voice is clearer than the actual words.

'You leave today?' The question is hard-edged, cold.

That was a mistake, I think. Alessandro may not deny me this last farewell, but now he knows I'm leaving. The less he knows the better. My anxiety is cut short by the phone being placed down on a hard surface. The next thing I hear is Louisa's voice. It is entirely without warmth.

'Goodbye, Jim. It was nice to see you again. Have a safe journey home. Make sure you have one last look at the Caravaggio, I know how much you love it.'

The phone goes dead. My mind quickly decodes her message. There are only two Caravaggios in Naples: one in Capodimonte, the other in her private chapel. She is saying, meet me there. She still thinks she has to give me the money.

I know I should call her back and tell her it's not necessary, but then I realize this will mean not seeing her again. I calculate the risk. Where was Alessandro when we spoke? Surely he wasn't going to let us have a private, intimate goodbye. He must have been standing right by her. What does he think has passed between us? He's far too canny to have misinterpreted her suggestion as genuine concern for my love of Caravaggio. I can't remember whether he knows about her refuge. So he works it out and catches us? It's nothing compared to being pistol-whipped by Lorenzo Savarese.

I decide to head back to the apartment, collect my things and go and wait for her at the chapel. I don't want to run the risk of her going there and not finding me.

I cannot help fantasizing that she has finally decided to leave Alessandro and wants to go back to London with me. Even though I know it's about the money, why can't it also be this? Everything has changed since yesterday, and yesterday she wasn't entirely sure what she wanted. These thoughts energize me. My heart races. We could leave the same way I was planning for Giovanna: train to Rome, overnight to Paris, then to London. A honeymoon of sorts. The absurdity is not lost on me and I laugh out loud. Passers-by stare at me. Then they notice the state of my face and turn away. I'm a man with a head wound cackling to himself – I am a madman.

I *am* a madman. Louisa is not going to leave Alessandro. Not for me. I keep forgetting, I'm the intruder here. For three weeks it might have seemed like he was the odd one out: different in age, culture, sensibility, language, all creating a feeling of distance between him and us. But I am the holiday romance. The three-week fling. Its abandon risk-free because of the certainty of its end. Only here it wasn't an affair with difference, mystery, the exotic; this was an affair with the familiar. Louisa didn't need to escape the humdrum for a few weeks; she needed ballast against the power of Alessandro to eradicate her. Motives not too dissimilar to Giovanna wanting to leave, except that Louisa has the freedom to control her sense of self with an adulterous fuck and isn't required to flee her family for ever.

Just as I reach the entrance to the alley Giovanna appears. No Vespa this time. A young girl in denim. Without breaking stride I turn into the alley and dip through the door. She follows.

We are in the lemon-and-lime courtyard. Giovanna looks at my head. There is no discernible reaction. Her bruises have faded further; the scabs are peeling away tantalizingly. Enough of the damage remains to show her beating was worse than mine. Multiple blows. Cracked cheekbone, brow, lips.

'Who?' she says.

I debate whether to tell her the truth or not, but don't see why I shouldn't. 'Your brother. Lorenzo.'

She covers her mouth with her hand – a reflex of horror.

I say, 'I'm OK, don't worry, it looks worse than it is.' I can tell she needs reassuring. She hasn't factored this in. She is also confused by the unexpected concern she feels for me mixed up with the selfish fear that I will not help her now.

Her fear is all powerful. 'You will not help me now?' she asks.

I want to explain why that's impossible, reiterate my earlier rationale for leaving alone, whilst also trying to reassure her with a promise that Louisa will help her soon; but I don't, I can't. Facing one another, our faces bashed in, I know with the money from Louisa we could both be gone today.

'Giovanna, do you understand I'm risking getting killed? Your brother will kill me.'

She nods – yes, she understands, but she doesn't back away. 'They will kill me.' We are the same, she is saying.

But we're not. I can be free of this.

With no more than a battle scar.

I look at Giovanna. A beautiful young girl also battle-scarred. And willing to risk worse to be free of this.

I only have to answer one question: will I be able to live with myself if I leave her behind? And the answer is, yes probably. I'm thick-skinned these days. I have had longer, deeper relationships with hundreds of patients and lost many of them: suicide, overdose, even murder. I know I can't save everyone. My success rate was high, higher than most, but I failed more often than not. But then what I'm being asked to do here is not my job. There are no responsibilities to fulfil. There is no therapeutic contract. What I'm being asked is something more primary – fate has elected me to help someone who can't help themselves and it comes with risk to myself. What do I do? It's not a test of my skills, my experience, my commitment. I'm not even sure it's a test of my humanity. It just seems to be a question of what I think is the right thing to do. For me. Now.

'Meet me at the station this afternoon.' I say it quickly to get it out, to force my own hand.

'Time?' she asks. Now I have been decisive, she wants decisions made.

'I don't know . . . I need to . . .' I am not a natural at this – I should be saying: station, 4 p.m., under the clock etc. But I want flexibility; I want to be able to back out.

I say, 'Look, Giovanna. This is a bad idea. They'll be watching you.'

Giovanna scans the landings and balconies; no one is watching. 'It is OK. They do not suspect. I *promesso*. *Promesso*. Stay. When I meet you I will not . . .' she mimes holding bags, 'baggage . . .' The use of the word 'baggage' under these circumstances sounds ridiculous. She is guaranteeing our safe passage on the basis of a promise and the fact that she won't attract attention by packing for the trip.

I ask, 'Where's a good place to meet?'

'At the station . . .' she says unsurely, worried she has misunderstood something.

'Where at the station? I don't want either of us wandering around.'

She understands, thinks, then says, 'McDonald's. My *famiglia* . . . my *famiglia* . . .' She makes the flick gesture.

It seems she is suggesting we meet in McDonald's because her family has issues with American fast food.

'McDonald's then.'

'You have tickets?' she asks.

I don't want to tell her that Louisa is giving me money because she won't trust her. 'Not yet. I will get them.'

'When?'

'I don't know. Trust me. I will get them and meet you.'

She looks at me suspiciously, her big eyes narrowing. She wants to push me on this but doesn't want to risk my backing out.

Eventually she says, 'I will be there at two and wait.'

'Won't that look strange?' I say. 'You might be there for hours.'

She shakes her head. 'I like McDonald's.'

It takes a second. She *likes* McDonald's. We have a plan that includes a rendezvous at McDonald's because she likes it and her family doesn't. I want to laugh. But Giovanna is crying. Her whole body trembles. The absurdity of the arrangement might be funny but in its absurdity Giovanna is beginning to believe she might actually be free. I take her in my arms. Hold her tightly. It is only now, with her body wrapped in mine, I understand how scared she is. She is collapsing into me. Almost breaking apart in my arms. All her strength and toughness have gone. She is no longer Giovanna Savarese; she is a rag doll of a girl ready to be reconstituted in her new life. And I realize right now I'm all she has in the world. Everything else she has left behind.

5

Time is a shape to me. I can see it clearly as a wedge, a sloping away, to the thin edge. The width of the wedge is vast, not allowing for any other way off. Nothing suggests the way down is anything but a way to end this. It is finite insomuch as it is the shape of time from now until the moment Giovanna and I leave Naples.

It is midday. The sun is directly above the lemon-and-lime courtyard. The tiles appear to melt into one another as if they are made of lemon-and-lime ice-cream.

When I enter the apartment Signora Maldini is listening to Italian opera. She raises a finger to her lips. A soprano wails – all vibrato and hysteria; she has just announced with unrealistic vigour that she has consumption and is about to die. It is painful, pathetic and agonizingly slow. At first the shrieks of passion, remorse, hope, despair, regret just irritate me, but by the end, her end, which is signalled by a darkly sad orchestral chord, I am almost in tears. My own private fear has been transformed into public sentimentality. Signora Maldini notices and smiles. She says something sombre in Italian and then quickly wipes away her own tears with two precise dabs of a handkerchief picked out of her sleeve. She turns on the television.

I head into my room. Prepare to leave. I look at my stuff spread out around the room. I am not going to take anything with me. As far as anyone else is concerned, I'm still here. All I need is wallet, watch, passport, money.

When I casually say, 'Ciao,' to Signora Maldini I know this is the last time I will ever see her. I will not come back today and I will never be able to return to Naples. I bend over and kiss her lightly on the forehead. This always pleases her. She says, 'Ciao,' without looking up and continues watching the television. I am tempted to have one last go at righting the beehive. It has been an oddly frustrating thing to live with. Its gravitational audacity has made me question the kilter of the world down here and at times convinced me that something is most definitely out, and it might not necessarily be Signora Maldini's hair. It just might explain how I got into this mess in the first place – some cracked fault line below the city causing everyone above to be a little cracked themselves. Only Signora Maldini's hair obeys Newtonian physics, everyone else is leaning towards madness.

On the landing I pat my pockets, making sure I have the little I need. I look up at the square of sky, high and blue and cloudless. Below me the lemon-and-lime courtyard is cool and watery. Before me the shape of time is sloping away . . .

The streets are beginning to empty, the shops closing. Siesta time. There is a faint echo as my shoes click against the worn stone. Every now and then I am almost knocked to the side of the street by a Vespa skidding past. I feel conspicuous. I am clearly no longer a tourist and no right-minded Neapolitan would be walking with such determination in the heart of the city in this heat at this time of day. If I am being watched, followed – I am making life easy.

It takes ten minutes to reach the chapel. It is closed, just like when Louisa first brought me. The heavy iron door – twenty feet high, ten feet wide – is forbidding. It is like a high-arched castle door. It looks as if it's been closed for centuries. There is no sign around its stone frame, around its huge iron hinges, that it has ever been opened. I don't want to wait out on the street, so I look for the door where Louisa previously must have collected the keys. There is only one side street and there are two possible doors. I knock, but my knuckles barely resonate. There is no bell or buzzer. I head further down the side street, away from the church, but there is no way in. I even ask an old woman leaning out of her *basso* doorway. We exchange words, gestures, we are clear about the information I need, but she just shakes her head, shrugs and retreats into the shade. I start back up to the front of the chapel, banging on every door and window I pass. Nothing. It's impregnable. Like a giant piece of granite with a sculpted baroque façade.

I give up. I sit down on a step a little way from the chapel. I have to place myself at an angle so my good eye can see the iron gates. There is no movement from my closed eye.

I wait. It is hard being still. Time is moving along and nothing is happening. Every moment in Naples is dangerous now. They were right all along – Naples is a dangerous place. Nothing has changed since the days of the Grand Tour. Except now there is McDonald's. Giovanna is probably setting out to wait for me there right now. With only a few lire and the clothes she's wearing. I shake my head wearily. How have I arrived at the point in my life where I'm in Naples watching a church, waiting for my lover to bring me money so I can meet a girl at McDonald's, so we can flee in fear of our lives? I can't be bothered to relive the events but I wonder how much is my fault. Falling in love with Louisa seems to be my only mistake. But that's not entirely correct.

I foolishly trusted Alessandro. A handsome, intelligent, seductive idealist. Yet also a vain man; a man who transposed all the trappings of old Neapolitan honour into a prestige job and a trophy wife. What's a judge if not the godfather of the law? It is a position of power, not a job of work, especially here where it is a career choice and not a reward for service or ability. The only difference between Alessandro and senior members of the Camorra is breadth of intellect and taste. He was too refined to be a gangster. Nonetheless the vanity, the power, are the same.

I have to admit to myself, I was blinded by Alessandro's charisma, which I mistook for being on the side of right, as if any human light must be for the good. It was naive. In the end he is little more than a man who needs to push people around. He might prefer the subtlety of a chess player to the brute force of a mobster but the perversity of the pleasure is the same. I can't now remember a single conversation where I wasn't in some way being manipulated, controlled or coerced. I must, of course, take some of the blame. I was flattered by his attention. It doesn't take a genius to work out all I was doing was displacing desire for Louisa onto her husband. In a way I was looking to be seduced by someone, by anyone.

This thought forces through my second laugh of the day. Irony is so much worse than absurdity and makes the laugh hollow. I almost choke on it. Please come soon, Louisa. I scan right and left, my one eye as keenly focused and directed as I can manage. Maybe she's not coming. I misunderstood her – it wasn't code at all. But then she knows you can't get into this place, so what was she telling me? I stand and peer through the railings of the chapel. To the doors. If I didn't know what was inside, I could imagine it contained the entire Dark Ages. All 400 years compressed.

I try the side-street doors again. Still nothing. It's three o'clock. Time now feels slippery beneath me. Stand, sit – it's the same. My head throbs. The energy it takes to ignore the pain weakens me.

I sit back down. Drop my head between my legs. Tiredness floods my brain, my skull. My body feels as broken as Giovanna's body collapsing in my arms earlier. I could fall asleep in an instant. List over and curl up. The temptation is almost overwhelming. I jerk my head up. Can't have this. Must be alert. I take three deep breaths and rub my face. I sense light in my closed eye. I can't tell whether it's from the inside out, or whether the swelling is subsiding and it's finally opening up.

There is movement to my right. A flicker beneath my eyelid. It is Louisa, jailer's keys in her hand. I leap up; my heart begins to race.

'Let's talk inside,' she says, her smile faint.

She unlocks the gates and ushers me in, locks them. She then selects a huge key from the ring and buries it inside the great doors. Unlocking them requires a two-handed turn. She pushes the door open with her shoulder. We walk in and both close it behind us.

Inside everything is illuminated. The sunlight powers in, reflecting off every surface. Only the altars have a shield of shadow, the altar-works barely visible. The Caravaggio is a misty rectangle of flesh tones and darkness. It could be an orgy rather than an allegory of mercy.

I want to hold Louisa, to kiss her, but she shows no inclination to be close to me. Instead she walks to the centre of the chapel, dumps her satchel on the floor and sits down on one of the chairs. She presses her hands, palms together, between her thighs and looks up at me. She has been crying. Her eyes are swollen; her cheeks pale, red, blotchy. It is only now that she sees the state of my face and head. Like Giovanna she covers her mouth – a cliché of horror.

I feel slightly embarrassed, standing there, pathetically injured. Wanting her love. Needing her help.

'It was Lorenzo Savarese. He broke in this morning. My guess is it was a warning of some kind.' I don't know why I try to make a joke out of it.

Louisa stays where she is. Her hands twitch: fingers stretch, clasp, stretch, clasp. This is becoming too much for her.

'Where does Alessandro think you are?' I ask.

She answers dully, 'I said I had to go to college. I knew he wouldn't stop me going there. He thinks it is important I take it seriously.' She laughs at the absurdity. 'He made me promise I wouldn't see you.'

'Where is he?' I ask.

She doesn't answer, just drops her head in her hands and begins to cry.

I drop to my knees. Peel her hands away from her face. Look up at her.

'Come with me. Today.'

She wipes the tears away with her sleeve. 'I can't. I can't. Not now. I'm not leaving him just like that. Remember, it's me who's been bad. He's the innocent party. Besides, we're going to China next week. It's all booked.' She is grasping onto arrangements made before all this started to help her through.

'Louisa, you're not thinking straight.'

She glares. 'Can you blame me?'

I shake my head; stand. I walk into the middle of the chapel, turn a full 360 degrees on my heels. The eight altars spin around me. I know I must get going, but now I'm in here I don't want to leave – it is a beautiful place, with misty, golden air, a place of daydreams. And Louisa.

'Jim,' she calls. A voice turning in the air around me.

'Yes.'

'What are you thinking about?' The question is plaintive, helpless.

'You, Louisa – you are all I ever think about.'

'Aren't you thinking how nice it is here and how you wish we could stay here for ever?'

It is a ridiculous notion, but not confined to her. 'I am,' I say.

'But we can't, can we?' she says.

'No.'

I hear her get up, walk over. She threads her arms around me, resting her head on my back.

'I wish I could come with you.'

I twist round, inside the wrap of her arms, and hold her. 'Then come.'

'I can't. It wouldn't be right. It would be running away. I need to think. I need to talk to Alessandro. Maybe I should go and stay with my parents for a while. Just until I work this out.'

I resist saying, you could stay with me.

She lifts herself on her toes and kisses me. 'If I see you in London maybe I'll never leave.'

It is important to remain silent when you are promised what you wish for: any utterance will destroy it. Our lips meet again and the promise is reiterated. But it is now about practical matters.

'I need to leave soon, Louisa. Do you have the money?'

Louisa pulls away from me, the promise suspended. 'I haven't got it yet.' It is petulant, resistant. I don't know whether to believe her.

'Louisa. This is not the time to act up.'

'I'm not. But I'm being left behind.'

It's a dramatic declaration. She wants to express something, but it's not about being left behind. She is silent for a moment, then says with a weary shake of the head, 'It wasn't supposed to be like this. He's a wonderful man, Jim. You remember when you first met him, how wonderful he is . . .'

I nod. She wants reassurance that her love for him hasn't been flawed from the start. She continues, 'He's funny and kind, and he's mad about me. I feel loved by him. That's so important.'

I have to stop her. Emotional exhaustion is making her maudlin, unfocused, nostalgic. 'Louisa. Yes, he's all those things. But he lives in a very complicated world. A world we don't understand. I was seduced by the glamour – real gangsters and all that. But glamour is the sheen of the vainglorious.'

'I don't understand.' She looks frightened; she doesn't want to have to understand anything new; she wants clarity, a solution – a solution that makes sense of the last two years but also makes the present comprehensible.

I look at my watch: time to go. 'Louisa. I have to go. Giovanna is waiting for me.'

Louisa looks shocked for the second time in fifteen minutes. It hasn't occurred to her I'm still going to help Giovanna after all this. She searches my face. 'Jim, don't be stupid. You're lucky to be alive. Look at yourself.' There is nowhere to look at myself, except reflected in Louisa's eyes. I don't see much.

I realize I haven't even contemplated whether I was supposed to survive the attack. Maybe the pistol-whipping, the sheer determination of the strike, was intended to be a silent killing. It is my turn to be shocked.

'Think about it, Jim . . .'

I am thinking about it. I'm thinking two things: Savarese doesn't make mistakes. Why not just cover my face with a pillow, press the gun deep in and be sure? And then, what if he has made a mistake and thinks I am dead; does that mean I'm in no danger? At least in the short term?

Louisa interrupts my thoughts, 'Just go to the airport and buy a ticket – you'll be home in a few hours.'

I only vaguely know what she means by home. I shake my head. 'I've promised Giovanna.'

'What do you mean you've promised? Promised her what?'

Promised to help her, but that doesn't seem to be the point. 'She doesn't have anyone else,' I say.

'Forget her, Jim. You're not her knight in shining armour.'

'I'm not trying to be . . .'

'Yes, you are.'

However accurate her insight, it's immaterial.

'Jim! I'm telling you, forget her. She's not worth it. These people are animals and she's no different.'

I retreat two paces. 'What?'

'You heard me.' She knows how it sounded but she refuses to retract or apologize.

I am horrified, but still want to defend my position. 'Giovanna is different. You don't know her . . .'

'And you do?'

I want to say I do, although I know I don't, but then I have to trust my instincts.

'Louisa, I'm going to the station to meet her. That's not going to change. What can change is whether you come with us. I want you to come with us.'

'Fat chance.'

It's an odd thing to say and it betrays her. I accept she doesn't want me to put myself in danger. I now realize she shares something like Alessandro's hypocrisy: compassion from an acceptable distance. But fundamentally the problem here is that she's piqued because I'm leaving Naples with another girl. I want to be furious, but I can't. Confused, out of her depth, scared of being left alone, Louisa has reverted to ugly demands. And right now she wants me to be entirely hers, even alone in London. She wants a clear picture of her options. Alessandro here, Jim there. And Giovanna Savarese is not part of this. Her presence disturbs the picture.

It is my turn to feel alone. Alone here, in the chapel. The person

I now feel closest to is sitting in McDonald's waiting for me, counting on me.

Louisa grabs her satchel off the floor, slings it over her head, straightens it on her shoulder, grabs the jailer's keys. 'We need to get to the bank.'

It's my turn to delay things. All warmth has left us. We are no longer parting lovers with promissory kisses to be lovers for ever. Her rejection of Giovanna is a rejection of me.

'Come on, Jim.'

I do not move. This is too hard.

Outside Louisa says, 'Wait here while I return these.' She jangles the keys and disappears around the corner.

I wait where I am told. I tell myself that Louisa will make sense of this soon and regret her selfishness. She will also realize she can't stay here and will have to come with me. I know I'm foolish for even thinking this way, but I do – she is more than the occasional hateful remark and love forgives the unkind. Louisa reappears and orders me to follow her. We cut through the dark, narrow streets towards Corso Umberto. We do not walk together; she is slightly ahead of me. We are like a couple after a row, unable to make up, displaying our anger, resentment, in the separation of our strides.

'I have to cash a cheque. We need to go to our bank. It will take ten minutes.'

I am being told this without asking. These are the practicalities of her helping me, she is saying. She is taking control, command. Despite the disparity in our moral positions, I feel small and Louisa looms large. Her contradictions give her size. We reach Corso Umberto quickly and deftly cross the four lanes of gridlocked traffic to the Banco di Napoli. The exterior is almost as forbidding as Louisa's chapel.

Inside it is darker. The air is heavy and only the odd glint of sunlight reaches us from the windows in the high, vaulted ceiling. At the far end of the marble floor cashiers sit behind a high counter; there is no window or screen to protect them. They look small, bored, irritable. There isn't a computer in sight. Louisa tells me to wait. She walks the length of the bank, heading straight for the youngest of the male cashiers. Good move, I think. He stands, smiles. I cannot hear what is said, but after a moment she is directed to a door at one end of the long counter. She looks around to me before following the instructions. I give her the thumbs up for encouragement; it feels inappropriate but I can't help myself.

An older man appears. He and Louisa kiss. I cannot tell whether it's just custom or if they know one another. My hope is that it's just custom; involving the family banker, some old buddy of Alessandro's, would be the wrong move right now. What's to stop him calling and saying, 'Your wife's just been in here and withdrawn a load of cash.' How would Alessandro react? Would he fly into a rage? Or use his influence calmly and pick up the telephone. Make calls. Exert his power. Most police officers will know who Louisa is, what she looks like – he could suggest a possible kidnap and have them on the lookout for her: *It's probably nothing, but could you keep an eye open . . .*

I look at my watch. Five o'clock. I think of Giovanna. Apprehensive, sitting upright, waiting. Peering at everyone who walks in the door. The thought of her exhausts me. The throbbing in my head returns in long oscillating waves.

Louisa reappears, ushered out of the office. A shake of the hands. She looks at me and gives her satchel a surreptitious pat. Got it, she is saying, no problem. She doesn't even break her stride as I join her.

The handover happens just inside the lobby. Louisa pulls the chunky envelope from her satchel and hands it to me. 'Three million lire. One thousand pounds.'

'Did you know that guy?' I ask.

'Which one?'

'The one that gave you the money?'

'He's the manager. I've met him a couple of times before.'

'Jesus, Louisa! What if he alerts Alessandro?'

'Why would he?'

'Because his wife's just withdrawn all this money. He might think it's suspicious.'

'Well, there was nothing else I could do,' she says, blushing, not wanting to have messed up; but then adds firmly, 'If I hadn't known him it would have taken much, much longer. Everything takes time in Naples.'

'Except murder,' I say with a mixture of irony and fatalism. I press the envelope deep into my trouser pocket. It barely fits and bulges conspicuously, temptingly. I pull it out, flick open the tucked-in lip, split the money into five and divide it between front and back trouser pockets, plus a thick fold in my breast pocket. I am now a perfect target for the most opportunist pickpocket but at least I won't lose it all. I hand the envelope to Louisa.

'What are you going to do now?'

She sighs and looks at her watch. 'I should go now. I've got to meet Alessandro.'

She hasn't told me this before. Didn't I ask where he was? Isn't he at home? 'Louisa, you didn't tell me this earlier.'

Louisa looks at me nervously, but tries to disguise it with a smile.

'Louisa?'

She doesn't respond; looks away.

'Louisa?' I say again. 'What's going on?'

Her face darkens. 'Nothing's going on.'

She's lying. Refusing to look at me. I tuck a finger under her chin and force her face up, her eyes to meet mine.

'Louisa, I want to know why you didn't tell me this before. Tell me.'

I'm trying not to shout. People going into or leaving the bank look at us. We're a couple rowing. We are only interesting because we are trying to keep it contained, a curiosity in Naples.

'Please, Jim. Don't.'

'Don't what?'

Her face has remained passively upturned, resting on my finger, but now she wrenches it free. 'He told me not to tell. That's all. So I didn't. What difference does it make, you'll be gone soon.'

To her it is just an arrangement that is happening in her life after I've gone, a life that existed for two years before me; the fact she was told to keep it a secret only now seems strange. At the time it was assumed the demand was just part of his anger and promising to obey him just part of assuaging it.

'Why do you think he told you not to tell?' I am incredulous that we could be this far and I don't know what's going on.

'I don't know, Jim. He often says things like that. To avoid people. The press.'

I'm not convinced. She knows this.

'I'm sorry, Jim. I didn't think.'

I can see she is frustrated and unhappy that our last moments will be spent like this. We stand together silently.

'You'd better go then,' I say eventually.

She nods. Her eyes are sad, intense, tired. 'Promise me you'll be careful. Promise me.'

All these promises, I think to myself.

She continues, 'You've got to think by now they'll know she's missing and they'll be looking for her. You've got to understand they've got connections all over the city. They'll be looking for you. And if they catch you . . .' She raises her hand to my face, long slender fingers fluttering over the bruising. 'They'll do worse than this. Jim, you have to understand, it's not a game any more. They'll kill you.'

It's said so calmly, distractedly almost, that for a moment I don't quite understand why she's telling me all this – it's just another warning and I've had plenty of those recently. But then as I look into Louisa's eyes I realize it's my final warning. No one is going to say this to me again. From this point on no one is going to care what happens to me.

I don't know quite what happens in the next few seconds, but following a last kiss, a whispered 'go', I'm weaving awkwardly through the traffic on Corso Umberto, the past three weeks scrolling through my mind: friendship with Alessandro, loving Louisa, fucking Louisa – a game; promises to Giovanna – a game; Lorenzo

Savarese opening up my skull – a game. But choosing to go to the station and help Giovanna – not a game. Because if they catch me, they'll kill me. And that isn't in the rules, not rules I understand. Threats, yes, even violence; I have experience of these. And I've talked my way out. Even now, even after Louisa's warning, I imagine that when it comes down to it this is what I will do: talk my way out of it, solicit understanding, reason, sense. I cannot believe this won't work. I realize I am at a disadvantage here because I don't accept they will kill me. But I don't *get* it. At least not yet. And right now I must make a decision based on the possibility that they will. Will kill me. Kill me. Me.

When I get to the other side of the street I turn. One last look at Louisa. But the steps of the bank are empty. I scan all directions, pulling focus on every detail which might become Louisa. I want to find her, run in a multitude of directions. To be with her one last time. Hope my perseverance will change her mind, and then tempt fate to offer us a clear way out. But she is gone. Gone to meet Alessandro. Her husband.

I head up Mezzocannone. I don't know why. My instinct is telling me not to stay still and right now the street is clear of traffic, people. But then the university doors open and within seconds I am surrounded by hundreds of students, spreading across the pavement, out into the street. I do not have time to move away before I am barricaded in: Vespas appearing from nowhere, the ground littered with rucksacks. Everyone is chatting, arguing, discoursing. The only real movement is a thousand hands making a thousand points, all equal in fervour, passion, certainty. I am being pushed, shoved, jostled. I'm too disorientated not to give way, not to obey the forces around me. I try to steady myself but hands, arms, elbows thrust me forward and back. I am not important. I am a tourist. Irrelevant. For a moment I find there is something comforting about this anonymity, but I'm burning up, unable to move, make my way out of the sun. Sweat trickles into the deep cut in my forehead and it's like the brandy poured into it; I almost wither from the pain. I start to press forward. Push my way through the knots of people. I barge through arguments. The students are pissed off, the flow of their declamations interrupted. They shout, curse, spit.

'Get out of my fucking way,' I say, my hands clawing at the last few bodies, through to the open space on the street just ahead of me.

From all sides I hear the word 'fuck' spat back at me. It has a new and impressive richness coming from the husky voices of young Neapolitans.

I finally push my way through. My shirt is soaking and clings to my skin. The money. Do I still have the money? I pat each pocket twice. All there. I cross over to the dark side of the street.

I lean against a wall. There is a police car twenty yards away. Officers sitting inside smoking. I am panting, sweating, hands on my knees; my fucked-up face is turned away from them. They watch me idly. The crowd of students blocking the road doesn't appear to concern them. Are they here for me? It's a fleeting, idle question, but it must be answered. Could they be? It would need Louisa to have told Alessandro where she'd left me, which I don't believe she would, and for him to order me to be followed – all in five minutes. Think straight. I stare down at the pavement, the dense, grey stone. I've got to make a decision. Leave now with the money? Save myself? Go to the station to meet Giovanna? Risk us both? My mind is as blank as the stone at my feet.

I push myself away from the wall and walk north. My beaten-up face arouses interest in the policemen. A cigarette is flicked out of the window. A few feet before me. Across my path. Why? Why do that? What does it mean? Probably nothing. I must ignore it. This is what I'm up against until I'm free of Naples – everyone is a potential assailant, everyone is connected. As I pass I try to look unperturbed by the fact half my face is bashed in, ignore the chronic pain that's been with me for hours now, fight the acute pain caused by the sweat seeping in. I am a tourist, that's all. Nothing special about me. The passenger side policeman rolls his head back onto the headrest and watches me. His hand reaches for the in-car radio.

I tell myself it's nothing. He's just curious about a tourist with a bashed-in face, something to look at, and he's just radioing in because . . . I don't know – he just is. Ignore it, you have more concrete things to worry about, where the connections are certain: Giovanna must have been at the station for some time now, and sooner or later Lorenzo will want to know where she is; and I'm certain that by now Alessandro has admitted to himself Louisa wasn't going to college – he's too smart for long-term denial. I'm only moments away from both men independently deciding that these precious women are with me; the moment has probably passed. And now Alessandro in his grand house up on the hill and Lorenzo in his *basso* at the heart of Forcella have converged. Naples has finally unified in pursuit of me.

I look over my shoulder. I am hoping the police car will have gone. But it's still there and the two policemen are now out, leaning on the roof, shielding the sun from their eyes and looking in my direction. One is talking into the radio handset pulled through the window. The students are dispersing behind them. I look around to see what, other than me, could be attracting their attention. There is nothing. Maybe I am being monitored, patrol to patrol, until I've left the city. Alessandro exercising his control, his reach over the city this way. Just make sure he leaves. And if that's the case, what do the police care if I take Giovanna with me. But of course that presupposes they have been instructed by a chain of command that starts with Alessandro, and why should it? What level of cash payment does it take to keep an eye out for some beat-up tourist and feed back the information?

Think: both want you to leave the city. Only one cares how you do it. I should just head to the airport. I satisfy them both that way. It doesn't matter then who the cops are working for.

That means leaving Giovanna. So who the cops are working for does count. Because if it's for Alessandro my options remain open.

But then my options are closed down. With a single glance across the street my situation is given perfect clarity. Gaetano and Salvatore. Stepping out from an alley in their Sunday best. Dark suits, white shirts open-necked, collars pulled over jacket lapels, the combed grooves of their slicked-back hair glinting in the sunlight. I try not to look over at them but none of us can resist sideways glances, and when our eyes finally meet Gaetano smiles. He's been practising this; he didn't want to smirk, it doesn't look psychotic enough. Salvatore wants to look meaner, more threatening. *He* smirks. Stares.

So the cops, if they are allied with anyone, are with Alessandro. What does this mean? Does it give me an exit strategy right now? Now it's clear Lorenzo is keeping this within the family and isn't relying on his earlier violence to have persuaded me. I've under-estimated Alessandro again, his subtlety, his understanding of this city and his facility to work it. He just wants me gone, and to do this he has put in place a mechanism to shepherd me out – the cops. There is no need to threaten me himself; he understands Lorenzo and knows he'll do that, and that will set me on my way. All Alessandro has to do is make me understand I'll be denied protection. Assuring my departure.

I stop. And as I do Gaetano and Salvatore stop with me. They are surprised and therefore their motion is interrupted mid-stride. They stumble slightly. They are amateurs at this, I can tell. I wonder how long they've been with me. I wonder how much they've seen. Louisa and I going into the bank, the handover of money in the lobby? What do they think? It doesn't implicate Giovanna. It's just money to go home with, obeying big brother. It doesn't even matter if they know she's missing, until I'm with her, seen with her, seen leaving with her . . .

But they are not thinking this way. They've been told not to think. They are just following me, watchful. I then realize Giovanna waiting at McDonald's condemns me. If they have found her. It doesn't matter what she says. She can't leave without me, they know that. Have they found her? If they have, I can make the decision to save myself. Accept that it's all played out. There's nothing I can do. Just double back to Corso Umberto, fall into a taxi, tell the driver, take me to the airport, avoid the station. Steer clear, literally. Make the point. I'm leaving and I'm not going anywhere near your sister.

But I don't. The decision doesn't have to be made yet. For the next fifteen, twenty minutes I'm just heading towards the station. For all they know I'm heeding the warning – leaving. And if I get that far, what happens next can be determined by me – if Giovanna's still there. What are they going to do – shoot us in a crowded McDonald's? All we have to do is front it out. Through the crowd and onto a train. Going anywhere. Milan. Florence. Rome. Venice. I play the scenario out in my head. Step by step. It can be done. But I must be focused. And without doubt. If I do not falter, I can out-think these two. I look across the street: the smile, the smirk. Two boys following their older brother's order. If I do anything unexpectedly, they will have to make quick decisions, alert Lorenzo, take instructions, compute the consequences, risk arrest. But I am making a mistake. Still thinking this is a game. Thinking I can beat them. But Louisa said, *This is not a game any more*. And I can't beat them.

We look at one another across the street, over the cars. Salvatore disappears down a side street. Gaetano stays with me, not even breaking stride. Again the smile. He's enjoying this, whatever this is.

It is now my turn to guess their intentions. They can't know what I'm going to do because I don't know. But they've a plan, they've revealed that much. Is Salvatore going to alert Lorenzo now? If so, what for? Again: what if they've found Giovanna? How long will it take to beat my name out of her? Again: this whole thing might already be over and I'm the only one who doesn't know. Giovanna's told them that it was me who was going to help her, even after Lorenzo's warning, and now I'm going to be punished for my arrogance. I stare across at Gaetano. What can he tell me? I don't dare risk a confrontation.

This really is my last chance to save myself. There's a cab beside me, without a passenger. No. I'm at greater risk in a cab than I am out on the streets. In a cab I'm a sitting target. Open the door. Lean in. Shoot. An easy kill. Out here I have people all around. A myriad directions to choose from. The shadows.

I want, somehow, to know what has happened at McDonald's over the last few hours. Giovanna arriving, a bag (she couldn't refrain from taking some stuff) slung over her shoulder. Finding a seat, far from the window. A table with remnants of food; empty packaging at least. Less conspicuous that way. Warm eyes trained on the doors. Time passes. She shifts around in her seat. Shouts at the staff when they complain she's been there too long and not ordered; they won't bother her again – she is a Savarese. She wants to go to the toilet but she cannot risk that moment being the moment I walk in. She fantasizes about her new life to distract herself but this only makes everything worse. Especially the waiting. Nothing makes time pass quickly. She has to change seat just to do something, eat up some time.

Then: Lorenzo walks in. The place falls silent. Everyone knows who he is. He's been in every paper for almost two years. Giovanna is scared, looks for a way out, but she knows he hasn't come alone. He pulls her out of her seat. She screams at him. She will not go quietly. He is impassive. He will not leave without her. After five minutes or so, when she cannot scream any longer, he slaps her down. Hard, to the floor. He wants to stamp on her, but controls himself. She is collected off the floor by . . . his men, her brothers, maybe he lifts her up himself. But she is gone . . . Or: she is still there. After three, four hours of waiting. Anxious. Nervy. At her third table. Closer to the window now. Taking the risk. She wants a view over Piazza Garibaldi. To see me coming. Because seeing me crossing the piazza is the beginning of the end of all this. And it's getting late. Soon the afternoon will be over. And that was the time I promised to be there.

But I cannot see any of this. I cannot know which it is. But I do know one fixes my destiny, the other . . . it's up to me. I decide something will happen which will make things clear. And I will only choose when I have to. It's the only advantage I can think to play – take the endgame to the end.

But this is not a fucking game, Louisa screams at me.

No, it's not a game. And because of that I'm learning something about myself. There are two ways of making decisions – thought and action. And I'm not giving up on Giovanna if I don't have to. I know this because my body is on the move – and my direction is the station.

I cross Piazzetta Nilo and head into Spaccanapoli; hang right. I only have to turn my head an inch to know Gaetano follows me. We are only a few feet apart now. There are no opposing pavements to this street, no road separating one side from the other. Only the slow passing of cars divides us.

If they have found Giovanna, every step I take implicates me further. I increase my speed fractionally. I am beyond walking pace now. If Gaetano stays with me it's the beginning of a chase – it's that straightforward. But he doesn't. He falls back. Instinct tells me he's still there. Behind me. Maybe that's the plan. Salvatore is going to come at me straight on, Gaetano from behind. I stumble on the lip of a paving stone. I begin to fall. I reach out, grabbing at anything to keep me upright. A shoulder, a sleeve. It's a hand. I am pulled up. I am expecting it to be Salvatore. A helping hand before a knife, a gun. But it's just an anonymous Neapolitan. I say, '*Grazie, grazie, grazie.*' My mind is scrambled. Where's Gaetano? Where's Gaetano?

He's still with me. He's not going anywhere. He knows the quickest way to get to the station is through Forcella. And he also knows that whatever he and his brothers have got planned for me can happen there with impunity. No one is going to call the police, no one is going to intervene. These are Savarese boys. He also knows if I'm heading for the station, and I'm not going to risk Forcella, I'll have to head north. To Via dei Tribunali. Is this where Salvatore will be? Ready to cut me off? I cross two more junctions; every side street is narrow, dark, empty – it is impossible to see if Salvatore is following in parallel, tracking me along the ancient blocks. I turn. I have no choice. Forcella is only a few streets ahead, Salvatore is north, and south is nowhere. Gaetano stops. The smile is gone. But I sense he has wanted this moment ever since he found out what I do.

We are five feet apart. He's waiting for his brother. He is unsure what I am waiting for. The smile is gone. He is tense. But he's not scared. I am. Whether it's visible or not, I don't know. It must be – the world is shaking before me. I look beyond him, to the very end of Spaccanapoli, to the sun dropping in the sky. This is what I'm waiting for. The obliterating light. I've seen it twice now. Does Gaetano know it's coming? All I can hope for is that you can live in Naples all your life and not know. Not know that there is a precise moment when the sun slots into the highest, narrowest point of Spaccanapoli and the fire is pierced open, its light flooding down like white hot lava. I know the moment is soon. Does he? The sun is golden, red rimmed, burning – falling. Its edge touches the rooftops, slung between the buildings.

Gaetano and I hold up the traffic. Naples' ancient artery is blocked. Pedestrians give us the flick; Vespas curve past, dangerously close; cars slam their horns. But I'm not moving until the sun comes pouring down and blinds us all. It's my last chance.

Gaetano steps forward. It's the most hesitant move he's yet made. I don't respond. I can't. My body is rigid. I cannot even turn and run; even if I wanted to. If the light doesn't come, I'm here until the brothers move me. Gaetano knows this. His next step lacks all hesitation. He's now teasing me. I'm his. I can barely make him out – the sun is a huge halo behind him, moments away from hitting the street, the sharp end of Spaccanapoli. I can't even lift my arms to defend myself. I've miscalculated. I thought I was more in control than this – braver. Gaetano reaches into his inside pocket. This is how it happens. Brazenly, on the street, pressed in by cars, blocked by swerving Vespas, people everywhere. The only thing I feel is the cut in my head throbbing; the pain itself is deep in my skull. The only thing I see is Gaetano, taking another step forward, his hand inside his jacket. Behind him the sun is pierced open and the light begins to flow down. It must arrive soon. Gaetano draws his hand out of his jacket.

I step back – self-preservation forces me. I'm only moments from an escape. My movement registers on Gaetano's face. He stops still. Am I going to run, he asks himself. No – I'm paralysed again. But the light is almost with us. It's a line on the stone; then a wall. A few seconds and Gaetano will disappear. I will disappear. He is no more than a silhouette now but that doesn't diminish him. We are only three feet apart. An arm's length. If he wants to stab me, he can, he can reach over.

The light hits Gaetano. Then me. Obliterating us both. This will last a minute – no longer. I must find a way out quickly. I search for darkness, a side street. Then I will run. I am pushed over, kicked. Maybe. I don't know. My head slams against the paving. There is no pain, my head just fills with the light – my skull broken open. I force myself up and press forward. Find a wall, follow it, run the moment it falls away. The light is thinning. I have a couple of seconds left. I brace myself for a knife, a silent weapon for a sightless death. I squint down at my feet, at other feet before me and try to sidestep every obstacle. I hear an American voice, 'What's going on? Where are you, Chuck?' There is no answer. I think, perversely but clearly, maybe Chuck's been killed by mistake. I turn my body sideways on and squeeze myself between a car and the wall.

The light begins to clear. Sucked up the street as the sun sinks behind the hill, its retreat swifter than its arrival. I feel it pass over me, revealing me, but as it does I fall back into a side street and into darkness. I turn and run. I can hardly see where I'm going but I know the way is clear – there is a rectangle of day ahead. Via dei Tribunali, I hope. I don't check whether I'm being followed; I have rediscovered movement and that's all that interests me. I spin around the corner and into a crowd of tourists. They part instantly faced with my determination to plough through them. Ahead of me is Vesuvius, way off in the distance. Via dei Tribunali. In the direction of the station. The sky above me is dark blue.

This is my chance. To beat them. They've got to think I've been scared off. I have been scared off. I can use that. It gives me an advantage. At the same time as I am saying, 'Good, good,' under my breath, I can hear myself thinking, 'Why? Why?' But again, action is determining everything. And I know why: there is nothing else to do. Giovanna needs me and I made a promise to her.

This is what I've been waiting for. What I've needed to understand. My promise. While I'm alive I don't exist independently of my promise. And it's this that makes me different from this city. Naples is a place where promises are made on constantly shifting ground, shifting with the next favour, the next threat, the next betrayal. Where a promise can be made with the subtlest of gestures and ended with the unexpected use of the Neapolitan dialect. Where everything is, in fact, a game. Louisa was wrong. Naples is a game where your survival depends on you reading the next man or woman's desire, greed, duplicity, mercy, compassion, honour and, perhaps most importantly, will to power, whilst at the same time trying to disguise your own. It's the reason for all the inscrutability. It's a tactical weakness to show anything. This is a game because everyone knows the rules – everyone, that is, but me. It's why my promise is a mistake – it's non-negotiable. And although the rules of the game allow this – only a fool plays this way.

I slow down past Castel Capuano, Alessandro's old workplace, on the outskirts of Forcella. My lungs ache. My throat burns. My muscles feel like lead one moment, liquid the next – I don't know whether I'm going to collapse from exhaustion or faint from fear. I scan the streets around me. Nobody is interested in me. People are going about their business, buying vegetables and meat, talking and arguing. If I am glanced at, it's merely from curiosity – I'm straying into streets beyond the old Tribunale that should hold no interest for a tourist. I'm not sure where I'm going, but I don't want to take a direct route to the station. I keep saying, 'Think, think, you can work this out. There are better and worse ways to go about this: to reduce the risk, improve the odds.' I recognize all this talk as an adrenal thing, but it's also about denial – if I stop talking I will really think about what I'm doing and I can't let this happen.

I reach Piazza San Francesco. I can feel my energy level begin to crash. Only so much adrenalin. I increase my pace; momentum is everything. I weave through the traffic. I am now an expert at this; it's all about anticipation: the drivers will use every inch of the road, any space, any opening, and speed will not drop until the very last moment. They expect you to understand this – to factor it in. I do. The perfection with which I manoeuvre gives me new confidence. I can do this. I turn right, following a sign to the Stazione Centrale. I can see the wide open space of Piazza Garibaldi. I slow down as I come to a corner. I am right by the Hotel Luxotica. I can see the station roof. Which is the best way? Across the centre of the piazza, over slip roads, car parks, through crowds of passengers waiting for buses and trams, or do I just use the pavement and navigate through hordes of Neapolitans heading home from work on foot?

The decision is made for me. To my left is Salvatore, leaning against a wall, waiting. He pushes himself upright. No urgency. But seeing me requires some action. I take a step back into the shadow of the side street. Does this mean there is a Savarese or Savarese soldier posted at the four corners of the piazza? It must do. I could have approached from anywhere.

I step out from the street into the middle of a group of tourists fresh off a tour bus. They've been told to be wary, alert, so they step away from me fearfully, but I smile and say, 'Hi,' and push through. This is all being done on reflex. I don't look back; I'm sure Salvatore is there, somewhere. More of the station is now visible up ahead. I half expect to see Lorenzo standing on the low, flat roof, right at the tip of the point, gun by his side.

I am only a couple of hundred yards away now. I can see the bright yellow and red branding of McDonald's. My heart is bursting through my ribcage. I feel like I'm choking on the burning sensation in my throat. I can't breathe; every ten steps I heave in air before I can go on. My stomach is contracted, petrified. Only a hundred yards to go. I can see an entrance to McDonald's, right off the exterior concourse. I can just walk straight in. If Giovanna is ready, we can walk straight out of the station exit and onto the main concourse. It's fucking simple. It's a straight fucking line. Just walk. Walk it.

Gaetano appears before me. Ten feet ahead. I swerve off the pavement and onto the road. Maybe it's just these two. Sent to do a job. I can beat these two, I say to myself again.

My straight line to McDonald's is now broken. I am walking between two lanes of cars; Gaetano walks with me, in perfect parallel, along the pavement.

They know Giovanna is waiting for me by now. But does she know? I think I can see her in the window. A girl with her back to me. I can't pass the window, alert her. I'll have to take Gaetano on. I'll have to swing round, via the station entrance. What will Giovanna do when she realizes her brothers are with me? She has to understand immediately: this ends when we falter. She must follow me. Mustn't hesitate for a second. If she panics, they'll lead her away. If she doesn't, and stays next to me, they'll have to fight us both, together. I'm sure it's her. Pressed up against the window, staring out, sure I'll be coming from that direction. Now all she'll see is Gaetano. And it will all be over.

Everything changes all the time – Gaetano is now gone. I look behind me – Salvatore is gone. I look back to McDonald's. The girl is still looking out. I narrow my focus into the brightness of the interior. Are they already inside, striding towards her? I can't see them. Maybe they just needed to be led to Giovanna; and now they've backed off, awaiting further instructions.

But the girl is still there. She can't have seen Gaetano. She would have reacted in some way. She must have seen him.

The entrance to the station is dark from the overhang of the roof. Although there is a constant flow of people in and out, few hang around. The first door is blocked by two young men talking, the subject of their conversation given away by the occasional involuntary, graceful mime of a ball being softly side-footed.

I stop just before the cab rank. There is just the station slip road to go, then the external concourse. I'm twenty yards from Giovanna. If she just turns and looks over her shoulder she will see me. 'Turn around,' I plead through my teeth. 'Turn around.' One glance, a simple gesture from me, and she can make her way to the platforms, ready to join me, heading for a train, any train. I can see the platforms and the trains from here. Their destinations. Firenze, Roma, Perugia.

I am ready. I check around and head for the entrance. I can hear myself saying, 'This is too easy – too fucking easy.' But there's nothing left to do. I manoeuvre easily around the sudden appearance of a baggage cart, my stride unbroken. I am three feet from the entrance. I am just someone going into a station to catch a train. Giovanna is now visible from another angle, over her other shoulder. This time I can see her face.

It's not her. It's not Giovanna. It's just some other girl waiting in McDonald's. Some other young Neapolitan girl who has set up a rendezvous there. McDonald's is a good place to meet.

I don't know what to do. Is this girl part of their plan? Is she a decoy? Have they got Giovanna? They must have. She'd be waiting. I need to check again. My eyes alight on every table, assembling all the information in my brain as fast as I can. Person alone? Girl? Anxious, panicked? No. No. No. Just mothers and kids. Groups of teenagers. The one girl. They've got her. And they're letting me go. What do I do? Leave and call Louisa as soon as I can. From Rome. Somewhere away from here.

It's the only thing. I turn back to the station. And as I do, I see her – in the corner of McDonald's, perfectly situated close to the station exit, far from the window. Reading. Head down, book open on the table in front of her. Reading and waiting. For me. I feel as though oxygen has reached my limbs for the first time since the moment I escaped Gaetano on Spaccanapoli. I feel completely embodied for the first time since leaving Louisa. We are close to the end. But this confidence lasts less than a second. A hand is raised in front of me – a palm. Its appearance is too quick to avoid. I slam into it. My chest slams into it. And for a moment all is still, as motion and energy evaluate the competing forces and who will win out.

It is Lorenzo. Here to see me off. I know this, because he is smiling, just like his brother. But he is smiling because he is pleased to have been able to come himself. I glance quickly across to Giovanna, a shunt of the eyes. She is still engrossed in her book. Is she still reading *Jane Eyre*, I wonder. It's a curious question right at this moment, and I don't particularly care about the answer. I am moving backwards, my feet tripping over themselves because of the speed at which they required to carry me. The only thing keeping me from falling over is the bodies breaking away behind me, clearing the way for us. Those who recognize Lorenzo say his name under their breath.

Lorenzo steps away. The pressure on my chest releases. All the oxygen I had left in my lungs has been forced out. I gasp for air. Lorenzo waits.

It's now just the two of us, surrounded, at some distance, by curious Neapolitans. Lorenzo is speaking; it's low, deep – a rattle. I understand what he's saying without recognizing a word. *Why didn't I do what I was told?* He is not angry. He is pissed off. Having to do this is pissing him off. He's been out of prison a day. I've been warned off once, I should have obeyed. Having to deal with me a second time is unexpected; an unwanted, undesirable and potentially messy chore. I look directly at him. I don't have anywhere else to look. If they haven't already found Giovanna, I don't want to give her away, and somehow appealing to those around me for help seems pointless. So I stare at Lorenzo because I've had enough and he's controlling this and what happens will be dictated by him. Gaetano is maybe looking on, but he's irrelevant. Salvatore – he probably just wants to get back to his computer games, if he's not there already. It's just me and Lorenzo.

I am still struggling for breath. I have to bend over. I clasp my knees to keep myself from falling. I need to get blood to my head, air into my lungs – without it I'll die right now, whatever Lorenzo has planned. I am half expecting a kick in the face, or to be punched to the ground. But nothing happens. I straighten up when my mind clears. Lorenzo registers my return, but no smile this time. No talk.

He just watches me. Every now and then his eyes flick to the right. Is he waiting for someone? One of his brothers?

Or a car? Am I going to be taken somewhere? This hasn't occurred to me before now, and it scares me. The reason we're standing here is that we're waiting for a ride. Is that where Gaetano has disappeared to? To get a car? Fuck. They're going to take me somewhere and kill me. The realization is so sudden I have no reaction. I am numb and dumb. Their plan was so simple, practical – professional. Follow him. Let him lead us to Giovanna. Then force him into a car. Take him somewhere. Kill him. Without resistance from me, it's easy; with resistance, just more awkward. But I'll give in – in time. Within seconds, probably. If not, knock me unconscious. Now I know.

Still we wait. I look to my left, to the set-down lane, waiting for the car to pull up. *Will* it be Gaetano? Another curious question. I suppose I know my death will be more painful if he's around; Lorenzo is not a torturer but Gaetano wants to play the psycho.

Running isn't an option. I'm not sure why. I'm not sure I can. Lorenzo is only an arm's length from me. Not close enough to be obviously threatening, but a microsecond away if he has to grab me.

Minutes pass. Our standoff is boring, it seems. The crowd has dispersed a little. Only those who recognize Lorenzo are prepared to give us a little more time.

'What's going on, Lorenzo?' I say. I am surprised at the sound of my own voice. Lorenzo is momentarily unsettled by my use of his first name. He steps forward, face, arms, hands tensing. *Don't speak, don't move, don't think.* I am being told this situation has not changed because the traffic in Naples has held up the car.

Is he wondering why I don't try to get away? No – he's as certain as I am; it's not an option. The waiting is incidental. He was supposed to drive me backwards to the kerb, where a car would glide up, a brother open the door, and I would be bundled into the back seat – and then away. The wait changes nothing. I am no more able to escape while we stand here than I was during the few seconds I was forced to moonwalk into position. This isn't a standoff. I'm flattering myself if I think Lorenzo and I are in some kind of existential showdown. This is a holding pattern. Everything waits on the traffic in Naples. Even this.

I look at my watch. I wonder how much life I have left. It's six-thirty-five. At least until seven. Wherever they take me they've got the traffic to deal with. Even if it's just to Forcella.

The specificity of Forcella shocks me, shakes me out of my compliance. I don't want to die in a basement in Forcella. Fear returns. Deep fear. Vomit arrives in my mouth. I choke to keep it down. It burns in my throat and this makes me retch again.

I'm not dying in a fucking basement. 'Fuck you, Lorenzo,' I spit.

His fist turns in the air towards me, but I manage somehow to lean back and duck it. I want to drive a punch into his stomach but opt to turn, to run. I am grabbed. Lorenzo has my collar. I am pulled back. The collar rips off, unwinding around my neck, causing me to spin around. To face him again. Lorenzo has the collar, hanging from his hand; for a second it looks like he's surrendering, my collar a white flag limp in his fist.

He looks to his right. The car. Almost got messy, he thinks. I turn. A big green Alfa Romeo gently glides along the kerb. Lorenzo punches me in the face just as it arrives. I turn again; my face turns, my upper body turns, my legs are still. I slam into the car. There is no sound. Me against metal, against glass. The crowd. The traffic. The plane in the sky. There is no activity. Crowd. Traffic. Plane. There is no pain.

I am against the window of the car, my face a smudge against the glass. I am an extrovert larking around: pressing my face against the window of a passing car, for a laugh. The glass is tinted. But through it I can clearly make out Louisa, and next to her, Alessandro. This is what we've been waiting for. This is who Lorenzo has been waiting for. Alessandro.

The slam, a dead noise inside the car, and probably no more than a gentle rocking of the suspension, has turned Louisa to the window. She recoils at the face looking at her. And for a moment

I am that extrovert larking around and she looks irritated by the unwanted disturbance. Recognition comes slowly. When she realizes she spins around to Alessandro. He refuses to register her. He has a file open on his knees. He has been working right up until this point. His serious eyes are now fixed forward. Louisa jams her hands under the door locks and tries to force them up, her fingers bent back with the leverage. I can hear her screaming, a whisper behind the reinforced glass, 'Alessandro, Alessandro. It's Jim. It's Jim. Help me. Help me.' Alessandro looks down at his work, flips over a page with his thick fingers. The car glides away and I slide down onto the kerb.

Lorenzo is standing over me. He places his foot on my chest, rests it there. He knows I am not going to move.

He asks, '*Dov'è Giovanna?*'

I stare up at him, and say, she's twenty yards away, in fucking McDonald's, you moron. The scream in my head is so loud I imagine Lorenzo hears it because he looks around for a moment, but he then returns his gaze to me and repeats the question, with a sharp stab of his heal into my chest, '*Dov'è Giovanna?*'

I laugh, with my mouth full of blood. I think it must be the irony or something. I don't know whether Lorenzo notices, or just assumes I'm choking. I am choking as well. I think his punch has broken my jaw, and the wound he gave me this morning reopened on impact with the car.

The question is repeated; there is no variation of message. '*Dov'è Giovanna?*' He wants an answer. This will not end until I give him one.

I attempt to pull myself up, but he pushes me back with his foot. I don't have to move to speak.

'OK, OK,' I say weakly.

What do I tell him? Do I have to tell him anything? I could point. Make it clear with a gesture we can all follow.

'Airport. She is at the airport.'

Lorenzo studies me for a second. I'm not sure what there is left on my face to read, but then he's probably adept at judging honesty on beaten-up faces. I picture Giovanna at the airport, by a long line at a check-in, sitting on a suitcase, waiting for me.

Lorenzo lifts his foot from my chest, bends down and pulls the money from my top pocket, holds his hand out and waits for me to hand him the money from my other pockets. He is expressionless during the transaction. It's not a punishment. He just wants the money. He divides it and slots it into the side pockets of his jacket and walks away.

I can't stand. I know this without trying. There is nothing left inside of me, so I just lie there, being watched. Someone offers to help me. I am heaved up. A second person is needed. My body is a dead weight; I can feel their struggle to keep me upright. I sway forward when released. They make a grab for me, to steady me. I wave them off. I can do this. I have to make it into the station, to McDonald's, if Giovanna is still there. I look about me. Everything is glassy, my eyes straining to see through a pink sheen – a mixture of blood and tears. I can just make out the people directly around me. I wave them away. They back off. I wipe my eyes with my sleeve.

Gaetano and Salvatore stand either side of the station entrance. Salvatore leaning back, arms folded – bored. Gaetano, nervy, smoking – disappointed. I am no longer scared of these two. They are just boys. Apprentices. I understand the chain of command now: Alessandro is at the top, and they are at the bottom. They might be able to push people around but their power is limited now their brother is out of prison, and as for Lorenzo himself, his power must be compared with the power of the man who can order him to wait for a precise moment in time before he may exercise that power.

Alessandro. My friend. All this because I made love to his wife. Cuckolded him. Insulted his manhood. His Neapolitan manhood. A betrayal that requires brutality. And in front of Louisa. An elaborate set-up to show his wife who is the real man. This display was intended for her. He didn't even have to look round. He knew what was arranged and knew with certainty that it would happen.

If he needed proof, it came when my face smacked against the window – the jolt of the suspension just hard enough to make him look up from his work. My blood will be washed off the car by his driver when they arrive back at the house. And that leaves only Louisa to remind him of what has happened, what he has done. And she will be told that if I am forgotten she will be forgiven. That will be the deal. A deal possibly being made now. In the back of the car, with my blood still on the window. A deal without words. That was the point of the display. To make it clear. So he doesn't have to argue or plead with her. Make any kind of case. Demean himself further. In her eyes. Will she accept? I picture Louisa: her beautiful, perfect face, her beautiful, perfect smile, her beautiful, perfect, teasing voice. Will she assent? I don't know.

I step towards the brothers. They both shake their heads. I'm not going home yet. Things need to be checked. I want to look over to where Giovanna was sitting but I can't risk alerting her brothers. Gaetano is wound so tightly he notices everything, however slight or subtle. I turn and try to take her in as my vision rotates, but everything is a blur.

I can't understand how she's been missed. Were they too busy with me or too certain our rendezvous would have been more obvious? Under the clock. By a platform. The ticket office. And when she wasn't there they didn't even think to check McDonald's because of their prejudice against the place, assuming it was a family thing.

I look over Piazza Garibaldi. It is dusk now. The air is thick with pollution. It is going to be a hot evening. I step into the road. Traffic is slow moving. I am unsteady and cabs swerve around me. No one appears to stop me from crossing the piazza – as long as I'm in Naples they can find me. Between Alessandro and Lorenzo, their networks, I can't hide for long. So I've got a few more hours. Until they realize that I lied. Then they'll come and find me. This is just a postponement. I have a little longer. A little longer in Naples. I can't say I'm displeased. A sense of calm has replaced my fear. All my options have been played out. All my responsibilities have been ended. I am no longer beholden to anyone but myself. It's just me and the city.

I head slowly towards the far corner of the piazza, towards the tram and bus stops, magazine kiosks, the rush-hour crowds on their way home, and the Corso Umberto, which will take me back into the heart of the city. I am tempted to return to Signora Maldini's and wait for them there, but that would get her involved and there is no need for that. I cannot think where to go. I don't have a favourite place. Not really. Down by the port, maybe. At least it is cool there. The port? Will they have the port covered, I wonder. Why would they? The ferries just go to the islands and Sorrento. But then there are the bigger boats – to Palermo, and the cruise ships. I can escape this, I think. I can get out of here. Get to the port. My calm is replaced by a rush of excitement. I am almost able to skip out of the way of a Vespa heading straight for me.

So this is how it happens. An anonymous killer. On a Vespa.

The bullet presses in, determined despite resistance to make it into my body. It works to get there. I can feel its effort. But its speed is hindered. Muscle, organs, human density.

Being shot is not quick. It is not a precise moment. It is a long, slow moment of long, slow unravelling. Of a life unravelling. A million moments spun in spinning out.

I can feel the bullet has yet to lodge. I must be stubborn and not let it in further.

I am falling. A single turn to the floor. There is a sharp pain. Cold air is sucked in. Ice-cold and filling me fast. I don't like this at all. I want to wish this away, magic it away.

I am turned over; a body washed up on the beach. I hear urgent voices. Neapolitan urgency – husky and breathless. A concentrated urgency, without hysteria, melodrama. My shirt is ripped away. Fingers are thrust inside me. I am warm again, spilling over with warmth. But then the cold returns. I hear sirens.

Above me an old man looks down. 'Napoli,' he says, shaking his head. 'Napoli!'

All I can see now is a patch of sky. Around me shoes and legs. Silhouettes of shoes and legs. I turn my head. My arm lies stretched out beside me, listless. A sleeping arm. My hand is open-cupped, as if a clutched apple has rolled from it. This is my thought.

My arm is folded in. Across me.

I levitate for a moment. A stretcher shoved underneath me. I drop back down. I am strapped in. My body is rigid.

I am surrounded by policemen. Hands on guns. Moving people. Making space.

I think: what about Giovanna – what about Giovanna waiting in

McDonald's? Sitting in a yellow moulded-plastic chair, waiting for me, reading Jane Eyre. She will think I have let her down. I have let her down.

I levitate again. Move off head first under a dark sky.

Light around me is fading. Movement is fading. My eyes take poor-quality snapshots of the world; my mind strains to make them comprehensible. Everything around me is like a pointillist painting pressed to my face: a soft blur – watery and warm.

Inside I'm cold.

I levitate once more but this time I don't stop.

Acknowledgements

To all persons listed below I would like to express my gratitude for their many years of support, patience, encouragement and belief.

First thanks must go to Keith Baverstock for placing Naples on my mental map and for being an indefatigable guide, and for introducing me to judges Massimo Amodeo and Eugenia Del Balzo, without whom this novel would be much thinner in many aspects, particularly in the courtroom scenes. Some novels would not exist at all without the inspirations of the real and therefore Massimo must be singled out in this regard for very special thanks.

More generally, Luke Meddings, Curtis Radclyffe, Valarie Smith, Mason Horstmann, Thomas Harding, Jim Poyser, Kate Moran, Emmanuelle Keita & family, Amanda Lane (for her very own brand of support, patience, encouragement and belief), Paul Barrow, Kam Raslan, Sally Abby, Special Agents Trewin and Ballard at PFD, Leo Hollis at Penguin and all at the BLINC partnership.

Finally, thank you to Joanna Anderson for her deep belief and invaluable advice, and my partner Bridget Macauley for all of the above and everything else in my life.